WEEK-END MARRIAGE

Faith Baldwin

WEEK-END MARRIAGE

TRIANGLE BOOKS · NEW YORK

TRIANGLE BOOKS EDITION PUBLISHED AUGUST 1941
REPRINTED SEPTEMBER 1941
REPRINTED JANUARY 1942
REPRINTED MAY 1942
REPRINTED MARCH 1943

TRIANGLE BOOKS, 14 West Forty-ninth Street
New York, N. Y.

PRINTED IN THE UNITED STATES OF AMERICA
AMERICAN BOOK—STRATFORD PRESS, INC., NEW YORK

FOR GONNIE

"Poor little devils, tearing off to work in the mornings, coming home dog tired. What happens to them, I wonder?

"I wonder, too. Isn't there a story in them, somewhere?"

WEEK-END MARRIAGE

Chapter I

"LA-DEES and gentle-men," roared the sightseeing bus guide, through the megaphone, which, since the advent of Rudy Vallée, has become so popular an aid to understanding, "on the left you will see the new building of the American Life Insurance Company. The largest insurance company in the world. In that building alone eighteen thousand people are employed. The number of employees in the main office and in branch offices all over the country total fifty thousand. Fifty thousand! The building is forty-six stories high. The tower—"

The bus moved on, lumbering like some prehistoric beast. The sightseers, out-of-town people for the most part, gazed backwards at the soaring tower, and its four-faced, enormous clock, looked over their shoulders at the ceaseless revolving doors which cast forth into the summer heat of afternoon an endless tide of people.

"Gee!" said the little girl from Newburgh, on her honeymoon, and moved her printed chiffon shoulder against the protecting serge arm of her young husband.

"La-dees and gentlemen—"

It was four-thirty. Many of the employees of the insurance company were leaving, hurrying homeward by trolley, bus or subway, some via ferries and trains to Jersey and Staten Island. They came to work and left work by the stagger plan. They would continue to pour through the gaping mouths of the many doors from now onward.

3

Men and women. Girls and boys. All ages, all sizes, all types; and all stamped with that four-thirty look of drawn eagerness. Standardized by that look. Pretty faces, ugly faces, faces with youth glowing in them, faces from which youth had been trodden out under the relentless heel of necessity. Faces turned homeward, some with relief, some with dread, some with anxiety. Faces which held secrets. Faces which had been touched with romance, deadened with grief. Clever faces, stupid faces. Plodding faces and faces that spoke to the observer in terms of Success Stories, Go-Getting, Rotarian measures. . . .

Faces . . .

Lola Davis and Connie Varesi came catapulting through the doors together. They always came out together. They worked in different sections, Lola as a secretary-stenographer and Connie in the personnel. They lived in the same neighborhood in Brooklyn, met, coming and going, were friends.

"Gosh, it's hot!" said Lola.

She wore a slim straight-line linen dress, navy-blue, with white collar and cuffs. She took off her rough-straw navy-blue hat and swung it in her hand. Her small feet were demure in low-heeled one-strap shoes and shimmering silk stockings. She turned a little, alert face to Connie. She was faintly flushed from the heat, her skin, that of a child, rosy and damp, her impertinent nose a suggestion shiny. Over a broad forehead her short hair, the strange, haunting color of raw gold, curled tightly. And the eyes she opened wide upon the world were deeply and darkly blue.

"You always look cool," Connie told her.

Not for Lola the chiffons and satins, huddled under bright smocks for working hours, of so many of the other girls. Lola dressed for the job. Lola had ideas about jobs. Lola was going to get there some day. Now she said, hurrying toward the subway:

"Holmes was in one of her take-it-or-leave-it humors today. Blue Monday, on Friday! I bet she had a row with her boy friend last night."

"Holmes" was Mrs. Holmes, Lola's present section head, to whom Lola acted as secretary. Holmes was married and forty.

"Married women," said Connie, as they plunged downward, jostled, shoved, pressed, smothered, in all the terrible impersonal intimacy of the daily subway rush hour, "married women—"

Her voice was deep. It was not accented. Connie— born of Italian parents in Brooklyn, New York, and named Concepcion—had learned English as soon as she had learned Italian. Had taught English, too, to her reluctant parents. But her voice was colored, warmed, rather than accented by association. She was a tall girl, high-breasted, with a slim arrogant nose, a curved, thin mouth, and great melancholy dark eyes in an olive-skinned face. Her hair under the tight hat she wore was very black, as nearly black as human hair may be.

Conversation ceased. The local pulled in. Flung forward, urged, pushed, the two girls won, gasping, to the center of the car and clung to the white posts, dingy now, slippery with the sweat of many grasping hands.

The electric fans whirred, stirring the stagnant air.

"Let's," gasped Lola, "let's not try for the express. This is bad enough."

Men. Collarless. Coatless. Men with collars wilting and ties under their ears. Men correctly and hideously buttoned into vests and coats. Men, straw hats shoved on the backs of their heads, or hatless. Men, frankly sweating. Fat men and thin. Men, aloof and remote behind the financial columns of their newspapers. Men, engrossed in the tabloids, foreheads beaded, eyes avid or amused over printed sagas of passion, death, accidents, graft, gossip . . . forgetting themselves and their differing problems in vicarious mystery, romance, crime, or lust.

Women. Women coming from work, women with packages in their arms, coming from the shops. Women with children, dragging them by their dirty, sticky little hands. Old women. Young women. High school girls, grouped, giggling. Child-bearing women, heavy, docile, too tired for resentment, standing on aching swollen feet. . . .

At Fourteenth Street there was a rush for the doors. An express train, already crowded, stood waiting, panting, on the other side of the platform. The guards, blue and gray, made their hoarse appeals: "Step lively, please—watch the doors." The guards put their trained knees against the backs of these herded strangers and pushed. The doors closed. Last-minute arrivals hurled themselves forward into that dangerous narrowing space. The doors kept on closing. "Hell," said a man, caught. He grinned, and the guard, swearing, pushed some more while hands from within the car pulled. The man was free. . . .

The local moved on. Connie and Lola found seats. The floor was white and black with strewn newspapers despite the polite signs urging to the proper disposal of such matters. There was a wad of gum on the window-sill next to Lola. She looked at it with disgust. She remembered a car she had seen this afternoon, waiting in front of the insurance building. A proper car, a foreign car, with a uniformed man on the box, waiting for a belated executive. A car which had been quite sure of itself. A car as modern as the building, the building which from the vastness and dimness of its stepped-backed structure, the long, strange beauty of its vertical shadows, hurled a tower upwards toward the sky in supremacy and challenge.

"Some people have all the luck," observed Connie. She was thinking, not of the car, which she had not noticed, being uninterested in executives' cars, but of the picture of an apartment-house penthouse that she had seen in a magazine that morning. A penthouse with a terrace, grass and flowers, and little trees in bloom; with lounging chairs and gay chintzes and awnings against the intrusion of the sun.

Lola nodded. She didn't bother to ask, "Why? . . . How?" It was too hot. She said, "It isn't all luck. What were you going to say about married women, Connie?"

"Married women? Oh, just that when they get the breaks—you know—a couple of girls under them—they take it out on them."

"Take what out?"

Connie was vague. She gestured, graceful, very European, for all her American standardization.

"Oh—upsets and fusses and rows and late hours. Men don't. That is, few do. They can't afford to, I think. They've got to keep it separate. The job and the home fires."

Lola said, leaning back, closing her eyes: "Lord, I'm tired. Look here, Connie, you're all off girls working after they get married, aren't you?"

"Check," said Connie. Her dark eyes were enormous. "I've seen too much trouble. Look at Agnes and Jim."

"All right, I'll look at them." Lola's eyes were open now, she laughed a little, she was ready for a battle. Not that it was the first time she and Connie had disagreed on this subject. "They seem pretty darned happy, if you ask me."

"I don't think so."

"Connie, it's just your family . . . the way they think . . . you can't get away from it."

"No, that isn't it. Mother's idea is—ten howling, giggling, underfoot, dirty children, enough to eat, a little garden, prayers and curses, kisses and blows. Oh, I know. That's not my idea. I haven't fallen for the Italian big-family notion. Women, of mother's race, do work. In little shops, over here. In the inns and vineyards, over there. But that's different."

"I don't see it." Lola was scornful. "Anyway, what with rents the way they are and everything else in proportion, how are you going to make out, tell me that? Unless you marry one of the Idle Rich. And where would you meet a guy like that who has ever heard of marriage— outside of his own crowd or maybe, the chorus? It happens now and then! Specially in the tabloids. But not for most of us. You either don't get married and spend your life slaving in an office and wondering if you'll have your job next week and listening to office gossip and rumors and learning to *yes* everybody, or else you marry someone you've been going with and like a lot and who doesn't earn much more than you. And you keep on working. Fifty-fifty. It's all right with me. I've worked too long and too hard," said Lola, "to want to be a kept woman. I want to pay my shot as I go along—if the right kind of man is willing to pay his."

"You're thinking," said Connie, and smiled, "of Ken—"

"Ken's all right," Lola told her. But she flushed.

"Seen him lately?"

"Couple of nights ago. I'm going to Agnes's tonight. He'll be there. You, too? Agnes said to tell you to come along."

"I have to go to confession," Connie told her, "and be-sides—"

"Joe doesn't like your going to Agnes's?" asked Lola shrewdly.

Joe was Connie's elder brother. The head of the family, after Connie's father. Really *the* head. And a hard head.

"It isn't that," said Connie uneasily. But it was.

A little silence fell between them. Lola was thinking . . . snatches of thought . . . tired . . . chaotic. Pay day today. Twenty-five a week, with the usual deduction for her group insurance. Seven dollars to her mother. And a dress she wanted to buy. She had seen it in a little shop on Livingston Street. Reduced. Blue. That lovely soft French blue; a dreaming sort of color. Ken liked blue. "Gee, you look sweet in blue, Lola." Any color as long as it was blue, men were like that. She must get Howard to cut the grass tomorrow. Howard hated cutting grass. He wasn't available often. Lazy, Howard was. Hanging around the poolroom, tinkering with the radio, holding jobs for a week at the most, running with a rotten crowd of loud-mouthed kids. And Millie, with her movie ambitions, her airs and graces, just out of high school and taking a job in the telephone company and kicking like a steer at her beginner's eighteen a week. . . .

Ken. She'd see him tonight. She thought of the way his hair grew back from his forehead and the funny, foolish freckles on his nose and the cleft in his chin and the eagerness in his gray eyes. He hadn't spoken yet. Not really. Said, of course, the things they all say. . . . "Gosh, I'm crazy about you, Lola." Singing, under his breath, "You do something to me . . ." or, "If I had a girl like you." Touching her hand when together they washed up dishes and pans in Agnes's little kitchenette.

Saying, "This is fun, isn't it, Lola? Boy, I'd like a kitchenette of my own! The kind you can fold up and stick under the parlor overstuffed. A girl of my own too."

Ken was sweet. He was lots of fun. She—liked Ken.

"Here we are," said Connie, later.

Eighty-sixth. They went, with the people who were left, up the stairs and out into the heat, which was surrendering a little to the wind that blew across the water, a wind straight from the ocean. They walked together for a block or so. Connie turned off.

"'By," said Connie.

"See you tomorrow," Lola told her. "Connie, come tonight, if you can."

Connie waved and said nothing, crossing the street. Lola, walking up a block or so, turned toward the water. She lived between Ridge Boulevard and Third Avenue. She walked along, stopping to speak to a woman who was raking her front yard, leaning on the little gate to hail her. "Hello, Mrs. McCarthy, how's Junior?"

"Measles," said Mrs. McCarthy. She wore a print dress and sneakers. She smiled. She had a round face and tired eyes but they laughed at Lola now. "Measles, no less! And Dorothy will be down with 'em too. It always goes double. Well," said Mrs. McCarthy, "it's all in the day's work."

Lola went on. Across the street a boy clattered down the steps of a frame house and waved his tennis racquet at her. "Hello, Bill," she called.

It was a pleasant street. Like the country, almost. Frame houses, one- and two-family houses, some with "rooms to rent" signs in their windows. Brick houses, too, with little enclosed porches and handkerchief lawns, with bird baths too big for their tiny plot, with rambler roses and lilac bushes, long since out of bloom, with rubber plants on front steps and fresh white curtains at the windows. There were children playing and sparrows in the gutter. City children were like sparrows, in their noisiness, their alertness, their quick, heady quarrels.

Near the corner, another one-family frame house, about twenty years old. It was brown. It was not quite shabby. It had been painted within the last four years. The window frames had been repainted—green—in the spring. There were flower boxes, a wide porch with old-fashioned rockers and a canvas swing, a bay window filled with plants, and a small side yard with a maple tree in it and a flower border.

Lola's father, bookkeeper for a wholesale drug house in New York, had bought the house before Lola was born, with the little legacy left him by his father. At the time he had bought it, it was one of three houses on the street. Mr. Davis was fond of telling about those days. "Country," he would say, sighing. "And farms. You could throw a stone and hit a cow."

"Who wants to hit cows?" Howard would inquire at that juncture. For a number of years he had preferred windows as targets.

Lola went up the steps. The screen door stood open. Howard was sliding down the banisters. Howard was eighteen. But he still slid down the banisters. He had retained, too, much of his gawky adolescence in his long legs and wild arms, his dramatics, his sensitiveness, his delusions of grandeur.

"Hello, kid!" Howard greeted her. He fell off the banisters and minced toward Lola with steps denoting elaborate secrecy.

"Could you—" he began.

"No, Howard, I could not. What," she asked, with

exasperation, "did you do with the money you earned last week?"

"Bought myself a Rolls-Royce," Howard replied solemnly, "and smashed it up the very first day outside one these here new night clubs on Park Avenue!"

He grinned. There was a dollar in Lola's purse. Left over from last week. She gave it to him.

"Gee, you're a peach," said Howard.

He always wanted money. He always asked for ten dollars and was satisfied with a quarter. Movies. Gum. Cigarettes. Motion-picture magazines. He'd lost the last job in a garage, because, sitting on a packing case tilted against the wall, he had been lost to the world's work, deep in the true confession of the newest star. Some day, said his mother when his father raved and stormed, some day he'd grow up. He'd settle down. Straighten out. Wait till he met a girl! But Howard wasn't interested in girls. He had been, at, say, fifteen. There was one, with unfashionable pigtails, whom he permitted to join the neighborhood ball team. She pitched a wicked ball. And if she couldn't spit a curve in the wind she had other equal accomplishments. But she grew up suddenly, and their rough-and-tumble, somehow infinitely touching courtship of harsh names, ice-cream cones, and baseball had ceased. Since that time Howard wasn't amused. He had a rooted contempt for the softer sex. He was excessively critical. Too much lip rouge or too visible powder on Lola's charming mouth and tip-tilted nose moved him to a frenzy. Any rouge or powder at all decorating Millie's almost incredibly beautiful little countenance sent him into dramatics, a form of male hysterics. And as for smoking! "If I thought that *my* sisters smoked—" Howard would begin gravely.

He had no hesitancy at "borrowing" from Lola. Or,

at least, at attempting to do so. If he got what he wanted, great. If not, well, he'd tried, hadn't he? No hard feelings.

Leaving Howard to fold up the dollar bill with an exaggerated neatness, Lola headed for the kitchen. In order to do this she went through the comfortable, shabby living-room, with its mission furniture and Morris chairs and radio, through the dining-room with its veneered walnut "suite" and into the big attractive kitchen. The walls were painted yellow. You could have eaten peacefully from the spotless floor. There was a gray cat on the window-sill and a pot of begonias. The china-closet was a bright green, and green oilcloth was on the open shelves above the shining sink. The gas range was very big and as Lola went in there greeted her an odor of cooking, hot, spicy, and, on a cold day, entrancing. But today had been very warm.

Mrs. Davis raised a flushed, pleased face. She was a plump little woman with frankly gray hair coiled on top of her head. She had Lola's blue eyes, a little faded and a little tired, surrounded by a network of fine wrinkles. Her skin was blond and delicate. She had taken no care of it, yet save for the lines of laughter and anxiety it was firm and smooth and charming as a child's. Around her trim waist were the inevitable apron strings.

Lola untied them, received the usual admonition, said, "Hello, ma!" and swung herself to the edge of the kitchen table, which was covered with a red and white checked cloth.

"Hard day?" asked Mrs. Davis, lifting a steaming lid and peering at the soup.

"Not very. Hot, though. Why don't you get up salads and cold things a day like this? What's the use of killing yourself over a raging gas flame?" asked Lola.

"Your father," said Mrs. Davis, "doesn't think he eats, unless it's soup and meat and potatoes. It doesn't matter about the weather."

She plucked a pan of biscuits deftly from the oven. Lola offered, "I'll set the table."

"Millie," Mrs. Davis told her, "was going to. Said she'd be back in time. She isn't. She never is."

Lola opened her purse, extracted seven dollars, a two-dollar bill and a five, and, reaching up, tucked them away in a fat little china teapot which stood on the shelf. Lola, as her mother often said, didn't *have* to pay her way. The roof over their heads was their own; and the little food the child ate—like a bird! But Lola preferred to help. So every Friday the seven dollars was hidden in the china teapot and sometimes more, for extras. Mrs. Davis pretended she didn't see; or, seeing, that she didn't know what it was all about. It was a strange little conspiracy between them, tender and awkward.

Lola went to the dining-room. While she was setting the table Howard lounged against the archway between dining-room and living-room and regaled her with neighborhood gossip. "Dogan," announced Howard, "came home drunk again last night. Didn't you hear it? It was enough to wake the dead. And the McCarthy brat has the measles. Old Fitzgerald's dog got tired of rummaging in the neighbors' garbage cans last night—why they don't feed the beast at home, I don't know—"

"It's obvious, isn't it?" asked Lola, with a clatter of silver.

"Gee, that's a ten-cent word! Well, anyway, after he had had a good meal he jumped the back fence into Lang's garden and tore up a lot of bulbs and things. Is Lang sore? I'll tell the world! He's raving about suing and boards of health and getting out the cops. And say, Lola, the kids have gotten into that empty house on the corner again and about wrecked it," said Howard virtuously.

"Well, you wrecked it yourself, three years ago," Lola reminded him.

"Oh, lay off that! I wasn't grown up then. Hello, Millie, how's the great big beautiful star tonight?"

Millie came in. She was small and slender. She had red-brown hair and great pansy eyes. She had a skin of strawberries and cream, and her every feature was beautifully modeled. She alternated between moods of languor and moods of fire. Languor was uppermost tonight. The heat had made her hair curl, as it had Lola's, and it lay in fine baby-ringlets on her lovely forehead.

"You bore me," said Millie, who was seventeen, to her brother. She said it in a voice that was low, and a little roughened, of the quality of heavy silk.

Mrs. Davis came in.

"Lola, I forgot to tell you, Ken called up."

"As usual," commented Millie.

"What did he say?" asked Lola, ignoring Howard's snort and Millie's weary smile. Millie had been six times to the last Garbo picture. She now registered weariness on every occasion; except when she was registering animation.

"Just that he'd call for you to go to Agnes's," her mother told her.

Lola went upstairs. Millie could set the rest of the table. It wouldn't hurt her. She heard her father's step in the hall and his voice. A moment later she heard Howard's voice, querulous and full of self-pity. Lola smiled. Howard and his father were having their evening battle without which no dinner time would be complete.

She went into the room she shared with Millie. It was a large room, with three windows. She stood at one of

them and looked toward Shore Road. The faint breeze
stirred the cross-barred curtains. The furniture was
painted in tones of pale yellow and leaf-green. She had
painted it herself. The twin beds had a night table between them, with a little lamp on it, a lamp Agnes had
given her, jade-green pottery with a frilled yellow shade.
It was a pretty room. As usual it was untidy, Millie's
belongings cycloned through it. A stocking hung limply
on an electric-light bulb. Lingerie decorated the low
chintz chair. A dress and a pair of shoes were on Lola's
bed. "Millie was born to have a maid," commented Lola.

She had just time for a shower before dinner.

Fifteen minutes later Lola was slipping on a sleeve-
less silk dress, a dusky pink. Downstairs her mother
called her: "Lola . . . Lo-*la!* Dinner's on the table!"

"Soup's on!" yelled Howard, remembering the Gumps'
astonishing maid servant.

"Coming," answered Lola.

But she stared a moment into the mirror. Cheeks
faintly flushed, lips brushed with a crimson pencil, eyes
dark with some dream under the fine-spun raw gold of her
hair. Millie's better looking, she thought.

Ken didn't think so. She'd see Ken tonight. Something brushed her heart; it was like the touch of a bird's
wing. Her pulse fluttered, startled. Warmth crept over
her. Flooded her body. She'd see Ken tonight.

"Lola!" called Mrs. Davis.

Ken came at seven. He came in a battered Dodge roadster. He drove it up in front of the frame house and
honked, outrageously. Neighbors looked from their windows or peered over their porch railings and said, "That's
Lola's boy friend." Some left it at that. Some did not.
Some went into a comfortable rocking-chair session. "If

she marries him," said Mrs. McCarthy, resting on the veranda after a tussle with Junior, "she'll have to go on working."

Millie lounged out on the Davis porch.

"For heaven's sake!" said Howard in high-pitched astonishment, appearing, "did that thing come over in the ark?"

"Hello, Ken," said Mrs. Davis, and Mr. Davis, his pipe going and his slippered feet on the railing, stretched shirt-sleeved arms and murmured a greeting.

"Well," said Lola, coming down the steps, "this is style—to go a couple of blocks!"

Ken grinned. He opened the car door and got out. He went to meet Lola with ceremony. Millie giggled.

"Thought we might take a ride first," he explained. "Jake lent it to me."

Jake was his good friend. They lived together in a rooming-house. Jake was a mechanic in one of the biggest of the Fourth Avenue garages. He was saving money for a garage of his own. Lola liked Jake although he was ill at ease with her. Or with any other girl, for that matter. No give-and-take about Jake. He was too engrossed, too single-minded. A garage of his own, some day.

Lola climbed in beside Ken. She was hatless and over her dusky pink dress she wore a little short black velvet jacket. "Gee, you look swell!" said Ken, and permitted his eyes to adore her.

It wasn't far to Agnes's. They rode down Shore Road first. A great liner had come in and was lying off Quarantine. Tugboats were jerking around fussily, like water-hens. An airplane soared overhead, with the pulse of its great heart roaring in their ears. They drove slowly around the curves of the road. Staten Island in the slanting golden light of early evening looked like a foreign country, somehow. Something adventurous about it. The air was very clear. They could see the outline of a Ferris wheel, not yet lighted, at an amusement beach across the water; they could see the fort and a white church steeple and hills of a rolling, velvety green.

"It's a grand night," commented Ken, comfortably. His hands were steady on the wheel. His gray eyes on the road ahead. He was hatless, too. His brown hair needed cutting, decided Lola. She told him so.

"Get yourself a hair-cut," she said. "Who do you think you are—John Barrymore?"

They drove past the ferry at Sixty-ninth Street, turned back and drove the length of the road again. Reaching the wide circle at the end, by the little park and Fort Hamilton, Ken parked the car. They sat there, looking out to sea. . . .

"Look," said Lola, "at that ship. She'll be all lit up before long."

"Not so the passengers," replied Ken. "Three-mile limit, you know!"

He laughed. He said, and put his arm about the back of the seat, "I'd like to go to Europe. France, perhaps, or Italy."

"England," said Lola, firmly.

"Make it England then. For two. On a honeymoon. You and me."

She said lightly, because her heart hurt her so—an ache of desire, a stab of pain!—"That will be elegant. Meantime, we'd better get on to Agnes's. They'll be waiting."

Ken answered, making no move to start the car.

"Plenty of time. Pretty darned nice couple. Agnes and Jim. Jim's a prince."

They worked together, Jim and Kenneth. Jim as an

engineer in a public-utility company, Kenneth in the sales-rooms. Kenneth said:

"I'm making fifty, Lola. As much as Jim. And Jim's a college man."

Lola said nothing. Her hands were clasped tightly to-gether. He was going to tell her. Really tell her. She wished he wouldn't. It had been *sweet* this way, waiting, wondering, fearing, hoping . . . caught up in a breath-less round-the-next-corner expectancy. But he was going to speak. To turn the corner. She would have to listen. To decide. She wasn't able to decide. She didn't want to. But . . .

"I haven't saved much," Ken told her. His gray eyes were very grave. "You know, Lola, I had my mother to take care of. It's just the last year I've been on my own. How long have we known each other?" asked Ken.

"Six months," said Lola.

"Is it long enough?"

"For—what?" But she knew.

"For—*love*—"

She had thought she wouldn't be able to decide. But she was able. Why hadn't she known there was only one way to decide?

"Yes," said Lola.

"Lola, Lola, darling—"

His arm went around her. Tight. Close. He bent his tall head and kissed her lips. It was, curiously enough, the first time he had kissed her. Not the first time she had been kissed, however. Yet, as it was Ken, somehow the first real time. He set his mouth to hers and held it there. A horn honked derisively. Someone leaned out of a car and yelled, "Leave the poor gal alone." It didn't matter. They were alone, on the road's wide curve, with the open sea before them and the murmur of trees and drowsy birds and the scent of roses from somewhere. This was their moment. Their romance.

After an interval.

"Fifty a week isn't much, but we'll manage," said Ken contentedly. "I'll work. Glory, how I'll work!"

"So will I," said Lola, and leaned her head against his shoulder.

He looked down at her. He asked quickly:

"What do you mean? Work? How?"

"At my job, silly! Did you think I'd take in washing? I get twenty-five now. I'm due," said Lola practically, "for a raise. That makes thirty. Thirty and fifty, that's eighty, Ken. We can have a cute place. We'll be on the top of the world. Jim and Agnes haven't as much. Agnes only makes twenty, you know."

"But," said Ken, and he stammered a little as he always did when he was excited or startled or worried, "but I don't *want* you working, Lola! At your job, I mean. I want to work *for* you. Have you at home . . . to come home to. I didn't think for a minute you'd want to go on working. I don't like it," said Ken, a little helplessly.

Lola drew away. She faced him. Her eyes were very dark. The light had waned so he could not see her eyes clearly, but her red mouth was intoxication in the pale oval of her face.

"But," she argued slowly, "what else can we do? With rents the way they are? And food? and clothes? And there's doctors' bills, maybe, and insurance and . . . good times. We can't do it on fifty, Ken, you know we can't! But if I work . . . Oh, it will be easy then," cried Lola, her words beating like small frantic hands against what she dimly sensed was the wall of his resistance. "And we'll be happy. Like Agnes and Jim. It won't be for long," she told him; "just till you get ahead."

"Gee," said Ken, "gee, I hadn't thought about that. I just took it for granted—the other way."

"Well," said Lola, "it's the only sensible thing to do. Unless—unless we wait," she said, very low.

"Are you willing to wait?" he asked her. His young good-looking face aged suddenly with the urgency of his question. "Lola, *are you willing to wait?*"

"Yes," said Lola. And sighed.

"I'm not!" He snatched her to him, kissed her again. The other parked cars had moved away, they were alone in their little world. "I'm not! My God, no! I've waited six months—"

"Six months?" asked Lola, laughing, trying—not very hard—to free herself.

"All my life, then, for someone like you. Six months, then, since the first time I laid eyes on you. Lola, I love you so much."

"You were in no hurry to say it," she suggested.

"I've said it every time we've met! You've known," he contradicted.

"Possibly. I meant tonight. I meant, you hadn't said . . . 'I love you.' "

"I love you," he said, quickly, ardently.

"I love you, too," whispered Lola. "Ken, for heaven's sake!"

"Is it settled then? When will we be married?"

"Well," said Lola, "in the fall? I was going to take my vacation late. In October. If you could get yours then?"

He said, suddenly worried:

"But working? I don't want you to work."

"Fifty-fifty," laughed Lola. "Partnership. We'll work together. What other way is there? It won't be for long," she said again.

He repeated it after her, salving, anesthetizing something which he, very vaguely, and very dimly, knew was a wound . . . a deep wound . . . He couldn't put a name to it, couldn't identify it. But there was an ache and a hurting, far within him.

Presently they drove the short way to Agnes's.

Agnes and Jim Read lived in a walk-up, overlooking Shore Road, on a side street. The little apartment was charming. The furniture was good, the atmosphere was better, the books that lined all available walls were best of all. Jim, out of M.I.T., had married Agnes when he found his first job, of cadet-engineer. Agnes, who had been expensively educated and then tacitly requested not to look for more help from parents who had three other girls to educate—and marry off, was working, had been ever since her marriage, in a very big department store. They managed, between them. Lola had known them ever since, directly after their marriage, they had moved to the Fort Hamilton district. That was three years ago. The girls had met first at a bridge party. And then had taken to visiting back and forth. Six months ago in this apartment Lola had met Kenneth Hayes. Jim had brought him home to dinner. "Doesn't get much home cooking, poor lad," he'd said to Agnes. "Well, he won't get much here, Lord knows," she told him. But had cooked for them both and for Lola, on Jim's suggestion to "get a girl for him—get Lola." Agnes didn't cook often, she was too tired. She and Jim ate out, at tea-rooms, a good deal. But she was a good cook because, being intelligent, she could do almost anything when she put her mind to it.

She opened the door to them.

"Hello, infants—" She stopped and stared, a dark, pretty girl, with shadows under her eyes and a gallant mouth. "Hello!" she said again, slowly. "What's happened to the two of you? Won a movie contest? Or a cut-out picture game? Or written a slogan for a new cigarette? You look as if someone had left you a million."

Jim appeared, looming up behind his wife, very tall, overslender, with a keen, hawk-nosed face and the eyes of a frustrated dreamer.

"What's up?" asked Jim. "For cat's sake, Aggie, must you keep 'em standing on the door-step? Ken doesn't sell vacuum-cleaners and toasters out of business hours. Not on his own time."

They went in. The little hall was crowded with the four of them. And Kenneth said, "We're going to get married."

"You are!"

There was the briefest silence. Agnes met her husband's eyes. They were questioning, they were demanding, they were baffled, somehow, and hurt. She looked away. There were exclamations, and back-slappings and a chorus of good-natured questions and answers. Presently Agnes took Lola into her bedroom with her.

"It looks—like Hades," Agnes apologized. "I was late. I didn't have time to clean up much. We were out to dinner. Look here, Lola, is it true?"

"Well, yes, of course."

Lola looked at Agnes. She asked, "Aren't you going to say something?"

She was frightened.

Agnes said quickly: "Of course. I wish you everything good. He's a dear, Ken. I like him so much. And he's lucky. You're—well, you're a wonder, Lola. I . . . I hope you'll be so happy," she said, and her voice broke a little.

Lola answered, out of her own dreams:

"We will be—like you and Jim."

Agnes was silent.

Suddenly she became brisk. She watched Lola combing her bright hair before the mirror, powdering her little nose, and laughing a little, with innocent defiance touching up the blurred curves of her lips with the squat little lipstick.

"When is it going to be? Where will you live? What do you plan to do? You will miss the office," she said, "I suppose. At first. They say you do. I don't know. I never saw the inside of one until after I was married. And you'll have to learn to cook . . ."

"Why?" asked Lola. "I mean, why more than—than you do? I'm going to keep on working."

Agnes asked, leaning against the bedpost: "You're going to keep on working, Lola?"

"Well, yes. What was it you called the idle rich ones? Para-parasites?" said Lola triumphantly. "That's it. I'm not going to be a parasite. And I've got to keep my job. It's twenty-five a week more. You know what that means, Agnes."

"Yes, I know," said Agnes.

In the living-room the men had turned on the radio. Someone was singing "A Cottage for Sale."

"I wish they'd sell it," said Lola, laughing.

She turned from the mirror, came and stood beside Agnes.

"Well," said Lola gayly, "pretty soon, I'll join the ranks . . . of the married women."

"Happy, aren't you?"

"So happy." She stretched her slim arms exultantly. "It's going to be such fun," cried Lola, "working—for Ken. With Ken. Keeping my job."

"Having your cake," said Agnes strangely, "and eating it, too."

Lola looked at her. Her heart sank. Agnes—didn't look happy.

"What's the matter?" she wanted to know.

"Nothing. The same old worry. It probably doesn't mean anything, but I worry each time, just the same. Lola, have you thought that if you marry and keep your job you—you won't be able to have babies?" asked Agnes, low.

Lola said slowly:

"No. I hadn't. I understand now, though. No. I hadn't thought. It's rotten, isn't it?"

The two girls stared at each other.

"I don't know," answered Agnes. "It's unfair, somehow. And you worry so. And get so nervous."

"Lola—?"

That was Ken, calling.

Lola turned her eyes from Agnes. She said:

"Well, you can't have everything."

Agnes put her arm about her.

"I didn't mean to be such a gloom," she said, with an effort at lightness. "I wish you lots of luck, Lola, you know I do."

And in her heart she added . . . God knows, you'll need it.

Chapter II

THE Davis family received the news of Lola's engagement with varying emotions. Mrs. Davis cried a little and smiled a lot—she liked Kenneth Hayes—and then became eminently practical. When would they marry? Wouldn't it be better at home? How about clothes? Where would they live? And taking Kenneth aside on that late Friday evening, felicitated him, and bound him over to keep the matrimonial peace, in the lovely, sentimental, somehow pathetic manner known only to the mothers of girl children. "She's a fine girl . . . You'll be good to her, Ken, won't you? . . . Her father and I have been very happy. . . . Marriage isn't easy, never think it, but if you really love each other—"

Mr. Davis grunted. Lola was pretty young to be getting married. "But," said Lola's mother, "I was just past eighteen!" "That's different," said her husband, with masculine lack of logic. But he was satisfied enough. He shook Ken's hand and went through all the awkward, touching male motions. He spoke of Ken's job.

"About fifty a week," Ken told him, red to the ears.

"Well," said his prospective father-in-law, "her mother and I had fourteen a week to start and we got along all right. . . ."

Howard was, of course, facetious. Howard would be. Howard, perhaps, conceded in his heart that it was better to marry than to burn; although why people were compelled to burn as an alternative, he did not, as yet, understand. Howard wise-cracked. And was a little rude to

26

Ken. But his eyes were startled and inquiring, as he turned them on his sister. "Hope I can snatch me a free lunch now and then down to your mansion," said Howard. But his boy's heart was dark with a nameless melancholy. There were, of course, no words for it. Not in his vocabulary. Howard's thoughts may have been long, but they were also vague, dim, a struggle for mental expression, altered and colored by the swift-shifting moods which were beyond his own—and a great many other people's—comprehension. He knew only that somehow this was the beginning of the end; the end of this closely knit little family—mother and father, and the three children, who, having grown up together, quarreled, demanded, fought fiercely, took sides, were nearer to one another than they knew. This was the first break in the pattern of their unity. Lola, married. Half a stranger. "Uncle Howard!" said Howard to himself, with what he termed a horse laugh. But it wasn't so funny after all. Lola, with other interests, Lola with a family of her own. It would be Millie, next! Gosh, that crazy kid! And then, some day, himself. Oh, not getting married! That was a lot of boloney. But growing up. He knew, vaguely, that he was growing up. He termed himself an adult. . . . "Hey, what's all the shooting for? I'm not a kid. Why can't I have a latch-key? Oh, for Pete's sake, you make me sick treating me as if I were a baby!" I'm a man, Howard told himself. But he knew that he wasn't. He very incoherently sensed that this polliwog stage of dreams and disasters, fevers and furors, boredom and enthusiasms, and above all the vast, rigid conservatism of his years denoted the growing-up stage. But with Lola marrying and the pattern shifting, the ultimate goal of youth, which is maturity, seemed to be too imminent.

"Why in thunder," he asked of the kitchen cat, "do girls have to get married and all that sort of blah?"

The kitchen cat, given to complacent stove and veranda sleeping by day and to wild untrammeled musical wanderings by night, looked at him from secretive amber eyes, yawned and said nothing. Born female, born feline, she was wise in any generation.

Howard deserted the family conference and drifted out on the porch. Most everyone on the street had gone to bed, he reflected gloomily. But there was a light up in Bill Downes's hall. Howard felt the need of companionship. Male companionship, young companionship. He was shut out from the living-room with its mission furniture and Morris chairs. He ambled across the street and whistled for Bill. They had never been very close friends, but they had gone to school together and had, in common, their boyhood. But Bill wasn't there.

Howard turned homeward; Bill, coming up the block, was vaguely discernible in the dusky light, pierced by the curiously effective rays of the street lamps. White flannels. Cake-eater! sneered Howard, and resolved to strike a blow for white flannels in the morning. Bill, he supposed, mildly scornful, had been hanging over the gate with Mary Norris, around the corner. . . .

"Hey!"

"Straw," Bill replied brilliantly. There was a swagger in his walk. He'd kissed Mary. She wasn't, he told himself, easy to kiss either. A nice girl . . .

They walked along together.

"What's new?" Bill wanted to know.

"Nothing. Oh, yes," remembered Howard elaborately casual, "Lola's gone and got herself a meal ticket."

"Who's the lucky guy?"

"Name's Kenneth Hayes. He's not so bad," Howard

told the other boy, suddenly boastful. "Pulls down a lot of jack. Betcher they get a car."

Bill said something suitable. Probably, "What kind?" Ensued a deep grave discussion of the relative merits of Cadillacs and Packards. "I wouldn't have a Rolls if you *gave* it to me!" announced Howard magnificently. "Overrated. That's what they are. Overrated. A Lincoln, now! That's my speed. Say, have you seen the new Fords?"

When he came home the family conference was still in progress. He whistled loudly, carelessly, and went on up the stairs. "Aren't you coming in to say good night?" his mother wanted to know. "Good night," responded Howard, hanging over the banisters for a moment. Then he went on his way. "That boy!" sighed Mrs. Davis.

Lola, had Howard looked at her . . . but somehow he hadn't wanted to look at her . . . by tomorrow it might seem right and natural . . . but not tonight . . . Lola was flushed. Ken was scarlet. Mr. Davis drew on his old pipe, making the liquid sounds which so disturbed his wife at normal times. Tonight she didn't notice. Mr. Davis had been saying, pacifically:

"But if Lola thinks that she should keep on working——"

"I don't believe in it," Mrs. Davis said flatly. "When a girl marries, she works, of course. For her home. For her husband. What kind of a home can a girl make for herself and her man if she's running to an office daytimes and skipping out to the delicatessen at night? I've seen 'em," she went on, scornfully, "bringing home dinner in a paper bag. A bit of salad, a cut of cold meat, sliced so thin you can read through it. A couple of pickles and a bakery cake."

"Marriage," Lola commented, "isn't all eating."

Mrs. Davis snorted. She sat very erect in her chair.

Her husband, thin, spare, furrowed across the high forehead from which the gray hair was retreating, looked at her with blue eyes in which a twinkle predominated.

"You'd be surprised," Mrs. Davis said, unconscious of her slang, "how much just eating marriage is! Good food! Hot. Nourishing. The kind of food that builds a man up and sends him off to work healthy and well fed and happy. Look at your father!"

Lola didn't. She looked at Kenneth instead. Her eyes were dark with appeal. Help me, she asked him silently. I belong to you now. The two of us, against the rest of the world. Against even these dear people who love me. Help me.

Kenneth said soothingly, forgetting his own disquiet, remembering only the appeal in Lola's eyes: "Lola feels that it costs a lot to live nowadays. She wants to be a partner. It will be only for a little while," promised Ken, smiling, "and then she can quit and live like a lady of leisure. I won't always be in this job. I'll be working for myself some day. There's nothing in working for another man all your life."

He stopped, embarrassed, conscious that he had stepped heavily on Mr. Davis's shabbily slippered toes. Frank Davis had worked for "another man" for thirty years. Davis smiled, waved his pipe, setting the younger man at ease.

"Oh, I don't know," Lola's father argued mildly. "Your own business is all very well, of course . . . but it's a risk. Feast today, famine tomorrow. There's something comfortable about wages that come in every week, about a boss that looks after you when you're sick, and pays you a pension when you're too old to work any more."

"Except when you get laid off," Ken suggested.

"Well, that happens, of course. But there is risk in everything." Davis's mild blue eyes had clouded. The fear of the wage-earner. Constant. Getting up with you in the morning, lying down on your pillow at night.

Mrs. Davis rose. She hadn't said her last word. Not by a lot of words. But it was one o'clock in the morning.

"Lola, you have to go to work tomorrow," she reminded her daughter.

"No, I don't," said Lola, "you forget."

"That's so." The insurance employees had full Saturdays from June until the first of September. "But Ken does. . . ."

Twenty minutes later Lola and Kenneth stood on the veranda. Inside the house Mr. Davis put out the cat, spanking her gently—"Get out, you, and don't be howling on the back fence the rest of the night"—and wound the clock. Comic-strip gestures. Real gestures. Human. Routine. He tiptoed about the living-room and kitchen, making an elaborate rite of turning out lights. Mrs. Davis was on the stairs. "Don't forget to lock up," called Mr. Davis to Lola, as he followed his wife, certain that all the windows had the catches on and that the screens were hooked.

"All right, father—"

Now they were quite alone. A light flared up in the front bedroom. They did not see it. A rambler, full-blown, clambered up one side of the porch and ran, on stealthy green feet, over the roof. Frank and Annie Davis had planted it when first they came to live in the brown house. Near it a clematis grew, thick and heavy, not yet in the feathered snow of its fragrant bloom.

Lola stood in the circle of Kenneth's arms. She asked: "It wasn't so bad, was it?"

"No—I'll say it wasn't! They're corkers. Lola, I love

you so much. You'll never regret it," he told her, and kissed her. . . .

"Of course I won't. Run along now, it's awfully late. What will the neighbors say?"

"You know as well as I do. I'll be around tomorrow. Early. We'll get Jake's car and go down to Lundy's for a shore dinner. How about it?"

The wind from the Narrows, faintly salt-scented, stirred in the tangled branches of the rambler roses. There was a silence on the dark corner of the veranda. Overhead the stars looked down and did not marvel.

Lola went upstairs, after locking the front door, dreamily. She went up lightly, her hand on the banister rail. "I'll get you a ring," he'd said. "No—you mustn't. . . . It's too extravagant. . . . We need all the money we can scrape together to furnish the apartment," she'd told him, regretful but practical. "I've something saved," he boasted. "We'll need that too," she'd said. "Then, there's my mother's. It's old-fashioned, Lola, but a good stone. I'll have it reset. You'd wear that, wouldn't you? She'd *like* it," Ken said, low.

She'd wear that, of course. Some day when their ship came in she'd have lots of jewelry. A dinner ring. A really nice pin. Meantime she'd wear the ring that Kenneth's mother had worn and she'd love it to death. . . .

Now that he had spoken she wondered why she had feared that he would. It was all so perfectly right, so natural. And as wonderful as she had known it would be. Or was it? Yes, just as wonderful, only a little different. You didn't know, really. You dreamed, you lay awake in the darkness with your arms behind your head and thought over every look, every gesture. You were wrapped, somehow, in a flame which warmed but which didn't burn. You slept thinking of tomorrow. Wondering, Will I see him?

Will he telephone? You awoke, first, to a vague, unformed feeling that something marvelous had happened, something marvelous would happen. Consciousness returned fully; you knew, you remembered, you sprang out of bed and went to your windows and looked out over the world. *Your* world. You were atiptoe, inside. Waiting. Expectant. Opening to life as a flower opens. . . .

That was over now. Gone. Now, you knew, now everything was settled. Now you belonged.

Marriage, thought Lola, that was the next step. You didn't know, either. You knew with your mind, with the knowledge people had given you, your mother, evasive, embarrassed, first, then the girls at school, then married women, and books you'd read. Oh, you knew! Yet, not really. Even when men kissed you and murmured things, and their voices grew hoarse, and their hands grew seeking, even then you didn't know. You were simply stirred, you were disturbed, you were warned. Girls, of course, cheated—before marriage. Lots of them. You knew them, listened to their light, brutal talk. You hadn't cheated. Partly because of your people, their decency, their self-respect. Partly because of your practical middle-class wisdom, which told you that you hadn't much to offer, no madness of beauty, no temptation of fortune, just yourself and your integrity. So you kept that. And then, too, you hadn't been tempted, very much. Not if you were Lola, keen on her job, happy at home, clever at eluding, and never really terribly stirred until . . . until Kenneth.

Now you were glad you hadn't cheated.

Mrs. Davis was waiting outside Lola's bedroom door. They couldn't go in Lola's room and talk. Millie was sleeping there. Millie needed her sleep. They couldn't go in Mrs. Davis's room where Mr. Davis, yawning widely, his heart inarticulately tender, inarticulately sorrowful,

was taking off his clothes and thinking how early he'd
have to get up in the morning. Thinking, damn it, it was
morning.

So they stood, Lola and her mother, just inside the
bathroom door together, the tiled bathroom with its pol-
ished nickel and bright bath mats and shower, of which
Mrs. Davis was so proud.

"You're happy, baby?" asked her mother.

Lola kissed her. No words were needed.

The girl looks tired. Her cheeks are flushed and her
eyes bright, but she looks tired, her mother thought.
There were many things to say. Many things to ask.
But that could wait.

"Run along to bed," said Mrs. Davis, and she smiled
and Lola realized how pretty Annie Davis had once been,
how pretty she still was. "He's a fine fellow," said her
mother.

That was what she had wanted to hear.

She went into her bedroom, walking carefully because
of Millie. She did not switch on the light; stood for a
moment by the window, looking out into the darkness of
the night—a darkness traveling so surely toward dawn.
She turned from the window, smiling secretly, and started
to undress.

"Lola," said Millie.

Millie sat up in bed and turned the button of the
bed-table lamp. Through the silk shade the lamplight
streamed on Millie and her almost unbelievable beauty.
Her rounded, slim shoulders in the voile nightgown. Her
red-brown hair with the light on it. Her skin of flushed
ivory. Her great eyes dark with excitement. Her mouth,
curved to a smile, shaped to a question.

"For Pete's sake!" said Lola, and ran to pull down the
shades.

"There's nothing," Millie told her, lying back against the pillows, "that the neighbors haven't seen already. What I know about Mr. Thompson since he got that sun-lamp last winter!"

Lola pulled her nightgown over her head. She has a lovely body, thought Millie, although she didn't phrase it that way. But Millie was complacent about bodies, she was so sure of her own.

Lola started for the door. "Wait a minute," Millie told her. She patted the side of her bed. She had a pretty hand.

Lola sat down. Millie stared at her. She demanded. "Well, why don't you tell me? I listened over the banisters."

"Oh, Millie! Then I don't have to tell you, do I?"

"No." Millie was silent. Then she asked . . . they all asked that. didn't they? . . . "I suppose you're awfully happy."

"Yes."

Millie said: "I like Ken. But you're too good for him. Too good for any man. Unless he has so much money that—"

"Money?" asked Lola. She lifted her chin. She said proudly: "We'll have enough! But it isn't everything." Sometimes Millie worried her. Harping on money.

"You'll go on working," Millie stated rather than asked. Of all of them she seemed to take it most for granted.

"Of course."

"That's your funeral," Millie decided, "not mine. I wouldn't work for the best man on earth. When I work, I'll work for myself. When I marry I'll quit working. And I won't be quitting the phone company either."

"Millie," said Lola with tired exasperation, "can't you

ever get it through your head that little unknown girls from Brooklyn don't become movie stars?"

"Don't they? How about Anita Stewart? And Clara Bow? How about the girls that started in business? Nancy Carroll was a stenographer, wasn't she? Ann Harding was working for an insurance company—like you."

"Go to sleep and forget it. Aren't you," asked Lola, suddenly wistful, "going to wish me—anything?"

The round arms shot up, pulled her down close. "*You know,*" said Millie, with difficulty. Millie wasn't sentimental. Millie might dream but she wasn't sentimental. Millie cared for her own, a lot. But she'd never let them know it. It made her feel queer and silly and babyish. So Millie was cynical instead. Millie cared for herself more. But that was natural, at her age and in her era. Millie knew all the parked-car technique but Millie was cautious. She knew more than Lola dreamed she knew; had experienced more. But was shrewd about it. Not from a dream with a man in it somewhere; not because of her family; but because she saw herself out of the brown house, out of the little street, out of the city itself. She saw herself with her youth intact and her beauty unimpaired. Millie was dedicated to very powerful gods, cry down the tinsel though you may. And as far as boys went—it wasn't passion that moved Millie to slip into difficult situations and with an incredible ease find her way out again and no harm done. It was a thirst for knowledge; for guarded emotion; for the spectacle of other people's emotions. For a sense of power. For a dramatic moment. Millie lived on dramatics.

Presently Lola slept. Not Millie. Millie lay there, thinking. "Some day you'll know," Lola had said. "I hope you'll be as happy as I am—some day."

Well, of course she would be! Differently. Flats . . . a walk-up—a gas range—furniture on the instalment plan, a man to cook for when he came home at night or when you both came home. Not for me! thought Millie. Babies and play pens and the odor of diapers drying, the tumbled hair and the flushed face and the marks of the can-opener and hot water and suds on pretty hands. Never! vowed Millie.

Chapter III

Kenneth telephoned the next morning. On his way to work. "I can't believe it," he said, over the wire, "but I want to believe it. So tell me it's true!"

It was true, she told him. She hadn't believed it either, waking, to that half-sleeping consciousness of something marvelous happening, something more marvelous about to happen. But it had happened. Last night.

She spent the morning with her mother. There were things to talk about. Clothes. "There's two hundred and fifty in the savings bank," Mrs. Davis said. "I saved it out of the housekeeping money. Ever since you were a baby. That's yours. To spend. Millie will have hers too, when she's ready. We've put a little aside, for each of you, when you marry."

Lola took pencil and paper. They made lists. "I can give you some furniture," her mother told her. "There's a lot in the attic. Some, you can use. And enough kitchen things, to start. And your grandmother's dishes."

Fun, planning. Knitting your brows, trying to be practical and matter of fact. "Lucky," laughed Millie, at breakfast, "that you don't wear many clothes nowadays."

Howard groaned. What a remark! He edged from the table and was gone. Baseball. Not too old for baseball, down by the sea wall, with Bill Downes and some others. Later, he'd go see the picture at the Dyker and laugh at the red-nosed comedians and the skit, on the stage, and applaud the acrobats.

After luncheon, Connie came around. Lola had phoned

her. Connie was happy for her, Lola knew that. But, "*Must* you work?" asked Connie.

Afterwards, sitting on a bench along Shore Road they talked of the wedding. She'd wear, said Lola, something simple . . . blue, perhaps, because Ken liked it so much. An afternoon dress. "The hem-lines are getting even again," Connie reminded her. And a floppy sort of hat. It would be, Lola deplored, between seasons, not summer nor winter. She'd buy her clothes to last over the winter, though. A street suit, a new coat with a furry collar, an evening gown, "black, I think, black's always good," a tweed dress for the office. Shoes, she needed shoes; and lingerie.

With what she had saved and what her mother would give her there would be plenty for clothes and for linens too, and she'd been up in the attic. There was a perfectly good bed there and some chairs and a couple of tables. Old-fashioned of course, they had belonged to her grandmother. "Everyone," said Connie, "is crazy about antiques."

Presently they went for a walk, turned off Shore Road and went up the hilly side streets. There was a house there which Lola loved. A fairy-tale sort of house, stone and built on several levels with a roof that simulated thatch. It had unexpected windows, steeply gabled. There were shrubs about it and conifers. Back of it, a garden. On the upper level, that garden—so situated that when you leaned from a bedroom window you looked into its radiant bee-haunted heart.

She thought, I'll never have a house like that. A car was standing outside the door. A sleek car, long in the body. A chauffeur in uniform was talking to a pretty maid. Her uniform was silk, pale green. She wore a sublimated apron. She was laughing up at the tall Irish boy.

I'll never have a car like that, either, thought Lola. Or a maid in a silk uniform to flirt with a chauffeur in puttees. Never.

But she might. Kenneth was clever, Kenneth would work hard. For her. For the future. Their future. Lots of people with cars and chauffeurs and maids and houses, like something out of the old dog-eared volume of Grimm, had started with walk-up flats.

Yet how many people, passing, said to themselves: I'll never have that. And never did.

Connie was talking about the wedding. "Just the family, and the girls from the office and some of Ken's friends. And of course you and Agnes and Jim," Lola answered, absently. She was thinking of a wedding she had seen, as an interested bystander. She had been shopping, one Saturday afternoon, in New York. Had passed under the striped awning, treading on the red carpet of a Fifth Avenue church. Her arms had been full of bundles. Christmas-tree trimmings and little silly, funny gifts from the big Woolworth's. She'd stopped, a little tired . . . cold . . . The December air was biting. People milled about the church, a woman with her bonnet on the back of her head, idle men with overcoat collars turned up, and girls, giggling, mentioning society-page names. "They say he's worth twenty millions . . ." "Polo," said a girl near Lola, "and the second biggest yacht afloat." She was quoting paragraphs.

The church doors were flung open. Here comes the bride. Down the red-carpeted steps, a white gown, a white veil, orange blossoms, orchids, lace. The bridesmaids a background, pastel-tinted, laughing. The groom, in correct morning clothes, a stocky man. The bride was smiling. "God bless you, lady," said the woman with her bonnet awry and the telltale breath.

Rose petals on the steps. Rice. Policemen pushing back the crowds. "Hey, what do you think you're doing?" Tall ushers running. A woman in mauve and lavender and a sable wrap. The bride had a sable wrap too. Pride feels no pain. She'd come down the steps in the whiteness of the wedding gown, smiling. Pearls at her throat. Not a very pretty girl, but a girl who made you believe she was beautiful because she thought so herself.

Cars waiting. Cops shouting. Music swelling.

Lola had walked away, with her Christmas bundles, a choked feeling in her throat. It was, she told herself, severely silly and wicked to spend money like that. She imagined the banked flowers in the church. There would be a reception somewhere. At the Plaza, the informed girl next to her had told her gaping companion. Money thrown away. Or was it? This was that girl's day.

Now, Lola was remembering.

Oh, it wasn't envy! Not envy as Millie knew it. It was a sort of sick, empty feeling. As if something had passed you by. And you wondered why. Why it had passed you by and other people had it? Not the money. Not that. Not even what the money could buy. But the power of lifting everything out of the commonplace.

Not envy. She smiled, looking back at the house. The chauffeur was in the car now, the maid had disappeared. The house dreamed in its garden. It would be cool inside, with the shades drawn, the summer curtains fluttering against the screen. Tea. There would be iced tea on the small terrace where, Lola had seen, there were lounge chairs, striped canvas, and things green and growing in pottery jars, and metal tables and a great gay umbrella.

No, not envy. But something hurting. A child outside a pastry-shop window, the nickel in her hand, to buy bread—not cookies.

"Perhaps," Connie was saying, "beige would be more practical. You could dye it, later."

"I know. But blue," said Lola firmly, "my mind's set on blue. I'm going to watch the sales. And Agnes will help. She has an employee's discount at the store. She'll get lots of the things for me."

Blue. Kenneth would love her in blue. Just as much as in ivory satin and that faintly yellowed intricate lace, just as much as in yards and yards of train and tulle, in orange blossoms, with orchids negligently in the crook of a satin arm.

That was all that mattered, really, wasn't it?

They went to Connie's house to talk to Connie's shapeless mother with the young face, the coal-black hair, the magnificent eyes, the difficult English. Joe, who ran a cigar stand and poolroom somewhere, was home. A short, broad-shouldered young man with a quick dark gaze, a sullen mouth, given to fits of anger and to bursts of laughter. His fingers were stained yellow. He dressed well. Connie was afraid of him. He had a car out at the door. They lived in a two-family house in a neighborhood of back yards, peeling paint, screaming children, and blowing paper. Yet the car outside was of a good make, in the four-thousand-dollar class. It was painted maroon, and the metal on it shone.

Connie's house smelled of cooking. Of garlic. It was vocal with the cries and quarreling of the younger children. Connie's father was upstairs sleeping heavily, fully dressed. He worked on a night shift. Joe took his feet off the round table and greeted Lola. He was pleasant to her. He approved of her—with reservations. Joe had been born in Brooklyn, but he had not yet become accustomed to girls who looked you straight in the eyes and who gave you as good as they got, who held out firm little hands for a man's casual clasp. The girls he understood best he understood racially. Slim girls, very young, with the lovely skins, the great eyes, the mouths that drooped at the corners. Girls who obeyed their fathers and brothers, and who went often to church and looked like the stained-glass windows come alive as they knelt, their beads slipping through their pale olive fingers. Girls who married men of their race and class and went to work with them in little fruit or grocery stores, who stayed at home, and went out only to haggle at the market or to gossip with the neighbors over the ramshackle fences. Girls who grew fat and—aging. Girls who had a baby every year. Girls hot with high temper, hot with ardor; girls who might use a knife on a man if he were faithless, but who loved their men; who had, in child-bearing, the incredible deep, voiceless patience of the Latin woman. Such a girl would Joe marry. And, if he had anything to say about it, such a man as himself would Connie marry. His partner, perhaps, Louis. Louis was all right. Drank too much, perhaps, gambled. But would be a good husband.

Connie didn't like Louis. "That little wop," she said; and Joe had asked, his chin thrust forward: "Wop, eh? What are you? What am I? . . . Wop!"

That was it. That was what came of giving a girl this American freedom. Wop—and dago. Nothing quite good enough for them. The house not clean enough, the food too rich, too much olive-oil. . . . "Can't you get mother to cut out a little of the garlic?" Connie would ask him, pushing away her plate. "It makes me sick. I can't go to work in an office with it hanging around me like—like—"

Nothing was good enough for them. Wanted the windows open when you had a cold. Wanted doctors. Wanted light, air, cleanliness. "The company nurse said so."

Who the hell was the company nurse? What did she know? Ma, thought Joe, had brought up plenty children. Twelve. Five had died, of course, but children always died. You expected that. Diphtheria, scarlet fever, measles . . .

"You might drive Lola home," Connie told her brother.

"Sure." His teeth were white in a dark face. "Sure, I drive her."

"No," Lola smiled back at him, no need to antagonize Connie's brother. "No, thanks a lot, Joe, but I'd rather walk."

"You staya to supper," asked Mrs. Varesi, in her sliding soft accents.

Lola shook her head. She was, she explained, going out.

Joe's face clouded. Lola was always going out. It wasn't good for Connie.

Mrs. Varesi rose and shuffled into her odorous kitchen. She came back with a bottle and some little glasses. "Good," she said, taking out the cork. "You have a little drink?"

It would hurt her if Lola didn't. "It's all right," Connie assured her. "Joe made it from our own grapes. It won't poison you or anything."

It was red and sour, a thin wine. Connie laughed as Lola raised it to her lips. Lola was, thought Connie, a good sport.

Later, Lola walked home. Down the shabby street, with its heat and noise and smells. Poor Connie! And she, Lola, had been standing in front of a stone house in

a cool garden with something like rancor in her heart.
Yet her own street was quiet, a breeze reached it, there
were flowers, and old frame houses each set in its little
yard.

Here, there were flowers too. Riotous. Roses, un-
trimmed, and forlorn lilacs, past their bloom, rhododen-
drons shaped to sturdy trees, dusty hedges, geraniums,
petunias. Now and then a pretentious bird bath, stones
piled about it, ivy struggling for a foothold. Now and
then small garden-truck patches. Or a fruit tree, undis-
couraged.

There were immemorial gestures; these cried a reaching-
out after beauty. Yet not so much after beauty as after
color. And not so much after color as after a certain
sense of communion with earth. Dark earth, from which
these people, and all people, had sprung, to which these
people, and all people, must return. These back-yard
gardens, shabby or tended, were symbols. Symbols of
man's need for earth, for the feel of it on his hands, the
taste of it on his lips. . . . This was the urgent desire
which sent home men at night to city houses, which sent
them out in their shirt-sleeves to dig, to cut a tiny handkerchief of grass, to tie back bushes, to use the pruning
shears.

Lola was aware of this. She did not put it in words.
Had she done so, she would have said: "Funny, how everybody, from the Shore Road people to the people on Connie's street, all have to have gardens, something growing."
She didn't put things in words, ever, save in the most
commonplace coinage of her age and day. What she
thought, secretly, was never verbally released. Sometimes she wondered at Agnes's incessant search for the
right word, the right phrase, Agnes's gift—or was it
curse?—of analyzing—Lola called it "picking things to

pieces"—Agnes's compulsion to argument. Perhaps, thought Lola, of Agnes, it was the way she was brought up.

She was right. Agnes had come from an environment that made more of the contacts of the intellect than of the flesh. So had her husband.

Lola looked at her little wrist watch. It was late. She quickened her steps. She must be home in time to take a shower and dress. If Ken got Jake's car again they'd have a grand time, at Lundy's.

If not, they could take a subway.

She thought about Jake. Jake was a queer creature, all red hair and freckles and square, never quite clean hands. Jake was always buying up second-hand cars that had been smashed up, and were in a desolate condition, and working on them, nights, in his shed garage back of his father's house, putting them together, taking them apart, taking a part from this one to fit into that, and then giving the finished product a coat of triumphant paint and selling it at considerable profit over what he had bought it for. She liked Jake. He hadn't had much education but he was a real person. Only, he ate, drank, and slept cars, garages, gas stations. He was fond of trying to persuade Ken to come into business with him. Ken, he said, was a natural—a born mechanic. More than that he knew figures—financial figures, Jake would add, flushing. He could run an office. White-collar stuff. With Jake on the garage end—if they got a garage—and Ken in the office, they'd get into big money some day. But Ken would laugh and shake his head. Selling vacuums and toasters was all right by him, he'd say.

Jake was going to stand up with Ken. And Millie with Lola. Lola would have liked Agnes or Connie. But she couldn't have just one. She would have to have both, and "this is no Vanderbilt wedding," she'd told her mother, laughing.

She was late getting home, and Ken had to wait. She could hear him downstairs, teasing Millie about her motion-picture ambitions. She could picture the exaggerated toss of Millie's head, the flaunting of her slim hips, the gesture of her eloquent hands. She could hear Howard saying something about a car . . . it must be a car, Howard was always talking cars, but it sounded like a cord. She could hear her mother. . . .

Presently she ran downstairs. She had a moment alone with Ken, drawn into the empty living-room, as Millie and Howard scattered, self-consciously, and Mrs. Davis went back to the kitchen.

"Love me?"

"Well, yes!"

"As much as last night?"

"More."

And then, from Ken, "Let's go."

It was like that the rest of the summer. Ken, in and out at night. Shore dinners. Trips to Coney, screaming as the boat shot into the water which boiled up around them, screaming as the roller-coaster took the steep hills and raced down them. Hot dogs. Funny prizes you got by shooting for them and paying more in the long run than a gross of them were worth. Dolls on sticks. Dolls with sleazy sophisticated clothes and a cigarette glued to the painted china lips. Motor rides along Shore Road. Once, a week-end trip to Jersey with Jake and Ken and Jake's married sister. Lola had wanted Connie to come too, but Connie couldn't. Suppers at Agnes's, with Agnes and Jim arguing about everything, and never getting anywhere and dropping the argument to go out for a soda, or to fix something in the kitchen, or because they were just too tired to argue any more. Clothes-buying at the sales, with Agnes. "This is prettier but this will wear better." Talks with her mother. . . . "But if you work, there can't be babies." "I know, mother, we'll have to wait." That embarrassed you, somehow. Not meanly. It simply touched on something you didn't want to talk about, even to your mother. You were crazy about babies. You had never told Ken so. He didn't guess. Men didn't. And talks with Ken, about furniture. And flat-hunting with Ken. And finding one, not far from the Davis house, between Third and Fourth avenues, a nice little place with a sun-room enclosed like a porch on the top floor of a four-family house, red brick, whitening with the weather. Furniture and furniture stores. And Ken giving his utility company for a reference, so that he could get things on the instalment plan.

This and more. The girls in the office whispering; envious, prying, or cordial. The ring, reset, the diamond very brave in its new platinum. That had cost a lot. Too much. "Not too much for my girl!" Ken had told her.

Holmes, the office boss, her eyes sharp behind glasses. "So you're getting married?" "Yes, Mrs. Holmes." "Quitting?" "Well, no." And Holmes had laughed a little.

There'd been no trouble about vacations. Jim had spoken a word for Ken, in an official ear which happened to be lenient to Jim. "Fine fellow. Fine family, Yale Sheffield, working his way up. Our engineers are all of a very fine type"—and Mrs. Holmes had somehow not spoiled Lola's plans. Her vacation was due her, of course. But if Holmes could have made her unhappy she might have done so, out of something that Agnes said, sagely, when it was discussed, was probably Mrs. Holmes's own unhappiness. "Never thought of that, did you, Lola?"

Agnes herself was all right again. The fear gone, the terror dissipated. "Until next time," said Agnes bitterly.

October.

The maples red, and the water deeply blue and the sky an arch of living azure. Liners sailing up the Narrows. Autumn in the air and summer in the sunlight.

The little flat had been furnished. "When you come back," promised Mrs. Davis, "you can walk right in, we'll have everything ready."

They were going to Atlantic City. For two weeks. On the last of Ken's savings, even if they could have autumn rates and live in a reasonable hotel, off the boardwalk. Oh, Ken, should we? You bet we should! And in her heart she had agreed. A little madness, a little extravagance, didn't they owe it to themselves?

Once in a lifetime.

Wedding presents. Linen from Agnes and Jim. From Connie a suitcase and a case of home-made wine from Joe. Astonishingly good silver spoons, six of them from Jake. The money from her parents. And an overstuffed suite. And a nightgown from Millie; she'd saved her money for it. "*Oh!*" cried Lola, gasping.

Chiffon, blush-pink, straps of real lace. A lovely thing. Insanity! Millie had put every cent she had into it.

"Millie . . . you shouldn't—you mustn't—"

Mrs. Davis, feeling the material between her worn hands.

"It's indecent, that's what it is! But it's beautiful," she said grudgingly, "but for what you paid for that, Millie, you could have furnished Lola's kitchen with the things she needs."

Millie said, merely, "I wanted her to have *this*."

October.

She was married in blue, in the living-room, the furniture cleared out, the rented palms in the corners. She had a wide hat and pretty slippers and sheer stockings. Ken, beside her, very grave, a little pale, in the new serge suit. The minister's voice, deep, questioning . . .

"Do you take this woman—"

Her own answer, clear, sounding very loud in her own ears. Ken's muffled, low.

"For richer, for poorer—"

For richer, she thought, oh, not in money. In . . . living.

Agnes, standing a little back, put her handkerchief to her eyes. Lola, Lola, so much to learn!

Jim put his arm about her. "Steady, old thing," he murmured. But he couldn't meet her eyes. Nor she his. If they could only go home and find a moment, an untired, unirritated moment in which to talk things out. Everything. All the things that troubled them, distressed and puzzled them, separately and mutually. But they never found that moment.

Connie wept frankly. Joe, uneasy in his stiff collar, cleared his throat. Mrs. Davis was crying too. Millie, in her bridesmaid frock, pale pink and very becoming, posed herself before the mirror. Her eyes were very bright. She wouldn't cry. She couldn't. But something in her, her sense of the theater said, dramatically, *My only sister!* She wept then, gracefully, tears rolling down her little face.

Then it was over. They had a buffet supper. Salad, cake, ice-cream, coffee. Home-made. All of it. They had decided against the caterer. To rent the palms and the chairs was enough.

It was early evening. Jake drove them to their train, in one of the good cars he had borrowed from his boss. Lola, in her little suit, wearing the very simple, very pretty fur piece the girls in the office had clubbed together to give her, slipped her hand into Ken's. Her lashes were wet, stuck together in points. But she was smiling.

"Feel very grand?" she suggested, patting the upholstery with her free hand.

"Swell. Some day we'll have one of our own."

He tightened his clasp on her hand.

"Sorry?"

"No, Ken."

"Afraid?" he asked, feeling her tremble against him.

"No—that is—not much."

"You needn't be," he told her, reverently, with tenderness.

Married.

Chapter IV

Lola, coming up out of the subway at Eighty-sixth Street, gasped as the bitter wind caught her, twisted her skirts about her knees and flung the soft, damp snow and stinging particles of sleet into her face. It was very dark, at six o'clock. The snow swirled about the lighted street lamps, feathery and unreal. People were hurrying home, bearing useless umbrellas, hailing taxis.

She was late. She had telephoned Ken that she would be. She was cold, hungry, and dead-tired. Every bone in her body ached like a bruise. She hesitated, in the shelter afforded by the doorway of a stationery and cigar store. People pushed by her, fighting to get inside where the space around the public phone booths was crowded, women standing on tiptoe at the transmitters, calling their homes, while men chewed cigars outside the dirty glass doors and glared, profanely vocal with impatience.

Lola thought . . . I'll take a taxi. But it seemed silly, for just that little distance! Besides, it was the middle of the week, two days, two lean days until pay-day. Things had happened. Ken had had to have some dental work done, there were the instalments on the electric refrigerator, which, even considering Ken's discount, mounted up, had to be thought of each month. Instalments on the rugs and furniture. The first of the month was gradually becoming a nightmare. She had never minded the first of the month before she had married. And her raise just before her marriage had seemed enormous, especially as she would no longer be contributing anything at home.

She thought—*home*—with a sudden nervous, sentimental longing. Shabby brown house and the smell of cooking and her mother's voice from the kitchen.

She looked out, across the shining slippery street where the snow was melting as fast as it fell. The lights of a radio shop pulsed through the sticky dusk, and a loudspeaker fastened above the door beat out a dance tune, accented by static and by code from somewhere. She thought . . . instalments on the radio, too. She had given Ken a radio for Christmas. He had loved it, spending most of his spare time taking it apart and putting it together again.

I'll take a taxi, she thought again. But even as she stepped forward a man brushed past her, hurried down to the corner and hailed the last cab left on the line.

I can't stay here all night! she decided. She clutched her umbrella and left the temporary shelter. The umbrella was quite without worth. She put her head down, struck out bravely. But the snow and sleet and the half-rain, half-snow were wet and cold on her legs above the galoshes. Her eyes were blinded and her cheeks wet, not alone with weather but with involuntary tears which the sharp wind forced from her eyes. She set her teeth and went on.

Ken would have brought something in from the stores. She'd asked him to. She was too tired, she thought, to cook. Too tired to do anything but get off her wet clothes. She wondered, worriedly, if she would have to send her coat to the tailor's. The fur collar lay about her throat bedraggled as an alley cat. It had been cloudy when she left for work but with no apparent signs of this sudden blowing storm.

She wondered if there would be any hot water. They had found the type of water-heater that they had been using dreadfully expensive, and had changed to a little coal stove, which had to be tended. She hadn't, she remembered, asked Ken to build up the fire when she had left that morning. They had both overslept, they had been out with Agnes and Jim the night before, going to the second show at one of the down-town picture theaters.

She reached her home, with very little breath left and to spare. She stood for a moment on the steps, let herself in, handling the key gingerly with her soaked gloves. She started up the steps, walking like an old woman, a little sorry for herself and so terribly tired that her feet in the clumsy galoshes dragged and felt heavy to lift. Half-way up the stairs she found voice.

"Ken?"

There was no answer. He wasn't there. Sudden disappointment swept over her, as damp and chilling as the snow.

She went into the apartment. The door was unlocked. Ken must be home.

The "sun" porch was empty. So was the living-dining-room. She saw that he hadn't set the table. It was pushed back against the wall as she had left it this morning after their hurried breakfast. The bedroom was empty, too. And the kitchen, with the breakfast dishes piled up in a corner of the sink.

The apartment was cold. They supplied their own heat, but made an arrangement with a man who took care of other apartment furnaces to look after theirs. He was a garrulous, voluble creature, much given to strong drink and mild language. Probably he hadn't been in today. But Ken might have looked. Still, Ken wasn't home.

Oh, but he had been, she saw his overcoat on a heap on a chair in the tiny foyer and his large masculine rubbers near by. He must have gone into the apartment next door, which was inhabited by three young men from the telephone company, whose radio was a fascination and a snare to Ken at all times.

She stripped off her wet things. She ran the water. It wasn't, of course, hot. She put on one of her summer dresses and belted a sweater coat about it.

Lola went into the kitchen. Yes, Ken had remembered. On the shelf by the sink was a little soaked paper box of potato salad, a roll of oiled paper containing, she thought drearily, either ham or roast beef. Some rolls in a bag. A coffee ring.

She got down plates and cups. She went into the living-room and pulled the gate-leg table away from the wall. She laid a fresh cloth upon it. She couldn't use the one they'd had that morning, she thought, after Ken's accident with a soft-boiled egg. And their laundry bills were tremendous considering that there were only two of them! Ken had a way with towels. Used them once. Bathing, he blotted himself dry and then threw the towel on the bathroom floor and stood on it, for no good reason. Their bath towels were a sight. Face towels were always sopping wet. Ken shaved merrily, wiped his face, and flung the towel aside. No use remonstrating. He always grinned and was sorry and forgot, next time.

Men were, she supposed, like that.

She heard his step in the outer hall. She hadn't gone to meet him. She was too tired. He came in whistling.

"Lola?"

"Here—"

He followed her into the kitchen, where she had gone to get the coffee-pot. He said gayly, "Hello, darling."

"Hello," said Lola, and turned her cheek to his kiss.

"Why the frozen face? What's the matter?" Ken wanted to know.

She hated being asked what's the matter. Most women hate it, whether anything's the matter or not.

"Nothing."

"Here, let me help." He was suddenly busy making himself useful in his awkward male fashion. He plucked an apron from the nail on the wall and tied it about his slim waist. He piled dishes . . . along his arm. . . . "Watch my smoke," said Ken.

"Look out!" cried Lola, too late.

A dish crashed to the floor. And another.

"Oh, gee, I'm sorry!" said Ken, with a rueful face.

He made for the little brush closet. Produced dustpan and broom. Knelt.

"Here, let me do that," said Lola.

She pushed him aside gently. She swept up the damage. She said, "My poor dishes!"

"Well," Ken remarked, "there's compensation in everything! They weren't the good ones. Just the five-and-ten fillers-in."

"Even," said Lola, "even the five-and-ten ones cost—five and ten."

"Why so downhearted?" asked Ken. "Give the bird another seed. Here,"—he thrust his hand into his pocket, pulled out two quarters, flung them on the kitchen table—"go down and buy yourself a banquet set!" order Ken magnificently.

Lola laughed in spite of herself.

"Bring in some spoons," she said.

Presently they were at the table. Ken looked about him with appreciation.

"Pretty good port in a storm," he observed, helping

himself to salad and putting top-of-the-bottle cream in his coffee.

Lola, a little relaxed, and very much ashamed of her recent humor said, on the breath of a sigh:

"Thought I'd never get here. It was awfully cold. I got soaked through."

"Poor kid. Why didn't you take a taxi?"

"Well, while I was wondering if I could afford it the last one took wings and flitted away. Some bloated pluto-crat from Shore Road, I guess."

"I guess not. They have their own cars. Or else are so busy paying taxes and holding on, in case the apartment-house boom does go through, now that the restrictions are off, that they haven't anything over for taxis. But you have. We have. I mean, it's better to pay a quarter and save yourself, than get pneumonia or something and be laid up."

"Don't I know it?" Lola's little tired face was very grave. She had been out, ill, several times since fall. More times, she thought, than in all the years before. Before, she'd had a very clean bill of health on the company records. Not now.

But she was so tired, often. Nervous. She caught cold more easily. She had headaches.

"What made you so late?" asked Ken, his mouth full of ham.

Lola pushed her plate away. She was still hungry but somehow too hungry—or was it sick?—to eat. She answered:

"Oh, Jameson. He had some letters to get out."

She had been transferred, directly after her vacation. The Central Bureau had taken her from Mrs. Holmes's department and she had worked there for a time. From there she had gone to be secretary to Mr. Jameson, one of the vice-presidents.

"He shouldn't keep you," grumbled Ken. "Slave-driver!"

"No, he's not, really. He's a peach. Nice as can be. But they're swamped with work. Holmes said I'd have to work like a slave."

She chuckled faintly, thinking of Mrs. Holmes. Holmes had been a grouch. Lola remembered the Black Monday moods. Holmes, as Connie had said, had taken out her personal grievances on everybody. But she was a good sort in her way. Awfully afraid of her job, of course. She'd been there, thought Lola, a thousand years.

"What's the joke? Let me in on it?"

"Nothing much. Only when I left Mrs. Holmes she was so full of good advice. 'You'll never get anywhere,' she told me sourly, 'and you'll work your fool head off. Women in business haven't a chance. Especially married women.' I said, 'Well, we can't all marry millionaires, can we?' And she shut up. You know, they said in the office that the man she married was supposed to be heir to a wad of money. But the uncle died and didn't leave him a cent. He fought the will and it cost him all he had and he lost his case. So now he clerks somewhere. They say he does the housework."

"What a sap!" Ken remarked deeply. "Catch me doing housework!"

"I thought as much," Lola told him, "when I came in and didn't find the table set or anything."

"Oh, gosh!" He was apologetic. "I didn't mean not to. I meant to have everything ready. But the boys in three forty-one have a trick new tube. They yelled at me to come over. What's the matter, Lola? You aren't eating."

"I don't want to. I wish we'd told mother we'd be down tonight."

"In all this weather? Besides, we were there night before last and we always go Sundays."

"I know. But they love to have us," Lola said.

He helped her wash up after dinner. They went into the living-room together. Lola relaxed into a big chair and put her feet on a little stool. Lord, she was tired! She was always more tired than ever when Ken insisted on washing up. Logic told her that in a fifty-fifty partnership he ought to be willing to do his share. And he was, despite his recent remark about housework. But drying dishes didn't seem beneath his dignity to him. Not yet, at least. He rather liked it. He would whistle about the kitchen, dropping plates and neatly catching them, until Lola's nerves were on edge. He'd remind her of their first meetings at Agnes's. "Remember how I said I wanted a kitchenette of my own and a girl like you in it? Well, I got 'em. I'm a lucky guy!" he'd boast.

He was a darling.

He was fussing at the radio now. Turning things on. Turning them off. "Hell, nothing but lectures and French lessons!" A snatch of jazz; a blurr of the Venetian Love Song; a man talking on conditions in China. Lola put her hands to her ears. "Wish we had a set like the one at three forty-one," said Ken.

"Please turn on something and leave it on or turn the darned thing off altogether," Lola begged him, a little shrilly.

He looked up in some astonishment.

"Sure. What's the matter? Something get on your nerves?" he wanted to know.

She suppressed a desire to shriek, "Don't always ask me

what's the matter. Take it for granted." She smiled instead.

"No, just tired."

"Poor kid," he said again.

He came over and perched on the arm of her chair. Stroked her hair back from her forehead with a careful, tender, clumsy touch. Lola set her teeth. She didn't want to be touched. Yet, insensibly, under his hand she quieted, relaxed and lay quite still.

"What do you say we call up Agnes and Jim and see if they'll come over?" Ken wanted to know.

Lola roused herself.

"Oh no, not tonight, Ken. They probably didn't go to the tea-room because it was storming. Agnes has a cold. Don't you remember how she sneezed last night? She'll be dead-tired if she gets dinner. She hates getting dinner."

"Well, she can buy it out of a shop window," Ken grinned.

"She can. But she won't. She can't bear cold food, thrown together. Neither can Jim. She'd toil over a cook-book for hours first. That's why they eat out so much. Even breakfast."

He rose, walked about the room talking. He'd seen Jake at lunch time. Jake was on the crest. Had sold several of his remodeled cars at a good profit. With the automobile business not so hot, since the crash, second-hand cars were bringing something. Buy a new car nowadays and they gave you a damned good turn-in price. Anything to keep the cars on their floors moving. Jake was looking for a gas station site. Lots of customers who'd come to the garage where he worked would throw him their trade. Only gas and oil and fixing flats at first. But he expected to expand. Of course, he'd have to rent at first, though. Your credit wasn't so good with the gas companies when you rented. You paid, on the nail. Own your own building and it was different. Jake, said Ken loyally, would own his own in five years. That boy was a humdinger!

Lola wasn't listening. He looked over at her. Her lashes were dark against the pallor of her face. He said quickly, forgetting his instant and instinctive resentment at her inattention:

"Gee, honey, you look white as a sheet."

"No, not really. Just too dog-tired to drag out the old compact and lipstick, that's all." She opened her eyes and looked at him. He was an awful kid, a sweet kid. His gray eyes were dark with anxiety, his brow furrowed. She smiled at him. His forehead cleared. He came over and kissed her.

She could forget a lot when he kissed her.

She said lazily: "Turn on your old radio, do. Wednesday, isn't it? There ought to be a good program. Rudy Vallée?" she teased.

"He's on Thursdays," said Ken, "and what you see in crooning!"

"How about the Maine Stein Song?"

"That's different. I'll say he puts it over," Ken admitted. He hummed a bar or two. He had a pleasant untrained baritone. He went to the radio and fussed with the station-finder and volume control.

"You listen to that," Lola told him, as a blues singer's throaty lament came drifting over the air. "I'll go and get the family budget-book and the bills and things."

"Must you?" Ken groaned. "What a note!"

"Has to be done," she said firmly.

She went into the bedroom. A pleasant bedroom with the old-fashioned bed she'd found in her mother's attic, and a low slipper chair. A fat squatty chair, chintz-covered. The lamp Agnes had given her, on the bedside table. A bureau she shared with Ken, his brushes and comb on the top of it. And her picture in a leather frame. Her vanity table, with Ken smiling from a tiny silver setting. A snapshot. She'd taken it on the Boardwalk in Atlantic City. On the other side of the vanity was the unframed absurd postcard they'd posed for down there. Herself, bolt upright in a straight chair, in an attitude of the not-so-gay eighties; Ken, standing back of her, one hand on her shoulder, the other thrust into his coat. How they'd laughed, how pained the photographer had looked!

Atlantic City. She sat down in front of the dresser and stared at the postcard, which was a bit limp about its edges. I must find a frame, she thought. The comfortable shabby hotel. The appetites brought to their meals. The miles they had walked, the movies they had gone to, seeing very little of the vicarious romance briefly living on the screen. Living their own. Happy. Wondering. Discovering. Quarreling once—no, twice—and making up again.

She opened the vanity-table drawer. It was a confusion. She must clean it out, straighten up Ken's things, too, look through all the closets. When she had time. Saturday afternoon maybe. Or Sunday, before they went to her mother's.

The bills were there. The budget books. The stout manila envelopes marked: rent . . . coal . . . light . . . gas . . . food . . . recreation . . . clothes . . . emergencies . . . savings. Into these envelopes went sums of money. "We should have a checking account," said Ken. "But we never have enough over to keep a balance, darling! Well, some day."

The savings envelope was flat, as deserted, as empty as last year's nest.

Eighty a week had seemed like a fortune.

Well, it wasn't.

She poked back in the drawer and found the instalment-payments envelope. It was wedged in. She loosened it and drew it out. Presently she went back to the living-room table and cleared a space, pushing aside book-ends and a tall green glass vase. Ken was still at the radio.

"Tell me the worst," he suggested cheerfully.

"Turn off that thing," said Lola, unable to add with the strains of "Soon" in her ears.

Ken switched off the radio. He came over and pulled up a chair beside her. The dentist's bill stared him in the face. In the teeth. He asked gayly, "Does this come under recreation?"

"Emergencies," Lola said absent-mindedly.

Half an hour later she gathered up the fatal papers, as Ken called them.

"There!" said Ken. "Here, give me the bills; I'll get money-orders tomorrow."

"Don't," begged Lola, "don't put it off. I mean, don't forget."

Once, he had forgotten. Two bills. Notices had come. Lola, who hated debt, had acted, Ken said, as if the sheriff were after her. "Don't be downhearted, girl," he had teased her. "Bigger and better women than you are have been in jail." He had mentioned Mae West.

When Lola had returned from the bedroom.

"There won't be much left over at the end of the month," she said, sighing.

Kenneth sobered.

"Lord, I wish you didn't have to go through all this!"

He thought, frowning, of her careful way of figuring percentages: "*I'll pay half of this; a third of that.*"

"Some day," Ken promised her, "I'll make a million. And all you'll have to do will be to sit back and watch your private secretary write checks."

He went to the window. The snow had stopped. It was raining steadily. He said, over his shoulder:

"Got a lift home tonight."

"That's nice," Lola murmured sleepily.

"Here . . . where's that new detective story from Womrath's?" He browsed about among their few books. School text-books of his, and Lola's. A few novels. A couple of "sets"—one had been a wedding present and was George Eliot. And finally he discovered the book among half a dozen weekly and motion-picture magazines on the table.

"Get set," he urged her. "I hope there are six murders, all in closed rooms with no exits or entrances and lots of blood on the floors."

Lola lay back in her chair. Ken, in a corner of the couch, adjusted the bridge lamp to his liking. Opened the book.

" 'As Mary Evans entered the door of apartment six to do her morning cleaning she stumbled over the body of a man lying across the threshold, his throat cut with some jagged instrument,' " read Ken.

"Oh," said Lola in a small voice.

"Gee, this looks like a lulu!"

He read on. By the time he had reached the middle of the chapter in which the titled amateur detective walked in, monocle in eye, topper in hand, and deduced that the murderer was six foot two, blind on the left side, and wearing specially made boots—these deductions all accompanied with erudite references to the Borgias, Cellini, the Mona Lisa, and the export trade to South America, as well as sales at Christie's—Lola was fast asleep.

"Well, I'll be darned—or something," Ken murmured. She was tired. He'd let her sleep. He went on reading to himself, stopping now and then to run a bewildered hand through his thick brown hair.

At half past ten she stirred and spoke his name.

Ken dropped the book, face down, and went over to her.

"Oh—I must have fallen asleep," said Lola, flushed and apologetic. "What time is it?"

"Time for little secretaries to vice-presidents to be in bed," Ken told her.

He picked her up and carried her into the bedroom, returning to lock the windows and turn out lights. Lola in pajamas and a coolie coat appeared, headed for the kitchen.

"Hey, where you going?" asked Ken.

"To set the table for breakfast."

"Leave it. We'll get up earlier."

She stood in the kitchen doorway, her hair curled about her forehead, her eyelids heavy. She looked very young, much of her weariness had vanished, she looked like a sleepy child. "Oh, Ken, we never do!" she said.

"Go to bed, woman! We'll go to the tea-room and have breakfast with Agnes and Jim," decided Kenneth.

"But, darling, we can't afford—"

"Another word out of you and a wife-beating will take place in this quiet residential section, near beautiful Shore Road," he threatened her.

When he emerged from the bathroom a little later after the strange raspings and garglings which marked his ablutions, he found her sleeping, one arm over her head, her cheek turned to the pillow. On the edge of the bed.

Later, he knew she would roll over to the middle and hunt for him drowsily. Later, he would lie on the extreme edge of his own side and suffer in patience and with some curious, wistful delight.

He was asleep almost as soon as he had climbed in beside her. So sound asleep that he knew very little about it until the alarm clock went off in his ear.

It was a clear, cold morning. Rained out. With few traces of yesterday's storm and snow save for the swirl of brown oak leaves, tenacious, trying to hold on until spring, in the gutters, and a glistening, washed look to the world. Ken and Lola walked the short distance to the tea-room.

It was rather like other tea-rooms. Beige curtains, green drapes, green painted tables, fair food. Very good food if you only used it occasionally.

It was occasionally with Ken and Lola. They went in, laughing, and made for the table at which Agnes and Jim always sat, waited on by the same waitress.

"Hello, infants," said Ken.

They had been arguing, low-voiced. One saw that. Jim got up hastily. A strange expression in his eyes; half relief, half regret. He said, "Well, if it isn't the newly-weds!"

"Thought we'd spread ourselves a little. Can't we all sit together?"

"Sure. We've just ordered. Here, let's take that table for four."

Ken, settled, picked up the menu. Club breakfast. He passed by the coffee and rolls with its modest price. He looked fleetingly at coffee, rolls, and cereal. He decided on coffee, rolls, cereal, ham and eggs. He said so, loudly, leaning back, tilting the chair on its frail legs.

"Coffee and rolls," said Lola.

"That's our meal-ticket," Jim remarked, nodding to the red-headed waitress.

"Lola . . . I insist," said Ken, in a husbandly voice. "You have to eat more, mornings. Remember the time you fainted going over in the subway? Coffee, rolls, orange juice, and two boiled eggs for Mrs. Hayes," he told the waitress firmly.

"Masterful guy," Jim commented, grinning.

Later, the girls talked . . . Lola of the new boss, Agnes of bad business in the store. "What *are* you whispering for?" Lola wanted to know, amused. Agnes flushed to the roots of her black hair.

"Oh, just habit. They know us here. The red-head is especially fond of Jim. Hovers over him like a mother. We can't say anything—confidential."

"I see. Well, Mr. Jameson isn't confidential," Lola laughed.

"What's that about bad business?" Ken wanted to know.

"People aren't shopping much," Agnes told him. "Necessities, yes. Luxuries, no. At the perfume counter no one has sold her quota for weeks. As for jewelry and furs—"

Ken said, low, to Jim:

"We're not doing such a hot business either. Did you hear anything about some of the salesmen being laid off?"

Jim shook his head. "No. Not worried, are you?"

"A little," Ken answered, glancing toward Lola, deep in conversation with Agnes, and dropping his voice. "You see, everyone else has been there longer than I have. And that's that."

"We're all right, in my end of it," Jim told him. "People burn more light in winter, thank God."

Agnes looked at her watch. "You'll have to hurry," she said to Lola.

The other three would get out of the subway down-town in Brooklyn. Agnes a station or so ahead of the two men. Lola gathered up her things while Jim and Ken paid the checks and tucked their modest tips under a plate in the shamefaced way of men dealing with waitresses and tea-rooms. They went out into the street together and down into the subway. Connie was waiting there. "I thought you'd never come," she told Lola.

The three girls found seats together. "Glad we live so near the end of the line," Agnes sighed. She stretched out her feet. "I'll have to draw on the family exchequer for new shoes," she complained. "My feet kill me. I can't get used to it. Running about all day buying an ironing-board cover, six glass plates, two fancy flowers, and a carpet-sweeper, for women who, generally, return them."

She had been transferred lately, from the selling end to the personnel-shopping service. She liked it, she told the other girls. "Only if business keeps on like this I'll be behind a counter again and lucky at that."

"Why?" asked Connie.

"Oh, shopping services are luxuries too and the first to go when they cut down the staff," explained Agnes. She added hastily: "Don't say anything to Jim. He hates me to be worrying about the job."

"Who doesn't worry about jobs?" inquired Connie.

She thought . . . *Louis*. She couldn't avoid him. Joe brought him around every night. An undersized man with a sallow skin and bright dark eyes. Sometimes he brought flowers. He sat and looked at her. He was, she knew, quick-tempered, overbearing. But a good business man. And humble, with her. She didn't love him. She never would. But—

"I'm tired of working!" she said aloud.

There was a silence. Agnes was remembering. Her father's old house off lower Fifth Avenue, small and gloomy, with a little yard. The shades pulled down in early summer, the furniture cloaked in white, the pictures covered with green net. She was remembering school. And matinées, after she graduated. Lunches. Dinners. Dances. She'd met Jim at a dance. Later, he had come down to Bellport, where her family had a cottage in the summer.

They spent their vacations there now, with the family. For the two years since they'd been married. It had been —quite a wedding. But the other girls were coming along. It cost money to dress girls, to keep a small car, to go away in the summer. Her father was a lawyer in a big firm but not of the firm. Now and then he gave her a little check with a shamefaced smile. "Sorry it isn't more, Agnes. But somehow we don't seem to manage . . ."

Lola said sturdily: "I'm not. I love it. I'm going to get somewhere some day, I'm going to draw down a salary I'm not ashamed of. Have a maid. Have lots of things I want."

Agnes asked gently, "Have you told Ken that?"

"Why, no—he knows, though, why shouldn't he? He wants to get somewhere, too, doesn't he? Why shouldn't I? I don't ever want to be a drag on him."

"Don't tell him," Agnes advised wearily. "Men are funny about ambitious wives; I was ambitious once, too. When I first went in. Was going to be a buyer some day. How I figured it, I don't know. But one of the girls from school, whom I used to know, is a buyer over at Best's. She's making good. Goes abroad every year."

"Is she married?" asked Lola idly.

Agnes looked at her, a bright, dark glance.

"She is not," said Agnes.

The car had filled up. Jim and Ken had given their seats across from the girls to middle-aged women. They hung on straps and read tabloids.

Presently, good-bys said, Lola was riding toward work. She was still tired from last night. But she looked forward to her work. It was new, being with Mr. Jameson. She liked it. She liked him. If he liked her, she might go far. She could earn much more than she was earning. And she was earning now so much more than most of the girls. Connie had shown her some statistics once, from her department. Of 305 married women only a little under twelve and one-half per cent were earning thirty dollars a week.

She thought: When spring comes I'll have to get some clothes. The last summer's ones wouldn't do. She thought further: We'll have the ice-box paid for then and the radio. But still, there wouldn't be anything in that envelope marked savings. We are saving though, she argued with herself; we both carry group insurance and disability. Yet it was different to have cash in the bank. Solid. Back of you like a friendly wall. An anchor to windward.

Other springs she'd managed clothes.

She thought: If we don't take a vacation this year? But if they were lucky enough to get theirs together they had planned to go to a place in Maine Jim had told them about. Where you could fish. Like a camp, it was. Ken would love that. Jake might come along, drive them up in the car. But summer was a long way off.

She got out at her station and presently the great doors of the building with its soaring, aspiring tower engulfed her, swallowed her up, cast her out again into the immense modern halls, with their indirect lighting, their black and white pattern. Messenger girls hurried past, gay smocks, green, blue, orange, over their dresses . . . dresses with uneven hem-lines, dresses of sleazy chiffon and satin and crape.

Lola looked down at her trim little tweed dress, one-piece and belted, the white collar and cuffs spotless. They should be. She washed them herself and sewed them on again, almost every day.

She got into the elevator and went on up to her floor.

The outer office was quiet. She picked up the mail and went into the private room. The telephone rang. Her day's work had begun.

Two weeks later she was hurrying home. Early. Her cheeks were flushed with excitement. Jameson wanted, he said, to use her permanently. He was satisfied with her work. She would have a raise immediately. She'd go up fast, he told her. She wanted to tell Ken, to surprise him. She'd have the very best dinner . . . She couldn't wait to see Ken, to tell him.

She got off at her station and went into a near-by butcher shop. She bought a steak, a little porterhouse. She'd be extravagant for once. There were priceless mushrooms in the window of the green-grocer's. She bought those too and, laughing at herself, a box of straw-berries. Ridiculous. But they were red and pointed and capped with green. They were fragrant as summer. She took them all home and the French bread, a long roll, that Ken liked so well, and a paper container of cream.

Ken was late.

Broiled steak and French-fried. A plain salad of the lettuce, now keeping fresh in the ice-box. Strong coffee and real cream. And biscuit shortcake! Her mother had taught her to make that. It would be hot . . . the cream would melt on it.

She was whipping the cream when Ken came in. He was tired. She could tell that by the silence attending the slam of the door, by the sound of his feet. He came and stood in the kitchen door and sniffed.

"Golly, that smells good," he said.

"We're celebrating," she told him, reaching up to kiss him jubilantly.

"Hey, mind the beater! Can't send this suit to the cleaner's for another month," he warned, backing away from her.

"Ken, I've grand news! Wait till you hear!" she told him. "After dinner."

"Yeah . . . ?" He thought: She's happy. Haven't seen her as pepped up for weeks. Just my luck to have things break when she's happy.

The steak was just right. Just the degree of pinkness he liked. The mushroom sauce was delicious. The potatoes were golden-brown, the salad crisp, the shortcake a culinary dream.

But Ken wasn't hungry.

He tried to eat, manfully. But pushed his plate away, beaten. "I've a headache," he mumbled.

Things went flat for her. Her surprise dinner gone for nothing. She had kept from telling him the news till he'd eaten. He was drinking his coffee now. So she told him, with little excited catchings of her breath, "He said"— and she repeated what Jameson had said—"forty beginning next week. And after that, fifty, perhaps, if he goes on liking my work."

"Gee, that's great," said Ken. His voice was dull. He looked at her. His eyes were hurt. There was shame in them and appeal. "You'll be making more than I do," he said, trying to laugh.

"Ken, don't be silly!"

"Well, it isn't so silly. I got transferred today," he told her.

"Transferred? *Transferred?* Why? How? Does it mean more money?" she asked him.

"No, it means less."

"Less? But, Ken!"

"It was either get transferred or get fired," Ken told her.

After a moment she recovered, rallying gallantly. But the strawberries were tasteless. Hothouse things. Stupid extravagance. She forced one down. Dry, and without flavor. The vision of spring clothes vanished.

"Dear, don't worry," she said, putting out her hand to him. "It won't be any time at all before you're doing just as well as you did before. And meantime I'll be making up the deficit."

"Yes, damn it to hell! I can't even support my own wife," said Ken.

They looked at each other across the desolate little feast. Their eyes were estranged and frightened. His hand was on her own, but for the first time since their marriage she didn't know that. She said, slowly:

"That's unfair."

Chapter V

It *was* unfair of Ken, Lola contended hotly and silently during the days which followed. Unfair not only to her but to himself. To sulk around, to act like a hurt, grieved child because his salary had been lowered and hers raised.

Of course they had "made up." They always made up. Ken's arms out, his ashamed, moved, "Gee, Lola, I'm sorry. . . . Please don't cry like that" . . . her instant response, her almost instant forgetting while in his embrace. But she was finding a certain nerve strain in these scenes of reconciliation, renewed vows, renewed tenderness and ardor. Afterwards—afterwards you lay awake and remembered. Nothing had been settled, not really. You hadn't eliminated the cause of the original difficulty. It was just evaded for a time, pushed aside, and smothered in brief forgetfulness. But it waited there, till the next time.

Things adjusted themselves. They had to. Ken's thirty-five and Lola's forty reached almost to that eighty dollars a week which had once seemed so stupendous and elastic and had proved so unsatisfactory after all. And it was funny, the difference the lack of the five dollars made. But Jake fixed that. Ken helped Jake nights sometimes, earned, that way, a little extra money, often more than the missing five-dollar bill. That helped. But it hindered, too. It left Lola alone, calling up Connie to beg her to come in and sit with her while she caught up on darning and mending, or running around to her mother's with her sewing basket. "Can I come in for a

74

while?" "Where's Ken?" "Oh, he's working with Jake for an hour or so." "It isn't right," her mother would say, worried, "after working all day to let him work at night. It will ruin his health." "Oh, don't bother the child, Annie," Mr. Davis would comment, over the old pipe. "Ken's young and strong and ambitious. It won't hurt him."

"Where's Millie, mother?"

"Out to a movie—I suppose. I never know *where* she is any more."

"Howard?"

"Running the streets—"

"He'll have to quit hanging around the poolroom," Davis would put in. "I'm still able to lay him over my knee and give him a piece of my mind!"

Lola would laugh. But somehow she felt—funny—coming home. She didn't belong. Oh, that was nonsense of course! They were always so touchingly glad to see her, they wanted her to come, they loved her as much as ever. But she couldn't share every minute of their time, she couldn't know what was going on inside their heads. Yet Millie came to the apartment often. Howard too. And her mother and father would arrive for an occasional dinner almost, it seemed to Lola, formally.

"If you'd only come oftener!" she'd beg. "It's no trouble at all. I *love* it. I wish I saw more of you, mother."

"You're out all day," Mrs. Davis would answer quietly. That was all. Lola knew what she was thinking, however. If Lola were at home—where, in Mrs. Davis's estimation, she belonged—her mother could run in and out all day; with a scrap of sewing; a bit of neighborhood gossip; a new recipe; a bowl of soup stock. Neighborly, in a close, intimate mother-and-daughter relationship. But Lola went to work early and came back late.

Mrs. Davis suffered in her maternal pride as well. Meeting an old friend:

"Well, so Lola's married, Annie! I declare, it doesn't seem any time at all since she was sitting up in her carriage and you wheeling her, as proud as Punch. What does her young man do? What's his name? Where do they live? How does she like housekeeping? Haven't been married long enough for—? Well, lots of time yet. How'll you like being a grandmother, Annie?"

Mrs. Davis would answer. And sometimes during the conversation she would be forced to say, her chin held high:

"Lola's working. She's staying on in her old job. Doing very well, too."

"Oh," the old friend would say blankly; and then rally. "My cousin's daughter is working too. She's been married a year. Her husband wants her to give it up though. He has a very good income. But she says she wants something to do. I don't know what's come over girls nowadays—as if they didn't have enough to do with house and children . . . I never have a minute to myself, with eight rooms to take care of and six to cook for!"

And so they'd part. And Mrs. Davis would go on her way thinking: She doesn't believe that Ken can support Lola. They never believe that.

She said so once to her husband. He answered mildly:

"Well, he can't—can he? Not in the way she wants to be supported. That's all that's the matter with young people nowadays. They have to have things we were able to get along without."

As long as Ken had been earning more than Lola he had been able to "laugh it off"; to concede her right to wage-earning; as time went on, to accept it. But things were different now. When, on the first of the month, the

budget-book came out and the manila envelopes, he no
longer made a comic ceremony of the routine. "Come on,
baby, let's hear the damage! Have you the stock-broker's
account handy? And the restaurant bill from the Ritz?"
No more of that. He'd get through it as quickly as possible or turn from the radio to say: "I think I've got St.
Louis. Go ahead, Lola, will you? You know more about
it than I do. Just write down what money-orders you
want me to get."

So, for the most part, she worked over their mutual
finances alone. But they weren't mutual. When they'd
first been married they had been able to tease each other
a little. "What on earth did you do with that twenty
cents which was over from last week?" "Ken, your hair-
cuts will ruin us yet." "Well, what about yours, darling?" "Now"—looking over the cash budget—"where
did that four-fifty go?" "Ken, I hate to confess it but
I had a Woolworth orgy last week." "Woman, it's over
the hill to the poor house now. Lucky you got your on-
time bonus this month!"

Not any more. Since his transfer Kenneth had scrupulously refrained from asking her what she did with any
surplus—not that there was ever any surplus—had once
even said, when she apologized for an expenditure, "What
of it? It's your money, isn't it?" She'd flared up at that,
hurt. "It is *not*. It's *ours*, and you know it." But he
hadn't answered.

In the spring, Lola had another raise. Coming home
that night her feet lagged along the streets. The locusts
were out, shedding their fragrance on the mild air; their
dusty blossoms lay thickly, a cream-yellow carpet, on
street and lawns. She didn't, she discovered, *want* to tell
Ken. There wasn't any kick in it, somehow. Just a feeling of—could it possibly be apology? But how absurd!

She worked for it, didn't she? It was hers; she earned it, every cent!

Why should she apologize to Ken? That she got the breaks and he didn't was his hard luck. He couldn't help it, of course. She'd never blamed him, never even held him guilty in her most secret thoughts.

It would be better, she decided, to tell him when other people were about. She hadn't been married very long but quite long enough to know that some things were more easily spoken in public. As it happened they were going to Agnes's that evening. Agnes's sister had come over for the night, and Jim was bringing in a couple of men from the company. Lola had planned to go over a little early and help.

Ken was in a high good humor that evening. He had reached home ahead of her, the radio was going full blast, he swept her off her feet as she came in the door and waltzed her gayly about the apartment.

"What's happened?" Lola wanted to know, plucking her hat from her head, which ached just a trifle. "Good news? Ken, let me go. I'm dizzy."

"Sure, I've been made president of United States Electric," he informed her.

"Ken?" Her eyes were bright. His way of telling her perhaps. It would be wonderful, wouldn't it, if they had something good to exchange, to share tonight. . . . *Listen to me, what do you think has happened?*

But Ken went on waltzing. She freed herself and, while he stood still laughing, reached up to kiss him.

"Ken, you've had a drink!"

"Check. I had three. One on the house. Garrison—you know—he's in my department—took me to a swell speakeasy. You'd never guess it. Bar and all. Old-fashioned frame house and a back yard plumb-full of the most innocent-looking lilacs and tulips and ramblers you ever saw. Chickens walking around. I don't mean what you mean. Regular chickens, the kind with feathers, not sables."

Lola went into her bedroom. So that was the reason for his high spirits. Not that she minded Ken taking a drink. He didn't drink much, as a rule. Now and then on a party. Never, till recently, when she wasn't along. Or hardly ever. But for the last few weeks he and the mysterious Garrison appeared to have explored every speakeasy in town. . . . "Just one, Lola, sets you up before dinner, I haven't had any appetite lately."

She was, she admitted to herself frankly, cross with Ken. She didn't see why he had to. And it was expensive. He couldn't always accept drinks. He had to set them up sometimes. He had to pay the check. Ken wasn't, she thought proudly, a sponge. Her second thought was instinctive: he mustn't get to be. Oh, he never would be. He was, if anything, too generous.

He was still gay at dinner. Lola tried hard to enter in. She knew from occasional experience how easily she could dampen his gayety. A raised eyebrow, a certain inflection, a tight, straight mouth, a silence when silence was the last thing he wanted. She had done it before, when she'd been hurt. She hated herself for doing it. Hated the look that came into his eyes. Hated the change of his mood to a sulky oh-very-well attitude.

Now, perhaps, when he was feeling this way, was the time to tell him. Why, she wondered wearily, did you always have to wait for moods? But she didn't tell him. Something within her held her back, silenced the words on her lips. . . . "Ken, isn't it great? I had another raise today; I'm getting more important work to do—and it isn't the end. Not yet! I'll keep on getting on."

Easy words, simple, childish. Yet she couldn't say them. *Why?*

They went to Agnes's. The bunch was already there. Millie was coming in. Agnes and Jim liked Millie. A type, said Agnes. A raving beauty, said Jim. Agnes's sister Marie was sitting on the little sofa, the two "company" men draped over it. One was telling something he'd read in the paper—"this fellow Winchell is a card." The men knew Ken, hailed him as he and Lola came in.

Presently Lola was in Agnes's kitchenette, helping with the sandwiches and the fruit punch. "Jim," said Agnes, "has some gin left. We'll let him pep this up after we're through. Marie looks pretty tonight, doesn't she?"

"She always looks pretty," Lola answered.

"Why shouldn't she? She hasn't anything to do but take care of her skin and nails and figure and wait for some man to come along and support her, if such a paragon is left in the world nowadays," said Agnes bitterly.

Lola looked at her. Agnes for a year or more had been making just such remarks. Yet Agnes loved Jim. Was happy. Or wasn't she?

"You shouldn't have had us in tonight," Lola began. "You're tired. You look half dead, Agnes."

"I'm all right. If people don't come in we go somewhere. I don't know why," Agnes said drearily. "And the evenings we do plan an evening at home we're either too dead or too bored to make any use of it. Get down the green highball glasses, will you, while I empty some ice trays. Lord, I wish they wouldn't play the radio so loud. Why do men always want that thing turned on to its fullest extent?"

"I think they're dancing," said Lola.

Millie came in. They heard her arrival. They could visualize her through the closed door, poised on the threshold. Millie never really came in. Millie always entered.

She held the kitchen door open a moment later. "Hello, Agnes. . . . Hello, Lola." She swung the door shut behind and came to Lola's side. She looked, thought Lola, as if she had been brought up on dew and weaned on rose leaves. There was a freshness to Millie's skin, a sheen to her hair, a radiance that was heartbreakingly lovely.

"How are the working girls?" Millie wanted to know.

"Working girl yourself," retorted Lola, not very brilliantly.

"The joke's on you, darling. I've quit."

"Quit?" Agnes and Lola stared at her; Agnes with a half-smile, a look almost as of silent applause, Lola as if the younger girl had suddenly gone out of her mind. "Quit?"

Millie perched herself on the edge of the sink. She clasped her hands about her knees. She was wearing, they observed, a new green dress. Very new, in cut. Better looking than her salary warranted. But she had a perfect figure. She could get sample clothes, for very little money.

"I've been posing," she said, "free time. For a commercial photographer. Oh, don't look so sunk, Lola! We wear clothes. Lots of them. Except the girls that do lingerie and even they are pretty well covered. There's more money in it than in excuse-it-please. So I've quit. And when I'm not posing I'm going to get extra work on the Long Island City lots and try for a screen test if I can."

"Does mother know?" asked Lola helplessly. She wanted to say, You mustn't . . . you can't! What right had she to say it? Millie would be eighteen soon. It was Millie's life. And she, Lola, no longer belonged in that life. She belonged in Ken's life.

"Not yet. She will though. Dad," said Millie affectedly, "will throw a fit. He'll show me the door, maybe. Mother . . . well, she won't like it either, at first," Millie went on more thoughtfully, "but I can't help that, can I? I've got to live my own life," proclaimed Millie dramatically from the sink-board perch, "haven't I?"

"Well, naturally," Lola heard Agnes say. "I think you're perfectly right, Millie. And you've a pretty level head. See that you don't get it turned by the first man you meet or it will be a walk-up and back to the phone company for you."

"Fat chance!" laughed Millie. "I'm going to get somewhere, I am!" She slipped down from the sink board and departed self-consciously from the kitchenette. Lola looked at Agnes and carefully set down the glass she was polishing.

"What do you know about that?" asked Lola.

"Very little. If I had Millie's looks I'd know a lot about it," Agnes answered. "Oh, don't get sisterly and stuffy! If you do, remember that part of it's envy. . . ."

"Envy? Millie and her screen-struck ambitions? Envy? I wouldn't change places with anyone in the world! The kid's crazy."

"I'm not so sure," said Agnes somberly. "I think she's going to make the grade. She has everything," added Agnes, "including a glorious vanity, magnificent self-confidence, and a perfectly wrought-iron little heart."

"She's just a kid," Lola said again, stupidly.

"I'm not so sure," said Agnes once more.

Ken stuck his head in at the door.

"Hey, are you girls going to hang around out here all evening?"

"Coming right away. Here, come carry this tray in,

will you? You look strong and willing," Agnes told him.

"Lady, I'm a fast worker."

He took the tray and pranced out again. Lola and Agnes followed.

There was radio, dancing, a round of mild poker. "Hell," said Ken, "there goes my lunch-money!" There were home-made sandwiches and cup-cakes, from the tea-room, and the fruit punch with a stick in it. Talk, laughter. "Company" gossip. Millie smiling over the rim of her green glass at one of the bedazzled young engineers, who began suddenly to think better of married life. Lola, laughing, watching Ken. Talk of money. Of jobs. Here was her chance. Say it clearly, laugh when you did, avoid Ken's eyes.

"Congratulate me, everybody, I had a raise today!"

Later, going home, "Why didn't you tell me before?" Ken wanted to know.

She answered evasively:

"I thought it would be fun to startle the gang." Then, at his silence, she thought, desperately, oh, why do I always have to fix things up—tell half-lies, explain things? She went on, in an impulse of utter and relieving honesty: "No, that's not so. The last time—Ken, you acted so funny! It took all the joy out of it somehow. So I was afraid, this time."

He answered, tightening his grasp on her arm:

"I'm sorry. I was rotten about it. Look here, it wasn't meanness or jealousy. Not really. Just . . . oh, I don't know, Lola—shame, sort of, that a little slip of a thing like you could shoulder so much of the burden and a big hulk of a man like me couldn't measure up. You sure deserve every cent you earn. I hope you get to be confidential secretary to the president. Honest I do. But more than anything I want you to forgive me."

Her heart was light again. She was flooded with a serene, joyous happiness. She told him, looking up, her face a dim blur in the spring darkness:

"There wasn't anything to forgive, stupid. We just misunderstood, or something. Look here, Ken; we can start saving a little now. Things are pretty well paid for—and we'll have a bit left over."

"That's great," he told her heartily, and tried to feel it as he said it. To himself, he said: I've hurt her badly. I won't again. She'd never understand. Women don't—or can't. Well, grin and bear it, Big Boy!

Lola went on:

"Ken, I went into dental clinic today. You have to, every six months. There isn't anything wrong. Miss Hicks—that's the girl I had, who cleans 'em and everything, said that if everybody had teeth like mine there wouldn't be any dentists. I didn't get through my last physical as well, though," she said ruefully. "I've lost weight. They said I'd have to go to the Milk Room every day and drink a couple of glasses."

"You don't feel—ill?" he asked in instant concern, horrible visions of anemia and tuberculosis flashing luridly through his perturbed brain.

"Well, no, of course not! I get tired, though. And edgy. When I'm cross sometimes, and have a grouch, it isn't me, really, Ken. I don't mean ever to be. I'm not that way, in my heart," she told him gravely, wistfully. "Just tired. It's all such a rush . . ."

"You didn't use to be that way," he said suddenly.

"No, I suppose not. Silly, isn't it? I wonder why—now."

But she knew, dimly. She thought of what the woman doctor, keen-eyed, trim in her white coat, her gray hair waved close to a fine head, had said to her . . . over at the company. . . . "You must remember that the first year of marriage brings certain adjustments—mental, physical, emotional. It's hard enough on any girl. Harder still on the girl who goes to work, outside of her home. She is holding down two jobs. And the adjustments aren't easy."

Well, doctors always talked like that, of course. That was their job. But, gosh, almost every girl she knew married and kept on working! Book talk, perhaps; the gloomy view taken by the medical profession.

Still, she was more tired than she had ever been; more easily irritated; given to finding her eyes suddenly filled with foolish tears—for no good reason; given to introspection, to contradictions . . . such as longing for Ken's arms about her, longing for the serenity of quiet tenderness, longing, when tenderness proved not so serene after all, for the bright release of young, unsated passion . . . and yet dreading it, somehow.

"Then, too," the doctor had told her gravely, "most of you young married women suffer under a nervous strain because of the fear of pregnancy."

Well, she knew that, didn't she?

You can't have everything, after all. But her heart turned over in her breast every time she saw a rosy, healthy baby kicking its bare toes in a carriage, out in someone's back yard, in the sun.

Why couldn't you have everything?

The next morning, before setting out to work in the clear sunlight of a perfect spring day, Ken and Lola went through their usual routine. While she was giving her little nose its last powdering and looking to see that the windows were shut—it made it stuffy, when you came home, but it might rain and if it rained and you were at the office, you went wild with worry—Ken carried out the garbage pail and then waited for her. Lola came out finally, locking the door. They set off down the street. On the next block a woman in a house dress, her hair, in curlers, partly concealed under a "boudoir" cap, was cutting branches of lilac from a small, rather dusty, frontyard bush. Lola said distastefully:

"Do they have to dress like that?"

Ken laughed. He'd never seen Lola in curlers, nor, indeed, in any fatal state of extreme dishevelment. She admitted to herself often that it was a hardship not to be able to let down occasionally, even with Ken there. But she'd read a lot about "holding the glamour," in magazines. *"If you don't some other woman will!"* She thought it true . . . with no reservations, but thought, too: That's easy for women with maids and money . . . not living under a man's feet all the time in a two by four.

"Hey, look at that!" Ken said.

The woman had turned from the lilac bush. In the open doorway of the brick house a baby was standing, heavy-eyed from sleep. She was about three years old. She wore one-piece pajamas, brightly patterned with prints of an enchanting circus—clowns, elephants, horses, dogs. Her yellow hair was all tousled from contact with the pillows. Her face was flushed and her lips drooped at the corners. She put a small finger in her mouth and eyed her mother with drowsy inquiring eyes, startlingly brown. Her mother said: "For goodness' sakes run back in the house, Eileen. I'll be there in a minute."

"Brekker!" demanded the baby firmly.

"Golly, isn't she cute?" asked Lola.

They walked on. Ken, deep in some speculation of his own, replied, "Uh-uh," absently. They stopped at the news-dealers on the corner. Ken bought two papers and gave one to Lola. Presently they had entered the subway together. Connie wasn't there. "I wonder," said Lola, worried, "if she's sick?"

This was on a Saturday. Lola had a half-day. When she reached home, Ken wasn't there. She went out again —leaving a note for him in case he arrived before she returned—and went around to Connie's. She must be sick. She hadn't come in to work. No use getting her out of bed by telephoning. Mrs. Varesi was very bad on the wire, Joe wouldn't be home, the other children howled at you over the phone so that your ears rang.

She arrived at Connie's and went up the steps. The door was open. A small dark child in soiled rompers crawled in the entry hall. The last Varesi. Lola stooped to speak to him. He had tremendous eyes and a grave, sticky, dirty face and features of a classic beauty. But his neck and legs and arms were thin and spindling, and he had a little pot-belly, the skin stretched tight and taut about the protrusion of ribs. He was two years old. Unweaned.

Connie's brother Umberto, who had been born on shipboard, coming over, and who was older than Connie and deformed, slightly hunch-backed, as often happens in a family of this size and situation, greeted her gravely. He spoke good English but stuttered.

"Connie's in bed," he told her.

Lola went on upstairs. Connie's room was at the back of the house. Its window gave on the overgrown back yard. The window was open, Lola saw with a little smile. That must have cost Connie a battle.

"Connie?"

Connie stirred on the pillows. The oval of her face was perfectly white.

"I'm glad you came," she said. "Sit down. The room's a sight, but I can't help it."

Her lips were straight, a thin red line in her face. Her eyes smoldered.

"What's the matter?" Lola asked, finding a chair.

"Nothing. A headache."

"Nurse in?"

"Yes. She came early. . . . Oh, I'll be all right, by Monday," Connie said.

She was remote. Not unfriendly, but terribly preoccupied with her own intimate thoughts.

Lola, faintly ill at ease, said:

"I wish you'd been at Agnes's last night." She went on to tell of the party. "And Millie! Connie, can you bear it? The kid's got herself a job, posing for a commercial photographer, and says she's going into the movies! She's quit the phone job. The family will have lace-tailed kittens. I'm going around to mother's now and see if I can pour a little oil on the stormy waters. I didn't know what to say. Agnes thought it was all right. So do I . . . in a way. In a way, I don't."

"Millie can take care of herself," Connie declared evenly.

"I suppose so. Naturally," Lola said, laughing, "I don't really think so. She's always seemed an affected, spoiled sort of a baby to me, but a darling too. What worries me isn't so much Millie, but the family. They're pretty old-fashioned. How they'll take it—"

"Oh, they'll fuss," Connie predicted, "and then it will be all right. American parents are all like that."

"Connie, what's the matter with you?" asked Lola, arrested by the tone of the other girl's voice. "You haven't had a run-in with your mother, have you, over anything?"

"Mother? She hasn't much to say. Cries over me, prays over me, storms at me, hugs me, and loves me. . . . Poor mother!"

"Then, what is it? Is there anything Ken and I can do? Oh, don't hold out on me, Connie! Something's awfully wrong. You can't fool me," Lola told her.

Under the pallor of the olive skin the hot color flooded up suddenly. Connie had been lying straightly under a sheet and blanket, her arms at her sides. Now she lifted her arms. They were bare under the cap sleeves of her nightgown. A pretty nightgown. Connie sewed beautifully. And on the bare arms there were dark streaks, dark spots. Bruises. Red with congested blood, turning black.

"*Connie!*"

"Look at my back . . ." cried Connie, her reserve going.

She turned on her side; shook with a tearless sobbing. On the smooth healthy skin, more red marks. Welts.

"He didn't," said Connie, turning back, "touch my face. There's that to be thankful for!"

Lola's heart was sick and tight. Her eyes enormous in a face gone colorless.

"Connie!" She clutched the other girl's hand. "Connie. *He? Was it—Joe?*"

"Yes. Joe. Damn him to hell," said Connie, steadily.

"But why—*why?*" asked Lola helplessly. "Where were your father and mother? Connie, you can have him arrested! You can go to law about this. . . . You mustn't stay here . . . it's terrible!"

It was beyond her comprehension. She knew such things happened. Low people. Drunken people. Slum people. But they didn't happen to people she knew. They didn't happen to *Connie*. Connie was afraid of Joe. Lola knew that. Afraid of his temper, his ugliness. He drank, sometimes. Still . . . things like this just didn't happen to your friends.

"Mother? What could she do? Father's away. Joe's the head of the family, in his place. He has a right to do as he likes with me," Connie said. She had herself under control now. Too much so, if Lola had only known it. "I'm not of age, you know, Lola, as they figure things."

"But—*why?*" Lola wanted to know.

"Oh, nothing much. Louis—you met Louis?—came here to see me. But I had a date. With Frank Mason. You know, he was at Agnes's with me last winter. I like him. He's a good scout. He sells automobiles. . . . He took me out in a car—we went to Larson's for dinner and to dance. We got home late. When we got home Joe was waiting. He'd seen Louis. He said things to Frank. I'll never see *him* again," she said bitterly. "Not that it matters; I wasn't crazy about him or anything. Frank took it. He had to. He's an American and Joe's my brother and I was in the room. Then after Frank went—"

She was silent, remembering.

"You must take him into court . . . scare him into behaving himself, Connie. It isn't safe for you here," Lola begged.

"I can't," Connie told her. "It would kill my mother. Remember, she thinks he has a right."

"This isn't Italy!" cried Lola furiously.

"Isn't it? A lot you know! How Americanized are any of them, except me and possibly Umberto? Look at mother! At father! Oh, Joe *talks* American, runs a cigar store, drives a bargain, and a car—dresses well enough and keeps average clean. But, Lola—*underneath?*"

"You'll have to get out. Go to Mrs. Richards; she'll find you a place to live."

Mrs. Richards was the company house-mother.

As Connie shook her head Lola went on urgently,

"The nurse? You said she was here this morning. Did she know?"

"Of course she knew. I lied. But she knew. Then I had to tell her."

"Connie, what *are* you going to do?"

"I don't know. Get out? I can't get out, that way. You don't know Joe. What he'd do. The money too. I have to give in money. We're a pretty big family; they need all I can make. And there's only Joe and me and two of the others working. Father doesn't work steadily."

Half an hour later Lola left, hot with Connie's wrongs, sick with her unsolved problem. She went to her mother's, suddenly glad of the brown wooden steps, worn and peeling. Glad of the house and yard and the smell of baking, glad of her mother's arms and kiss. . . . "I've a cake in the oven for you, for over Sunday. But you'll come to dinner as usual, you and Ken?"

"Try and stop us."

"Millie," began her mother.

"Don't fuss, darling. Millie will be all right."

Let Millie go her way, thought Lola suddenly, remembering Connie. She'd be all right, she really would. She'd have them back of her, the brown house and the pleasant sunlight through the windows and their father, grumping over his pipe, and their mother, fussing over food and wet feet and colds in the head. She'd *have* to be all right. It was her life. If you didn't give them freedom they took it and things went wrong.

She stayed an hour or so talking to her mother. "I'll talk to dad tomorrow," she promised, "and get Ken to."

"It's not that I am afraid. Only she's pretty young."

"Well, so was I when I started to work. This is really the same. Just different work. Look at it that way.

Millie would never have been happy as she was.   And unless she's happy, you'll have trouble," Lola said.

Mrs. Davis looked at her.   You carried them in your body and nourished them with your blood; you bore them in shrieking, grinding pain; you tended them, helpless, innocent, demanding, selfish; you watched them grow up; you sat up nights and slaved days; you washed and cooked, scolded and comforted, agonized and worried and rejoiced.   Then they matured.   They left you.   They fought their own battles and made their own decisions. Why couldn't you think of them as adults?   But you never could.   You loved them terribly, without demonstration.   You didn't have time for demonstration.   You just loved them and watched them go from you.   Yet in a sense, they didn't go.   You had memories.   You had them in your heart, as you had had them in your body.

Children . . .

Lola went home.   Ken was there, fussing round, not knowing what to do with himself.

"Fiend!   I thought we'd go to a movie," he reproached her.

"Let's not.   It's late.   I've been to Connie's and mother's.   I stopped to shop for dinner.   We'll have an elegant dinner!" she promised, pacifically.

"Drive afterwards?   Jake will let me have a car.   It may fall to pieces and then," said Ken, grinning, "you'll walk home.   Ever walk home, baby?"

"I wouldn't tell you if I had," Lola remarked primly. "It isn't good for you to know too much.   Ken, do stop prowling around.   Come, sit down here."   She patted the sofa, beside her.   "I've lots to tell you.   Connie—oh, Ken, what do you think has happened to Connie?"

To her utter amazement she found herself crying.

"Hey . . . what's up? she isn't—seriously sick, is

she?" asked Ken, horrified. "Quit that! You drive me goofy."

He sat down beside her and took her in his arms. Presently she told him. She felt his muscles tighten. He made a few terse, profane comments. He told her what Joe was and where he would go. Lola expostulated, half laughing again.

"Ken . . . such language! But . . . check," said Lola, "to every word. Ken, we'll have to do something for Connie."

"I'll trim that adjective so-and-so within an inch of his misbegotten life," promised Ken, enthusiastically.

"Darling, no! It wouldn't help Connie. It would only hurt her. And we've got to help her. Why, she's one of the finest people I ever knew."

"Well, we'll cook up something. See here, couldn't she come stay here for a while? If she wouldn't mind the sofa? She'd get cramps and probably fall out on the floor, but that's better than what she has to put up with at home. If she's afraid to leave I'll go and fetch her," Ken declared.

"Ken, you *are* sweet!"

They sat there for a time, in silence, perfectly content, perfectly relaxed, in a wordless communion of understanding. Ken *did* understand. It was only about silly trivial things they quarreled. Jobs. Money. Things that didn't matter, essentially.

Lola roused herself and talked of Millie. "Silly kid," commented Ken, grinning, "more power to her! We'll belong in the I-knew-her-when class yet."

"Oh, Ken, do you really think so?" asked Lola, seriously.

"Sure I do. With her looks. And ambition. And level head."

"That's what Agnes said. I wish I looked like her," Lola sighed, truthfully enough, but obviously baiting her hook.

"Well, *I* don't! No magazine-cover beauty for me. Helen of Troy never mended any guy's socks that I ever heard of. Anyway, you're better looking than Millie."

"Don't be dumb, darling. And you're contradicting yourself."

"No, I'm not. Millie's a knockout. Death to the innocent bystander and all that. But you—you've got something in your face . . . and eyes—"

"Cinders?"

"Who's loony now?" asked Ken.

"I'll bite—"

These were the intervals that made everything so worth while. Understanding moments of awareness, keen and wonderful, of each other. Moments of nearness. Little interludes of foolish talk, so trivial, so idiotic in the ears of a third person, so meaningful in their own because what they felt, the intimacy cloaked with laughter, went so much deeper than words. Interludes of sharing . . . "What do you think has happened?" or, "Someone told me downtown, today . . ."

They agreed that something must be done for Connie. But Connie came back to work the following week. "Forget it," she told Lola. "I'm sorry you had to be in on it. Sorry I let down and told you. I hate a squealer."

So there was nothing that Ken and Lola could do for her. Besides, about a month later Connie married Louis, her brother's undersized, hot-tempered, very shrewd partner, resigned from her position, and sailed to Italy for her honeymoon.

Chapter VI

Connie, thought Lola sadly, was lost to her. She had given up the battle. "Battle?" asked Ken, when she said it to him. But it was hard for her to explain. Agnes, when they discussed it together, could put it into more adequate words.

"She couldn't stand it," Agnes said thoughtfully, "couldn't stand being pulled both ways. By her people, her traditions, her racial instincts one way; by her own standards and ambitions and ideals the other. Perhaps she will be happy. I hope so."

Ken couldn't see things in that light. Why was Connie married any different from Connie unmarried? Of course if she'd married someone else—he did acknowledge vaguely. "Still, I don't see that it will make any great difference."

But it would. Connie, thought Lola, would Americanize to a certain extent the man she had married. Louis, Lola knew, had saved money. Would, she imagined, make more. They would have a big house. Connie would keep it well. She would dress well. They would have children, with clean clothes, who would attend good schools. She would get her husband out of his present business. But Connie would also adjust herself to Louis. She would have to. She would make her friends among his friends; or reach out and make friends for him; but not, Lola thought, in her old circle. Connie was ambitious. She always had been. When she could no longer be ambitious for herself and in her own job she would be ambitious for Louis. "You wait and see," Lola told Ken.

It was strange, going to work without Connie, coming home without her. Lola missed her more than she had realized she would. The brightly colored postcards, conventionally scrawled upon—"Having a fine time . . . wish you were here. . . . This is a beautiful place"— gave their recipient no satisfaction, told her nothing. . . .

Spring slid into summer. In the Davises' back yard the honeysuckle on the garage sent out an amazing, overpowering fragrance, the essence of a thousand summers, the scent of a hundred country lanes, rain-wet and languorous. Going out in the evening with Ken, Lola would see the little girls going up to the big church near by for confirmation, the children of well-to-do parents, all in white, white shoes and stockings on small feet and spindly legs, white roses binding the virginal veil above grave, awed small faces. Others, as awed, if a little envious, contenting themselves with just the veil and a bunch of wired roses held tightly in their hot, clean-scrubbed hands. The little boys were touching too, with their best suits brushed and their round white collars and the white bows on their arms.

Sparrows chattered and quarreled in the miracle of green leaves. Standing at her mother's gate, she saw a scarlet tanager flash by, a streak of flame in the summer dusk. And remembered how once, in early spring, lying in her bedroom at home she had heard the incredible sound of a flight of ducks winging and calling their way across the Narrows.

A nostalgia for the country she had never really known was upon her. Except for a summer spent on a relative's farm up-state when she was nine—the time Millie had nearly died of the measles—she had never been away from the town, unless one counted the Boardwalk at Atlantic City and week-ends in suburban Jersey or the hot trips to the Island on a Sunday picnic, coming back in the close-packed, scarce-moving, nervous mass of traffic.

Ken still talked of Maine. She said reluctantly, "We mustn't . . . we can't afford it." Yet she knew that they must afford it. It seemed to her that she saw so little of Ken. Yet that was foolish, for when they were together they were always under each other's feet. She said something of the sort to Agnes.

"I know," said Agnes, "a lot better than you do."

Vacations were finally planned. She and Ken would have the same two weeks, in August. Once in a while you did get the breaks. Jake would drive them up, and there'd be a friend of his along. They'd go to the camp; it wouldn't cost so terribly much, even sharing the expenses of the car and of the nights spent along the road. It seemed to Lola that she couldn't get through the time intervening. To get away—from the apartment, the office, the hurry, the incessant worry and rush and fever heat . . . If only, she thought, something doesn't happen to spoil it.

Ken might spoil it. Ken was changing, very slowly, almost imperceptibly. But now and then she looked at him with the eyes of a stranger, clear, startled eyes, and realized how he had changed. He no longer seemed hurt or made ashamed by her wage-earning ability. Once or twice she heard him boast about it. He began bringing men home. . . . "Can I throw a stag poker tonight, Lola? Oh, of course, I don't mean you to go out." But she would go out. To Agnes's perhaps, or to her mother's, to listen to Millie chatter about her experiences as extra girl in the big new picture, to hear her sophisticated gossip of the studios, which set her somehow miles apart where Lola could not follow or with which she could not cope.

"But I read in a movie magazine that John Gilbert—"

"Press-agent stuff. That's all boloney. This is the low-down—"

And so on, far into the night. Or far enough until Lola, dead with sleep, would ask Howard to walk home with her and would wander into the apartment, into a living-room blue with smoke, foul with the smell of opened bottles and sticky glasses and extinguished cigarette butts.

The men would greet her noisily. Sometimes Ken would bring her forward, his arm about her waist. "Here's the little meal-ticket," he would say, theatrically proud, and they would laugh. And she would laugh, too, and go into the bedroom and shut the door and lie down fully dressed, half dead for sleep, knowing that when they had gone she would have to wash glasses and empty ash trays and open windows, for there was never any surplus time in the morning.

Garrison came to these parties a lot. She didn't like him. He was too sleek. His hair was sleek and his face and his brown eyes and his clothes and his hands. He had a girl who was working in a big real-estate office. She was making sixty a week. They were going to be married, the end of July. "Wish *my* girl worked," said one of the other men one night.

It was as easy, proclaimed Garrison, for a single man to trot around with girls who held down good jobs as to go calling on 'em in the sanctity of the home and hear the old man ask, "Can you support my girl in the luxury to which she has not been accustomed?" A man had sense who picked his crowd. Then, when you fell in love with one of the girls who paid her way—and it was as easy to fall in love with such a one as with any other—you could be assured that she'd go on paying her way. Otherwise, why marry? with the cost of living as it was and jobs scarcer than hen's teeth and raises a bright dream of the future that never materialized? When Garrison and his Amy were married they were going to save every cent. Put it in good stocks and hang on to them. Put it in an occasional bond; or a building-and-mortgage concern. Garrison, said Garrison, would have his own business before you could say Jack Robinson. When they got five thousand together he knew another man who would kick in five thousand more, and then they'd start in in the contracting business. On a shoe-string. But they'd manage. He had pull in the city. He knew politicians. He'd own his own home and a six-thousand-dollar car yet, said Garrison.

But a man who married a girl who'd never done a lick of work in her life was a fool. He tied a millstone about his neck.

It was a lie that two could live cheaper than one.

No, Lola didn't like Garrison. She told Ken so. Ken looked at her in astonishment. "Garry's a great guy," said Ken. "He'll get there, some day."

"I don't doubt that," said Lola, "with Amy to fall back on."

Ken was getting a little careless about himself. Not his clothes, not his appearance, exactly. He was simply letting down. Sometimes the extra money he made, through Jake, wasn't forthcoming for the manila envelopes. He'd spent it, he'd say, casually. Or—"A fellow has to stand the drinks now and then, you know."

She couldn't understand Ken. Perhaps when they were away on their vacation, when they'd be a little more alone, when they'd have more time together, she could talk to him and find out why he was different. He was, and she could not tell why or put her finger on it, exactly.

So they locked up the flat, one hot August evening, and stood on the steps, their luggage heaped around them and Jake's car waiting. "Did you close the windows, Ken?" and, "Oh, wait! did I remember to stop the milk? Yes," said Lola triumphantly, "I did!"

Ken caught her about the waist and gave her an excited little squeeze. They were going away. The city street was hot and dusty. Papers swirled vacantly in the gutters. There was a smell of rubbish burning. A baby was crying down the street. The Davises were there to say good-by. Howard, with a new necktie he had bought out of his recent earnings. He was an errand boy in the drug firm now; Mr. Davis had insisted—to get him off the streets, he'd said. Millie had brought Lola a little summer hand-bag. Millie was getting such steady extra work that she had about given up her posing. "Have a good time," called the Davises, as the car moved off; and Lola leaned out to wave good-by, very trim and pretty in the little linen suit she had picked up at a sale, through Agnes.

They were going to drive out of city traffic that night and put up somewhere on the road after midnight and get an early start the next morning. Jake and his friend, a middle-aged bachelor named McKenzie, sat in front. The luggage was piled in, tied on. Jake's new fishing-rod was his chief concern.

The trip was pleasant. Jake drove well and carefully and maintained an even pace. Lola loved every minute of the long days, although they rose before dawn and drove until long after dark in order to make time. And presently they had reached the log cottages and the central log house on the rim of a lost blue lake, deep in great murmurous trees.

They had their own little cottage, Jake and McKenzie

putting up at the "bachelors' house." The place was well run, few conveniences but all the necessities and excellent, hearty, simple food. It was out of the way and was not maintained for the wealthy. Lola was perfectly happy. She tramped with Ken, she fished with him, she went to bed early and lay in his arms, listening to the wind in the trees and the sleepy, sliding sound of water on the little beach; and she was shaken with a simpler, more primal ardor than she had ever known—less complicated with remembrance of fear, with cerebral reluctance.

The days went by in a blaze of blue and gold, they were like pure, minted coins flung in a bowl of turquoise, set on a stand of jade. They were coins one spent and could not keep; but Lola said, under the dark cover of night to Kenneth: "We'll always remember, won't we?"

She was a child of the city—as he was. Asphalt was more familiar under their feet than the yielding carpet of the pines, the undefiled monotony of sand. Their trees were dusty in summer, stunted of growth; their flowers an extraordinary example of the will to live; their beaches harsh with the noises of something sardonically called civilization, and strewn as far as eye could reach with the evidence of man's ugly carelessness. This immaculate purity of leaf and running water, of sky and blowing wind, was new to them. They grew tanned and strong, and laughter was oftenest on their lips. If there had been differences between them, born of the close, smothering economic pressure, of the intimacy of four walls—so much less and so much greater than the intimacy they now experienced—these differences were forgotten. Nerve strain relaxed to a smiling and almost mindless peace. They walked and fished, swam and ate, loved and slept in a vacuum of serenity. And Jake said, grinning, "Ain't it the life?"

Jake was ecstatic. He and McKenzie out in a punt in disreputable khaki, pursuing the agile fish all day, coming in to supper burned, happy, triumphant, were good companions. Lola and Ken saw rather less of him and his friend than they had expected. And as the other people in the little camp interested them little they were constantly together, without the outside pull of obligaions to others.

They talked a lot and said very little. Kenneth, sitting on the beach or swinging his bare legs over the rather rickety pier of the bathing dock, would speak now and then of his childhood; of his mother. Lola, lazy and relaxed, would talk of Millie, perhaps, without her usual obsession of responsibility and worry; of Agnes and Jim; of her parents; of Connie, lost to her. It was as if these people were no longer so bound up with her life that they could not move without pulling at some chord within her; as if she loved them deeply but they no longer mattered; as if nothing mattered but the sun seeping through the green network of the trees, steeping her very blood, soaking into her bones.

It was all like one of her intervals of laughter and relaxation with Kenneth translated into terms of trees and water, wind and weather.

But there are only fourteen days in two weeks.

They came back to town to one of the hot, sultry periods in September which always occur and for which no one is prepared. But Lola returned to the office bronzed against the shining contrast of her hair, lithe and vital. "Gosh," said her fellow workers, "you look like a million!" And Mr. Jameson peering over his bifocal glasses commented kindly: "I've never seen you looking as well, Mrs. Hayes . . . your vacation certainly did you good."

She smiled. "We were up in Maine," she told him.

"Very beautiful country," he replied absently. "Will you take a letter, please?"

Back to the routine.

But you could, she thought erroneously, live on the vitality and memories that two weeks had given you.

They'd been expensive, the two weeks. She and Ken hadn't thought about it then. Now they had to think. But they looked across the budget books and the flat manila envelopes and said, "It was worth it."

Lola's tan had not worn off, nor had the spring departed from her step the day in early October that Peter Acton came into the office. Lola when he telephoned had been down on another floor on an errand. Returning, she found Dorothy, one of the typists in the outer office, and Gladys, who presided at the telephone there, with their heads together, one blond and one dark, and with their compacts usefully employed. "What's the excitement?" asked Lola.

"It's Mr. Acton," said Gladys. "He's coming in to see the boss."

"What of it?" Lola wanted to know.

"You'd be surprised," Gladys replied. "I forgot you hadn't seen him. Girl, you don't know nothing yet!"

Lola went into Jameson's office. Acton, she knew, was a director. She knew further that he was a close friend of Jameson, although much younger, and that often when he had been at a directors' meeting he stopped in to see the older man. He was, she had heard, very attractive and very rich. She frowned, trying to remember all she had heard of him, scraps of office gossip. And then forgot him promptly.

She was, as it happened, in Jameson's office alone when Acton walked in. Jameson had gone upstairs and had not yet returned. Lola, her back to the door, was looking through some files. Someone came in from the outer office and said pleasantly:

"Mr. Jameson is somewhere in the building, I understand. I'll wait for him here, if I may."

She said, "Certainly," and turned. He was leaning against a bookcase, looking idly on the pictures which topped it. He was tall, he had a lazy grace. His hair, she saw, was prematurely gray, a thick cap of silver. He had a square face, very tanned, and excessively blue eyes. His clothes had achieved that perfect state which is neither new nor well worn. He had very white teeth, startling against the dark face. He smiled at her now and asked:

"I haven't seen you before, have I? My name is Peter Acton; I'm a friend of Mr. Jameson."

Lola said: "I haven't been with Mr. Jameson long. Yes, he expects you, Mr. Acton."

Acton sat down by Jameson's desk. He said:

"Please don't let me disturb you. Do you mind if I smoke?"

She said that she didn't, faintly astonished. Other men —Ken, Jim, certainly her father—didn't ask. He lighted a cigarette and leaned back in the big chair.

"I generally barge in at odd times," he told her, "and upset office routine." He added: "I was in a couple of weeks ago—or more—I didn't see you here then."

His tone conveyed that he had suffered an irreparable loss. Lola smiled faintly. Men. She'd known lots of men, before Kenneth. All very much alike. The technique differed, the approach, that was all. And if a man was attractive, you liked it; if he was not, you were annoyed. Things went that way.

She answered demurely:

"I was on my vacation, I imagine."

"Is that so? Vacations are great, aren't they? until you get back again and then you feel terribly let down. Where did you go?" he asked with the friendly interest that characterized him. You felt always, even if you were sane enough to know it wasn't really true, that while he was talking with you you were the only person in the entire world who mattered to him.

"Maine," said Lola, "to a camp, on a lake."

"Maine's wonderful," he agreed. "But the swimming is colder than I like it. Once, when I was hunting——"

He launched without pause into a saga of the hunt. Lola listened, turned from the filing case, the letter she had come to find in her hand.

Jameson came in.

"Hello, Phil," said Acton, rising. "I've turned up again. Come on out to lunch, can't you? I've been making myself at home and boring Miss——"

He halted and looked inquiringly at Jameson. "Hayes," said Jameson mechanically, and Acton went on smoothly ——"Miss Hayes with some of my Richard Halliburton tales. She's been very courteous though and never once told me I was boring her."

Lola flushed and laughed. She had never heard of Halliburton. She wasn't accustomed to this exactly. A good many men, some of them very important, came to the office to see Philip Jameson. But they never knew she was there; or, if they did, they indicated it by no more than a glance, recognizing her as a human being, or sometimes as a pretty girl, and a word or two of business-like inquiry.

Lola murmured something and went into the outer office where she had her desk. Gladys and Dorothy were in the state commonly known as all agog. They rushed at her and bombarded her with questions and comments.

"Isn't he too marvelous-looking?" "What did he say?" "Gosh, you were alone with him a long time!" "What's he like?" "Can you imagine any woman ever leaving him?"

"I can imagine any woman leaving any man," said Lola firmly, sitting down at her desk. "Yes, he's very good-looking. And *did* a woman leave him?" she wanted to know.

"Don't you ever read the papers? Sure, he's divorced from his wife. She married some Englishman with a title. Probably," said Gladys cynically, "on *his* money."

"For heaven's sake," Lola implored both girls five minutes later, in despair, "will you keep quiet? Mr. Jameson will be out in a moment and it might be well to look as if we were working or something."

Jameson did come out then, followed by Acton. Jameson stopped at Lola's desk to give her some instructions. Acton stood at the door. His exceedingly charming smile included all the girls and lingered a special moment on Lola. Lola smiled back. The door closed behind the two men.

"Well," sighed Gladys, "I'm all of a flutter!" She produced a motion-picture magazine and began to rustle its pages. "Who does he remind you of? Is it Richard Dix? But he's built something like Gary Cooper."

In the elevator, as they stepped out at the main floor.

"Darned pretty secretary you've got. She *is* your secretary, isn't she?" asked Acton.

"Yes. Mrs. Hayes, you mean?" said Jameson. "Nice girl, very capable."

"*Mrs.?* Alas, poor Yorick! What does a girl like that want to get married for? No, don't answer! I suppose I know. But why is she in the office? Some modern idea? They all get that way. Did you know that my sister had opened a hat shop?"

"Well subsidized, I take it? No, Lola Hayes works because she has to. I don't approve of it, for perfectly sound biological reasons, but quite a number of our women employees are married," answered Jameson. "Lola has been with the company for several years and is doing very well. If she sticks to it and can stand the gaff she'll do even better."

"A girl like that," said Acton firmly, "should sit on a cushion and sew a fine seam. Or should be glorified by Ziegfeld, or someone. It's a damned shame."

"You'd better," suggested Jameson, laughing, as they got into Acton's car, "stay away from my office. I can't have you demoralizing my force."

"Oh, why?" asked Acton innocently. "I know I'm a nuisance but I'm very much attached to you, Phil," he said gravely, while his eyes laughed, "and I'm at a rather loose end just now. In between drinks. Held here in town by some estate stupidities. Lawyers and trust companies should be included among the plagues. Sometimes I grow so bored I think I'll go to work."

"You'd be better off," suggested his friend.

"I don't know. Just because you started at fourteen or some ungodly age and haven't a lazy bone in your body, you're no judge. Besides I'm a director on a lot of important boards," remarked Acton solemnly. "I sit around a long table and yawn dutifully. No one can ask more of me, can they?"

"Possibly not. Here we are. I'm starved, if that's any consolation to you."

"I love to feed you," Acton told him, "although I'd a damned sight rather feed your secretary."

At home that night Lola told Ken:

"Acton—Peter Acton came in to see Jameson today."

"Gee, this ham is good," said Ken. "Who's he?"

"I don't know exactly. Director or something. Very good-looking. The girls said he has houses all over the place, yachts and things."

"Some people get all the breaks. How old is he? And how fat?"

"About fortyish, I imagine. And he isn't fat at all. He's as thin as you are and a couple of inches taller."

"Don't, you're breaking my heart!" said Ken amiably. "I can't stand hearing about handsome guys, lousy with money. Glad you're not working for him though."

"I'd love to work for him," said Lola, out of pure mischief.

Ken eyed her sternly across the gate-legged table.

"You have a lot of funny ideas," he said, and added contentedly, "but I'm not worried."

"You needn't be," she told him, and smiled at him.

Millie came in unexpectedly.

"The door was open," she said mildly, "so here I am. I'm the gas man."

"Have you had dinner?" Lola asked, jumping up from the table.

"No. I was going home." Millie walked over to the table and sniffed. "Broiled ham . . . and vegetable salad . . . and one of mother's chocolate cakes. And coffee. Why go home? Can I grab me a plate, Lola? Wait, I'll phone mother."

Presently she was at the table, but she ate very little. Her eyes were enormous in a small flushed face.

"I've had a screen test . . . and a voice test. I'll know tomorrow. If I make good——" said Millie, and you knew that she knew that there was no possibility of her *not* making good. "Gosh, it was funny," she said. "I don't mind lights and things any more or even the tomb-like silence. But when it was just me . . . speaking into that contraption. My knees shook so—"

"Lucky you didn't have on puttees," Ken commented.

"Millie!" cried Lola, "when will you hear? And if you go over all right, what will it mean to you?"

"Oh, in a day or so. What will it mean? A little part, to start with, I think. In a new hot technicolor revue thing. After that, the sky's the limit."

"Pipe down, Mil," Ken advised her. "You've got to have everything, you know. Besides looks and speaking voice. You have to dance and sing."

"Well, I've won a couple of cups already," Millie said, aggrieved. "I can dance enough to get by. As for singing, I can do that, too. But let me tell you both if I get this chance I'll put every cent of my salary back into lessons."

Lola said,

"Don't tease her, Ken." She thought: Why, she really cares about it! It isn't just kid stuff. She really *cares*. She's ambitious. She means to make something of herself . . . something big.

Millie stayed for an hour and regaled them with studio gossip. Then she rose. She had always walked well. Now she carried her small person as one imagines a queen carries herself. But only imagines.

"I'll run along," said Millie, "and break the big news to the family. Father has already had me ruined, disgraced, and out in the cold world with the unfathered child. And mother is worrying about late hours and orgies. . . . She thinks my health will be all shot."

"Well, it would be in that case," Ken told her reasonably.

She swung around on him.

"You certainly must think I'm a sap," said Millie, "as

if that sort of boloney ever got you anywhere! You've got to train for this job like a—like a prize-fighter. Catch me slipping, like most of 'em after they've got somewhere. Not me," said Millie, "I've too much sense."

She left. Kenneth stared at the door. "There goes hard-hearted Hannah!" he commented.

"She's right, though," Lola told him.

"Sure, she's right. You don't have to read the success articles to know that. But how many of 'em stick to it after they've made the grade? Darned few. And she's nothing but a kid. If she were really my sister—I'd—"

"You'd what?"

"I'd forbid it!" said Ken.

Lola, who had been wishing that she could forbid it and wishing it without, as she admitted to herself, any good reason, flared up instantly in Millie's defense.

"Well, you're not her brother," she declared. "I didn't think you were so narrow-minded."

"It isn't narrow-minded," Ken told her. "Hey, don't get all hot and bothered. I just spoke an opinion. I'm entitled to that. And if your father and mother can't stop her and you won't try, certainly I can't. Only she's riding for a fall, that's all," he prophesied gloomily.

"I don't believe it! You said yourself she had a level head."

"I thought so; I'm not so sure now," he argued stubbornly.

Lola cleared the dishes, her mouth a straight line and her hands performing a clatter of exasperation.

"What gets me," burst out Ken suddenly, tilting his chair back and stretching his long legs, "is a kid like that, without any real training, can walk into a big salary, just on the strength of her looks . . . and earn in a week more money than I'll ever make in a month."

"So *that's* it!" commented Lola, carrying the things to the kitchen.

He rose and followed her, lounging against the door. "So that's what?" he wanted to know.

"So that's what's worrying you," said Lola. "You're afraid that Millie will make more money than you do."

"It doesn't worry me," he began impatiently. "I only said—"

"I know what you said. Well, I hope she does," said Lola savagely. "It will serve you right!"

Ken turned and walked away. When Lola came out of the kitchenette, after a frantic washing up at which he had not offered to assist her, he asked her, wonderingly:

"Gee, what were we fighting about anyway, Lola?"

"I don't know," Lola told him, as astonished as he. She came over and perched on the arm of his chair. "Millie, I suppose."

"Forget it, I didn't mean it. About Millie I mean. I just thought—things were unfair sometimes, somehow. I hope she makes a million," said Ken.

Peace again.

And during that autumn and early winter Millie had her contract, Connie came back from abroad, and Agnes and Jim separated.

Chapter VII

LOLA couldn't believe it. She kept saying to herself, But it isn't possible. Yet it was.

During the early winter she had seen very little of Agnes. She was working hard, and was more tired than usual. Her mother had been wretchedly ill with an attack of the flu, and Lola had done what she could for her, evenings and over Sundays, as Millie was rarely, if ever, to be depended upon. Millie had had her "little bit" in the revue and was already working on a second picture, in a better part, and was beginning to complain about the distance to the lot and wondering if it wouldn't be better if she took a small place in New York to be nearer. This proposition was hotly debated in the family; and it was Millie herself who finally decided to stay at home until the time came, which it eventually would, for her to go out to Hollywood. She said frankly: "It's an awful bore, the long subway trip, but not much longer than from New York I guess, and it will cost me less to live at home." She was as good as her word about lessons. She was taking dancing lessons, fencing, and voice culture. And so, although her startling salary seemed enormous to her astonished family, most of it went out as quickly as it came in.

Lola was worried too, about Kenneth. He saw Jim as rarely as she saw Agnes. He was going out with Garrison's crowd almost exclusively. He had come home, not in the happy parlance of the day "tight" or "plastered" but decidedly and miserably drunk, three times since their vacation. And although he had been apologetic enough the first time, on the following morning, the times thereafter he had been merely sullen and on the defensive; and, before he sobered up, amazingly frank.

"What's your kick?" he had asked thickly and defiantly, sitting on the edge of the bed, struggling to pull off his shoes, while Lola lay in her bed and watched him, anger drying the tears in her eyes and steadying the quivering of her lips. "A fellow has a duty toward prohibition," said Ken, "and I don't question *you*. Why question me? Fifty-fifty. That's us. Modern. Modern marriage. Pay your own shot and go your way." Ken laughed. It was an unpleasant sound. "You're a great girl, Lola," said Ken sleepily, "even if you do wear the pants!" And fell sound asleep, just as he sat there, one hand tugging feebly at a refractory boot-lace.

She asked him the next morning:

"What did you mean by what you said last night that I—'wore the pants'?" she demanded, distastefully and resentful.

"I don't remember. I don't remember anything. Oh, for God's sake, Lola, don't start nagging at me! I've a head on me like the Zeppelin and I'm late to work," he had groaned, turning pale green at the sight of the coffee she had kept warm for him. And Lola was late, too. She couldn't leave him to fend for himself in his miserable condition, and she arrived at the office breathless from hurry. And cross. She snapped at Dorothy and lectured Gladys until both girls raised plucked eyebrows. It wasn't like Lola. What had got into her? "Had a row with the poppa?" Gladys wanted to know. Lola said, "Certainly not," stiffly. Then, sitting at her desk, she took stock of herself. She was getting just like Mrs. Holmes. Taking out her anxieties and her domestic trouble on other people! She said, presently, over her shoulder, "Sorry I was such a grouch, girls," and let it go at that. It mustn't happen again, she told herself. But it did. And she was beginning to understand Holmes. She would like to tell Connie so. But Connie wasn't interested in the office any more. Connie had changed.

But more than by Connie, Lola was distressed by the situation in which Agnes and Jim found themselves.

Lola had heard nothing, knew nothing. Millie's first picture, the review, was opening in New York. Lola and Ken and the Davises were going. She wondered if Agnes and Jim wouldn't go, too. She stopped in at Agnes's one Sunday morning on her way to her mother's. Ken had been out late and wasn't up yet. She left him, the shades drawn, sunk deep in the profound innocence of sleep.

She knocked at Agnes's door. It was open, and as no answer reached her she turned the knob and walked in. She called, going through the hall:

"Agnes . . . It's me . . . Lola."

"I'm in the bedroom," said Agnes.

Lola came in. Her cheeks were bright from the crisp winter air. She had her hands tucked in her pockets for warmth. She talked all the way down the hall and into the room.

"I'm on my way to mother's. Ken is sleeping like the dead. Where's Jim? Agnes, Millie's picture opens next week. Why don't you and Jim come? It would be a lot of fun." She stopped dead, on the threshold. "Agnes . . . what *are* you doing?"

Agnes was packing.

She was on her knees before a bureau, the drawers gaping, stockings, lingerie, blouses hanging over the edges, tossed on the beds. The beds were stripped. Now Lola remembered that coming through the little hall there had been something strange about her glimpse of the living-room. "Why, *Agnes!*" she said, in bewilderment.

Agnes got up. She was quite white. There was a streak of dust on one cheek. Her eyes were red and tired. Her mouth lacked color. She was no longer a pretty girl. She was a tired woman with disillusion and failure in her eyes.

"Where are you going?" Lola wanted to know. Her knees gave way from sheer astonishment, and she sat down on the edge of a bed and stared at her friend.

"Home," Agnes answered briefly.

"Home? To your people? What's the matter? Are you ill? Is Jim? Oh, Agnes," cried Lola, thinking that perhaps after all she knew, "are you going to have a baby?"

"No." Agnes tried to smile. She sat down beside Lola. She said evenly:

"I'm going home for good. We have subleased the apartment. The furniture is to be stored. Jim and I are breaking up, Lola."

"No. No." Lola thought if she said it often enough it wouldn't be true. "*No*, Agnes, you can't! Have you— is it just a quarrel? Oh, Agnes . . ." Lola was crying now, with little catches of her breath. "I'm so sorry. Can't it be fixed up? I don't understand. I thought you were so happy. I thought you loved each other."

"We were for a little while. We did, for a little longer. We can't go on, now. That's all. Don't cry, Lola. It doesn't," said Agnes oddly, "mean anything to you, really. Don't cry. I don't. I can't. Not any more."

Her eyes were dry; and her lips. She was tearless. Her voice was steady.

Lola mopped at her eyes with a handkerchief. She fought back the panic that was sweeping darkly over her—a panic that had to do with Agnes and Jim only by indirection. She said:

"It's your own business. But I feel—I can't tell you how I feel. Could you tell me about it, perhaps, Agnes?"

"I'll try." Agnes touched her hand briefly. "You've been a good friend, Lola. We've had some good times . . . all of us." She stopped and then went on. "I don't know if I can make you understand. It's different with you and Ken. Ken grew up without much family, made his own way, shouldered his responsibility. You had a brother and a sister. You went to work, early. It was expected of you. You were trained for it from the beginning. I wasn't. I led the usual life of a daughter of a middle-class lawyer, with a good income he more than lived up to and whose expenses never kept pace. But I always had clothes and went to parties and went to a school that cost my father a couple of thousand a year. I wasn't trained for anything. I met Jim. He came from the same sort of people that I did. People who talked a lot about themselves; about other people; analyzed; 'pulled things to pieces,' as you once said. People who had to talk and discuss and—and come to some sort of intellectual grips. Then we married. Jim wasn't making much, and so I said I'd work. I was sure I could. I had education, background, all the rest of it. I had a lot of modern theories and ideas. I thought I could begin somewhere and work up. I wanted a modern marriage. A partnership. Each of us working, each of us helping build a home, each of us coming there at night to share everything, to—to create a new world by talking about it, I expect. Each of us awfully in love."

"But you did that," Lola told her helplessly.

"No, not after a time. You know how it is, Lola. Coming home, dead-tired. Talking trivialities. Talking money. Worrying about things. Bills. Possible pregnancies, which would be impossible, in the circumstances. Trying to entertain. Getting so you felt you *had* to go out for relaxation or have someone in. Feeling the monotony get on your nerves so that you could scream. All Jim and I had after more than two years was a shared burden of work and finances and a—a bedroom. Love?" she asked. "We wanted more than just a physical marriage. And that was all we had. And even that lost its magic, its glamour. We were tired, we were afraid. And when we were alone together, what happened to all the books we were going to read to each other, all the things we were going to talk about? I don't know. We were just too damned tired. Jim looked at a paper and I cleaned up the apartment and we went to bed. Or I talked about the shop and he talked about the company. And we went to bed. And we began to quarrel. About money. About a lot of things. About my people. If he hadn't married, he said, he could have gotten on faster. If I hadn't married him, I said, I could have married a man who could support me."

She leaned forward suddenly and clutched at Lola's hands.

"If you love Ken," she warned her, "never say that to him! If I had it to do all over again I'd live on Jim's fifty a week and slave and do my washing and let him feel that there was one head to a family. Sex pride, Lola. You don't know what it is until you see it in operation. Take a woman's dependence away from the average man and you've crippled him. I could have gone without a lot of little things I thought I had to have. I could have changed my standards. Why did I have to bring my old standards into marriage? I could have grown old and fat and had children and been—oh, perhaps not happy—

but less discontented. This way, we were neither of us content. And we needn't have started out in New York. We could have gone to a small town somewhere, where living is a little easier and simpler, where we didn't know anyone and would have had no old ties and no rich friends by whom to draw comparisons. Jim had an offer just before we were married. To go to the Middle West. I wouldn't, I said. I couldn't bear Main Street. My God, Lola, it's all Main Street!"

She fell silent, twisting her hands in her lap.

"But," asked Lola slowly, "if you *know* what the trouble is, can't you do something about it, Agnes? Begin again? Give up your job? Get Jim to take a position somewhere else?"

"No. It's too late."

"But, if you know——" began Lola stubbornly.

Agnes turned on her. Color flared up in her face and died away again, leaving her whiter and wearier for that brief moment of vivacity.

"People like Jim—and like me—always know," she said, despairing at making the other girl understand; "we know all along. We see things coming. We know with our minds. But it doesn't do any good. We struggle and try and in the end it gets us. It is too late. We—don't care any more. Or if we do care there is such a layer of bitterness and resentment and hatred, not of each other but of ourselves, that it's corroded the caring. We can't scrape it off and get to what's underneath, if there's anything left underneath, anything that hasn't been eaten away. We have said things to each other we can't forget. And thought things. Nothing's left. I can't live that sort of life, the sort it would be if we went on from here. Sharing bills and a bed. Quarreling with a man and sleeping with him. I can't do it, Lola!"

"Where is Jim?" asked Lola after a moment.

"He's gone to a boarding-house where the bachelor engineers live, in this district. They are talking of getting an apartment together. Eight of them. If so, he'll take some of the furniture out of storage. I don't want it."

"What do your people say?" Lola wanted to know.

"They are wild, naturally. Back on their hands! Damaged goods. They hope, I think, that someone will marry me, after I get my divorce."

"You'll really—divorce Jim?" asked Lola, her last hope going.

"Some day. I can't afford to go West. Here, perhaps. He said he'd give me the manufactured grounds. He's been very decent."

"Doesn't he—care?"

"Of course, he cares. He hates failure. But he'll get used to it. He wasn't any happier than I. We were, people said, perfectly mated." She laughed aloud. "We liked the same things. That was perhaps the trouble." She brooded, her chin on a curved wrist, her dark, tired, red-rimmed eyes remote. "When I think of the things we were going to do. Lectures. Reading. Cheap concerts. Take up some home study courses together. Go away on week-end trips. For vacations. Hike. Buy a cheap car and rattle away like gipsies to the four corners of the earth. Save and go to Europe, student class . . .

"It didn't happen," she said dully, after a pause. "It couldn't. Too many things came in between."

Lola said, inadequately, "Agnes, I'm so *sorry.*"

"I know you are, Lola; don't look at me that way . . . What is it?"

"It frightens me," Lola said, whispering.

Agnes understood. She had that sort of mind.

"For you and Ken? It needn't. You're different," said Agnes.

"I'm not so sure. We have the same problems."

"Not quite. You were not spoiled, either of you, before you married. You didn't expect as much. I don't mean money. Of course you expected a lot—romance and all that—we all do. But there were other things—" She was silent again, then she went on, abruptly: "I am going on working of course. I won't take money from Jim. I can't live on the family. They have a hard enough time as it is. Town house, country cottage, servants, a car, the other girls to dress and put out on the bargain-counter, theater and occasional opera, entertaining, father's clubs. They never have enough money, somehow. I wonder if anyone has, except very poor people who don't want very much. I'll get a job in one of the New York stores. I've several friends working in them, and the shop has been very decent about my leaving and about recommending me. I'll work because I have to and maybe I'll want to, after a while. I used to be very ambitious. I thought I could go a long way. Perhaps I can—alone. We'll see. I'll be able to buy my own clothes, at least. I can live in town while the others go to the country next summer; they always keep the house open. I'll manage."

"I won't see you any more, Agnes," said Lola.

"Of course, you will! I'll come over as often as I can, and then we can have dinner together and we'll meet often for lunch."

But they looked at one another with a sudden, hurting shyness. They would see each other of course. Especially at first. "Often," perhaps, at first. But not afterwards. They would drift apart. It was bound to happen. Life went on and you went on with it. Agnes, living at home and working in a New York shop, and getting a divorce, and meeting other men, and going out with them, and picking up old threads of acquaintanceships that she had dropped since her marriage, would be different from Agnes round the corner from Lola, with Jim to open the door and call: "Come on in, folks. How about a little round of stud? Aggie, is there anything valuable in the ice-box?"

"Let me," Lola begged unsteadily, "help with the packing."

"It's all done, almost, except for my things. The storage people are coming in the morning."

"Can't I," Lola wanted to know, "spend the night with you? . . . You'll be all alone."

Agnes looked at her strangely.

"Not any more alone than I've been with Jim asleep in the bed beside me," she said. "No, it's dear of you, Lola. But I'd rather not. Oh, God," she cried suddenly, "why can't women be reasoning adults instead of sentimental animals? I want to stay here alone, one night. And luxuriate. And say good-by to things. And remember. I keep remembering all the happy times and forgetting the wretched ones. I keep on writhing in my mind, a sort of suicide of the heart. I'm a fool. Yet I wouldn't go back to Jim. Not for anything. I never want to see him again. He's—a stranger. Why do I keep on remembering?" she asked frantically.

Lola left her, after a time, and walked to her mother's. The sun had clouded over, was the round, pale yellow disk of a sea-shell behind the graying sky. An aimless flake of snow or two drifted down.

Agnes thinks too much—thought Lola.

But she thought too. She didn't put it into words. Perhaps when you had to put your thoughts into words something happened; something vital escaped from yourself. Agnes and Jim's marriage had gone on the rocks. Why? It wasn't all lack of money, was it? Yet it must be. If they'd had money they would have had leisure and if they'd had leisure they would have had their books and their trips and their intellectual diversions, their mental passions, which seemed so important to them; and their keen-eyed, alert talk, which seemed more important than anything else, to them. Yet if Jim came into a fortune tomorrow Agnes wouldn't go back to him, thought Lola, shrewdly, correctly; Agnes had lost something. Something within her had been too bruised and too beaten. "We said things . . . We thought things . . ." she had told Lola. Agnes couldn't forget. Neither could Jim. Everybody wasn't like that. No matter what she, Lola, said to Ken in anger, and he to her, she could forget if love survived. But Agnes and Jim's love hadn't survived.

She went into her mother's house. Millie was home, quarreling with Howard as usual. Howard couldn't take Millie seriously. It was nothing to Howard, or at least not yet, if Millie became fifty motion-picture stars. She was still Millie. He was unimpressed or behaved as if he were. Mrs. Davis and her husband were as basically unimpressed as Howard, yet persisted in regarding Millie as if they had hatched out something strange and beyond their understanding.

Millie's lovely speaking voice was lower. She had tricks of accent now.

"*Bean*," said Howard in a clear falsetto and shuddered with a bitter amusement. "Dear Millie has *bean* out to the lot where she has probably taken a bawth. Oh, deah me, deah me!" raved Howard, all angular arms and legs. "Isn't that just too divine? I cawn't get over it," he mouthed.

"Shut up," said Millie absently, still somewhat herself

in the bosom of her family—a rather cactuslike bosom, in Howard's case.

She hadn't heard Howard say carelessly to Bill, across the street, half an hour earlier: "Millie's working for Unimount Pictures now. She's got 'em all stopped. Watch her smoke." Howard bragged, "She's going to get me a job too. Out in Hollywood."

"Doing what?" asked Bill, awestruck.

"Oh, I think," Howard replied carelessly, "I'll write scenarios. I know what's wrong with the pictures. Lousy stories. I'll tell 'em what's the matter and draw down a wad of jack doing it. I'll have an office and a secretary and sit in on conferences, some day," Howard announced deeply. "Pretty soon too."

"Cripes!" commented Bill, not believing but not quite daring to disbelieve openly. After all, Millie *was* in the pictures. Millicent Davis, she called herself now. All the neighbors knew that. The neighbors kept dropping in and finding out.

Ken, Lola found on her arrival, was in the back yard tying up a long cane of a rose bush which had been whipped by the stiff winter wind of the previous night. "Where in heaven's name have you been?" he wanted to know as she appeared on the little back porch, hugging herself to keep warm in the breeze from the Narrows.

"At Agnes's."

"Coming with us next week?"

"No. I'll tell you later, Ken," she said.

She didn't want to tell him now. With the family around. Or at the family table. She knew beforehand how everyone would take it; Millie with a superior smile; her mother with real distress and incomprehension; her father with disgust . . . "crazy kids—marriage isn't worth anything nowadays—it doesn't mean anything—

not any more than human life does, with gunmen and all!"

They left the Davises a little after six and walked home. "Want to go to a movie?" asked Ken, yawning.

"No, let's go home. We can have a late supper. I left plenty in the ice-box. I want to tell you about Agnes and Jim."

But they were not to be alone for a time. As they reached their door a car stopped in front of it. A closed car, a good sedan. Connie was driving. Fur was nestled about her face. She had grown heavier, more placid. She asked, leaning out: "Can I come in? I was driving by; I have to pick up Louis at seven, we are going out."

They welcomed her volubly and Ken helped her out and drove the car into the driveway for her. "The people downstairs are away, they won't be using the garage today," he explained. Connie and Lola went upstairs. Lola had seen her several times since her return from Italy. Not often. She and Ken had been to a party at her new house, over in the Bath Beach district, once. A stucco house, set back with a large yard around it. Trees, bushes, shrubs—too many of them—carefully landscaped. A little bronze fountain and some strange cast-iron animals on the lawn. Inside it was all very new. Furnished very much *en suite*. Louis's taste showed there, despite Connie's careful planning. Lace curtains, overdrapes. Gay cushions. Statuary. Lots of velvet and plush and overstuffed things. A canary in a cage. A bowl of goldfish. . . .

Louis had left the cigar store. With what he had saved, he was now in a contracting business of his own. Joe, explained Connie, was pleased.

Ken came in and they sat and talked. Connie was, in a sense, herself, friendly, smiling, pleasant. And she had never looked so well. The extra flesh became her. She seemed happy and content. She asked Lola about the office. She hadn't, she said, seen anyone from there save Lola since she left. She talked a little about her trip.

One of the young men from next door came knocking, to ask Ken's advice about the eternal radio. Ken departed, glad to escape. Connie relaxed a little; so did Lola. Lola asked, out of long friendship:

"Connie, I never see you alone. Are you happy?"

Connie said, yes, she was. She added that Louis was a good husband. She added further, frankly, looking directly at Lola and seeming very well dressed, well powdered, very comfortable in appearance:

"He gives me anything I want. As long as I fall in with some of his ideas everything is all right. I've grown very fond of him."

Lola stated, abruptly, determined to speak out:

"You weren't in love with him when you married, Connie."

"No. I didn't dislike him." Connie flushed suddenly. "And I was tired. Tired of working. Tired of fighting Joe. Tired of the treatment I was getting. I didn't care for any other man. Louis would take me away from all that. I'll be a good wife to him. After all a woman doesn't get much else even if she starts out with love, does she? I mean, she doesn't get much more than a roof over her head and meals on the table and a man and children. No matter what she starts out with, that's what she ends up with—if she's lucky. I'm going to have a baby," said Connie.

"Oh, Connie, so soon!"

"Yes. I wasn't happy about it at first. Too soon, I thought. But Louis is so pleased. He's crazy about children. Most Italians are. I'm content enough now. I'd

just as soon have several quickly and get it over with.
I've a girl to help me with the work. I've been to a good
doctor. It will be all right. Louis never comes home without bringing me a present and one for the *bambino* . . ."

She laughed easily, smoothed down the flat crape of her
dress, and looked at Lola. Lola said:

"I'm glad, if you are. I—envy you, a little. Connie,
Jim and Agnes are separating. They'll be divorced pretty
soon. She wouldn't mind my telling you."

Connie wasn't astonished. She said so. She was sorry,
she said, but it was apparent to Lola that she cared very
little. Jim and Agnes belonged to another part of her
life. She rose. She mustn't, she said, keep Louis waiting.

Lola went to the door with her.

"You haven't," she said, "much freedom, have you?"

"No. Have you?" asked Connie.

Lola was silent. Connie went on while Lola was search-
ing frantically for denials—of course I have . . . a fifty-
fifty marriage . . . an American marriage . . . are you
out of your head?

"I didn't have much before I was married. Just freedom, permission to work myself to death and hang on a
subway strap coming home. I've all I want now. Real
freedom. Freedom from worry. From struggling."

She laid a cool cheek against Lola's, kissed her. "Come
see us soon," she said.

When Ken came back, "Where's Connie?" he wanted
to know.

"Gone. Ken, she's going to have a baby!" Lola told
him, still amazed.

"She is?" He whistled. "Pretty quick work. Is she
sore about it?"

"No, she doesn't seem to mind. *He's* tickled to death,
of course," said Lola.

"He would be. He isn't a bad sort. Look here, I heard the other day that he made the money he put into the contracting business by bootlegging. I had it pretty straight. I thought there was something more to it than a cigar store. I forgot to tell you."

"Bootlegging? Oh, poor Connie!"

"Perhaps she doesn't know. Or doesn't care as long as she's safe." Ken sat down and lighted a cigarette. "What's this about Agnes and Jim? You sounded mysterious."

Lola told him, briefly enough. Ken said, after a pause: "Poor old Jim!"

Lola had been feeling very sorry for him. In a boarding-house. Alone. Without Agnes. Now she flared up in Agnes's defense.

"What about Agnes? She had a lot to put up with, too."

"Oh, I don't know. Probably she rubbed it into Jim about how much she had before she married him. Pretty high-hat she could be at times. I like Agnes, but she's selfish as the devil. We'll have Jim here often now."

"Of course," Lola agreed; then thought and added, "if Agnes doesn't mind."

"Why the hell should she? Does she want to cut him off from all his friends?"

"No, she wouldn't. That's the last thing she'd want to do. But she's my friend. More than Jim ever was."

"Well, he's mine," Ken said stubbornly.

"Ken, we can't take sides!"

"Who's taking sides?" he demanded. "It's mutual on their part, isn't it? Of course, it's just like you women to stick together and see that a man doesn't get a decent break . . ."

They were quarreling again. Hotly, eying each other like enemies.

She said, after a while:

"Oh, Ken, *don't!* What does it matter? Of course we'll see them both. Go on liking them both. But why do we fight so? I'm so tired of it. And I'm so afraid."

She was close to tears. He said, taking her in his arms:

"I guess we're both edgy or something."

She whispered: "Ken, do you remember, up at camp— the big moon shining through the trees and the water on the beach?"

He remembered. He held her close. He said, worried and awkward:

"I'm sorry I got all wrought up about Jim. It doesn't matter. Nothing matters but us. I love you, Lola."

She answered, her cheek against his own:

"And I love you. Oh, let's stay so, Ken! Let's not go about trying to hurt each other. I get so frightened when I hear of people breaking up. It doesn't seem fair. Something's awfully wrong somewhere."

"Not with us," Ken told her strongly. "We love each other. They didn't. Not enough. That's the whole story, Lola, they didn't love each other enough."

She said, and wondered while she said it:

"I suppose that's it. It must be. There couldn't be any other reason. Could there?" she asked him.

It was not a question. It was a cry in the dark. It was a cry for a reassuring hand, for a final word, for the tenderness and oblivion of lips on her own, for the assurance of security.

Chapter VIII

I⊤ was spring once more when Lola met Peter Acton again. And it was perfectly obvious that, in the meantime, he had forgotten her. Coming into Jameson's office without heralding, he looked at her with a puzzled knitting of the brows, and then, as she spoke his name, with a face clearing to delighted recognition. He had a direct method of attack which she found amusing.

"Do you know," he said happily, "I had almost forgotten you! Almost, I repeat. Not quite. Something has teased me in the back of my mind for a good many weeks. Something kept saying to me: 'You've had a charming experience which you'd be a fool not to repeat.' Now, I know. You. How I could have forgotten, even for a little, is beyond me," he said, in apparently honest astonishment.

Lola answered with gravity, although her eyes danced: "You must see a good many people, Mr. Acton."

"I never—or rarely ever—see a girl with raw gold hair and blue eyes and a mouth that wants to smile and doesn't dare," he retorted amiably. "Look here, isn't Phil coming in?"

"Not until afternoon," she told him. "I'm sorry."

"I'm not. That is, I'm not if you'll have lunch with me. It must be about time, isn't it?"

She thought: A fast worker. She said aloud: "Thank you. But I can't. I have an engagement."

"To eat upstairs with the crew of the ship?" he wanted to know.

"No—to meet a friend, outside the office," she answered.

"Lucky fellow!" Suddenly he stopped, disconcerted. "I forgot! You're married! Don't tell me," he begged in mock horror, "that you are going to meet your husband?"

She said no, and laughed because she couldn't help it.

He added, with the winning quality that disarmed you and made you forget impertinence: "I wish you'd explain to me how come that your young man permits you to work? Oh, I know you girls and your ideas about partnership marriages. But *you* are a menace to public peace. You should be kept, you know, in a glass case."

"I'd hate that," she laughed, and evaded his question. He did not appear to notice the evasion but he did.

"Lola—"

Lola looked at him. Now it was his turn for laughter.

"I'm sorry. I couldn't remember the other part but the Lola remained, however, in some dim gray cell."

"Hayes," Lola instructed him inflexibly.

"Where do you live—Mrs. Hayes?"

He was sitting on the edge of Jameson's desk. His eyes were as young as Howard's under the shock of gray hair. It was fortunate, thought Lola swiftly, that he had closed the door to the outer office behind him. Otherwise Gladys and Dorothy would be in convulsions; they were probably not far short of that tragic state—because of the closed door.

"In Brooklyn. Bay Ridge."

"Brooklyn?" He looked smitten. Then remembered, gayly, "Well, I've been to polo games at Fort Hamilton."

"We're not far from there," she said.

"Tell me, would your husband object if you went out to lunch with me?" he urged. "It would be a tremendously kind thing to do. I'm alone," he complained mournfully, "in a big city. No mother to guide me."

Lola answered quickly, "Kenneth's not the objecting sort."

"Good. But unusual, even today. How about tomorrow?"

She shook her head.

"Next day then? Saturday? Oh, I suppose not Saturday. Well, Monday? Blue Monday?"

There was nothing for her to do. She couldn't pretend engagements indefinitely. She said, steadily:

"I'm sorry. I'd rather not, if you don't mind."

"But, of course, I mind!" His face was a rueful one. He asked, gently: "Don't you like me? I've always been told I was a pretty likable person. What's wrong with me?"

He was incorrigible. She replied, laughing:

"Nothing, of course. But well-behaved secretaries don't go out to luncheon with friends of their employers."

"I see. They go out with their employers, though, don't they? I've read it in books; and seen it, in restaurants. How about being my secretary?" he suggested gravely. "I really need one. I have a couple but they don't count. They are earnest boys who keep track of my bills and my check-books, fondly hoping that such responsibilities constitute stepping-stones to Higher Things. I think," he said, "I need a social secretary badly. How about it?"

Lola said, wishing that he would go, "I like my job."

"You do? Really? Lord, that's odd!" He regarded her solemnly. "Imagine a pretty girl—imagine you—liking any job! It's too absurd! Do you know I don't believe I ever knew a girl who worked—I mean . . . my sister runs a hat shop, of course—and there's a girl I know in a decorating place and another on a magazine but it's different . . . that is to say—"

He was actually floundering. Embarrassed. A new situation for him, she decided, enjoying it very much. She helped him out, evenly:

"You mean you've never known a girl before who *had* to work, is that it?"

"Well, I fancy it is. Thanks a lot," he said, once more unabashed.

"That's curious," Lola told him. "You must have had manicures, and waitresses, and people to do your house-work—"

"Oh, I say!" He looked at her, his eyes brilliant. He said: "I deserved that. I didn't mean it the way it sounded. Look here, why *won't* you go to lunch with me?"

"I've told you," she said, sighing.

"Oh, no, you haven't!" He tried a bit of table-turning. "Confess now, be honest, even if I have made you sore, that you're *afraid* to go; afraid your husband will be angry; afraid that he'll be after me with shotguns and things. So much for modern marriage!"

She was annoyed. Her color rose. She asked swiftly: "It's done, in your class, isn't it?"

"Well, yes," he answered before he realized where she was leading him, and Lola went on quickly.

"But not often—in mine. You see the difference? I'm sorry to be rude, Mr. Acton, but I really must get to work."

She was moving toward the door. Her head was well up. He followed her, and spoke to her urgently:

"I'm sorry. What a—poor creature you must think me! Class, indeed! Look here, I'm not going to give up. Of course, if you'd get in wrong at home—I mean that;

I'm not joking—it's a different matter. But think it over."

She opened the door and walked out into the other office. Dorothy and Gladys sprang apart, ceased their whispering and became tremendously occupied, one at the telephone desk, the other at the typewriter.

"Good morning, Mrs. Hayes," said Peter Acton gravely. "You'll tell Mr. Jameson I dropped in."

Lola answered pleasantly and sat down at her desk. She was astonished to find herself shaking. Anger? She didn't know. Yet she liked him. He was—different. He had charm and a certain smooth, but disarming audacity. What had he meant about Kenneth? Kenneth wasn't— old-fashioned. Kenneth wouldn't mind. Or, would he? Anyway, she didn't want to go to lunch with Peter Acton. Or, did she?

Five minutes later she was on her way out of the building to meet Agnes at a down-town Schrafft's. Agnes was working in a Fifth Avenue shop. Lola had seen her several times. She had come over to Brooklyn, as good as her word; but had said despairingly, as she left: "I can't again. For a while. Don't ask me to. You and Ken come to dinner. At the family's. Or we'll eat out somewhere amusing in the Village. And I'll ring you up, for lunch."

At Schrafft's, looking very trim, rested, and much prettier than Lola had ever seen her, Agnes talked about her job. She was going out a good deal, too. And having a good time. But a quiet one. She asked abruptly:

"Do you ever see Jim?"

"Yes. He's been to the house, twice . . . no, three times."

"Has he said anything—"

"No, we don't talk about it. He's working hard," reported Lola, "and looks, I think, very well."

Agnes answered, crumbling her tea-biscuit and looking idly about the crowded room:

"I'm glad. I've nothing but friendship in my heart now. And a sort of sick grief. Yet I'm happier than I've been in months. Not happier, perhaps. But—relieved. I can't tell you. It isn't easy at home, of course. Later, when I work up a bit further I may take an apartment with another girl I know. It would be better all around. But not until I can swing it without deadly anxiety. I have had enough of that."

She liked her work, she added. She was selling. Later, she expected to be made assistant buyer in the gift shop. It might lead to a buyer's job. She was taking outside courses. There was a chance in advertising, she thought. She spoke of the brilliant young woman whose advertising copy for a certain well-known shop had made her famous and independent. Agnes said:

"There's no limit to what you can do, when you're working for yourself."

Lola asked, a little diffidently:

"If you hadn't had to work? If there'd been money . . . it would have been all right between you and Jim, wouldn't it?"

"I suppose so," Agnes told her. She added: "It's sort of unfair, isn't it, that money, and the things it can buy can make such a difference? I don't exactly understand. When I think of the ideals with which we went into marriage; when I think of the way we cared . . . real caring. Where has it gone? Why? It can't all be money. Lola, there's something the matter; I don't know what it is. Perhaps women aren't meant to lead that double sort of life; perhaps they can't stand it. I don't know. Yet thousands do, successfully. We only hear of the unsuccessful ones. Or are the ones we don't hear about just standing the gaff and keeping a close mouth and trying to make the best of it? Pick up any magazine. Read the articles. By business women. With husbands. With children. Read what they say; how successful they are, how happy. Perhaps I'm made of different stuff, shoddier, more fragile. Perhaps it frayed more easily than they did; wore through. I don't know," she said again.

"It can't all be money," Lola agreed after a while. She was thinking of Peter Acton. His wife had left him. Yet he had had money. Lots of it. His wife had had leisure, amusements, coddling, beautiful clothes. . . . She had had him, a good-looking man with great charm. She had had social position. Nothing to fight for, no worries. But she had left him. They hadn't been happy. What was it then?

She spoke of Acton impulsively to Agnes. Found herself, once launched upon the subject, unable to stop until she had told all there was to tell. Not much really. A well-bred, attractive man coming into the office of a friend and trying to begin a flirtation with that friend's paid secretary . . . that was all. It sounded, put into words, less like an amusing adventure than like something stereotyped and cheap.

She was sorry she had mentioned him.

Agnes regarded her with shrewd dark eyes.

"Don't start anything you can't finish," she warned her. "I'd advise you not to go out with him—not that it's any of my business."

"I haven't any intention of going out with him!"

"I suppose not. Anyway—don't. Not because I'm— what was it he called Ken?—'old-fashioned.' Most of the married women I know have other men friends, for the most part innocently enough. Good clean fun," explained Agnes, and laughed without malice. "But in your case—"

"It all comes back to what I said to him, doesn't it?" asked Lola a little bitterly. "Class."

"Don't be a fool. You know I didn't mean that. I didn't mean Ken, either, although, if I know Ken, he would be terribly annoyed. I mean for your own sake. It would be a temptation, you know."

"Agnes!" Lola's eyes were enormous—and hurt. "As if—caring for Ken—"

"Dumb bunny, I didn't mean a physical temptation. Not while you do care for Ken. I meant that all this man stands for is a temptation . . . comfort, leisure, luxury, the means to loaf and invite your soul. It—would make you discontented, that's all. Why do you suppose I stayed away from the men I used to know? From their wives too, while I was living with Jim? Jim wouldn't have cared if I had gone out with the old crowd, either with or without him. He isn't the caring kind. But I cared. I knew I'd come home grouchy and bothered and wishing and . . . out of my depth. So I stayed away, that's all."

"Don't worry about me," Lola told her. "Golly! We've talked so much and eaten so little, I'll be late for work."

She did not see Acton but she heard from him. He called the office every other day or so. He would ask for Jameson. If Jameson were out he would ask pleasantly, "May I speak with his secretary, please?" and Lola would be summoned to the wire. He had not had to give his name to Gladys. And it wasn't necessary to give it to Lola.

"Free for lunch today?" he would ask. And she would answer, "No," in as stern a tone as possible. "My loss," his voice would come to her over the wire, "but Peter

Acton never gives up. You'd be astonished! Bulldog Drummond isn't in it. I'll try again. You know the old legend about the drop of water wearing away the stone? Sure you won't change your mind? It's so inevitable. Eventually, why not now? Sorry. Good-by."

She would have to laugh. The other girls would look at her curiously. Well, it was none of their business. She planned to tell Ken: What do you think? That man Peter Acton—you know, Jameson's friend—has asked me to lunch. Several times. Isn't that absurd? I think he wants to know how the other half lives or if heaven really does protect the woiking goil.

But somehow she never said it; started to, half a dozen times; stopped. She couldn't say it unless it was spontaneous; a good joke, shared. And somehow it wasn't. Why? Silly of her. She loved Ken and he loved her and they ought to be able to laugh it off.

She wouldn't go out with Acton. He was wasting his time.

She went, of course, just as spring was slipping into summer, in a riot of pale green leaves and clear blue skies.

She had quarreled with Ken. One night, as they were leaving a motion-picture theater in their neighborhood, a girl touched him on the arm. A little blond girl, all soft curves and pretty, commonplace features, too heavily made up and a little cheaply overdressed.

"Why, Ken," said the girl, "we haven't seen you for years! Where've you been keeping yourself?"

Ken was startled. Lola saw that. He even flushed a little. He answered with some laughing banality and introduced Lola. "This is Miss Smith—my wife," he said.

"Oh," said the girl, and giggled, "I forgot you had a wife." She looked at Lola from head to foot. She said, "Some girls have all the luck!"

She laughed and spoke to Ken over her shoulder, "Give my love to Garry," she told him.

She went back to her escort, a tall, overthin young man who was glowering near by, and Ken and Lola walked on. For the life of her she couldn't keep the edge out of her voice.

"Well, who's the girl friend?"

"Who?" asked Ken with overelaborate innocence. "Oh, *her!* That's Shirley Smith."

"And *that* sounds fishy!" Lola commented, still trying to speak lightly and not succeeding. "I could have fallen for Jones. But Smith! *And* Shirley!"

"Well, it's her name," Ken replied reasonably. "There are a lot of Smiths. Not all of them are aliases, you know." He grinned. "Want a soda?" he asked.

She said she did. They went into a candy and sandwich shop, narrow, brilliantly lighted, a radio turned on full blast. They sat down, facing each other, at a marbleized table in a little stall-like section. A girl swung herself hippily up to them, and looked inquiring.

"Chocolate sodas, one with vanilla cream, the other with chocolate," said Ken.

"One black, one black and white," the girl called to the white-coated gum-chewing boy at the counter.

Lola said, regarding the menu:

"Where did you meet her?"

"Who—oh, Shirley?" asked Ken. "Oh, one night with Garrison. She's a friend of Amy's. I told you I'd met Amy?"

"Yes, but I was under the impression that these parties with Garrison were stag," Lola told him.

"Well, they are generally. But now and then. . . . For Lord's sake, Lola," he said with exasperation, "I can't go out with a gang and say: 'Hey, be sure that you don't have any dames along; I'm a married man and my wife wouldn't like it.' What a sap I'd be! Comic-strip stuff. You know perfectly well that I don't know another girl's alive, don't you?"

"Of course. But you might have told me."

"Why should I? It wasn't important enough. We've been out now and then for something to eat—we can't hire a private dining-room, you know, not being in the millionaire class. People come in. Girls sometimes. And sometimes someone at our table knows one or two of them. And they sit with us. And we dance, maybe. That's all," said Ken.

"I see."

She smiled at him, a little ashamed.

"Hurrah for our side," said Ken, much relieved, as the sodas appeared. "Here, sister." He gave the girl the money and added a tip.

"Ken, that wasn't necessary. You don't have to tip girls in places like this."

"What's ten cents?" he wanted to know. "Gosh, Lola, you're getting to be a tight-wad!"

"Oh, don't let's fight!"

She felt tired. She felt the tears rush to her lids. Always silly tears. Why? So that Ken could soothe and kiss her and they could be reconciled? She didn't want that. It wasn't enough. Wasn't fair of her, somehow, wasn't fair *to* her. She winked the tears back resolutely—said, her small face flushing and her eyes appealingly on his own:

"I was cross about the Smith girl. Perhaps I'm jealous."

That delighted him. He didn't mind. No man does mind—at first.

"Glad to know it," he said comfortably. "Hate to have

you get so sure of me that you don't know I exist. But there's nothing to worry about. Gee, Lola, half the time we go out on parties we run into girls someone knows. No one thinks anything about it. And they rarely even ask you if you are married. They don't care. You don't mean anything to them but a sandwich and a drink or a ride home maybe. That's all."

"I know it is," she said.

They walked home, arm in arm, through the warm spring night.

Silly of her to mind, of course. This was modern marriage. Ken hadn't done anything, after all. First names didn't mean anything nowadays. It didn't mean anything either that the Smith girl had looked at him as if he were as strong as Dempsey, as handsome as Gilbert, and as wise as Solomon. It was the type. The type looked at every man like that. The type went to work reluctantly because it had to. It powdered its nose and rouged its lips and scamped through its jobs somehow and prayed to Heaven that a man would come along soon and support it. The type didn't work after marriage. It stayed home and sometimes had babies and drove its husband, by its demands and extravagance and clinging, kitten ways, into suicide, despair, defeat, divorce or—quite often —into making a great deal of money in order to satisfy the blond and whining Moloch in the home. That was all.

"How big you are! . . . How strong you are! . . . How wise you are—how stupid I am! Poor little me!" said the type, and cuddled.

But when the type found out a man was married it turned its attention elsewhere. Unless the man was very rich, in which case marriage didn't count. Marriages can be unmade.

Lola understood. She had often heard Agnes discoursing on the type. And Lola read novels. She got them from the loan library or bought them in the reprint editions. She read serials in the magazines and she read news in the papers. She knew the type. It didn't matter. She had been crazy to be upset.

So she bought a new spring suit and went out to lunch with Peter Acton.

He had phoned, of course. And this time she said, laughing:

"I give in. If only to prove to you how silly it all is. I have just an hour. May we go somewhere near by?"

"I belong," he told her, "to a down-town club. What time did you say? Good. I'll wait at the elevators."

He seemed astonished; so much so that she was annoyed. Meeting him—

"This," said Acton, "is a great pleasure. Nothing's worth anything unless you have to work for it!"

He took her to his club. She thought, with a feeling of pride: Well, he isn't ashamed to be seen with—Jameson's secretary.

Men nodded to him. He nodded back. He installed Lola in a window on the thirty-third story of a business building and ordered a perfect luncheon. Mostly cold things, the day being very warm. "Sorry I can't offer you a drink," he apologized, "but we don't do it here. Afraid someone will get hold of some good gin, I suppose, and throw themselves out of the window."

He offered her a cigarette though. She smoked very little. It cost too much. Ken smoked two cartons a week. Lola had said: "I think I won't. I don't like it enough and if it gets to be a habit, I'll go broke." But she took one now from the slim gold case, the name of another famous club stamped upon it.

"What made you decide to come out with me?" he asked her.

"Nothing. Perhaps because I grew bored with saying no," she answered, and added seriously, "But I really don't think Mr. Jameson would like it."

"What he doesn't know won't hurt him," retorted Acton, "and, if you are worrying, he never comes here."

He regarded her inquiringly.

"Oh, I wasn't," she said, and flushed. She had been.

"Somehow," said Acton, "I don't think you're telling me the truth. Did you have a row with your young man? Did you catch him going out with a blonde?"

Lola almost choked on some tomato aspic which is not as a rule a dangerous article of diet. She started to say: How did you know? And wondered why, for she hadn't even acknowledged it to herself. She said smoothly:

"Well, of course not. He'd go out with brunettes, if he went at all, wouldn't he?"

She was a little afraid of Acton. He knew, she decided, too much. She regarded him with something like awe, as if he had suddenly produced a rabbit from the pocket of his blue serge suit.

Sublimated blue serge.

"Would he? He'd have very poor taste, I think," said Acton.

The hour went by very quickly. Acton had been abroad after the first time they had met. Was staying home, for once, for the summer. He had a place in the Hamptons. He said carelessly:

"I'll be in town a lot. We'll lunch again, won't we? And perhaps do a roof garden, some night."

She shook her head firmly.

"No, I couldn't, really."

"I thought not. Look here, are you going to tell your husband?"

"Well, naturally!"

Until she had said it, she hadn't known. Hadn't thought. Purposely.

Acton said heartily:

"Good. It's all so perfectly harmless. You only make it—shall we say dangerous?—by not telling."

She was a little late to work. Jameson, for a wonder, was late too. And her mind wasn't much on her work, either. It was on—not Acton; but Ken. She would tell him. "Well, naturally!" But how?

She told him at dinner. She had a very specially good dinner for him. She hadn't realized how—was it clever? she was—until she found herself marketing for all the things he liked best.

"This," commented Ken, contentedly over coffee, "is a feast. What are we celebrating?"

"I had a grand lunch today," she told him suddenly, "and wanted to make it up to you. I knew you hadn't."

"Nice girl. See Agnes again?"

"No, I went to lunch with Mr. Acton."

"Acton? Who's he?" asked Ken, puzzled.

She was impatient. Only women know why.

"Oh, Ken, don't be stupid! You *do* know. He's a director of the company—a great friend of Mr. Jameson's." She found herself lying—"He dropped in at lunch time. And asked me to go out."

Why had she lied? She hadn't meant to. Ken's eyes? That was why. Ken's eyes.

"Isn't this something new for you?" he wanted to know. "Where did you go?"

She told him.

"It was so hot," she explained, a little more pleadingly

than she realized. "Oh, Ken, don't look so cross! It was"—she found herself repeating Acton—"perfectly innocent, perfectly harmless. Why shouldn't I go out with another man to lunch, if I like? Most all the girls do. And you go out with other women."

"No, I don't. I don't *ask* 'em out. I don't plan it. I run into them—with a crowd. That's different," said Ken. "I don't like this, Lola."

She rose and began to clear the table.

"I'm sorry." She added, "I needn't have told you, you know."

"If you hadn't it wouldn't have been so harmless as you make out, by a long shot. Look here, honey . . ."

He rose, put his arm about her waist.

"I do want you to have a good time. But I don't like the sound of this Acton. He—he isn't our speed, Lola. He has money, he has—everything. He doesn't take other men's secretaries out to lunch out of charity. And you're too damned good-looking."

She cried angrily:

"Oh, why do people always have to put it on that— that sex basis? You make me sick, Ken!"

"Because it always is on that basis," he retorted. "I'm a man, Lola. I know."

"Then you can't tell me," she flung back, "if you feel that way, that Shirley and her crowd aren't on the same basis. Even if it is a gang. You don't dance with her in a gang, do you? like the Lancers or something?"

"Don't be dumb," said Ken shortly. "Of course we don't. It's different, I tell you!" And now he said the last thing he had expected to say: "I forbid it! You're not to do it again, do you hear me?"

She hadn't intended to do it again. I really hadn't, she

told herself. She said now angrily, wrenching herself away:

"I'll do it as often as I wish! And you'll like it. If I carry half the expenses of this house I'm entitled to as much consideration and freedom as you are, Kenneth Hayes. I'm my own boss!" said Lola.

"Thanks a lot," Ken told her, white. "You needn't rub it in. I know it without your telling me," he said.

She had hurt him. Terribly. She didn't care. She walked into the kitchen with her tray. She did care. She came out again, swiftly—ran to him. He was still standing as she had left him, hands sunk in his pockets, staring at the floor.

"Ken, I'm sorry. I didn't mean it," she began.

"Yes, you did," he contradicted, without moving.

"Perhaps. But not in that way. I—I won't go out again, like that," she promised impulsively. Anything, just so they wouldn't quarrel. Anything just so he wouldn't look like that.

He said: "You needn't bother. I know how you feel. If you feel that you are entitled to do as you please, you may just as well do it. Sacrificing yourself won't help. It doesn't change the way you feel, does it?"

She said despairingly, sitting down on the couch to look up at him:

"Ken, can't you understand? Yes, I do feel that way." Now she knew that she did. Nothing could change that. "I do feel that as long as we went into a partnership sort of marriage I can have the same privileges that you have. But I am willing not to take them if it bothers you. You," she went on, "wouldn't be willing to give up your pleasures for me though."

He said sullenly: "Why should I? A man has to have

some freedom. He doesn't jail himself when he marries, does he? Besides, they're harmless enough."

"I don't think so. You drink too much. You gamble. You lose more than we can afford—"

"Not always. I win," Ken boyishly defended himself, "a lot of the times."

"If you can't afford to lose you can't afford to win," she told him. "I have never liked Bert Garrison and his crowd. Do you think it was pleasant for me to have you reel home after a party with that gang? It wasn't, and you know it. I don't call that sort of business harmless. Yet, when I go out to luncheon in a perfectly innocent way with a perfectly decent man, you make a scene!"

"I don't. Who is this Acton anyway? He's out of our class. I told you that. A man like that doesn't take out somebody's secretary for innocent reasons," said Kenneth stubbornly.

They were back where they started.

Before they went to bed they had been reconciled after a fashion. That is to say, both had said they were sorry. They had kissed. They had drawn what comfort they could from each other's arms and lips; from assurances and reassurances of each other's love. But the issue remained unfaced, the problem unsolved.

Lola had never thought much before about her rights as wage-earner. Until she had put her rights into words she hadn't considered them. Now, lying sleepless in the bed beside Ken's, she did think. She was, she argued, perfectly justified. If Ken could go out when and where he pleased, so could she. If Ken were the sole wage-earner, he might have a right to dictate. But he wasn't. She did her share and more. Hence, she was as free as he was. He was blind not to see it. He was unreasonable. Of course, she probably wouldn't go out with Acton—or any other man—again. But she would reserve her right to do so without question. Why couldn't Ken trust her? She trusted him. She really did—despite the drinking and the things drinking did to a man—despite all the blond Shirleys in the world.

Why did men think that because an attractive man asked a girl out to lunch that he immediately planned a trip to Atlantic City? If the girl was unmarried no one would think that. But if she was married, an entirely different construction has to be put on it.

Ken was of Today. Ken was modern. Ken had married a girl who had continued to work for her living. If it had been her father who objected she could have understood, could have dismissed his attitude as outmoded. But it wasn't her father. It was Ken.

She fell asleep wondering. Woke to spring sunlight and the smell of coffee. Ken had awakened earlier and had started breakfast. Now and then he did. She liked those occasional times. Liked to lie there and hear him moving about, ridiculously tiptoeing so that he would not disturb her. She lay with her arms behind her head, smiling drowsily, loving Kenneth very much. She heard him come to the door.

"Hey, lazy, aren't you ever going to get up?" he inquired.

It was as if their quarrel had never been.

She thought: He's ashamed. He's sorry. It's all right between us.

But Ken was neither ashamed nor sorry. He was hurt. Not emotionally alone but basically. He'd said to himself before he slept, *I won't have it*. But he had known in his heart that he'd have to have it. Take it or leave it.

So he went out with Garrison a night or two later and

along about one in the morning he confided in that shrewd, worldly-wise young man.

"Women are the limit," said Ken solemnly.

"Sure, why not? What's on your mind?"

"Nothing." He wouldn't discuss Lola with anyone, directly, he thought. But he asked, "Look here, do you think it's all right for a married woman to go out with other men?"

"No. And the only guy that says it is, is a pansy," announced Garrison.

"That's what I say, Garry." Ken leaned across the table in the little speakeasy. "Take my word for it, don't let Amy go on working after you marry her. It's . . . it ruins a woman. A man hasn't any come-back."

"Oh, I don't know. If she wants to marry me," said Garrison, "she'll *have* to go on working. I've all I can do to support myself decently, let alone a frau. And I've already made plans. I'm going to get somewhere. But if she wants to be in at the finish she'll have to help ride the nag. See? Some guy—Kipling, I guess—said that a fellow travels faster if he travels alone. He was darned tootin'. But Amy draws down a good salary. Between us, we'll get to the goal-posts. But a man's a fool who just marries one of these sit-down-and-do-help-me-off-with-my-overshoes dames."

"Perhaps you're right," Ken said. "Still—"

A little mellow he was, he thought, making a mountain out of a mole-hill. Lola, sweet kid, was probably worried to death. Well, she knew where he stood. She wouldn't do it again. He'd put his foot down. Poor Garry, he was getting into a hell of a mess and didn't know it. Didn't know how to handle women, either. Ken had heard Garrison's Amy speak to him acidly. She was rather a hatchet-faced girl. The blond battleax, someone had called her. Ken chuckled. Garry was in for more than he knew. He felt a glow of kindly sympathy and sly understanding. Lola wasn't like that. He was a lucky guy, he was. Lola was a darling. There wasn't a girl like her.

A wave of perfume invaded their table.

"Oh, hello, Shirley," said Garrison, not rising.

Ken got to his feet.

"Hello, Big Boy," said Shirley to Ken, "and where have you been for the best part of my life?"

She sat down and beckoned to the people with whom she had come. They came over to the table, three or four of them. "Let's go where we can dance," Shirley suggested to Ken. "This is a lousy dump."

"Anything you say, sister," he agreed, smiling at her.

She said, looking into the mirror of her compact:

"I love to dance with you, Ken. You take me right off my feet. Gee," she said, "you're a swell dancer."

Not as pretty as Lola. A little cheap. Too slangy. Too self-assured. Ken knew that. But a girl like Shirley made a man feel—like a man. Not like half of a budget-book and the thin side of a manila envelope.

"You shake a mean ankle yourself," he told her.

Lola wouldn't like it, of course. But Lola couldn't have her own way, always. Not even if she paid for it.

Chapter IX

During that summer Lola and Kenneth's vacation did not coincide. Because of a shortage in her section she was unable to arrange her vacation as she would have wished and was forced to take it early. Kenneth, if he took any vacation at all, was to take it in September. The result was that Lola stayed home during those two hot weeks in July except for a week-end at Agnes's in Bellport, where Ken joined her for Saturday and Sunday and returned home alone Sunday night, while she waited over and came in on an early train with Agnes on Monday.

She had had rather a good time. She had gone down Friday afternoon with Agnes and they had the house to themselves, more or less, as the other girls were away on visits and Mr. Harvey was in town. Only Agnes's mother remained, a vague, plump, perpetually worried woman, with an habitual air of mild astonishment and fluttering anxiety. Lola had met her before once or twice, and she was uniformly amiable to her.

They swam, they played a couple of rounds of golf on Saturday, and had time to talk before Kenneth's train came in. Sitting on the sand, half buried in its white-gold warmth Lola said thoughtfully:

"I hope Kenneth will behave himself while he's here."

"How do you mean?" Agnes asked her.

"Oh—he's been drinking a lot," Lola said distastefully, "and going around with a bad crowd—Garrison . . . You remember him?"

"Well, yes. As to drinking, he won't get it here.

Father is scared silly of bad liquor. So we haven't any.
The supposedly good stuff he gets through the steward
of one of his clubs—'right off the boat'—Staten Island
ferry-boat, I suppose—he saves for state occasions. So
don't worry. But that doesn't sound like Ken."

"He's changed," Lola told her.

"I don't believe it. Defense mechanism, that's all,"
Agnes said.

"What on earth is that?" Lola demanded, sitting up
and clasping her bare arms about her knees. "Agnes,
I'll burn to a crisp—hand me that towel, will you?"

Agnes tossed her the towel.

"Protective coloration, if you like it any better. Ken
has never been happy about your working. He's the he-
man sort of person who wants to be the Big Boss, Head of
the House, and all that. Well, he can't be, with you on
the job, and a better job than his own, and with more
future to it. He can't dictate to you—"

"Well, he'd better not!" Lola flared up. "Not if he
were earning a hundred thousand a year!"

Agnes laughed.

"If he were he wouldn't dictate to you," she explained.
"Can't you see? He'd wouldn't feel he'd have to. He'd
know his own position and importance. This way he isn't
sure. He wants to tell you what to do and how to do it,
simply because he *isn't* sure. Can't you see that? And
he can't do it, because you have as much right as he has
to say what you'll do and where you'll go. Understand?
So he drinks—a little, to escape and to give him a false
sense of security. And he runs around with people who
tell him he's a big shot and all the rest of it."

Lola shook her bright head.

"It's all too deep for me," she said. "I only know

that— Oh, well, what's the use? The first hundred years are the hardest!"

"You are changing too," Agnes told her. "Was Ken angry at you for lunching with Peter Acton?"

"He was."

"I see. I thought he would be."

"Well, I didn't. I thought he'd have more sense. There are girls on these parties Garrison takes him to Blondes for choice," said Lola.

Agnes raised her pretty, dark brows.

"That's where the shoe rubs, is it?"

"No, it isn't. . . . As if I care what he does! Only he needn't lie about it."

"You *do* care. And blondes, on parties of Garrison's type, are apt to give Ken a lot of his self-respect back. Don't shake your head! I know what you are thinking. But if they tell him what a marvelous person he is— You don't tell him that, do you?"

"Oh, but I thought he was. And he isn't," said Lola. "So why should I tell him—any more?"

"Lola, you're headed for trouble! . . . Here comes mother," said Agnes, and rose to her feet as Mrs. Harvey made her slow, fluttering way to them, a parasol over her gray head and sand in her little, useless slippers.

Ken arrived in the afternoon. That night Agnes had several young people in for dinner, and they went over to one of the Hamptons to dance.

"Gee," said Ken, his wife in his arms, "this is the life! Great music, isn't it? And you look lovely, Lola."

She wore blue, which was his color. A faint, hazy, powder-blue with a little fitted bodice of chiffon and wide, full skirts of tulle. She had spent more on the frock than she could afford. But, after all, she wasn't going away, and she had her vacation money and why shouldn't she have a pretty dress now and then? Other days, she had been able, even on the smaller salary, to dress well.

She smiled up at him. He was frowning down on her, out of sheer intentness, his gray eyes very serious. Flannels and a dark coat became him. New flannels. "You'd better," she'd said, waving a manila envelope at him, "buy some flannels for Agnes's over the week-end."

"I'll look like a cake-eater," he had told her. But he didn't.

"Gosh, I'd like to have a place down here for the summer," said Ken, and added anxiously, "and we will have some day, won't we?"

Once she would have said, *Of course we will.* But to-night, she didn't. She thought: Another dream. Ken's dreams. They don't come true, do they? But she was spared the necessity of answering. Someone touched Ken's arm, he stopped dancing, automatically, thinking it was one of the members of their party, and found himself looking at a strange man who was beaming delightedly at Lola.

"Mrs. Hayes! I thought so, I couldn't be mistaken. May I cut in?"

It was Peter Acton.

Lola presented the men. "My husband," said Lola, "Mr. Acton." They shook hands. They looked at each other, a long measuring glance. Kenneth thought, sulkily, unprintably: Good-looking ——! And Acton thought swiftly: Here's a nice kid. Not half good enough for her. Talk about the white woman's burden!

Deftly he extracted Lola from Kenneth's hold. Deftly eased her into his own arms. He danced beautifully. He said:

"What luck! I couldn't believe my eyes!"

"If a cat may look at a king," said Lola, "even working girls may come to the Hamptons!"

"Why do you always pick me up like that? Cactus plants are fashionable but not as pretty as you are. Why be on the defensive? I didn't mean anything like that— I meant—I had been thinking about you. I had stopped in after a dinner party to see what was going on at the club. I was bored. And I had telephoned Jameson on an excellent excuse last week, only to discover rather cleverly that you were on your vacation. And so I stood there tonight in the doorway, and wished myself—wherever you were. And for a wonder, my wish came true. For I saw you . . ."

She said, laughing, "I had forgotten you came down here, summers."

"To be sure. Why should you remember? Are you staying long?"

"Only until Monday morning. I am visiting Agnes Read. Her mother, Mrs. Harvey, has a house in Bellport."

"I don't know them. I'll make it my business to," he said carelessly. "Perhaps you will present me."

"I'd be glad to."

She did so, after they had stopped dancing. Agnes said, casually, "I met Mr. Acton at Southampton about four years ago, but he doesn't remember."

"On the contrary," said Acton, "I remember perfectly. Naturally."

Lola thought, What an accomplished liar! He was looking exceptionally well, very tanned, his gray hair and vivid blue eyes startling by contrast. She walked out on the veranda with him at his insistence.

"Mr. Hayes is on his vacation also?"

"No, not until September."

"Oh, and you will be alone at home? and will need consolation? I expect," said Acton, "to be in town a great deal in September."

"Kenneth," said Lola, "will probably stay at home."

But she knew he would not. He was already talking of going somewhere with Jake. He'd said:

"I'd go crazy, lobbing around with nothing to do all day and you at work."

She'd reminded him that she would be home early; they could have late afternoons and their evenings together; and the week-ends. But he hadn't seemed interested.

"I'd probably go to the movies until I had the jitters," he told her. "No, if Jake can get off we'll go fishing somewhere."

"I could have gone away," said Lola, "on my vacation, and didn't."

"That's different," said Ken.

But now she told Acton:

"Kenneth won't be going away, for vacation."

"No? That's a pity," Acton said gravely. "Every man needs a change."

One of Agnes's friends came up to claim his dance. Acton released Lola reluctantly, and later his own party must have spirited him away, for he disappeared from the dance floor. Lola found herself looking for him; and found herself wavering between disappointment and relief when she saw that he had gone.

Presently Ken danced with her again.

"Where's the social boy friend?" he wanted to know.

"Gone, I guess," she answered, determined not to be annoyed by his tone.

"Acts as though you were his long lost childhood love or something," Ken commented.

"Don't be silly," said Lola, without conviction.

His arm tightened around her.

"Am I being silly? I hope so," said Ken. "You see, Lola, you're just about the prettiest thing that ever walked this earth and I'm jealous of every man who looks at you."

Her heart lifted. She could understand this. She couldn't understand the things Agnes had said. Lola was a practical small person. She was not analytical.

She said, lifting her eyes to his own:

"You needn't be, Ken." She laughed a little. "You're all there is—there isn't any more," she told him.

She was silent after that. They danced, Ken stooping his tall head to the bright softness and fragrance of her hair. He thought, remorsefully, She is a darling. . . . I'm a mess, he told himself. Yet he hadn't done anything wrong, really; just taken a drink or two too much; and listened to a lot of stupid wisecracking; and let a girl or two tell him, against his better judgment, how misunderstood he was.

If it could always be like this, Lola thought, conscious of their nearness, of his arms about her, of their heartbeats timed to music. But the music stopped, and they stood there looking at one another, a little self-conscious, a little dazzled, somehow, by that swift silent moment of unity.

On the following evening Kenneth returned to town. His return was not made any happier for him by the knowledge he took with him of Peter Acton, stopping his big, imported roadster in front of the Harvey cottage and brazenly announcing that he had come calling. He had been almost too well received by Mrs. Harvey, who after all had several daughters on her hands, including Agnes.

Ken, in the crowded train, wished he had taken Lola up on her offer.

"If you'd rather, I'll go back tonight with you," she'd said.

"No, stay here. I wish you could stay longer, it would do you lots of good," Kenneth had answered, instantly and sincerely.

So she had stayed, with Acton. Acton had offered to drive him to the station. Agnes had sat in front with Acton, Lola and Ken in back.

"Lost very little time, didn't he?" Kenneth had commented.

"Oh, Ken, don't be silly. He lives near here," she had whispered.

"Not so damned near——"

"Well, near enough. And he used to know Agnes."

"Not well enough to remember her!" Ken replied.

"Darling, don't be dumb. I couldn't help his coming, could I? Do be quiet."

She had slipped her hand into his own. Now he was on the dusty hot train headed for the dusty hot city, and Agnes and she were driving back to the cottage with Acton. Probably, thought Kenneth gloomily, he'd make some excuse to get Lola to himself, soon enough. *Not that I blame him, damn him!*

Acton didn't, however. He was perfectly correct. He did not stay long, sat on the porch with Lola, Agnes, and her mother and talked about nothing with consummate charm and ease. And was sorry, he said, that they were returning to town so soon. Couldn't they wait and let him drive them back, later in the morning? But no, Agnes told him, to her mother's horror. "You forget I am a working girl!"

Couldn't, he wanted to know, Mrs. Hayes wait over then? He'd come for her at ten.

But Lola was firm. She must get the early train, she said.

Agnes shot her a mirthful look in the darkness, and Mrs. Harvey rocked and plotted how to allure this brightly gilded fish to her maternal net. Nancy and Barbara would be coming home at the end of the week.

Going into town the next morning—"He's pretty far gone," Agnes commented.

"Who is?"

"Oh, Lola, please! Have it your own way, and be innocent and wide-eyed. Even Millie couldn't improve upon your current facial expression!" Agnes told her with affectionate exasperation. "All I want to know is how you are going to handle it?"

"There isn't anything to handle!" Lola denied, dropping pretense.

"Perhaps not now. But if you want it, there will be."

"I'm not interested in Peter Acton," Lola told her. "No, that's not true. I *am* interested in him. That is, I like him. I think he's amusing. If I weren't married, I might even lose a little sleep over him. But I am married and I'm not getting hot and bothered about anyone but Ken."

"Wise girl. But watch your step. He's a very attractive man," Agnes reminded her, "and he has a great deal of money. I wish he'd turn his attentions to me. I wouldn't be so casual."

"Why, Agnes!"

"Well, why not?"

"But—Jim?" asked Lola. "I don't understand. . . . I mean, I know you no longer care for Jim but . . . so *soon?* Agnes, you haven't fallen for Peter Acton, have you?"

"Love?" Agnes laughed. "No, little simpleton. But I shan't be looking for love—next time," she said bitterly, "if there *is* a next time. And, believe me, there won't be unless it is awfully worth while. I can get along with a lot less love and a lot more other things, I think," she added.

Returning home, Lola went straight to the apartment and found it, as she had expected, in a condition of wild disorder. She straightened things up, sighing, for the heat was heavy and enervating, and planned a cold dinner. She fixed her salad and her ice-box dessert, after marketing, and after a solitary luncheon of milk and crackers went around to her mother's. She found the Davis house upside down with excitement and Millie at home, her last picture having just been finished.

"What's the dope?" Lola wanted to know, greeting her mother and sister, finding them in Millie's bedroom, where things were strikingly chaotic.

"I'm going to Hollywood!" Millie told her.

"You're not!" Lola sat down limply on a bed and stared.

"Yes. I've been offered a chance—and a good one," said Millie, her own excitement well under control, "a lead with ——" she named a well-known male star. "It's my big chance," she said.

Mrs. Davis wept.

"I want to go with her," she said, between sobs, "but she won't hear of it."

"You'd only be unhappy there, mother," Millie told her, "without father; and he couldn't get along without you. Nor Howard. I'll be all right," she said. "You need never worry about me."

She flew at her mother and kissed her soundly. "And when I'm in the thousand-a-week class—" she exulted—"and it won't be long now!—you can sell this shack and you'll all come out."

"That," said Lola practically, "sounds great but it isn't. I've heard too much about transplanted families. Mother and father will do very nicely here, where they've always lived and where they're contented. I can't see 'em in Hollywood somehow." Lola laughed frankly. "And as for you," she said, and threw a bedroom slipper at Millie, "you certainly get the breaks."

"I intend to. And I work for them," Millie told her.

Lola spent the rest of the afternoon helping to plan Millie's packing, listening to plans, story scenarios, contracts, and ambitions. At five she went back home, having been of some comfort to her mother. Millie would be leaving in a few days. They'll miss her terribly, Lola thought. There's one good thing about this vacation, I can see more of the family.

She told Ken, when he came home.

"Gosh," said Ken, "that's an earful. I can't understand though," he said, shedding his coat and taking off a wilted collar, "how she got where she did so quick. Oh, she was good in the revue!" he added. "I'll admit that. But there must be thousands. . . . Lola, do you think . . ."

"No, I don't!" said Lola angrily. "Millie's a straight kid. Get that in your head for keeps. Oh, *men*—you make me sick! just because a girl gets somewhere you seem to think that there has to be something rotten in Denmark."

"I don't. I didn't say anything. Hey, pipe down! I only wondered, that's all."

"I don't like your way of wondering. Why, it wasn't

very long ago that an extra girl was picked to play opposite Maurice Chevalier! There's nothing so very remarkable about Millie's sudden success. She has had extra parts and the part in the revue, and a better part in 'Soul Sinners.' Why shouldn't she be ready for the breaks now? You men hate to hear of any woman succeeding at anything, don't you—unless you can say that she climbed there on a man's shoulders? That's old stuff," said Lola scornfully. "If Millie rides in a Rolls-Royce she'll pay for it herself . . . and not *with* herself, hear me?"

"I could hardly help hearing you," Ken replied reasonably, "as you are shouting at the top of your lungs! Forget Millie. I'm tickled to death. And, now, when do we eat?"

But he kept on wondering. And Garrison when he told him said, "Heigh-ho!" and raised an eyebrow and afterwards remarked: "You picked the wrong sister, didn't you, Ken?"

They saw Millie off for Hollywood. There were photographers at the station also. Lola whispered, clutching Ken: "Oh, get mother out of the way, do! and let's go on. We don't want to be in the pictures."

Ken said suddenly, "Hollywood sounds pretty good to me." He went to where Millie was standing on the platform steps, an eastern-office publicity man from her company hovering near. "Millie, when you get settled," said Ken, grinning, "find me a job, will you? I'd like to winter in California."

Going home, in the car Millie had engaged for "the family"—sort of a funeral-coach business Ken remarked —Ken said seriously to Lola, who, her mother's hand in her own, was trying, as she afterwards remarked, to be as comforting as if Millie really had died:

"Why don't we give it a try? I could get into something out there and living is cheaper. There's money to
be made in pictures if Millie wanted to look around for
us. And you'd like it there, and to be near her."

"What about my job?" Lola wanted to know tartly.

"Well—*what* about it? It isn't so vital, is it?" he
demanded.

How vital she couldn't remind him, at the moment;
nor ask him where they would get the money to go West.
Perhaps he meant Millie to advance it, she thought acidly.
Well, Millie wouldn't have her—or Ken—to support—
ever. What she might want to do for Howard or her
parents was another matter.

She was with her mother every day until the end of her
vacation. And then returned to work, glad to be back
at the routine again, somehow. It hadn't been much fun,
hanging around home. She began to appreciate how
Ken would feel about it.

In September Ken went on his vacation with Jake,
back to the camp where he and Lola had been the previous
summer, for fishing. And returned brown and healthy,
steady of hand and clear of eye. In July, Garrison had
married and had set up housekeeping not far from Lola
and Ken. Ken said, early in October:

"Oughtn't we to ask Garry and Amy over?"

So Lola did so, rather against her wishes. Nothing
would induce her to change her mind about Garrison and
she was not in the least drawn to Amy, who chattered
ceaselessly of money made on the stock market, of the
"right" sort of investments. ". . . when the stocks are at
rock bottom . . ." and the "right" sort of speculations.
Amy was a good business woman. She admitted it herself. After an evening of Amy, Lola felt as if she had
been under a steam-roller.

Connie's baby, a boy, was born in November. Lola went to see her in the hospital, where Louis had "spared no expense." Connie had a private room and bath, nurses, a specialist.

The baby weighed nine pounds. He was temporarily dark red, he made aimless gestures with his hands, he had a mop of black hair. He looked like no one or nothing to Lola, regarding him in his swaddled condition.

"It was pretty bad," Connie confided, "but it was worth it."

Louis came in while Lola was there. He came in all the time, Connie told her. Each time with a present. A diamond bar pin, first; then fruit; then baskets of caterer's food; today a bunch of roses, stiffly held in his hand. He was shining of countenance, his clothes ruthlessly brushed, his dark face anxious and proud. He tiptoed in, awkward and happy and a little touching.

Connie's eyes, on her husband's face, were not apologetic. They were content, even fond. Lola went away, conflicting emotions stirring her. What on earth did Connie see in this man? She hadn't cared for him when she married him. She was complacent about him now. Complacent about the baby. A little, somehow, superior. Didn't she know that people said Louis was a bootlegger, on the side? Or had been. Or, if she knew, didn't she care?

The baby had not been pretty. But Lola had held the warm, talcum-smelling bundle in her arms. Her arms felt curiously empty now. She went home to find a note from Ken.

"Have to go out," wrote Ken. "You weren't in when I got here. . . . Don't wait up."

It was Saturday afternoon. She went around to her mother's and returned about ten o'clock and went to bed, with a book. At midnight, she snapped out the light and lay awake a little longer. Finally she slept.

Waking, she thought: I wonder what time Ken got in? He must have come in very quietly so as not to disturb me, or else I was sleeping like the dead.

She sat up. The sunlight streamed in through the open window. The place next to her own was empty. It had not been slept in.

She sprang up and started to dress. As she dressed she grew increasingly angry. He had never stayed out all night before. He had a nerve! He had—oh, but something might have *happened* to him! She had visions of him robbed, blackjacked, lying senseless in some dark alleyway; visions of him in the hospital, nothing on him to identify him. Oh, but that's silly; he always carries an identification! She had further visions of him run over by a hit-and-vanish driver. She was frantic.

She called up the Garrison house.

Garrison answered.

No, he hadn't been with Ken the night before, had no idea where he was. Hadn't come home? "Well, don't get hysterical about it, Lola, it happens to all of us now and then."

She telephoned Jake. Jake knew nothing but, if she needed him, would be right around.

No, of course she didn't need him. She was being silly. Ken would come in at any moment now. Of course, he would, Jake agreed.

She was angry again, her terrors forgotten. What right had Ken to frighten her like this? She thought of the days, the two weeks he had been away on his vacation. She thought of Acton, phoning her twice and coming to the office; and of her steady refusal to go out with him again—on Ken's account, because Ken wouldn't like it, although she wouldn't give Acton the satisfaction of admitting that. Now she wished she had gone; now she told herself that the next time Acton asked her she *would* go.

A little after ten, Ken called her.

It was a simple enough affair. A party. A speakeasy and a raid. Ken, with several others, was in jail. Ken admitted there had been more to it than a raid. There'd been some girls there. And something of a fight. She was to get hold of Louis. . . . Louis Carmino. Connie's husband. He'd know what to do.

She hung up the receiver. She was sick all over. After a little she called Connie's house. Mr. Carmino was at the hospital, she was told.

Was anything wrong with Connie?

She got him finally at the hospital and explained. She repeated all that Ken had told her to say. Louis listened. "O.K.," said Louis, "I'll fix it."

"Is Connie all right?"

"Sure, she's fine."

Early that afternoon Ken came home. He was unshaven, his clothes were soiled, his linen crumpled, a slit torn in his coat. He was haggard and hungry.

"They don't give you Ritz meals in the hoosegow," he told her, trying to grin.

Lola set her lips. No use fighting. Just sit down later and talk about it quietly.

"I'll get you something to eat," she told him, "and there's lots of hot water for a bath."

"Gee, that's great! You're a peach, Lola." He looked at her wistfully, shyly. "Louis stepped on the gas," he told her. "I knew he was the guy to go to. He knows all the politicians in town. But he was too late to keep it out of the papers, damn it," said Ken.

Later, shaved and bathed and dressed, he came out to

the living-room, where the table had been set for him Lola was standing beside it. He took her in his arms, but she was rigid. After a moment, he let her go, and sat down.

"I don't blame you for being sore," he told her, "but it wasn't my fault."

"Perhaps not," said Lola.

He said a little sullenly:

"I went out with Garry—"

"No, you didn't. I called him up this morning. Why do you lie to me, Ken?" asked Lola, in despair. "I was so *worried*—"

She began to cry. Kenneth said pleadingly:

"Don't, Lola, please. I did go out with him. He left early, that's all. I went on with the crowd. We went to this place. A fight started at a table near us. One of the girls with us was sort of in it. We all mixed in. You know how it is. Then there was the raid. That might have been all right if it hadn't been for the damn-fool fight. . . . One of the other guys was hurt, some. I didn't have anything to do with that. But we were all held. Louis got me off."

Lola said evenly, getting herself in control:

"You might think of me occasionally. It wasn't very pleasant, you know, waking up and finding you hadn't been home all night. I was nearly crazy. I—I called up everyone. I was going to call the hospitals. I didn't," she said, "think of jail."

"Gee, I'm sorry," he told her, inadequately.

He pushed back his chair and came over to her. He lifted her out of her own chair and carried her over to the couch and sat down with her on his knees. He held her close. He said:

"Lola, I won't do it again. I promise."

"Oh, promises!" she said scornfully. But she stayed where she was. He might have been seriously hurt. He might have been killed. But she had him back; he belonged to her. She thought, her cheek against his own: After all, nothing matters but that.

"I never promised before," he reminded her. "I—I don't know why I go out on these fool parties. I wouldn't if you'd come," he said absurdly.

"Ken, I always go with you places. When you want me to."

"Yes, but lots of times *you* don't want to. And I get fed up, sitting around listening to the radio, going to the movies."

"Fed up—with me?" she asked him, on a half sob. "Oh, *Ken!*"

"You know I don't mean that. I'd never mean that. But lots of evenings, Lola, you are so tired—and on edge—and we fight . . . God knows why. And I get restless and want to go where there's lots of noise and lights and excitement. Well, I got it all right, last night," he said ruefully, "especially the noise and the excitement. Right up to the neck, I got it. Never again. I swear it!"

And it might have ended there, save for the papers. The papers were full of it the next morning. The fight had concerned a rather well-known Red Hook personage; the speakeasy itself was pretty notorious. There were editorials and things, and grave people made statements to the papers. And the prohibition question came in for a few thousand more futile "signed" remarks.

The utility company by which Kenneth was employed prided itself upon being "conservative." One of its executives had political ambitions and was a dry. So the result was that Kenneth was given a month's pay and his freedom.

Lola had that to face. She had also to bear with his remorse, which turned, in self-defense, to anger against the company, against corporations in general. And she had her family to reckon with.

"It was," said Mrs. Davis, "unforgivable of Ken." She added quickly that Lola must forgive him, however. She reminded Lola of her wedding vows. Mr. Davis was a little more lenient but hardly pleased at the escapade and its outcome. Howard was frankly curious. And Lola had the office to face as well.

"This Hayes . . . he isn't any relation of your husband's, is he?" Jameson wanted to know.

"It is my husband," she was forced to say, a little proudly. "It wasn't his fault, Mr. Jameson. He was . . . an . . . an . . . innocent bystander."

"I see," said Jameson. "I'm sorry." Gladys and Dorothy wanted all the "dirty details." "Golly, weren' you scared sick?" asked Gladys.

Agnes telephoned. And at the office there was a box of flowers and a note from Peter Acton. "I'm awfully sorry if anything has happened to hurt you," he wrote on his narrow card. "Can I do anything?"

She put the flowers in the waste-basket. She fished them out and put them on her desk. She tore the card to pieces.

"Never mind, kid," Ken said gayly. "I'll find a job and a better one. Jake's looking around for me. I'll get something. Don't worry."

But she did worry.

The days went by. Weeks. Kenneth hadn't found a job. She said anxiously:

"I can't swing this place alone, Ken; we'll have to move if you don't get something to do."

The instalments were all paid, that was one mercy. She could manage the rent. They would have to be careful about food. They ate a good deal, at her mother's. They managed. "I'll get something tomorrow," he promised.

"Don't take the first thing you find," Garrison warned him. "You'll only be stuck with something phony. Shop around. Lola can keep things going until you do find something."

So he "shopped around." Called on people. Answered advertisements. Refused commission-only berths. Couldn't afford to take that chance.

Insensibly, he was falling in with Garrison's advice. After all, they did have a roof over their heads and food on the table, a place to sleep, a place to eat. Insensibly, because of his position, his attitude was slowly changing. If he was out of a job, Lola could take care of them for a while. If the positions were reversed, wouldn't he take care of her? He was the type of man who needs responsibility. He hadn't had it since his marriage. He had had it, with his mother. But Lola paid her way. There isn't a man alive who is entirely noble. Nor one who cannot be influenced, however subtly, by circumstances.

He'd hated her working. But the only way he could have her was to permit her this indulgence—"temporarily." How much his self-respect had suffered, only he knew. He wasn't the type. He lost face, with himself. He couldn't stand up under it. He had to go down to defeat. Insensibly, too, the advice of his companions, the wisecracking, the cynicism had had its way. Why worry? Lola would run things till he found a good job.

She said, "You aren't in much of a hurry to find one, are you?"

"Do you want me to be an errand boy?" he asked her. "I've got to wait till something turns up. Business is bad."

"You should have thought of that before."

"How in hell could I? Oh, can't you stop nagging, Lola? You're enough to drive a man goofy."

"Ken, I don't mean to nag. But we can't go on this way. We can't! You *must* take something. If you'd let me ask Mr. Acton I'm sure he would——"

"The day you ask Acton," he shouted at her, "I'll be on my way. Somewhere else. I'll be through."

That much of his self-respect he had retained. You don't get jobs through your wife's rich admirers.

Lola didn't come home to dinner a few nights later. She telephoned Ken that she wouldn't be in. She arrived home shortly before eleven. Ken was waiting for her.

"Where were you," he asked, "if I'm not being impertinent?"

"I had dinner with Mr. Acton," she told him.

"That's nice," said Ken savagely.

"It saves money, too," said Lola, taking off her hat.

They went to bed and to sleep without speaking again. The next day Millie's letter came by air mail. Her mother had written her, she said. She enclosed a check for two hundred dollars. "It may help," wrote Millie, in her flamboyant scrawl, "and I can afford it. If you're so darned proud you can pay me back another time. But if you get up against it I wish you'd tell me, Lola. Direct."

Lola told Ken. She had to. He said genuinely:

"That was white of her. Now, we needn't worry. I'll find something before that windfall's gone, Lola."

Lola said, her lips a straight red line and her eyes dark with anger:

"You'd better! I'm not crazy about sponging on my sister. Nice headlines that would make. Almost as nice as the ones you drew. 'Motion-picture actress forced to support sister and jobless husband.' Well, she doesn't have to support me," said Lola evenly. "I can make out all right alone."

The following day Kenneth, through Mr. Davis, got a job behind the retail counter of the drug firm. At eighteen dollars a week.

Chapter X

Tʜɪs arrangement was, Ken said, temporary. Until he could find something better. He intimated that if Lola had "given him time" he could have found the elusive something better eventually without resorting to the eighteen-dollars-a-week expedient. At the end of the first week he gave Lola fifteen dollars of the eighteen, with some ostentation. He had to eat lunch, pay carfare, and buy cigarettes, he told her, a little too humbly. She pushed a five-dollar bill across the living-room table to him and tucked the ten away in one of the inevitable envelopes. "Three dollars won't carry you through the week," she informed him evenly.

Their eyes met, very hostile. His lowered first. He put an arm around her, said, more himself than she had seen him in a long time:

"I'm sorry. Getting to be the world's worst grouch, I guess. I'll get along on as little as I can until something decent turns up."

"You mustn't," she told him, "grab a malted at a counter for lunch and let it go at that. Do take the money, Ken, and eat sensibly. We'll manage all right."

He took the money, folding the five-dollar bill with the three ones, creasing them carefully before putting them in his pocket.

"What an oil-can I turned out to be!" he told her ruefully.

But he was more than rueful. He was galled. As the days went on and nothing "turned up," he acquired a swagger in his walk and speech, and the hard-boiled veneer, adapted from Garrison and his ilk, thickened slightly, or congealed. Deep within him was a sort of dogged resentment. Lola, and all her talk of freedom! Lola and her dinners with Acton! Lola, who could make more money than he could, who was dependent on him in no way! It didn't matter any more about that "million" he had been going to make. He couldn't get the breaks. Now and then he met men from the old company. "What are you doing now, Ken?" "Oh, carrying messages to Garcia—catnip tea and camomile flowers, iodin, senna," he would tell them gayly. "I'm nursemaid to a flock of drugs. And I'm learning to mix up a very fine side-car of castor oil and sarsaparilla!"

They laughed, and then they laughed at him, he supposed, after they'd left him. A guy who could just about keep himself in collars, cigarettes, razor-blades, and lunch money! A guy whose wife went to work and brought home the financial bacon and kept a roof over their heads and food on the table; whose wife was "free" to go out to ritzy places with another man, one who had most of the money in the world!

Christmas with the Davises, with Millie's extravagant gifts to make it unusually merry, and Millie herself, between pictures, rushing home to stay two days only, and rushing, moreover, part of the way by airplane—to the despair of the motion-picture company officials, who hadn't thought to include "no air joy-rides" in her contract—was a wildly merry occasion. Too merry. Ken looked at the string of beads and bit of frivolous lingerie which, by difficult saving and by working nights with Jake, he had managed to buy for Lola, and shook his brown head. Millie with her perfumes and lace and little sable scarf for Lola more than put him in the shade. And Millie herself, delicately made up, superlatively well dressed, was a stranger to him. "You've got to do it," she explained, as the turkey smoked on the table and the family, even Howard, exclaimed about her. "The bigger bluff you put up, the harder it is for them to call it."

Lola saw her alone for just a few minutes. Millie was at home only a matter of hours, and her father and mother claimed her attention as well as the stream of old school friends—"Half of them didn't know I was alive last year," commented Millie scornfully—who came ostentatiously "calling" to wish her a Merry Christmas. But in the short time they were alone, Lola tried to thank her for her check. Their positions were curiously reversed now, or so it seemed. Hitherto, Lola had been the older sister, ready with help, advice, scoldings loans, and Millie the recipient. Now she seemed years older than Lola somehow, poised, a little hard, very sure of herself, but always sweet.

"Forget it. More where it came from, if you want it. I wish you'd let me know. All I ever hear about your troubles comes through sob stories from mother. What's the matter with Ken, anyway?"

"He can't get work. That is, he has gotten it, but it's a pretty poor substitute for what he had."

"Oh, men," said Millie, bored. "Once take a shot at supporting 'em and they'll lie down and permit themselves to be supported for the rest of their natural lives. Although it *isn't* natural, at that," she added thoughtfully.

"I can't believe it, especially of Ken. He used to be so eager—so ambitious."

"Two eager and ambitious people in a family may not work out," Millie told her suddenly.

"I didn't," said Lola, "think Ken was so—small."

She was seeing a good deal of Peter Acton. Lunch. Dinner. A theater now and then. Well, why not? Ken had ceased to "make scenes." He contented himself with a sneering remark now and then. At first she had gone out with Acton from sheer weariness, spiced with a little bravado. Now, she admitted that he both rested and stimulated her. He was amusing, he was interesting. And it was pleasant to go places and do things with a man so easily correct, so effortlessly good-form; with a man to whose side captains, waiters, maîtres-d'hôtel flew anxiously; with a man who knew how to order a dinner, who procured the best theater tickets in town, who did everything just enough and not too much.

She said to him, shortly after New Year's:

"You're spoiling me, Mr. Acton."

"Peter, please."

"Mr. Acton or Peter, the fact doesn't change. You are spoiling me."

"I intend to. Why else do you think I hang about New York with the wide world to rove over as I please? I had planned to go to Italy this winter and to England in the spring. And—here I am."

She looked at him, blue eyes, dark blue, the bright hair curled against the healthy pallor of her cheeks, the red mouth curved to half a smile. She never meant to flirt with him. One never does. But she did nevertheless. He had a way of making her ask questions. And answer them.

She said firmly: "Nevertheless hard-working secretaries have no business going to the Plaza and the Ritz and being driven home afterward. It's bad for character."

"I'd like to spoil you so much that you would get very bored with being a hard-working secretary and give it all up to sail around the world with an old man who works pretty hard, most of the time, at being idle."

"Old!" she mocked lightly.

"These gray hairs— Lola"—he leaned across the table in the big, softly lighted restaurant—"did I ever tell you why Marie—my wife—left me?"

"No," she said. She had wondered, for a long time.

"I wasn't romantic enough. I used to work hard, you know. The Bigger Business Man. She complained of that. So I stopped working. I had never needed to, God knows, but I liked it. I liked making money even when I didn't need it. The power. That's what gets you, the power. But I stopped. It didn't matter, however. It was too late. She'd got all she could get out of money and the social position I was able to offer her. She wanted to live in Europe. In England. I didn't. I like to travel, I like to stay away a year, two years, perhaps, at a time. But I like to come back. She wanted the European leisure as opposed to American. She wanted to be called Lady This, or Lady That. I refused to expatriate myself and give enough money to charity, so that eventually I might be on the honor list. I didn't want to give up my citizenship, my birthright. Why should I? So she found herself a title, a good one, aged in the wood. There was a man attached to it. Somewhat younger than herself. A decent enough boy, only a little weak. I could have broken him, physically, across my knee. I didn't. She divorced me. I made a settlement on her, and she has what she wants. How long she'll continue to want it, I can't say."

His tone was even, but his eyes, as blue as Lola's own, were bitter. She said, sorrowfully, because she liked him very much:

"I—it must have hurt you, Peter."

"It hurt—like hell. You see, I loved her. As a youngster I was crazy about her. Through college and all that. Then we married. And I was crazier about her than ever. I wanted to give her the world. It—settled down, of course. I had my absurd little business excitements and she her own interests. But I loved her. And there were no children. I would have liked a son. So we drifted apart, very slowly. But underneath I cared as much, perhaps, as ever. Then, it all happened. She said, 'I don't love you; you can't give me what I want. I'll take a divorce and Cecil, if you don't mind.' Or words to that effect. Well, I did mind. But what was there to do? I let her go. I suffered, a good deal. Remembering. And through pride. Masculine pride. That's something to contend with. I don't pretend there hasn't been anyone else since she left me. There have been. Several. Makeshifts. I'd rather not talk about them except to be honest and say they didn't matter basically. But they gave me something of escape, something of warmth, some fleeting, transitional emotional release. But no one has mattered to me until you came, Lola."

She had had a hard time keeping him in hand for some time now. Ever since the beginning things had led inexorably to this. She wasn't a child. She had seen this coming since—she thought back—since the first day he came into Jameson's office. Nevertheless she heard him out with a sense of sick shock, of failure. Why had she permitted it? Why had she gone on seeing him? Why had she been such a fool? She could see, mentally, Agnes's half-smile, her lifted brows. Agnes had been right. You didn't, however, have to be very clever to be right. What had Ken said? She remembered all he had said, with a little shudder.

That Acton was serious she didn't in the least doubt.

At first it had all been light, gay, flirtatious, enchantingly shallow. Now it was different. Still light at times; but deadly serious beneath.

He had never attempted to touch her. But his eyes had become possessive, demanding.

He said, as she didn't answer:

"You don't believe me? Lola, I'm very much in love with you."

She said, flushing, one cheek against her curving palm:

"You don't know me. Except as Mr. Jameson's secretary. Married."

His face darkened. He lost his oddly youthful look. He looked mature, sharpened, a little angry.

"What has that to do with it? Secretary! Don't be silly, Lola!"

She murmured something about class . . . education. He rapped his hand down on the table. The crystal and china and silver clattered. A waiter standing near by, with folded arms, looked at them curiously, startled. The orchestra was playing.

"I still remember," played the orchestra.

He said sharply: "Be good enough to stop this idiotic sort of conversation. You've said only one thing that has much bearing on the subject. That you're married. How much does *that* mean to you, Lola?"

She raised her eyes candidly. She answered honestly. She said, troubled, "I don't know—now."

The eyes regarding her lighted swiftly. Acton leaned nearer. He asked, "Now? Does that mean—*me?*"

"No," said Lola, crumbling her bread and not looking at him. "No, I don't think so, Peter. I don't think it has anything to do with you. I think it lies between Ken and me. We—haven't been as happy—lately. And we've only," she reminded herself, distressed, "been married a little over two years."

Acton asked, masking his disappointment: "This—trouble? Have I caused that? By my friendship with you? Please tell me the truth, Lola."

"No, not exactly." She drew a long breath, glad that she need no longer pretend that Ken was complacent. "He doesn't like my seeing you, of course."

"Why, of course?"

"Why not?" she asked, amazed. "Oh, it may be all right, in your—circle. I know you don't like me to speak of that, but it stands to reason, doesn't it? But he can't help it. Our lives are supposed to be based on a partnership. . . . I thought they would be. I mean, we both worked, didn't we? Lately, Ken's had hard luck. He was transferred from the job he had when we were married and so made less money. Then he lost that job—when—when all that nonsense was in the paper. And now he has one that doesn't bring in much of anything. It gets on his nerves . . . and mine . . . and we quarrel."

Acton said swiftly, "If you had come to me—in the first place."

"I wanted to. He wouldn't hear of it," she answered, remembering. "And now, of course, I wouldn't."

"Why not—*now?*" he asked her.

"After what you just said?" She regarded him, astonished. "I couldn't, I couldn't."

"Your scruples," he told her, smiling, as the waiter cleared their practically untouched plates and brought the coffee, "are very charming. I love them . . . and you."

She said bluntly, "Ken and I don't get along because I make more money than he does."

"I understand that," Acton told her, "and being a man

I understand him. But my sympathies are diverted to your side. He should be a better sport."

"Are men—sports," she wanted to know, "where women are concerned?"

He replied slowly: "Perhaps not. Yet I flatter myself that I was—once."

Lola said, contritely: "I'm sorry. I didn't mean you, of course. I was thinking of Ken."

"How much do you think of him?" he asked her urgently.

She did not answer for a moment. Acton went on:

"I mean—look here, Lola, do you love him? Or do you care for me at all?"

Lola said, her heart shaking in a sudden sick panic of fright: "I—do love Ken. I like you very much, Peter."

He said, and sighed: "I suppose you do care for him. Loyal. You've always been. From the first time you flared up in his defense when I asked you if he'd mind my taking you to lunch. I hoped you didn't care. I hoped you were fed-up. You see, I happen to want you—very much."

She looked at him with great troubled eyes. She was easily, he thought irrelevantly, the prettiest woman in the room, the most desirable. The little dinner dress she wore was exceedingly simple and not new. But it was well cut, and any frock worn with her figure was a triumph. He thought of the clothes he could buy her, the furs, the jewels. . . .

He said: "Thank you for not misunderstanding. For not getting up and saying, 'Oh, Mr. Acton!' For not imputing the usual motives. Lola, if the day comes when you find you do not care for this boy you married, will you come and tell me so? You can get a quiet divorce; we will be married immediately . . . and—"

She whispered, paling, "You want to *marry* me?"

"I do. I didn't, at first. I do now," he said honestly, "and so, all along this evening, you haven't believed that? You've imputed the motives, just the same? Well, that's funny. And you weren't—what is the word—insulted?"

She said, deeply distressed, "Please forgive me, Peter. I thought"—she remembered Ken's words—"that when men went out with women who weren't of their own station—and sometimes who were—women who were married—"

"Never mind," he interrupted hastily. "I know. You thought thus and so, yet weren't angry?"

"No," she answered gravely. "Why should I be angry at you? Only at myself for having placed myself in that position. I'm not a child, you know. If what I thought—just now—had been so, I had only myself to blame."

He commented lightly, "It sounds like a ballad."

"Maybe. I'm not very good at expressing myself," she said, hurt.

He put out his hand and covered hers, there on the table.

"Forgive me—darling," said Acton.

She responded to the emotion in his voice by a quiver, a deep flush. She didn't love him. But she loved . . . the darkness, the depth of his tone, the tenderness. She had always liked him. He had never been physically unattractive to her. Now she told herself, frightened: Be careful . . . here is danger.

He said, taking his hand away:

"I won't badger you. If you love your husband . . . well, that lets me out, doesn't it? I won't say . . . we can be friends. It is impossible. I ask instead, let me go on seeing you. I'll"—he smiled at her—"behave. . . . You are—how old *are* you, Lola?"

She told him. Twenty-four, she said.

"And married two years? Were you so sure of love? *Are* you so sure? Sure it will last? I can wait. I'm not trying," he told her, "to play Faust. But I can give you so much. Not only things money buys, unlimited money, almost. But understanding. Companionship. The lad you married— Well, two things, desire, propinquity, the mating season. That's easy to comprehend. But I'm twenty years older than you are, Lola."

She said frankly: "You'd be mad to marry anyone like me. Everyone would say so."

"Mad not to. Mad to do so," he corrected her. "You're the loveliest thing—you have so much, youth and fire and self-reliance and . . ." He was silent, drumming on the table. "I've thought of marrying again," he told her briefly. "Girls . . . one meets them everywhere. And anxious mothers. Pretty girls, and young girls, sophisticated, charming enough. But—"

She said hastily, "Why not?" She looked at him, slipping back to childhood in her puzzled regard. "Those girls," she said helplessly, "they—*fit in*. Can't you see? As—as hostesses. As everything. Brought up to it. I'm not. I am," she said, laughing at herself, "a little like the girl in the advertisements who always orders salad—chicken salad! Only you make it easy, you order for me. Oh, I don't make many grammatical errors and I use the right fork. But I don't fit in. I wish you could see that."

He said: "You have one reason only for refusing me. Or rather, that doesn't matter either. I could, I think, teach you, although that's a pretty fatuous remark. Put it this way—you love someone else. That's the real reason, the only one that can silence me. But people have been known to fall out of love. If you ever fall out of love, Lola, let me know, will you?"

She did not answer. Presently they left, and he sent her home in his car, the oblivious chauffeur sitting straight and still behind the wheel, his face impassive.

"I'm not coming with you," said Acton. "I wouldn't quite—dare."

She knew what he meant. Not Ken. Not conventions. Himself. Herself.

She let herself in on reaching home. It was not late. Ken wasn't there, however. He came in after she had been in bed an hour. He'd been at the Garrisons', he said. He asked her briefly, "Have a good time with the boy friend?" and added that the Garrisons expected them over Saturday night. "Unless," he added, with a deadly courtesy, "you've made other plans?"

She hadn't, she said.

Kenneth went to bed and slept, almost instantly. Lola lay awake, staring at the dark blur of the window. She heard the trolleys go by over on Fifth Avenue. Heard cars. Voices. Laughter. Heard an unlikely rooster crowing, there in the city, shortly before dawn.

She did love Ken. Yet when they were—as they now were—he was strange to her. A stranger. Yet she loved him. She belonged to him. You didn't un-belong very quickly. She began to understand Agnes, no longer caring for Jim but remembering. Remembering with her physical memory, the memory of her habituated sense.

She, Lola, didn't love Acton. But there was temptation there for her. As Agnes had said. The temptation of leisure, of luxury, of freedom from worry and anxiety. The temptation of vanity . . . preening itself softly upon a capture, a matrimonial prize. And he was not repulsive to her. He could easily become perilously attractive; had perhaps become so already, if she would be honest with herself. Yet it wasn't *love*. Love was what she had felt for Kenneth, before marriage, after marriage. Was what she still felt for him now, under all the smothering, blanketing pall of irritation and exasperation, anger and estrangement; something hurt but undefeated, lifting a living head, something pulsing with unconquerable life.

Dawn was white at the windows. Lola was cold, she was inexpressibly weary, she was tired to agony, she was catching her breath, tears stinging her lids. She must love Ken. If she didn't, the solid earth would rock beneath her feet.

She looked over at him. He was sleeping, one arm flung above his head. She could see the pale outline of cheek, the brown hair tousled, the strong hand outflung, the mouth a little relaxed, boyish, serene, the closed lids. If Ken were dead? She thought of Ken—*dead*. She sat up, pushing the hair from her forehead, a forehead cold with sudden sweat.

"I'm cold," she complained, like a child, "cold—Ken!"

She lay down again close beside him. Kenneth stirred in his sleep. She nuzzled against him like a frightened animal, tucking her head into the curve of his arm. His body beside hers was warm, vital, living. She was still, feeling the warmth, the comfort seep into her veins. She said, to the ears which were sealed in sleep, I do love you —I *do*. And, presently, slept.

Ken said, as the alarm-clock went off and the bright sunlight pointed a reproving golden finger:

"Well—for the love of mud—how did you get here, old lady?"

"Crawled. An hour or so ago. I was cold," said Lola, laughing.

He sat up and took her in his arms. Kissed her hard, in the little tender hollow of her throat, on her smiling mouth.

"Good morning. Gosh, Lola, you look all in. Stay here." He eased her back among the pillows. "I'll put the coffee on," he told her.

He exhibited no astonishment at her gesture toward reconciliation; did not even admit its necessity. Took it all in his stride. And went whistling into the kitchen. Lola lay back against the pillows and closed her heavy-lidded eyes. She ached from weariness. But she was happier. This was part of marriage perhaps, this acceptance, this evasion of issues, this refusal to talk. You took things for granted, certain motions, certain negotiations toward peace.

That morning they shared a happy sort of breakfast, as they had used to do. No, not that exactly. As they had first done, as later they had often done, if less frequently. He was, Ken said, working on an idea with Jake. If he could only get the job he wanted and save money, he and Jake might make a good thing of it. Lola listened, believing again.

But a week later, after the party at Garry's, when she approached him timidly, disliking to do so, hating herself a little, for many subtle reasons, and asked him if he didn't want her to speak to Acton about a position, he turned on her furiously with sharp and stinging words.

He'd forced her to it, she answered, forced her to try and give him the impetus he apparently needed—in the right direction. Not that money mattered, as much, for she had been raised again. That very morning. And Jameson had hinted of certain changes and shake-ups which would affect her favorably. No, not that the money mattered; she could manage, more than manage. But his self-respect.

He couldn't, he told her savagely, see much self-respect in having her beg jobs from a so-and-so who was crazy about her. "You needn't think you pull the wool over my eyes!" said Ken.

Lola was very white. She asked him directly:

"You think I'm unfaithful to you? If you think so, why," asked Lola bitterly, "do you stay here another moment? For room and board?"

He swung around on that. And dropped his raised hand at the dreadful look in her eyes; a look as if she had died a little death, but not from physical fear.

"I don't think you're unfaithful," he shouted, whipping himself up to a frenzy of anger and shame. "If I did I'd—I'd—"

"What?" asked Lola, cold.

"I'd kill you," said Ken sullenly, "and him."

"Don't be silly. If I were, I wouldn't be worth killing," said Lola.

He came over to her, took her roughly into his arms.

"Lola, why did you say that? As if I'd ever believe— I don't mind your going out with Acton. Yes, I do mind; but it's your own business, you can do as you like. I haven't any right to tell you what to do, I guess," said Ken, loathing himself for his humility. "But I didn't think such things. I haven't for a moment. Ever. If I did . . . it wouldn't be you I'd kill, I suppose."

She said gently: "Then, if you don't . . . why won't you let him help us? He's a good friend, Ken."

Ken said instantly: "That's different. He's all right. I—I want you to have a good time, Lola. Go places.

Places I can't take you. But I won't ask any favors.
Understand?"

Lola's raise was authentic enough, deserved enough.
That Acton, through various channels open to him, had
been able to put a little pressure to bear was another
matter. He had been clever about it; so clever that
Jameson believed he himself, uninfluenced, was responsible. Acton's reasoning was quite normal.

He did not think Lola loved him—yet. But neither
did he believe that she loved her husband. A nice kid,
was the way Acton dismissed Kenneth Hayes from his
thoughts when, if ever, he was able to think of him dis-
passionately. Thinking of him in relation to Lola was
something quite different. Acton believed that Lola was
tiring: of her husband, of her job, of life as she was living it. Give her enough time, and she'd be tired enough to
want to break away. Part of her trouble with young
Hayes was caused, on her own authority, by her wage-
earning capacity, which seemed to be in excess of his.
Very well, the more she earned, the more trouble there
would be. All's fair, thought Acton. He wouldn't urge
her, he would do nothing to distress her personally. But
if the marriage was going down-hill and a judicious little
push could be added, without hurting her, well and good.

And Jameson had said to him recently:

"There's talk, you know, of reorganizing the St. Louis
office. I'm to go out and start things. I'll take a picked
staff with me."

Would that mean Lola? Perhaps. If it did, St. Louis
wasn't so far from New York. Not from Acton's viewpoint. But it might as well be six thousand miles away so
far as Lola's husband was concerned. Absence? The old
rule didn't work. If Lola went to St. Louis, if she could

be persuaded to go, if Hayes stayed at home, if Acton made it his business to be in St. Louis often—well, why not?

Lola, of course, knew nothing definite. Rumors reached her, in the underground way of a great organization; that the coming project would affect her, however, she did not dream. When she heard that Jameson might go west to inspect and to reorganize, it occurred to her merely that she would carry on in New York with Jameson's successor until his return.

She had stopped seeing Acton so frequently. When he told her, carelessly, that he was going south for the tail end of the season she was relieved rather than sorry. Better so. Being friends wasn't easy, not when the other person was by his own admission unable to be friends. One couldn't carry the burden of friendship alone. It had to be borne by two.

She saw less of Agnes, and very little of Connie. Agnes had her divorce now. She had been made assistant buyer in her department. And was busy socially into the bargain. "It's the life," she told Lola, on their infrequent meetings. "Keep on going so you haven't time to think. Then, when you stop, you haven't anything left with which *to* think." She no longer asked about Jim. When in the spring Lola of her own accord told her that Jim had given up his position and procured a similar one in Chicago, she was frankly uninterested. "I wish him luck," was all she said. Lola asked curiously, "You don't feel . . . more than that?" And Agnes told her no, why should she? There were one or two eligible men interested in her. Half a dozen willing to take her out. "But I'm not interested. I like my job. I'll get somewhere in it. After all, that's half of life—getting somewhere," said Agnes.

Connie, engrossed in her baby, was not often available. Lola saw more and more of her mother. And of girls whom she had known for some years, but with whom she had never been intimate. Of Amy Garrison, with decreasing reluctance. Amy was amusing in her way, and it did Lola good to see how she handled Garrison. He was a subdued and different person in the masterful presence of his wife. Less boastful. Almost cringing.

In her own section a girl whom she knew fairly well dropped out of view; and resigned. Lola went to see her, over in Flatbush. She was going to have a baby, Rhoda told her resentfully. She couldn't go on working afterwards, because there wasn't any relative she could leave it with. And she wasn't making enough money to pay anyone. So she'd have to stay home and get along on what her husband earned. That was that. "A girl's a fool to marry," said Rhoda, heavy-eyed and drawn, already a little disfigured.

Lola went home, thoughtful. She told Ken. Ken had the usual masculine comments ready. But that sort of commentary didn't mean a thing after something had happened.

She thought of all the married women she knew, the women holding down jobs and deadly afraid of pregnancy. And yet even Rhoda, angry, rebellious, not at all resigned, had shown her the clothes she had ready, and as she talked of them her face had softened and the haggard look had gone, erased by a transient smile.

During that spring the Davis household was flung into a state of argument, excitement and expectancy. Mr. Davis hadn't had a vacation, or rather hadn't taken one, in the memory of man. The firm was giving him a month with pay, and as much longer as he wanted, during the summer. Millie had written asking her father and mother to come to Hollywood on a visit. She would pay their way. The trouble was Howard. Why, asked Howard, couldn't he go on out and find something to do there? But Millie was against that. She was, she stated firmly, in her slanting, big hand, and telegraphically also, against anything but visits. Couldn't Howard stay with Lola? Couldn't Lola and Ken close up the flat for a couple of months and live in the Davis house and look after Howard?

Mrs. Davis was torn between the acute desire to go and see for herself that Millie was getting proper food and proper rest, and her maternal reluctance at leaving her son to the perils of Bay Ridge and points east or west. Lola added her quota to the family argument.

She wanted, she said, a bigger apartment anyway. She was earning enough to warrant it now. Even without Ken's help, she added mentally. Their apartment had been leased by the month only. They could give a month's notice, take Millie's and her old room at her mother's, and live there while the family were in California. Then when they came back, Ken and she could find another place to live.

Somewhere, she decided, nearer her mother's. Perhaps the Downes house, next to the corner. Their present tenants in the big second-floor apartment were leaving, and the rent would be no more than where they were living now. The Downes house, big and rambling—a one-family house until the children had married and moved out, leaving the upstairs vacant and too big for comfort—would provide them with an extra bedroom and a porch as well. Lola was enthusiastic. Only Ken demurred.

"What's the matter with where we are now?"

"It's too small," said Lola. "We're under each other's feet all the time."

"It used to be big enough," he reminded her.

"The rent's the same," she said carelessly. "I'll have to have a cleaning woman in, that's all."

Ken wondered, sullenly, if his salary would reach to cleaning women.

But in the end it was left at that. And in the early summer Mr. and Mrs. Davis set out for Hollywood. "Don't let dad meet Greta Garbo," called Howard as the train was pulling out.

There was room in the Davis's big cellar to store her furniture. Lola moved back home. Her old room looked strange to her with Ken in it. Ken was strange, too. He worked in the back yard, fussed with vines and flowers, painted porch furniture. But it wasn't, he said to Lola, like their own place. Having Howard with them made a difference too. It was easier . . . and harder.

Lola consulted Mrs. Downes and arranged for a probable lease at the end of the summer. Until the tenants moved out in September nothing could be done about it anyway. She decided against a vacation, and planned to use her vacation money for redecoration and new furniture.

She spent two week-ends with Agnes at Bellport. Ken stayed at home. Someone, he explained, had to be with Howard. But he didn't want to go. Probably Acton would be there. And he couldn't meet Acton without reserve. It was one thing to sit still and take it on the chin when your wife went out with another man; but another to meet that other man with outstretched hand and a hearty grin. He'd not do it.

Acton was there. He came to Bellport and took them out. He made no attempt to be with Lola alone. "Wish I had a look-in," said Agnes regretfully.

But in August Jameson told Lola that he was going to St. Louis at the end of the following month and taking half a dozen picked people, from different sections, with him. Later of course he would return, leaving the St. Louis office fully staffed and under a new manager. If Lola cared to go with him as secretary, and later in a position of more executive possibility, it was up to her. Such a position would carry seventy-five dollars a week as salary. And there were possibilities that it wouldn't end there.

She went home, almost bewildered. "Think it over," said Jameson, "and let me know by, say, next week. If you can arrange it . . . ?"

Would Ken go? Would Ken be willing? There must be jobs in St. Louis. As for herself, she couldn't afford to refuse, could she? It was real money. A real chance. She could work up even higher. She had visions of eventually managing the office alone. Why shouldn't she? She knew a good deal more about the business than just taking dictation. She'd work for it. Work hard.

But, would Ken go?

He must go. He had no right to stand in her way. She wouldn't stand in his.

It simply happened that this was her chance. If it had been his chance, she wouldn't have hesitated. Nor would he have expected her to hesitate. He would have said merely: "Here, we're going to pull up stakes and go to St. Louis. When can you be ready?"

Fifty-fifty. It wasn't any different because she, and not he, had had the opportunity, was it? And anyway he hadn't anything to leave here. Hadn't an important job. Just a makeshift one.

Of course he would go, she thought—running up the steps of her father's house and calling for him, her cheeks aflame with excitement, her eyes dark stars—of course he'd go!

Chapter XI

O F course, he'd go, Lola told herself, opening the front door.

Ken wasn't home yet; nor Howard. She busied herself with getting dinner. Everything went wrong, her hands shook so. She cut her thumb on the potato knife, she left the steak too long on the broiler, the coffee was mostly water. But she was too excited to care.

The table was set and the meal was ready when they came in, Howard with his amazing, incredible adolescent appetite and his way of talking with his mouth full and receiving reproof with an irritated "Oh, gee . . . *women!*" And Ken, tired from the heat, complaining that his feet hurt him. "Standing behind a counter all day is not my idea of a good time," said Ken, and suggested that they go to the beach that night, for Mr. Davis's ancient Ford stood in the garage and they could run down after dinner and cool off. "I'm all for it," declared Howard, r'arin' to go.

Lola had found the running of the big house a rather expensive proposition. She couldn't possibly do all the work and a cleaning woman had to come in. And there was more to clean and plenty of it. Ken and Howard between them managed to look after the yard and the porch. A window-washing company came around once every two weeks. Howard paid board, with ostentatious pride. Not very much. "But," Lola said, when her mother offered to make up any deficit, "don't be silly, aren't we living rent-free?" They were. There was that

194

much saving, but there were bigger light and gas bills to pay. And Howard could eat, all around the clock.

She looked around the pleasant shabby dining-room, mellow in the late sunlight. The Narrows breeze blew in at the bay-windows. She hadn't, she thought, watered the window-boxes for several days. Howard was talking about a letter he had had from his mother that morning. "She sure is stepping out," said Howard, tossing the envelope across the table to Ken. Ken read, between mouthfuls of steak.

"Gee, that's rich!" said Ken; and asked Lola, "Have you seen this?"

She hadn't. He gave it to her, and he and Howard hilariously discussed the possibility of their departing from home and becoming stars overnight. Lola thought, her eyes but not her mind on the letter, it isn't the time yet. But—

She couldn't hold back any longer. She burst out:

"Ken . . . I've a chance to go to St. Louis. With Mr. Jameson and some of the others. A picked staff. To work out there—reorganization, the end of next month."

"St. Louis?" said Ken stupidly. "I never heard of such a thing!"

She explained, leaning across the table, her face flushed, her eyes very bright:

"It will mean seventy-five a week, Ken. Isn't it wonderful?"

"What," asked Ken coolly, "do you propose to do with me?"

His mouth had hardened. Howard looked from one to the other, swept the remains of his shortcake into his capacious mouth, mumbled, "Well, folks, I'll see you later. . . . I'll be outside when you're ready to go," and vanished hastily and relievedly from the room. He felt a storm brewing. He preferred not to be near lightning at any time. Married people, he mused out on the porch, a cigarette in full blast in one corner of his mouth and a stick of gum exercising his teeth on the other side . . . married people. The day I get married you can take me out and shoot me like a dog. Yessir, like a dog.

But he strolled down the street a moment later to hang over the McCarthys' front gate and pass the time of day with Edna, who was sixteen and red-headed.

Edna would make a good wife for some wise guy, he mused. She sure could dance. A fellow could take Edna out—if he had the money—and be proud of her. She was a darned cute kid. He jingled the few coins in his pocket. "Want to walk around and have a soda?" he suggested to Edna hopefully, secure in his amazing capacity for eating anything and at any time.

By the time he got back home, ready to go to the beach, Lola and Ken, he devoutly hoped, would be over their quarrel, symptoms of which, he prided himself, he was swift as the next man to realize.

St. Louis. What in time had she meant by that?

That was what Ken wanted to know, leaning across the cluttered table. Funny, thought Lola, irrelevantly, how good a table looked, set and ready for a meal when you are hungry, and how desolate and almost repulsive it appeared when the meal was over.

"You aren't serious about this?" he was demanding.

"Well, yes. Why shouldn't I be? It's my chance. Our chance," she corrected herself hastily. "And, as it happens, it couldn't have come at a better moment. We are rid of the apartment. Mother will let us store our things here until we send for them. We could live in rooms for a time, or at some good boarding-house or an inexpensive hotel, until we'd looked around, you know.

We haven't signed a lease with the Downeses as yet. We're all set to go. It would be wonderful. We'd have a lot of fun, too," she pleaded, "getting away, going to a strange place, meeting strange people."

"We?" he inquired. "And just where do you think I come in?"

"But, Ken," she regarded him helplessly, "why not? I don't want to go without you. You know that!"

"Not much, I don't!" he interrupted swiftly.

She said, paling: "You've only my word for that, of course. But—your job here isn't important; it doesn't amount to a thing."

"I know that without your telling me," he retorted sullenly. "You needn't rub it in. It was you who urged me to take it in the first place. I didn't want to. I knew something better would turn up, if I waited long enough. But you weren't willing—"

She said, touching his hand: "Ken . . . please, dear, don't be so—so angry. So far away. I thought you'd be better off doing something until you got a really good chance. Well, why shouldn't you get a better break in St. Louis? There must be jobs there. We'd find one."

"This *we* stuff!" He laughed shortly. "Who do you think you are—Lindbergh? You make me laugh!"

"Don't speak like that," she begged, shivering with a cold resentment and a colder despair.

"How else shall I speak? Yes, ma'am, no, ma'am, whatever you say goes? Look here, what kind of a bird do you think I am, anyway?" Ken demanded furiously. He had never heard the word *maquereau*. If he had he wouldn't have known what it meant. But still its meaning was in his mind now. "When we married I was willing for you to go on working, because that was the way you wanted to have things. It wasn't my way, see? We could have gotten on on what I made if you had been willing to give up a few things and work a little harder around the house . . ."

She said angrily:

"I work as hard as any woman who hasn't a job besides! I'm half dead with working, most of the time! Suppose we *had* gotten along on what you were earning when we married. And you'd lost your job. Where would we be now without *my* job? . . . which you hate so much. But you don't hate it enough not to profit by it just the same!"

"That will be about all from you!" Ken told her. His boyish mouth was set. There were lines about it. His face was gray with anger. His eyes were gray too, the hard, cold gray of steel. "That will be about all," he told her. "If you think you can order me to leave my position, no matter how rotten it is, and pick up and follow you around the country like a pet poodle you have another guess coming. Crazy, that's what you are! I'd look great, wouldn't I," he asked her acidly, "sitting in a furnished room, biting my nails and reading advertisements, while you went out to work and kept me in cigarette money? 'Here's your week's allowance, darling.' Swell, wouldn't it be? A hell of a note!"

"You mean—you won't go?" she asked him quietly.

They had, a moment past, been shouting at each other. Like angry strangers. Now she dropped her voice, steadied it, clasped her hands to keep them from shaking and spoke through bitten lips, "You mean—*you won't go?*"

"Well, I'll say I won't go! What do you take me for?" he demanded.

"For a poor sport," said Lola. "Look here, if our

positions were reversed and you got a chance in another town, you'd expect me to go with you, wouldn't you?"

"Of course," said Ken quickly. "That's different."

"Why is it different?" she wanted to know.

"Lola, be your age! You're a woman, I'm a man. Whether you work or not, I'm the head of the house," said Ken.

"You are? And even if I were working you'd expect me to give up my job and go to wherever you had to go?" she asked further.

"Naturally. Look here, when you promised to marry me, when you did marry me," asked Ken, suddenly as quiet as she, "what did you marry me for? To sleep with me?" he demanded brutally.

"Ken . . . *Ken!*"

"Well, what else? You keep house—after a fashion. You bring home more money than I do. You complain all the time of being tired. What are you getting out of being married to me? What are you giving me?" he demanded. "You aren't giving me a damned thing except the privilege of sharing a bedroom with you. You're not a real wife," said Ken. "A part-time wife, that's what you are. A—a legalized mistress. Mistresses cook meals for their Big Moments now and then," he reminded her absurdly.

She was very white. She thought: It isn't Ken. It isn't—me. We can't be sitting here saying these things to each other. It isn't possible. She thought—I mustn't cry, mustn't faint. She said:

"Are you trying to tell me I don't mean more to you than—a mistress?"

"The shoe," said Ken with bitter humor, "is on the other foot. What I suppose I am trying to tell you is that I don't mean more to you than a kept man. There are kept men, you know. Well, I'm one of them."

She said, rising, "I won't sit here and listen to you talk like this."

"You will. Till I'm through. Sit down," Ken ordered, "and take your medicine. When I married you I expected a wife. But you thought more of your goddam job and your pin-money and your—earning capacity. Thought more of your boss and your little authority and your contacts. Contacts like Peter Acton, I suppose. The sort of wife I knew anything about, and was a fool to expect, worked with and for her man all right. But not in an office. She did her job at home. And she did it well. And she made a man feel that he had something to come home to besides a worn-out, grouchy girl, thinking of nothing but money and career. . . . Career"—he laughed shortly—"and making it pretty plain what a grand sport she was to dust a room and set a table and get up a meal—part of it out of a paper bag—and then go to bed with the man who married her. *Wives* are different," said Ken, "and wives go with their husbands, wherever they're told to go. They don't come home and say, 'Well, I've a nice job in St. Louis. . . . We leave next week, Big Boy.'"

She had sat down when he'd told her to. She couldn't have done otherwise, her knees shook so—from shame, from anger, from a deep, and, she thought, enduring hurt. He had risen now and was walking up and down, turning abruptly, his hands buried in his pockets.

After a moment Lola said faintly: "Very well. I understand perfectly. You won't go. That settles it."

He was by now very much ashamed. He loved her. He'd not been able to get away from that. From loving. Not all habit. But the sort of loving that a very decent boy grows into after possession, after marriage. He'd hurt her terribly. He had said unforgivable things. But he had meant them. All along through the past two years and more his sex pride, his male tradition, had taken severe punishment. First, he'd grinned and borne it. Then evaded it. Then covered it up with the veneer of what's-the-use? and cynicism. Now it broke through.

He came over and dropped to his knees beside her.

"Lola . . . Baby, please forgive me. I didn't mean half of what I said. Only you do understand now, don't you? Why I couldn't go? Why I won't go? Of course, you understand," he told her confidently—as confidently as she had told herself, "Of course, Ken will go"—"And you know I love you. I swear I'll get out of this job and into something decent . . . swear I'll take the burden off you. You don't know how I've hated your carrying it, Lola. I'll make it all up to you. You'll never regret not going."

"But I *am* going," she told him, in a sort of bewildered astonishment that he could have thought anything else.

"You are—going?"

"Yes—"

"Without me . . . without me?" he repeated, incredulous.

"So it seems. As you've said you won't come."

He rose and stood over her, tall, his shoulders a little stooped, his hands buried again in his pockets. And his attractive young face was dark with amazement and unbelief.

"You'd go—*anyway?*" he repeated stupidly.

She got to her feet somehow. She went close to him and put her hands on the lapels of his coat. She looked up at him. She knew his face. Ken's. The least expression that crossed it, she knew. He belonged to her.

And she to him. Or did they? Did you ever belong? She thought: I mustn't remember what he said. . . . I'll have to remember, soon. I'll remember whenever I want to be angry. Not now.

She said, holding him there:

"Ken, you say you love me. If you really did, wouldn't you make this sacrifice? It isn't a sacrifice really, not of anything that matters. Just of your pride."

He told her, awkward with his effort at self-expression:

"It's *because* I love you that I can't. Gosh, Lola, you talked about self-respect the other day. Well, what sort of self-respect would that be—if I tailed out there at your heels?"

She remembered a line in a poem she had read at school. She spoke it now, idiotically, hysterically:

" 'I could not love thee, dear, so much loved I not honor more.' "

"What? What's that?" asked Ken uncomfortably.

She said: "A poem. It doesn't matter. It's how you feel, isn't it? That your honor won't let you—make a concession for me."

Honor. His face cleared. "That's it," he said, knowing somehow that it was but unable to explain.

"It's a comic sort of honor," said Lola, and dropped her hands to her side and turned away.

From the porch, Howard shouted: "Hey, you fellows! Aren't you ever coming?"

Lola said, swiftly: "Go with him. I'll stay home. I've got to clear up."

Ken looked at her. He turned away, all he would have said or tried to say unspoken. He went to the hall screen door.

"Lola isn't coming. She has to clear up," he told his brother-in-law.

"Oh, gosh!" Howard thought deeply. That meant a fight, all right. They'd probably be hard at it all night, quarreling, and the walls were pretty thin. His room was next to theirs. He wouldn't get any sleep, even if he put his head under the covers, unnecessary on such a hot night. He catapulted into the house.

"Oh, sis, come on! What's eating you? We'll help clear away. Hey, give me that dish." He grabbed it from her, and half a dozen more, and rushed with them into the kitchen, arriving mercifully without accident, and reappeared to confront Lola as she stood by the table, not moving, the butter knife in her hand. "Here, leave 'em lie! Ken and I will wash up when we get back. Come on," coaxed Howard, "it won't be any fun without you," he lied gallantly.

Ken said nothing.

"Oh, all right," Lola decided suddenly.

They'd stay late perhaps. It was fireworks night at Coney. And when they got home they would be too sleepy and tired to argue—or to think. Maybe things would look different in the morning.

They got into the Ford. "Could we," asked Howard, "could we take the McCarthy kid? Not that I care," he explained hastily, "but it would make four and, gee, she's keen on the beaches."

So they took the McCarthy kid, much to Howard's relief, which was a mixed emotion. Howard sat with her in the back, his long legs draped over the scraped sides of the car. Lola was in front with Ken, who drove. They drove in silence, while Edna and Howard alternately giggled and indulged in puppylike antics behind them.

Fireworks at Coney. The buildings all lighted up. Radiant. A land synthetically enchanting. The great Ferris wheel, a circle of light, turning slowly. Crowds.

Girls in gay pajamas, girls in sailor trousers. "Look at that one, Howard. Isn't she the limit? Must weigh a ton," said Edna.

Barkers. Boys and girls, arm in arm. Sticky, dirty, tired children, fagged with the heat and press, crying, dragged at their mothers' hands. "Let's go for a boat ride," said Howard.

Into the boat. "You balance the boat yourself." Howard and Edna giggling. "Holy cat, it's dark!"

The boat rocked through the tunnel. Musty. Damp. Smelling of darkness and stagnant water. A duck quacked from somewhere. There were small red lights ahead . . . a little panorama of a foolish, impossible city. A man and a girl in the front seat were kissing, pressed close together . . . murmuring . . . sighing . . .

Lola felt sick. All these people . . . furtive . . . with a stimulated ardor—a tentative mating.

She'd never felt that way about things before. She'd always loved the beaches, their rowdy magic, their foolish, charming glamour. She was a child of the city.

Ken sat, unhappily silent. Bored. Restless. Trying not to think. Trying not to worry. Bluff. That's what it was! Bluff! She wouldn't go. It wasn't possible that she'd go. Why, they loved each other! He leaned nearer and took her hand. It quivered in his own, rebellious. Then lay still.

Howard back of them was wondering: Should he hold Edna's hand? He'd never wanted to before. But Edna was the snake's hips. She was perfectly O.K. Should he? He'd feel like a fool. Nothing in that mush stuff anyway. Who did he think he was, Gilbert or Chevalier or someone? But she was a honey.

Edna made up his mind for him, slipping a cool little

paw into his awkward own, which engulfed it. "Gee, it's dark! I'm scared," said Edna gayly.

They emerged, blinking, into the light. Howard a bright becoming red to his ears, Edna cool and collected in her printed chiffon, her red hair bound with a ribbon.

They went on a scenic. Lola loved scenics, although they took her breath and terrified her. She clung to Ken's arm. The long pull upward, the swift rush down. "Whoopee!" yelled Howard and Edna behind them. "Whoopee!"

You couldn't think, on scenics. You just felt. Terror and a wild sort of rapture.

They shot the chutes. The water rose up to meet them at the end of their swift, smooth descent. Splashed all about them. The boat rocked perilously on the troubled breast of the little pond. "Whoopee!" yelled Howard again.

They drove in the drive-yourself cars, bumping each other on the track, laughing. They went to cycloramas. They sat in a little open-air café and had sodas and coco-colas and hot dogs. They had their fortunes told. Lola snatching her palm away as the woman said, "You are going on a journey—I see a blue-eyed man in your life . . ."

They went out on the Midway and into a freak show. "Oh, poor things," said Lola, shuddering, as Howard and Edna gazed, wide-eyed and open-mouthed, never tiring of such spectacles of disaster and deformity.

"I want to see the babies in the incubators," pleaded Edna, a lollipop in her mouth, a balloon in her hand.

So they went to the incubators. Stood there. Red-faced atoms, tied in blankets. Blue for boys, pink for girls, the voice of the guide explained, behind them. Howard commented, disgusted, "Aw, gee, worse than the freaks!" but Edna spoke out of a deep traditional conviction. "Aren't they too cunning?" she said.

Lola turned away, leaving Ken to listen to the scientific explanations. She thought: It's too hot in here. I want to get out. . . .

One thing he hadn't said to her that wives—not part-time wives—stayed home and had babies. Like Connie, choosing motherhood, choosing wifehood, and without romance; like Rhoda who hadn't chosen; like her own mother, who had had no choice. No, she couldn't bear to look at the babies.

They had their pictures taken. They stood at a shooting gallery and watched Howard shooting wild, burning his fingers, swearing his strange ferocious boyish oaths; watched Ken shooting steadily and aiming straight and with a sort of savage determination; watched a woman shoot, better than any man in the crowd about the gallery. While the bystanders, pressing in closer, whistled. "Jeez, see the lady! . . . Glad I ain't her husband. . . ."

Laughter.

The streets were packed. You couldn't walk on the sidewalks. It was stifling. Cars shot by. Policemen sweated and cursed. Out there, a few yards away, the ocean beat against the dirty, dusty sand, strewn with papers, bottles, luncheon and supper remnants, and black with people, lying full-length. . . . People who loved and hated, quarreled and argued, complained and wept and laughed, swore and suffered and rejoiced.

They went out on the board walk. There was a moon. The ocean swelled in gently. It looked oily, tired, beaten, as if it longed for lonely sands, for beaches swept clean of humanity. "Nature," remarked a tall man, walking past Lola with a woman, "nature is clean, take it by and large. But humanity is dirty."

It was very late when they reached home. Howard and Edna had insisted on dancing. "One dance . . . please?" But they'd danced six, Howard solemnly revolving about, conquering his wayward feet somehow. Edna pressed close to him in the charming instinctive allurement of youth which at her age and given her nature was perfectly innocent . . . as it happened. Other couples, less innocent, revolved past them, cheek to cheek, eyes half closed, lost in the little marriage of the dance, forgetting temporarily. And the room smelled faintly of salt air, sand, heavy perfume, strong soap, and human sweat.

Lola said, "Shall we dance, Ken?"

"If you want to," he told her.

She didn't. Yet she, too, wished to forget. They danced easily and beautifully together. He held her a little more closely after their first circling of the room. Her hair brushed his cheek. He bent toward it, there was an odor of cleanliness and sunlight, orris root and health about her hair. He loved it. He had often wished she would let it grow.

She felt the response of her body to his own, welded together in music. She knew the pulse of music in her blood. She was angry with him, and he with her. They were disillusioned, disappointed, and estranged. But they loved each other. And so, while the music played, they did not think, merely moved rhythmically about the crowded floor and permitted their senses to think for them.

When the music stopped they looked at each other with slightly dazzled eyes, faintly shy.

But it was time to go home.

Up in their bedroom she turned from the window.

"Ken . . . let's not say any more tonight," she begged him.

He looked up, relieved, yet knowing that this was only postponement. "O.K.," he agreed, briefly.

Yet, later, he took her in his arms and stammered that he loved her and that she could not leave him. And she lay relaxed, her fingers drawn along his throat, still hearing music, that other melody of love and sorrow, and wept for love and for sorrow, and felt his lips upon her drenched eyelids; and slept.

But morning was waking and a scamper to dress and a rush downstairs to the kitchen and a clatter of dishes. Of course, they hadn't washed the dishes from the night before! So, while the coffee was on the stove, and while the toast was being browned, she washed them. Howard came in heavy-eyed. "When do we eat?" he asked, and Lola sent him to set the table, and listened to him grumble as he did so. Ken came down, having cut himself shaving, vocal because he couldn't find the sort of shirt he wanted. "Don't they ever come home from the laundry?" he demanded. Morning was all haste and hurry and getting to the office late. Morning was a time of staccato impersonal speeches. Morning was no time for confidences, for pleas for understanding . . .

But that night, while Howard ranged the streets upon his own personal affairs, they sat and talked. Not angrily now. That was over. Not with recriminations. But sanely, each from his own viewpoint. And at the end of the evening they went on upstairs, having arrived exactly nowhere.

She had a week to think it over. She wrote her mother, by air mail. She wrote Millie. She thought of Agnes, telephoned her and begged her to lunch with her. "It's important," said Lola.

But Agnes was not to be consulted over a luncheon table. "It's your own funeral," said Agnes. "I see your point. As a matter of fact, I suppose I agree with you. I see Ken's, too, and you'll never get together on it. Never. He's a bad sport if he doesn't go—he's a darned fool if he does. I know that doesn't sound sensible. But it's true. Take it or leave it," said Agnes.

She left it. She saw Connie one evening when Ken was at his lodge. Connie said—interrupting the conversation half a dozen times to look in and see if the baby was all right—Connie said: "I think you'd be foolish to go. There's Ken. After all, you care more for him than for the job, don't you?"

"Of course I do. It isn't that. But . . . I can't feel that I can go on caring for him more than the job if he's going to be so small and petty about it," explained Lola, confusedly.

"There are other women," Connie warned her. "You know, Lola, being a wife is a full-time job. There's so much competition."

Well, that was Connie, married to Louis, mother of his son, not caring much whether her security came from bootlegging or contracting . . . not worrying about romance and love and passion, just content to be secure and anxious to hold on to that security at any price.

"Connie, are you happy?"

"I'll say I am!"

Louis was out; they were alone. In the back of the house the maid of all work sang, off key, at her dishes. The baby stirred upstairs in his crib. Connie rose and Lola followed her. Connie, in a green negligee, her black hair waved, parted in the middle. Connie, placid, with the placidity of her race, which endures only to be shattered suddenly by anger or ardor and then settles down again. Connie, happy. "I'll say I am!"

They bent over the crib together.

"He's pretty sweet," said Connie. "I'm going to have another just as soon as ever I can."

Ken called for Lola. He looked at Connie with admiration. He said:

"Gosh, you look great. Can I see the nipper or is he snoozing?"

"He is, but of course you can see him."

She turned to Lola. "I'll wait here," said Lola. She didn't want to see Ken looking at the nipper, discussing his weight and the length of his brown, fat legs. Ken and Connie came laughing down the stairs. "Give my best to Louis; he sure helped me out of a hole," said Ken.

Before her week was up she had a letter from her mother. Mrs. Davis was expostulant. Lola must be mad. Did she seriously expect Ken to give up his work and go with her to a strange city? Did she seriously contemplate going without him? "Oh, why," wailed Mrs. Davis, through the medium of pen and ink, "why will you be so headstrong and foolish? Your father is very much against it. He says he doesn't know what the world is coming to when wives prefer their jobs to their husbands. He says to tell you he will write. Lola, please think this over very carefully."

Millie wrote, a laconic line. "Whatever you do, you'll be wrong," scrawled Milly, "but I'm with you, kid."

She added that Hollywood was a madhouse but that she was holding her own.

And then Acton walked into the office.

"Mr. Jameson isn't here," said Lola.

"Well, I knew that. Come on out to lunch. You look," said Acton, "pretty tired."

She was.

She went to lunch. He said, after he had settled her at a table on a roof-top, where funny fan-tailed goldfish swam in a pond and there were flowers growing and an absurd rustic bridge: "Not a word out of you! I'm going to order idiotic things in aspic and lots of iced coffee and some of the elegant heart-of-cream cheese and bar-le-duc which is a specialty here. And after you've eaten a little I'll let you talk."

He had never seen her look so plain. Her eyes were heavy, half shut, the lids drawn. Her mouth he imagined was pale under the brush of lipstick. Her oval face very white, haggard. She had lines between her eyes. She looked done, with heat, with fatigue, with worry. No, he had never seen her look so plain. He had also never loved her more or wanted her so much.

Why? He hadn't seen her more than twenty or so times in all. They had never talked . . . not really. They had chattered, for the most part. The usual male-and-female-created-he-them conversation. He knew very little about her. Oh, he knew her background and some of her stereotyped ideas. He knew that much. He knew what she liked and didn't like. But of the Lola who lived and thought and suffered and rejoiced and was darkly silent he knew nothing. He had known a hundred far cleverer women, and twenty perhaps more lovely to look at. He had known a dozen with whom he might be sure to find tastes and wants and needs in common. With her he had, perhaps, nothing in common. Why did he love her? God knows. How had it started? A pretty girl working in a friend's office. A pretty girl, and so the usual reaction. . . . "Will you have lunch with me?" Why did you always want to feed pretty girls? Then the amusement of sounding her out, of trying to find out why and how the wheels went around. And then the awakening interest, based, as he well knew, on physical attraction. But almost any pretty girl could be physically attractive to him given the right mood. Not that it went further than that, very often. A man doesn't ask every physically attractive girl to go to Atlantic City with him, despite women's current beliefs to the contrary. No, your senses respond to beauty in women as they respond to anything which charms and which you forget—flowers, sunsets, music, perfume. And after that perhaps the thought, not admitted: a pretty girl, and a husband . . . a girl who has to work for her living . . . a girl who might be tempted, not as you were tempted perhaps, but in the end arriving at the same result, by a different road. Just a thought. Then, love. Without rhyme or reason . . . without thought.

He looked at her across the table. Her hand was listless on the cloth. He said: "Do eat something, angel. . . . I've never seen you look so tired."

She told him: "I'm not. Just worried."

"Tell me, won't you?"

She told him, haltingly at first, then fully. It was unfair. She knew it. Unfair, because this man loved her, because this man, for that reason and for reasons of his own, would be on her side. Unfair. Unfair to Ken. But couldn't she be a little unfair to Ken, just once, if, just once, she could derive some comfort from it?

Acton said slowly, "He's right, of course."

"Oh—Peter!"

She stared at him wide-eyed. He had failed her then. They all failed her, beginning with Ken.

"And you're right. It's a question of values. You are entitled to your opportunity. You do care a lot about that, don't you? I am correct in assuming that?"

She said, "Yes, I care."

She did. She had worked hard. She had liked her work. Before Ken had come she had cared more about her work than anything. It wasn't creative perhaps. It was nothing that would ever gain her spectacular recognition. But it was peculiarly her own, no matter how many thousands of other girls were engaged in the same occupation. She had made it her own by what of herself she put into it. She wanted to get ahead. Before her marriage she had planned . . . a career. Stenography, secretarial work—all stepping-stones. The best stepping-stones a girl could find, if she hadn't been born gifted. The stepping-stones with which all the executive-job women began. The best equipment. Hers.

After marriage, she'd had to forget a lot of that; had to concentrate on the earning part, had to think, if she did think about getting ahead, that getting ahead meant just so much more in her pay envelope. But now she had proved that she could carry so much of the burden— alone. That had a kick in it somewhere. She could get on, alone, even without help, even without encouragement.

Acton said, "You'll have to make up your own mind." He smiled at her, dropping his gravity for a lightness which masked a deeper gravity still. "Of course, if I were your young man I'd pocket my pride and follow you to the ends of the earth. I'd never let you out of my sight. Not I!"

She said, desperately, pitifully: "Peter, would you think it too dreadful of me, if I did go—even if Ken won't?"

He answered, jingling the ice in his tall glass: "You poor little kid! If you want so much to go and don't, you'll only make it miserable for him by reminding him what you gave up. Even if you don't remind him," he added, Celtic. "Go—if you want my advice—"

"Oh, I do!"

"Go, then—and if it doesn't work out you can always come back," he told her.

But he knew that he was being not wholly truthful. It is easy to go, even when it is difficult. Far easier than coming back. You don't come back, except by a miracle. And Acton didn't believe that there was enough magic left in Lola's love for her husband or in Ken's for her to work that miracle.

Two days later she told Mr. Jameson that she would be ready to go to St. Louis whenever he wished. He congratulated her, and himself, and asked:

"Mr. Hayes is going, I assume?"

"No, not now. He can't leave his work here, at present. Later, it will all straighten out," said Lola.

Jameson looked at her with shrewd, elderly eyes. He said:

"Be sure you aren't making a mistake. I tell you this against my will. I want you to go. You are invaluable to me. But I don't want you to hurt your life in any way."

She said steadily: "That's all right, Mr. Jameson. Ken and I are perfectly agreed."

And so they were, after a fashion. She had said, "I've made up my mind to go to St. Louis, Ken," and he had answered:

"It's up to you, of course, Lola. But I'll stay here."

Chapter XII

S<small>HE</small> told herself desperately: I can't go through with it. But I can't back out of it now. I've got to go through with it.

There was no one who could make up her mind for her. Agnes had had her say; and Connie. Howard, hanging about her when she came home with his awkward, "Aw, sis, what's all the shootin' for? You're kidding, aren't you?" was less than a help. Ken, with his superimposed control and his estranged eyes, was someone she had never known. Acton—was out of the question. He would tell her to live her own life; and that, she was shrewd enough to surmise, because of reasons of his own. If Ken would only—tell her he needed her, beg her not to go, perhaps, perhaps she would reconsider. She said as much to Agnes, and Agnes replied:

"He won't. Do they ever *really* need us, I wonder?"

Perhaps Agnes was right; perhaps Ken didn't need her. Perhaps Ken was right. Perhaps, the way marriages went nowadays, men and women didn't need one another, not basically. Or, rather, perhaps men needed only the sort of women who stayed at home and absorbed themselves in their husbands and families. But that wasn't fair. They couldn't, she still insisted, have married on that basis. In order to marry at all they had had to work out this fifty-fifty arrangement. Only it hadn't been fifty-fifty, after all. Perhaps nothing was; perhaps no scales balanced that evenly under the weight of human emotions and frailties.

But St. Louis meant her chance. She clung to that. If Ken had been generous—she called it "broad-minded" —they might have gone out together and made a new life for themselves, discovered together a new adventure. She kept on telling herself that, had their positions been reversed, Ken would have not only expected, he would have demanded her to go with him, whether or not his ambitions took him to the South Pole or the Orient. "Pack our bags. We're leaving on the midnight." Something like that.

There were a few weeks left before she would have to go. She went about her work mechanically. Jameson looked at her often, a fold between his eyebrows. Not so alert, not so eager, not so happy-hearted as she had been. Was it the coming change? The wrench? He didn't, of course, approve of it personally. But he couldn't run his share of the business on his personal theories, approvals, and disapprovals. She was the best secretary he'd ever had; she was executive, too, and to be trusted. But the snap had gone out of her work. Was he perhaps making a mistake in selecting her to go, with the rest of the staff? The men he was taking were unmarried; and the other girl, Jenny Jones, the typist from the medical section. Yes, the snap had gone from Lola's work. Come to think of it, it hadn't been very apparent since her marriage. But her work was good, thorough and painstaking.

Acton dropped in at the office one day when Jameson was out. He generally managed to arrive when Jameson was out. In the outer office Dorothy and Gladys exchanged glances. In the inner office Acton, sitting on the edge of Jameson's desk, said persuasively:

"Come out to lunch? No? Why not?"

"There's so much to do," she answered evasively. "Mr.

Hobart—that's the man who'll carry on here in Mr.
Jameson's absence—has asked me to go over the routine
with him and his secretary. There isn't enough time
really to do all that should be done. I'm staying late,
evenings."

She was standing by the desk. Her bright hair was
tumbled about her colorless face. Her eyes were strained,
and the lines of cheek and chin chiseled to overslender-
ness. Acton jumped down and, before she realized the
import of his gesture, took her abruptly into his arms.

"Give over, Lola," said Acton, blue eyes blazing.
"You're not happy about going away. Not happy about
staying here. Forget this nonsense. Marry me and let
me take you away from all of this dusty, drab existence."

"It isn't." She freed herself gently. "Please don't,
Peter. I—I like my work. I'm happy in it. Besides—"
she made a miserable failure of smiling—"besides, I'm already married."

"It isn't a life-term nowadays," he told her. "Well,
think it over. I'll come to St. Louis to see you, you know.
You can't really keep me away. And I'll keep on asking
you."

"It's not fair," she said, breathless.

He smiled at her from the doorway.

"Perhaps not, darling," he said; "but I can't stop to
think about justice now."

After he had gone she sat down at Jameson's desk and
put her head in her hands. It seemed to her that she was
standing at a place where four paths met. One path led
to Acton; there was no love ahead on it, but there was
ease and perhaps peace of mind and a certain weary surrender; and one road led to Ken, to all their common
memories and their common hopes and their common mis-
understandings; and one road led to St. Louis, and to

work and to the fulfillment of ambitions; and the fourth road was dark, she could not see down it.

Her mother wired briefly that she was coming home, leaving Mr. Davis out in Hollywood for a time longer.

"I'm sorry," Lola told her, meeting her alone. "I— you shouldn't have come on. It shortens your time with Millie."

"Millie's all right," Mrs. Davis said in naïve astonishment. "She can take care of herself. But I didn't come home to talk about Millie. I came to talk about you. You don't really mean that you're going to St. Louis and leave Ken to shift for himself?"

"Why doesn't he come with me, then?" Lola evaded.

"It isn't a man's place," Mrs. Davis declared, "to go trapesing all over the country because his wife changes her job. You know it isn't, Lola Hayes! What do you expect him to do while you're gone? How long will you be gone, anyway?"

Lola said, "I don't know." She didn't. She knew however that Jameson considered that the job might be permanent.

She said, trying to believe it: "Ken will join me. He's pretty sore at me now. But he'll get over it."

"He's working here," her mother reminded her.

"That job doesn't matter."

"After all the trouble your father went to? Lola, jobs aren't to be picked up in the street. Ken might get to St. Louis and not find anything to do."

"That's happened right here," Lola reminded her, in her turn.

"I don't like it," said Mrs. Davis helplessly, "I don't like it at all."

Her eyes filled. Lola put her arm about her.

"Please don't. Here, take my handkerchief. Tell me

about Millie and the picture she's working on. Is she well? Happy?"

Mrs. Davis talked about Millie the rest of the way home. "She sent you a letter. I have it . . . here. Where is it? I'm sure I put it in my handbag!"

She searched frantically and finally produced Millie's letter and put it into Lola's hands. She had said: "Millie, you write her . . . try and persuade her not to be so foolish." But Millie had written something else.

"If you don't care for Ken," wrote Millie, "and are set on getting away from him, this is as easy a way out as any other, I suppose. I take it you've thought it over. I'd like to tell you to come on out to me and break into the pictures. You're good-looking and carry yourself well, you have a swell figure and a good speaking voice. But it isn't as easy as it used to be. They're getting a lot of their material from the stage, hiring people who have some sort of experience. I tell you it's no joke. In the days of the silent pictures it was hard enough, but not as hard as now. So many of the old stars, who seemed pretty fixed, are falling and falling hard. Hollywood is overrun with stage people. I can't see yet how I got the breaks. But it happens now and then. And even if you did come and made the grade you mightn't find it worked out, very long. I suppose you have too many principles. You couldn't *yes* them. You couldn't be nice to people you hated, some of them. I can be. I don't care about anything but getting ahead or at the very least staying where I am now. So I can be nice. Darned nice. Yes, Mr. So-and-So; of course, Mr. Somebody-Else; just as you say, brother! I don't mean that I've lost my virtue. I haven't, if that's what you're thinking. It isn't, you know, absolutely necessary. But I've learned to skate on thin ice. You'd never learn, Lola."

At home, after Howard's noisy greetings, which he tried so hard to make casual, and couldn't quite, Mrs. Davis shooed him out of the room and regarded her daughter and son-in-law gravely.

"I want to talk to you. Ken, do you approve of Lola's going to St. Louis?"

"I haven't," Ken answered sullenly, "anything to say about it. She doesn't care whether I approve or not."

"I *knew* you didn't!" Mrs. Davis said exultantly. "It's all nonsense! Tell her she can't go! I have no control of her any more, she's married; I'm only her mother. But you are her husband."

"Hardly that," Ken modified smoothly. Mrs. Davis looked at him, puzzled. Lola raised her hand in a gesture of hopelessness and dropped it to her lap.

"I mean," Ken went on, "I haven't any control over her either. Being a girl's husband nowadays gives a fellow damned few rights."

"Marriage is marriage," said Mrs. Davis severely.

Lola said wearily: "Mother—please—we aren't getting anywhere. I've asked Ken if he'd come with me and make our home out there, where my work will be. He won't. He thinks more of his man's pride than he does of me, that's all. But he only remembers it at times convenient to him. Other times, he doesn't care."

Ken said furiously: "Speak up, can't you? No use talking like a cross-word puzzle. You mean that I lolled about at home and didn't break my neck looking for a job and let you support me? Well, that was true enough. I might as well have the game as the name, I thought. Most fellows don't like their wives working; after a while they get used to it; then, maybe, they count on it some. Who's to blame? Answer that!"

Lola did not reply. Mrs. Davis said, after a moment:

"Ken's right, in a way, Lola."

Lola jumped to her feet. "Everyone," she said, "seems to be against me. It isn't like you," she cried childishly, turning on her mother, "to take Ken's part that way."

"It's only what I think right, dear," her mother said. She added: "Children—isn't there some way you can settle this without everyone getting angry and without fighting and everything?"

She seemed younger than both of them, in that moment. Ken replied, evenly:

"There's one way of course. Lola can get a divorce—"

"*Ken!*" That was Mrs. Davis, going white. "Ken," she said. "Lola . . . Divorce? with her upbringing? her principles? Are you out of your mind?"

Lola asked, a little wildly:

"Do you hate me that much, Ken?"

"I don't hate you." His gray eyes met hers intently. "I love you. Dammit, you know that. But what other way out is there?"

Lola said nothing. Peter Acton talked of divorce— but that didn't matter; he had been divorced before, he took such things casually. She didn't. When Acton spoke of divorce in connection with herself, it hadn't sounded real. But this was Ken speaking.

She said dully, "I married to have it last."

"Of course you did," her mother said hastily. "Ken didn't mean that. Did you, Ken? He was angry . . . worried. Lola, give up this crazy idea. . . . You must."

She was going to cry. She mustn't cry. I can't, said Lola to herself. She turned and ran out of the room and upstairs, colliding with Howard on the way, murmuring something, anything, from a throat which was choking. She held her hand to it. "Jehoshaphat!" murmured Howard, looking after her.

She reached her room. Flung herself across the bed. Downstairs her mother looked at Ken. Ken flushed, shuffled his feet uneasily. "You've upset her," Mrs. Davis told him unnecessarily, and with severity. She went over to where he was sitting, hands lax between his knees. She touched him on the shoulder. "Go upstairs, Ken," urged Mrs. Davis, "and make it up with her. There's a good boy."

"Oh, all right," he said, after a moment. He rose, hands thrust now into his pockets and looked down at his mother-in-law. He liked her. She was a peach. But she didn't understand. This that was between Lola and himself went deeper somehow than jobs and St. Louis and talk of divorce.

He turned and went from the room. Mrs. Davis sat down in a chair limply. She said to herself: It will be all right now. Children . . . ! She smiled. Howard came in, tiptoeing exaggeratedly. "Hey, ma, what's up?" he began. "I met Lola on the stairs. She all but knocked me down. Now I meet Ken at the door. He knocks me down too. What do they think I am?" grumbled Howard, "one of those what-you-may-call-it toys—hit it a kick and it bobs up again?"

"Don't be silly. They were in a hurry—"

"I'll say they were!" Howard agreed, heartily.

"Come here. Sit down. Millie sent some of her new pictures. I want to show you Millie's little apartment," began Mrs. Davis cozily.

Howard resigned himself to an evening of Millie.

Upstairs, Ken sat on the edge of the bed and tried to draw Lola into his arms.

"I'm sorry. I didn't mean that. About divorce. Of course I didn't. Please forgive me, Lola."

She permitted herself to be taken into his embrace.

It was comforting, it was safe, it was something so far removed from these last weeks of torture and hurt and anger and indecision. She said, sighing, her heart heavy:

"I won't go to St. Louis, Ken."

"You won't? Say, that's great! That's my own girl—" He broke off.

She said anxiously, her heart curiously empty and yet clouded with melancholy: "What's the matter, Ken? What do you want now?"

"I want you to go," he answered incredibly.

She sat up in the circle of his arms. Pushed back the heavy, curling hair from her wet eyes. She said, flushing, eyes burning with eagerness, with hope—

"You mean you'll come with me? Oh, Ken, that would be wonderful!"

He stared at her.

"No, I didn't mean that," he began uncomfortably. A half-sob escaped her. All the newly awakened radiance left her face. He said urgently: "See, it means that much to you, doesn't it? Look here, Lola. We've been going at this wrong. I won't come. You know why not. But you needn't stay here. I'm not going to spend the rest of my life having you tell me how much you gave up . . . on my account."

"I wouldn't, I wouldn't ever," she told him, hurt. She thought of what Acton had said. Funny—she thought further, irrelevantly—how men's minds work alike. The minds of quite different types of men even. Acton had said that she would only make Ken miserable by reminding him what she had sacrificed. Even if she didn't remind him. And Ken was saying it now.

"I know you wouldn't, perhaps. Except when we had a row or something; or things didn't go right. Or you were tired. But if you never opened your head to me

about it again, I'd *know*. You said to me, this was your
chance. All right, Lola. Take it. I won't stand in your
way."

"Oh, oh," she gasped, trying to break through the wall
of what she considered his misunderstanding, "you can't
see . . . you don't understand. I don't want to go without you, Ken."

He said stubbornly: "You'll have to. You go. I'll
stay here. It will be all right. I'll make out."

Perhaps he was unconsciously wistful; perhaps not. In
that moment she loved him terribly and hated him cruelly
for making her feel as she was forced to feel—hard, selfish,
demanding . . . the person at fault, the one on whose
shoulders the onus of all blame must rest.

She drew away from him. Out on the river a great boat
whistled, a deep, eery sound. Someone was laughing
down in the street. She said:

"You make me feel—rotten. Putting it up to me. All
of it. But where does it get us, Ken?"

"Here." He took her back again, her head against his
shoulder. "I'm not very good at explaining things. But
everything's been wrong somehow. We've been living,
like you said once, under each other's feet. Haven't we?
Too close. And maybe too far away. I don't know.
Perhaps if we do separate for a while, like this, we'll see
clearer. See what's important. Damned if I know what's
important now. I don't want to go on living the way
we have been living, any more than you do, Lola. Take
the job. I'll stay here. Maybe we can find out what's
wrong and what matters. We won't be all sort of cluttered up with each other. You see," said Ken, trying so
hard to find the words, "I get sore and ugly; and you get
peeved and tired. And then we make up. And I kiss you
and I forget all that's happened. And it isn't fair. I

mean afterwards—we are just where we were before. We haven't cleaned up anything. I can't see us going on forever quarreling about things . . . and making up. There must be more to it than that. There's *got* to be if it means anything . . . our marriage, I mean. So— perhaps if we aren't together for a while . . ."

She spoke, after a long pause:

"I understand. I didn't think you did. Ken, will you promise me something? Will you promise me that—if things go wrong here—and you need me, you'll come out —to St. Louis?" she asked.

"I don't know. Perhaps. I'd rather," said Ken, "that you came back. If you found you needed me. That we needed each other. If you found out what matters most, after all. If you don't, well, we can make it permanent and unanimous after a while, I guess," he told her.

She told him, holding him with her small, strong hands:

"It all comes back to this: your pride or whatever it is. You won't give me a promise. But you'll ask *me* to give one. I have to be the one to go; and the one to come back. Isn't that right?"

"I suppose so. I will promise, though," he told her, his cheek against the silky, fragrant hair. "I will. I promise I'll come out. If I can't stand it. But it will be to bring you back. I won't come out to loaf around and let you feed me while I beat the pavements for jobs. I'll make good here first," said Ken. "God, I've *got* to make good!"

It was after all a sort of compromise. She sighed. She said, "All right, Ken."

Later they went downstairs and told Mrs. Davis that it was all right; but drowned her complacent joy in consternation by explaining. Lola must have her way. And

Ken would have his. A temporary separation, then, in order to think things over.

Mrs. Davis shook her head; added to her arguments. It was late that night when she said, surrendering and beaten:

"I haven't any call to tell you what to do or what not to do. When your father hears this, Lola, I don't know what he'll say. Ken, you'll live on here, with us?"

"No, Mother Davis." He smiled at her. "No, Jake's got a place of his own now. A room. I'll bunk in with him. He wants me to."

Lola thought: He's been talking this over . . . with Jake. With Garry perhaps. And others. She was amazed at the dart of anger which went through her. She told herself: Not that it matters. I talked it over with Agnes and Connie, didn't I? And with Peter. Fifty-fifty, said Lola to herself, trying to believe it. Sauce for the goose, sauce for the gander—

Ken was saying, over Mrs. Davis's expostulations.

"But I'll come around often. You know I will. And I'll expect to get a free meal now and then. Don't think you're rid of me that easily. Not with the sort of pie you make!"

"But why won't you?" began Mrs. Davis.

"I can't, Mother Davis. Better this way."

Wild horses couldn't have dragged from him the public admission that he could not endure to be in the Davis house, with Lola gone, could not bear alone the room which they had shared together.

But upstairs he said something of this to Lola, awkwardly, anxiously.

"I hope I didn't hurt her. Get her sore at me. But it would be pretty damned hard, Lola, with you not here. Better I go with Jake. We'll make out."

"Of course," she agreed, "if you'd rather. But you'll eat crazy things and drink too much and catch cold. . . . Oh, Ken."

She hadn't thought of those things before. Of such possibilities of disaster. Or rather she had thought of them all along during their life together in a mechanical, routine, irritable, responsible sort of way. Now that she would no longer be able to urge, nag, advise, beg, she thought of them clearly, as detached from herself, as possibilities out of her reach to remedy.

"I'll be all right," he said again. "Don't you worry. Think of yourself. You'll have to. You won't have me to crab about rubbers and ice-cream-cone lunches and working too hard, you know."

Before she slept, she said: "I have your promise? I didn't ask you to promise anything else. About other women."

He told her: "No one matters but you, Lola. I haven't asked you anything about—other men. You'll meet men. I'd rather not think about it."

They left it at that. During the rest of her time at home, during the feverish, hectic time of saying good-by to people, of packing, of getting Jenny Jones, whom she knew slightly, over to meet the family and of planning with her what they would do and how manage—for they had decided, wisely enough, to manage together—during the time of getting the office straightened out and of trying to straighten herself out, she and Ken were outwardly on excellent terms. Not only outwardly. They were loving each other, secretly; afraid to say how much; afraid of what was ahead; afraid of sorrow; afraid of everything. But they were walking delicately as Agag, as carefully as strangers. Trying to make a joke of it. Trying to make it all natural and right and expected.

Trying to keep on keeping on. "It's just," they told people, "temporary separation." "I'll be going out and fetching her home again, soon," Ken told his skeptical friends. "Ken will join me, after a while," Lola told hers.

"I'd a darned sight rather not go to the station with you," he told her, when the time approached.

"Ken, *please!* What will people say?"

"Well, have it your own way," he said.

Acton phoned her, "Shall I come see you off?"

"Please, no! What will people say?" she found herself asking again.

"It's not what they'll say but what they'll think! You don't want me then?"

"I'd rather not. You see, my family—" she slurred and hesitated.

"I understand," said Acton.

He sent over a medley of books. Books in gay wrappers, stuck in a charming suède bag with handles. A cushion, also in suède, for her head. Candy. Nuts. Giddy foreign magazines, all packed in the suède bag and tied with ribbons. His card attached.

Ken said, "Must have set him back something!"

In a way he was glad she was going after all. Acton, thought Ken, would have to quit hanging around and would forget her. Or would he? Could a man, once having known her, forget her? Ken thought not. He glowered at the books and the candy and the ribbons.

At the station they crowded around her. Connie and Louis; Agnes; her mother, Howard, and some of the people from the office—"seeing the gang off." Ken stood a little to one side. He thought: Pretty picture I'm making! He wondered: Are they laughing at me? He thought: They probably are, and dammit, I don't blame them!

She kissed him. "I'll wire when I have an address. You have the office address all right?"

"Sure—"

"Ken, you promised . . ."

"You, too, baby," he said.

"I know." She whispered, "I do love you, Ken."

He kissed her briefly, but hard. A hard pressure. Enough. Couldn't say more now. They'd said good-by, last night. She'd cried in his arms. "Good-by," he said gruffly. "Don't take any wooden money."

The train pulled out.

Jenny, red-headed, straight, and slim, was chattering. Jenny's folks had come to see her off. All she had. A married sister and her husband. Jenny said: "Gee, isn't it exciting? What do you suppose St. Louis will be like anyway, Lola?" Jenny's eyes were big as saucers. St. Louis from Jenny's expression might have been peopled with Indians. Lola said, "I don't know, Jenny."

Jenny shot her a shrewd brown-eyed look.

"Feeling pretty low? You'll feel better when we get settled. I hear there's work to be done," said Jenny, with mock melodrama. "Nice of Mr. Jameson to find us that place to live. When we get our bearings maybe we could get a little apartment or something. I'd like that. I'm a good cook," said Jenny. "And say, Lola, I know a fellow in St. Louis. An automobile salesman. I met him when he was up for the auto show. I'll give him a buzz. Gee, won't he fall over backwards when he finds I'm in his town? He'll take us out."

Lola said mechanically, "I won't feel much like going out."

"Gosh, you can't live like a nun!" said Jenny in frank

astonishment. "About the apartment. It would be nice, wouldn't it? And if Ken came to see you? You don't mind if I call him Ken? Gee, Lola, he's a knockout. You must be pretty darned sure of yourself to leave *that* all alone and unguarded in a big city!" Jenny rattled on.

Lola closed her eyes and leaned back against the hot plush of the seat. Ken? Ken, who wouldn't eat right and who'd drink too much, perhaps, and who was careless about bare feet and overcoats and catching cold. Her heart felt as if a tight band were around it. A band which, strangely enough, constricted her throat.

"All right?" asked Jameson, stopping beside them.

"Fine," said Jenny, "just dandy, Mr. Jameson."

Lola smiled. "All right," she said.

Wonder if Mr. Jameson's wife minded his going away? But she was in Europe. And by the time he got back again for good, she'd be home. Anyway, wives didn't have much to say. Not wives who didn't have to take care of themselves.

Twice on the trip she had wires from Acton. Silly wires, cheerful and amusing. "Ken?" asked Jenny. "Well, of course," lied Lola, folding the yellow slips and tucking them into her bag.

She couldn't sleep. The train rolled a little. Everything creaked. She lay in the upper berth and listened to Jenny, sleeping audibly in the lower. Everyone seemed to sleep audibly on trains. Her sheets were right and her pillows, and the berth was comfortable. The car gave to the speed of the engine. Cinders rattled on the roof. They whistled, going over a trestle or something. She wished she had taken the lower berth after all. She would have liked to look out of a window at the houses they passed, at the stretches of country wrapped in sleep. Cinders rattled again; the whole car creaked. More whistles. They were slowing up—they were entering a station. People were running along the platform. She heard voices. It was lonely and strange to her. She looked out into the car at the swinging green curtains before the berths. The porter passed by in his white coat. Lola lay down again.

No, she couldn't sleep. Ken? She was frightened. Why had she come? How had she dared? But it was her chance. Her *chance*. She must hold on to that. Presently she slept, wet cheek against the pillow.

Mr. Jameson took them to the boarding-house. A pleasant one, on a side street, with a German landlady who, obese and friendly and accented, made them welcome and showed them their second-story room, with windows on the back, showed them proudly the twin beds and the shiny new furniture. It was, she said, her best room.

"*Sehr gemütlich, nicht?*" inquired the landlady. "Comfortable, ain't?"

They agreed with her, and went about their unpacking. Tidies on the chairs. Little china ornaments on dresser and bureau. Plush. Everything spotless. The counterpanes, heavy, with knitted lace. Bolsters.

One of the clerks whom Jameson had brought with him and who was also living at the boarding-house took them to the office the next day. He had come from St. Louis originally. Happy-go-lucky town, he said.

The office was housed in a great business building of noble proportions. Lola said to Jenny, "I'll be glad to get to work."

In a week she knew her way around. In a week she had accustomed herself to the heavy, hearty breakfasts and dinners, to a drug-store lunch. It wasn't after all so different from any other city. In a week she had had five letters from her mother, a postal from Howard, a wire from Millie, an air-mail note from her father, and two short letters from Ken. "I'm all right," said Ken. "I miss you like the devil."

In two weeks she had been to a number of the many parks. She had been to the movies with Jenny, her automobile salesman, and a friend of his. She had spent a Saturday afternoon alone, exploring the old Walnut Street cathedral, wandering through the Broadway courthouse to look at the frescoes by Wimar. She had gone to a matinée by herself, she had walked along the narrow streets of the old French settlement, and had begun to know something of the town.

During her third week Ken wrote her that he had given up his job and gone to work in a garage. He'd seen, he added, her father, who had just returned.

Ken in a garage? She couldn't imagine it. She said so. She wrote him by air mail. "I can't understand it," she said.

He replied that he was, as she knew, a good mechanic. He wanted to be better. He was taking a night course. He and Jake had big schemes. Jake was dickering with someone to get hold of a gasoline station near Fourth Avenue. He wanted to go in with him. "I want," wrote Ken, more truly than he knew, "to be my own boss. Nothing in this working for another fellow. If I can get some money saved and go in, after a while, as partner, it will be swell."

No word of coming out. No word to urge her back. He wrote a poor letter. Slangy and expressive enough, yet it told her very little. She wrote to her mother. "Is Ken all right?" she wanted to know. And Mrs. Davis replied: "Yes. We don't see much of Ken any more, though."

Connie, writing, didn't either. She'd had him up to dinner once. All he could talk about was cars and the gas station.

Lola had been away for four weeks, and the office was sufficiently organized to permit Jameson to return to New York—planning to come out for several days every other week for a time and leaving the force in the capable hands of a younger man, Mannering—when Acton arrived, without heralding.

He came straight to the office.

"Lafayette, we are here!" he announced.

She was glad to see him; gladder than she had realized she could be. She jumped to her feet and gave him both hands. "Peter!" she cried astonished.

"In person. When do you close?"

She looked at the clock. "Half an hour."

"I'll go to my hotel and clean up. Where are you staying?"

She told him. He wrote down the address. "I'll pick you up about six," he told her.

He was there for a brief week-end. He said, the second evening that they dined together:

"Like it as much as you thought you would?"

"Better. I've more work to do," she confessed. "Mr. Mannering lets me run the office pretty much, you know. Yes, I like it."

"Lola"—he leaned across the table—"Lola, aren't you about ready to give it up and listen to me?"

"I do listen to you. Most of the time," she told him, laughing.

"You know what I mean. I am beginning to think," said Acton, "that I am wasting my time. Look here, Lola. In the early spring I have a chance to go along as excess baggage on an expedition into Tibet. I'm helping finance it. And if I can make myself useful, they'll take me with them. It's up to you whether I go or stay."

"How long," she asked, startled, "would you be gone?"

"A couple of years. I'm fed up with doing nothing. I'm . . . If you say the wrong word—I'll resign from all the boards and directorships and start out to look at nature in the very raw. If you say the right word, I'll stay on here," he told her.

She shook her head. "I don't love you, Peter."

"You would. I swear you would! I'd make you. I'd make you happy," he told her eagerly, blue eyes on her eyes, lean face intent.

"I don't," said Lola, "think much about happiness, any more."

She missed him when he went back. But was relieved to have him go. Gradually she was making contacts. Jenny's automobile salesman, Frank Lansing, took it upon himself to show the girls the town, and to introduce them to his particular circle. Frank, who was an artist *manqué*, had made his friends in circles allegedly "artistic." Through him Lola met a number of people, very different in type from the people she had known. She was busy every moment of the day, and Jenny was having the time of her life. She was glad, once the wrench was over, to be away from "the folks."

"Mary kept too eagle an eye on me," she told Lola. "Not that I was doing anything I shouldn't. But if she'd looked long enough I might have, out of stubbornness. I like this town. It has it all over New York. Easy-going. Doesn't give a darn. Doesn't mind if Cleveland grows faster. Likes itself the way it is. I'm glad I came," said Jenny.

After Christmas they moved to a small apartment. Lola didn't like to think about Christmas. There were wires from home, boxes of presents, letters; and she and Jenny and Lansing shared the tree of friends of his. But it was a dismal season just the same. She was glad to plunge into flat-hunting and finding.

They took a furnished apartment, and in February Mrs. Davis wrote her that Ken was very sick.

Chapter XIII

"I've got to go home," Lola told Jenny, rather white.

She explained. Jenny pursed her lip-sticked mouth to a rosy whistle.

"Of course. I'll bet you're all hot and bothered. Don't worry so. He'll be all right. You know how men are. Think they're dying if they cut their finger. Goin' to ask Mannering to let you off?"

"I'll have to," said Lola.

She couldn't stay. She couldn't work; and not know the truth. Ken? He belonged to her. "Ken very sick," wrote her mother; "they are afraid of pneumonia."

She spoke to Mannering, a prematurely gray, aggressively slender, and rather nervous man. Mannering, with a troubled frown for the work piled up on his desk, had a smile for her. "Why, of course, Mrs. Hayes. I hope it isn't anything serious. I'm sure it won't be. Go, by all means, and get back to us when you can." He didn't say, "as soon as you can." But he meant it. Why did all the good secretaries get married, and either quit or keep on? One, he mused gloomily, was as bad as another. Something wrong with economic conditions. Coolidge prosperity, Hoover Hope, everything, didn't seem to matter. Richest country in the world. Highest wages and all that sort of thing. Yet the young women went out to work. Married, and kept on going out to work. Something wrong somewhere. Still, they had to. You couldn't get around that, Mannering agreed glumly.

Lola wired her mother and took the first train out. Ar-
236

riving home, she thrust the taxi money into the driver's hands and ran up the steps. Her mother opened the door. "Lola! We didn't look for you so soon."

"Ken? How is he—where is he?"

She was frantic, her eyes dark with terror. Her mother said comfortably:

"He's better. Out of danger, they say, if he's careful. If they'd tried my onion poultice in the beginning we wouldn't have had any of this fret and bother! But they wouldn't. New-fangled! Yes, he's better, Lola. Where is he? Why, in his room of course. I go over, twice a day. The landlady looks after him meantime. Dr. Carr said if he were worse he'd have to go to a hospital. I said, hospital nothing, I'd bring him here. I don't believe in hospitals."

Just inside the hall, her hat and coat still on, her bag clutched in her hand, Lola demanded:

"Why isn't he here now? Why didn't you bring him here in the first place?"

"Easy does it," advised her mother. "At the start he had a cold. Just a naggy sort of cold. Looked peaked. But we didn't think it would amount to anything. Then when he got really sick he wouldn't come. I couldn't bring him against his will. Not till he got delirious and too sick to know, anyway. And he didn't get that bad."

She added: "Lola, you look white. Let me fix you a cup of tea."

"I'm going to see Ken," Lola said, "right away."

Her mother sighed, shrugged and nodded.

"All right. We'll expect you back to supper. Your father wants to see you, Lola."

Lola went out and walked rapidly in the crisp February air the ten blocks or so that brought her to the brick rooming-house on a small side street off Fourth Avenue.

She rang. It seemed incredible, going to see Ken. As a stranger might. In a strange house. The landlady, spare, with a wild pepper-and-salt coiffure, let her in and listened to her explanations, listened, it seemed, disapprovingly. She volunteered, leading the way: "It's high time someone looked after him."

Lola climbed the stairs. The house was dark, but as far as she could see scrupulously clean. But not cheerful. Decidedly not cheerful.

"My mother——" said Lola, "she comes every day. She wanted to move him to our—her—house."

She was uncomfortably aware that she said it defiantly.

"That's as may be," said the landlady cryptically.

She knocked on a door on the third floor. She opened the door, said, "Your wife to see you," with a flourish as of trumpets. She left the door open. And lingered.

Lola stepped in and shut the door. Ken said, feebly . . . "*Well!*"

She ran across the room. Two cots, two bureaus, two chairs. Clean. Little curtains. Her picture on one bureau.

Ken, on one cot. He was gaunt. He was blue about the jaw, with that unshaven look which makes a well man look ill. His temperature having left him he was gray-white and shaky. He smiled at her as she leaned to kiss him, to take him in her slender arms, and cry—"Ken, Ken, you're *sure* you're all right?"

"I'm fine. Gee, it was great of you to come!" he said. "Sure, I'm all right. Jake looks after me. And Mrs. Bronson. And Mother Davis. She's here a lot, brings swell chicken soup and custards. Sure, I'm all right. You shouldn't have come, Lola."

"I couldn't help it. I was so worried," she said.

"You needn't be. Can't kill me. Only the good die young. Only," he added, "the young die good."

"Ken, why won't you let them move you to mother's?"

"Not on your life! Fine guy I'd be! She has enough to do. I'll be up in a few days. Out in a week. I—they're keeping my job for me. I like it, Lola." He regarded his big, thin hands. "Should have seen *these* a little while ago! Couldn't get the grease off 'em. Bleached out now some."

He talked about his job. His face flushed, darkly. She asked anxiously, going to the washstand and soaking a towel in water and sponging his face and hands, "Should you be talking so much, Ken?"

"You talk then. All about St. Louis. Letters are all right. I love to get yours, Lola. But talking's better."

She sat in a low chair, his hand in her own. She told him about the boarding-house. The German food. The office. The city. The parks. He asked:

"Hope you don't mope in the boarding-house all day? You do get out, don't you?"

"With Jenny," she said evasively. Yet an unconscious evasion.

She made no mention of Acton's visit. It stuck in her throat like a fishbone, she thought, in homely simile. But she couldn't help it. She couldn't tell him. He'd hate it.

The doctor came in, rubbing his hands. "How's the boy today?" he wanted to know, looking down from a height of six feet.

Lola made herself known. The doctor said, regarding her with a masculine admiration tempered with a masculine disapproval:

"It was, you know, nip and tuck. Looked as if we'd get a neat little lobar pneumonia out of it. But we didn't.

Still I wanted to send for you. I hadn't," he explained, "known at first that my patient here was married."

"Pretty much so," said Ken, essaying a grin. "Here's the little old ball and chain to prove it."

The doctor said to Lola, "You're staying on, of course?"

She answered haltingly: "No, I think not. That is, I can't. I'm working, you know, in St. Louis."

"She commutes," offered Ken hastily.

The doctor raised an eyebrow.

"If, as you say, there's no danger now?" Lola asked him.

"No." He was short with her, markedly so, "No, not if he behaves himself."

Presently he was gone, leaving a new prescription, diet dictated, heart and lungs gone over, temperature taken. "He's a fine guy," said Ken to Lola as the door closed. "He pulled me through great." He seemed to be explaining the older man, apologizing for his attitude.

Lola said absently, "He seems to be a good doctor."

She hadn't realized it would be like this; the pull, the wrench; the fear. She hadn't known how it would all come home to her. Of course, during the time she had been away she had known longing and had cried herself to sleep many nights, out of sheer weakness, out of a normal desire for Ken's arms around her, his mouth upon her own; for the escape from reality which their young healthy passion promised and provided; for the sheer physical comfort of his physical nearness. Many nights, many days. But this was different . . . the actuality of fear. She'd said, she'd thought—*if he should be ill?* And now he was ill. She remembered how she had felt when she saw him for herself, reassured as to his peril but sick with pity to see him looking so ill, so entirely wretched. She thought, angry at herself, but admitting her frailty: I can't go through with this. She thought: Tonight, before I go back, perhaps I'll tell him. I can't go through with it. I'll resign. I'll go back and clean things up and help Jenny find someone to share the flat with her. And I'll come home. I'll hate it, in lots of ways. But I'll have to.

Ken was talking. She listened, answering. But all the time her mind spun around in foolish circles. She'd have to give it up. Not eagerly, but rebelliously. For nothing was really settled between them. And yet—how could she give it up? How was it possible that Ken could support her on the wages of an unseasoned mechanic? He could not. Give up St. Louis and then try and get another job? Perhaps they'd have room for her at the home office. Jameson might find her something. It would be then as it always had been. Was that good enough?

Toward evening, her mother plodded, puffing, up the stairs and came in with a basket covered with a napkin. There were soups in it, jellies, junkets.

"Ken's supper," she explained. "Run along home, Lola, and have yours and see dad and Howard. I'll spell you for a while. You can come back afterwards."

Lola obeyed docilely. She kissed Ken. "I'll be back soon," she said. His eyes followed her little slim back to the door, hungry, wistful. She turned there and smiled at him and her mother. The door closed. "She hasn't changed," he said aloud, in some amazement. What, he wondered, had he expected?

"Well, no, why should she, a grown woman?" Mrs. Davis was busy heating the soup on the little canned-heat apparatus she had bought for such emergencies. "Let me shake up your pillows and wash your face and hands— There. Feel better?"

"Why do women always want to wash your face and hands? Wish you'd shave me, Mother Davis," said Ken.

"Well, why not? I'll bet I could. Dad could anyway. Here, you've got to eat. Nourishment. That's half the battle in a case like yours," she told him briskly.

Lola at home was talking to Howard, playing with her food, and listening to her father. He had a long speech to make. At the conclusion:

"And furthermore, my girl, I don't like it at all! It's downright unnatural. What's going to happen to you and Ken anyway? It can't go on like this. Your place is here."

"Woman's place is in the home," Howard intoned solemnly.

He seemed to Lola to have filled out, grown bigger, heavier, since she left. She said so, hastily, as her father shot his only son a lowering glance.

"That will be all from you, Mr. Wisecrack," said Davis. "Heaven knows you're never home, always hanging around that McCarthy kid."

"Well, well!" commented Lola. "Howard, the woman-hater? Not really."

"Aw," said Howard, and presently, unable to do more justice to the situation, slunk from the room.

Lola said evenly:

"I'm sorry you feel this way, father. If Ken had been willing to come with me things would have been different. This was my chance. I took it. I am getting a good salary, more responsibility and valuable experience. I couldn't pass it up. Ken wouldn't have either, had the chance come to him. And he would have expected me to go with him, no matter what my job was here, you know."

"That's entirely different," Davis declared.

"Oh, why?" She faced him defiantly; cheeks blazing.

"Why do you all say that? Different? Because I'm a woman? Because it's my job, a woman's job, and not a man's? That's unfair. Terribly unfair."

"Maybe, but it's true. Look here, Lola, think it over. Better stay on home, hadn't you? Ken"—he hesitated— "Ken, he's a good kid. He didn't like this business of your working. And then he got used to it and maybe you spoiled him a bit. I don't like some of his crowd. Jake's all right, a fine lad, hard-working, ambitious, and saving. Like to see Ken go in with him. Offered to help," said Davis uncomfortably. "We've got a bit put away you know, and Millie's always sending money home—not that we need it. But he wouldn't hear of it. Said he'd lived on the Davis family too long." He stopped suddenly.

"He said that?" asked Lola.

At her, that shot had been aimed. She knew it as well as her luckless father did. Her lips tightened. Ken was impossible. Putting the worst construction on everything. Wasn't a partnership in marriage attainable? Evidently not. She cooled down, thinking that Ken wasn't alone in putting such a construction upon their financial relationship. She had herself, when angry. Her father was answering her.

"Yes, he said just that; can't see's I blame him. But he needn't be so blamed stubborn. This Garrison, now, he don't see him much any more. But still and all, Ken misses you, Lola. He's lonesome. Hard for a fellow in his position to fill up time. Can't sit home with a book every night. He has been taking night courses too, you know. But he's free, some evenings. We get him here as much as we can. Not often though. He's restless here. Don't seem to be happy. I can understand that. Funny position for him to be in, Lola," said her father on a long breath.   He had talked more this evening than he had in years.

She thought miserably, I'm making them all unhappy— Ken, mother, father.   Perhaps even Howard.   I don't know.

She said: "Isn't that a new picture of Millie?   I saw her last release the night it opened in St. Louis.   She was wonderful in it.   I was so proud.   I wanted to get right up and tell everybody, 'That's my sister . . . there, on the screen.' "

Her father said, distracted, and knowing he had been, but unable to do anything about it:

"Sure, that's the way I feel.   And your mother.   Seen the show six times, we have.   Got tickets to the opening in New York.   It was swell.   Lots of picture people there. I'd met some out in Hollywood.   Mother wanted me to buy a soup-and-fish for the occasion, but I've gotten along pretty well with blue serge all these years.   Millie's a great girl, Lola.   She works hard.   It's a dog's life, that's what it is.   I couldn't stand it.   Don't see how she can. Work all day and wait over to see the rushes from the day before," said Davis, conscious of his professional jargon and enjoying it.   "I was on the set quite a lot after they'd gotten through rehearsals.   Saw some of the scenes shot and the retakes, too.   Once she had to work nights.   Pretty hard on her.   But she's pretty as ever and full of pep— Say, that Lupe Velez girl hasn't a thing on our Millie for pep—and she's getting temperamental, too," concluded Lola's father, with odd satisfaction.

"Go on," said Lola in honest amusement.   "Not Millie! Or, at that, she always was, around home."

"Wait a minute!   Round home she was because she didn't have anything to do with her temperament," her father explained, shrewdly. "Now, she puts it to work and she'll be drawing a thousand a week pretty darned quick, I betcher. But this temperament business about the studio—that's what it is—*business*. Pure and simple. She throws a couple of fits, but her mind keeps working on all six. And she gets what she wants. She's going to buy a bungalow, she writes me. Investment. Wants us to come out there again sometime," he added wistfully. "I'd like to stay there always. But I'm not old enough to quit my job and too old to find another one. Besides," said Davis, with deep, parental, rather tragic wisdom, "she's better off without me and your mother fussing and nagging at her. Better off to stand on her own feet."

Lola said: "Of course. Then why shouldn't I be?"

Davis looked at her. He pushed away his big coffee-cup and lit his pipe slowly. He said quietly:

"I got that all right, Lola. But it's different. Millie belongs to herself. You're married."

Lola rose and started to clear the table. "Did mother have anything to eat before she went to Ken's?" she asked.

"Yes. . . . It's my night for bowling," said Mr. Davis, "but if you'd like me to stay home?"

"No, run along. I won't be gone till tomorrow. I'll see you in the morning." She straightened his tie and kissed the top of his head. "It's good to see you," she told him.

"That goes for me too. I've missed you. Missed both my girls. But," said Davis, "that's life, I guess. Tell Ken I'll run in to see him sometime tomorrow."

Lola washed up. Howard had long since disappeared. She heard her father leave the house. She was quite alone in it. Her mother, she thought, had a key. She would lock up. But Howard returned before she left and was hanging around the street, his breath smoking in the bitter wind . . . "Going to see Ken, sis?" he called.

"Yes . . . right away."

"All the same to you if Bill and I come in and practice on his saxophone?" asked Howard anxiously. "Seems like we always have to do it when there's nobody home."

She left him and Bill emitting sounds of brazen agony in the living-room and picked up a taxi to drive her to Ken's. Arrived, she told the driver to wait. She went in and upstairs after the landlady had grudgingly opened to her, and found her mother placidly beside Ken, reading the Brooklyn *Daily Eagle* to him. "Well, I never! Did you ever hear anything like that?" asked Mrs. Davis of her listener, eyes popped over a particularly classic murder. Ken agreed, his own gaze on the door. "Time Lola came, isn't it?" he would ask every three minutes, trying to appear casual. "Here she is now!" he said on the heels of one such question.

Mrs. Davis rose. Lola put money in her hands. "Here, the taxi is waiting. It's slippery out, and awfully dark. You mustn't walk. I'll be back soon. Where's Jake?"

"He knew I'd be taken care of this evening," answered Ken. "He's gone to his sisters'. Back later. Thanks, Mother Davis. Good night."

Mrs. Davis was gathering her dishes and muttering about the extravagance of taxis.

"Father's gone out to bowl," Lola told her, "and Howard and Bill are doing saxophone scales in the house."

"Good land," said Mrs. Davis. "I'll get right along home and stop that before we have the neighbors and the police on the porch."

When she had gone, Ken said: "I'm glad you came

back. But you look tired. You must go home and get some sleep."

Funny to go "home." And leave Ken here. The strangeness of it took her by the throat. Better, after all, to give in; at least part way. To explain; I can't give up working altogether, Ken. Not till you get on your feet. But—I'll come back and get a job in the home office, or somewhere.

She said, rather timidly, "Ken, if you need money . . ."

His face darkened perceptibly. "Thanks a lot. I don't. I'd rather you didn't offer it, Lola."

You and your pride! thought Lola.

The door opened. Garry, spick and span in a gray suit and a woolly overcoat; Amy in black, with fox fur and a bright red hat; and a blond girl.

Shirley Smith.

They exclaimed. "Lola!" cried the Garrisons. Now Amy was kissing her. "Why, Lola, I had no idea you'd come back!" Garry was shaking hands with himself in the idiotic fashion he had, thinking he was better at it than Jack Oakie and being much mistaken. The blond girl's mouth was drooping but she was saying primly, "I've had the pleasure."

Then they had gone over to Ken's bed. "Hello, folks," said Ken uneasily.

"You old turkey!" Garry was saying. "Jake told us the doc said you could have visitors. You look like the devil, by the way."

"All my fault," remarked the blond girl, sitting on the edge of the bed. She wore a thick white coat, with a white fur collar. She wore a white hat banded with black in modernistic patterns. Her dress was sheer and black; her stockings sheer and beige. She had stilt heels, for walking in the snow, perhaps, rather run over. Her face was perfectly white under a mask of liquid powder. Her mouth was a curved red dash, for punctuation. Her lids were shadowed with blue and her eyelashes extravagantly curled and thickened with black mascaro. She repeated, "All my fault, poor darling!"

"Don't be silly, Shirley," said Ken. But Shirley went on being silly. Or, wasn't she? She flicked a blue look at Lola, standing with Amy at the foot of the bed. She said: "We danced so hard . . . and so much—and I made you go out on the porch for air. And it was freezing!"

"You don't catch cold that way," Garry announced. "It's a germ, that's what it is. A form of infection," he finished solemnly.

"Well, he didn't catch it from me, did he?" laughed Shirley. "Or"—she stopped and pouted gravely—"did he?"

Amy laughed.

Lola said, "I hadn't heard how he got it."

Shirley explained further:

"We were out on the Island, the four of us. That all-year-round-roadhouse place on the Merrick Road. We danced a lot. And Ken and I went out on the veranda to look at the moon. It had been snowing."

"I see," said Lola.

Ken didn't miss her so much. He could get pneumonia. Blond pneumonia. She thought: I've been a fool. Connie's right. Well, a man isn't worth keeping that begins to look over fences the moment you're out of sight. She thought: Do I look over fences? She acquitted herself: I can't help Peter thinking he loves me. I don't love him. I've told him so. I don't go hunting for moons on snow.

Garry was making warning faces at Shirley. Shirley was oblivious, powdering her nose. Amy was talking about St. Louis to Lola. "I knew a girl from there once . . ."

They made no motion toward leaving. Ken looked at Lola, in despair. She thought stubbornly, "It's his own fault." Amy said, finally, "We'd better step on it . . . the patient looks tired."

Good-bys. Smart cracks. "We'll come in often now and soon as you're well enough to crawl around we'll have dinner." And Shirley said:

"I'll come again, Ken. We've missed you."

They left. Outside the door they chattered . . . their voices diminished. Out in the car they'd come in, Garrison asked:

"What's the idea of spilling the beans like that and being all over Ken, Shirley? You're a prize idiot. With Lola there. You made him feel like hell."

"Well, why shouldn't I? He's given me something of a rush," Shirley defended herself.

"Don't be so damned innocent. You knew all along he was married!"

"Course I did. To what? To a sort of human type-writer and adding-machine who has jobs out west and runs home to see him when he's sick?"

"She wasn't," remarked Amy, "very crazy about seeing you with us. Or us, either, I guess."

"She's always been a high-hatter," commented Garrison. "Suppose it's because she has a sister in the movies. So have a lot of other people."

"Millie Davis is wonderful," said Shirley. "Funny Ken didn't pick her out instead of this Frigidaire!"

"She was just a kid then," Garrison reminded her.

"Maybe. But she'll always have too much sense to get married, I guess," Amy contributed.

"What do you mean by that dirty crack?"

"Nothing. By the way, darling, I paid your dentist's bill today. You owe me thirty-six dollars and don't forget it!"

"Fat chance with you around," said Garrison.

Inside, the room they had left was quiet. Ken said:

"I'm sorry they had to barge in like that, just now when we have so little time together, Lola."

"Oh, that's all right." She added, uncontrollably, against her will: "Did you get your cold that way, really? Out on the Island, I mean?"

"I don't think so. I already had a little head cold. Maybe it helped."

She said, "I thought you were taking night courses."

"I am. This was a Saturday night," he answered mechanically. "We motored down. Garry knows the man who runs it. The liquor is supposed to be good. Look here"—he regarded her, something in her tone reaching his ear belatedly, something in her attitude arresting his attention—"you aren't sore because I go out and dance now and then, are you?"

"No, why should I be?" She laughed, and touched his hand. "I don't expect you to sit home any more than you'd expect me to." She waited. He let that pass, although his eyebrows creased. She said lightly, "Shirley Smith seems to see a lot of the Garrisons."

He said, "Yes," abruptly. He added, with some violence: "I don't do anything that need worry you. But a guy's got to have some relaxation. I can't sit home with the *Saturday Evening Post* and your picture every night, you know—even if it is Saturday."

"Well, who said you should? And I'm not worried," denied Lola. She rose. "You were right, I'm tired. I'll go home to bed. I'll be in in the morning, just to say good-by."

She kissed him, her lips a little tight. He caught at her hands in an agony of tenderness and drew her close. . . . Lola . . . *Lola* . . .

She said, "Here . . . that's not good for temperature!" She disengaged herself, smoothed the sheets and patted the pillows. "Sure you'll be all right till Jake comes in?" she asked.

Ken indicated the bell by his pillow. "O. K.," he replied briefly.

At the door she turned. "Sleep well," she told him.

The door closed.

"Oh, yeah?" said Ken to himself. The room was thick with the perfume Shirley affected. Damn her anyway! No, that wasn't fair. She was a pretty, silly, soft little thing, always making up to him. Looked like a tart, but then a lot of girls did nowadays; and she was, he knew quite well, strictly virtuous, obeying the letter of the law if not the spirit. He liked kidding with her, dancing with her. Had kissed her once or twice. That was all. No deception about it. She knew he was married and in love, dammit, with his wife.

His wife.

He turned on his pillows. Lola would be leaving tomorrow. He had thought—had hoped, wildly—had watched her eyes and dared to hope—that perhaps she wouldn't go away. But she would. She always would.

"Jake?" he asked as the door opened, hoping that it wasn't Jake—that it was Lola, come back to say—what? To promise—what?

It was Jake.

The doctor was there the next morning when Lola went to say good-by. It made it easier somehow.

She had phoned Agnes and Connie. Agnes, said Agnes, had news. She would write it, but not yet. Lola cried,

"You're engaged." But Agnes said, mysteriously, "Wait and see." Connie was fine, and was going to have another baby. "Oh, Connie, so soon!" "Well, why not?" asked Connie. "Louis makes good money, I'm healthy as a clam. Joe? Oh, Joe's all right. He's married, didn't I write you? Sure, Joe's fine."

Her mother said, as she was leaving:

"You're really going . . . I'd hoped you'd change your mind."

"Why should I? I haven't given it half a try yet," answered Lola lightly.

Presently she was in the train. Back to St. Louis. No, he didn't need her, either in sickness or in health.

Once in St. Louis she found Jenny very glad to see her. Jenny had met a "swell couple," studio and everything. "She writes and he paints," said Jenny, awed. "We're to go there Sunday with Frank, if it's all the same to you."

Everything was all the same to her.

Lansing asked Jenny later:

"What's wrong with the girl friend? She's got the looks all right and the bean. But something is missing from the get-up."

"Well," said Jenny wisely, "you know she's married."

"Since when was that an obstacle or a drawback?" asked Lansing. "And she can't be very much married at that or she wouldn't be here and the Big Secret somewhere else."

"It's because of her job," said Jenny.

"Well, catch me getting married," declared Lansing, "until I can find a sweet mamma who'll make *me* her job. I'll keep her busy!" he promised.

Mrs. Davis wrote that Ken was up and better. He would be back to work soon, she said. Millie might be in New York in the spring, to make a picture at the Long

Island studio. If so she would arrange to stop off at St. Louis.

"Millie Davis, is she your sister?" they wanted to know at the Sunday studio party. The host, Dana Crossman, beamed down on Lola, sunk in a great chair. "She's very pretty," said the artist, "and so, my dear, are you."

His wife laughed. She was a small dark woman, her hair cut in heavy bangs; she had quick birdlike movements and restless hands. Her eyes were very bright. She came and perched on the arm of Lola's chair and looked up at her big blond husband. She called him something like that. "Don't believe the big blond beast," she said, "but as a matter of fact it happens to be true in this case."

"I can't hold a candle to Millie," denied Lola, laughing.

She knew she looked well. A new dress. Pale flesh, under black net. "You mean," said Crossman, "a Kleig, or whatever they call it now?"

The studio was big and very attractive. Rugs. Cushions. Divans. Rough plastered walls. Crossman's fine work hanging against them, strange, remote landscapes in oils. The coloring blazing, the workmanship nervous but true. There were a dozen or more people in the room. A new, young musician, just gaining recognition, was playing the piano. Someone said, "Let's dance—" and he broke obediently into pure Gershwin. Jenny got up from her sofa-seat beside Lansing and shook out her slim tulle skirt. "Come on, Frankie . . ." she said.

Frankie and Johnnie . . .

A colored man servant was passing drinks, frosted in tall glasses, sprigged with mint. Was passing sandwiches. Lola smiled at her host. She said: "I *like* this. It's different from anything I have ever seen."

"And you from Manhattan, city of penthouses and studios," he mocked her, leaning against a mantel—very tall, very blond. "But we like it too, don't we, May?"

May Crossman nodded. She was a successful novelist. Nervous in gesture, placid in disposition. She said, "I think the infant is weeping," and departed.

"Infant?" asked Lola.

Crossman nodded. "She's seven, really. A very good infant. Given to nightmares. Not that I blame her, in the age we live in," he added.

Across the room another striking couple attracted Lola's attention.

"Isn't that the man," she asked, mentioning his name, "who does the illustrations?"

"Peterson? Sure."

"His wife's an actress, isn't she?"

"A good one. She's 'resting' now," said Crossman, and added, "It's been a rotten season in the theater."

Going home late, Lola pondered. It did work out. The fifty-fifty marriages. Or did they have to be in the professions? Crossman was happy. So was his wife. They looked it. They seemed it. She was sure they were happy. The thought obsessed her.

She asked Lansing outright, going home. "They're happy, aren't they?"

"Sure, noted for it," he answered easily.

If, thought Lola, they were "noted" for it, it must be the exception and not the rule.

Two weeks after she had been in Brooklyn she wrote Ken and enclosed some money. She said: "Please don't be stuffy about it, Ken. I do want to help."

It came back to her by return mail. "You needn't," wrote Ken, in his black schoolboy scrawl. "Awfully sweet of you, Lola, and all that. But I'd rather not. I'm fine now and working again. Jake expects to get into the gas station by summer. I'm going with him. Your father offered me some money to help buy my way in. I refused. It was darn silly of me. I'm going to ask him now, and if he sees his way to do it I'll give him notes. He'll be paid back, all right. I should have taken him up on it the first time. But he was your father. That made some difference. Jake has persuaded me that no matter whose father he is it is just a business arrangement."

In April Millie came through. Lola stayed two days with her at her hotel. Took her the second night to the Crossmans', whom she had come to know rather well by that time. On leaving, Millie asked, looking like herself, yet unlike, in her very simple and attractive traveling tweeds and the sleek little fur jacket, "Happy, Lola?"

"Of course," said Lola. "I'm having a marvelous time."

"Anyone," said Millie, boarding the train, and waving away photographers and publicity people—*Motion-Picture Star Stops in St. Louis to See Sister*—"anyone who is such a good liar ought to be in the pictures!"

Chapter XIV

Sʜᴏʀᴛʟʏ after Millie's stop-over, Ken wrote again.

"I've changed my mind," he said, "about asking Dad Davis for the money. Louis is giving it to me. Better, I think. No family in it. He's a pretty good scout and a good business man. He's coming in with us as a sort of silent partner, by buying my partnership. We have to have cash, you know. Can't run it on a shoe-string. The gas companies aren't giving credit to the little fellows. You have to pay as you go, pretty much. We'll make our biggest profit on oil and repairs. We can manage simple repairs, even at first. Later—but that's another story." He added that he felt all right again, and sent his love.

Men were inconsistent. He'd shilly-shallied about borrowing money from his father-in-law; made up his mind to do so; justified it; and then changed his mind. He'd rather, thought Lola, borrow from a comparative stranger . . . bootleg money, she thought further; and then wondered why that mattered. Still it did matter, in a sense. Ken had nothing in common with Louis. The fact that Louis had married Lola's friend was the one basis for relationship, or perhaps that Louis had once reached out his fine Italian hand and dragged Ken out of trouble. She thought worriedly: I can't see why he'd rather be in debt to Louis than to father—but in a way, she knew why.

During that spring he wrote her once or twice a week. Things were going along all right, he was working like the devil; he saw the family now and then; and Millie.

Millie came over to Brooklyn Sundays, sometimes. She was a knockout. Hadn't changed, since going into the Big Time, except perhaps for the better. He said nothing about coming out.

It was hot in St. Louis that summer. The office ran well, on oiled wheels. Mannering had it in hand. Jameson had ceased his visits of inspection. Lola felt entirely cut off from life back home. Letters of course. But letters were mutilations somehow; they gave you just parts of the pattern. Howard had left the drug firm and had managed to get himself a job in Wall Street. She didn't know what. He scrawled, on a postal of the New York sky-line: "Bigger and Better Business Man, that's me!" She gathered he was working in some capacity for a stock-brokerage concern. Messenger, probably. She wrote her mother anxiously. Mrs. Davis replied that Howard had been restless and that he thought he had more future where he was now placed, through, she added, "a well-connected friend of Millie's." Lola laughed aloud, visualizing Howard, dreaming of a sky-rocket Wall Street career; of the messenger boys and telephone clerks who in a few years' time became the "boy traders" of the Street and owners of expensive gold-plated seats on the exchange. "Well-connected friend of Millie's"? A broker, perhaps? A motion-picture executive? Lola didn't know, probably never would know. She felt lost, cut adrift. She knew so little of anyone any more. Agnes's letters were infrequent. The "news" she had promised when Lola had been home during Ken's illness had turned out to be her new buying job; twice a year she'd go to Europe. She was immersed in it; even her letters, unsatisfactory as they were, proved her changed. Connie rarely wrote.

But Acton was faithful enough. He wrote, he wired.

There were always flowers for her over the week-ends; and candy. Books, lots of books, sent out from New York. Novels, poetry, biography, popular psychology. And he came perhaps once in three weeks to see her. Jenny raised her downy red eyebrows, which were disguised under a slim, severe streak of black, but said nothing. When Acton arrived, Jenny went out. But Lola kept him away from the apartment, meeting him generally at his hotel or a restaurant or "club."

"I've never read—much," she confessed to him. "No time. Too tired. Oh, papers and magazines, going to work and coming home. And detective stories."

She stopped—remembering the mystery tales in their bright jackets from the loan library and Ken, browsing among the litter of papers and periodicals on the little dining-and-living-room table, back in the apartment. . . .

"Where's that book you took out yesterday? You know, with all the murders? Want me to read to you, honey? All right, let's go!" . . .

Acton said, across the table of the hotel in which they were dining:

"You'll have to read more. I'm going to make you. It may open your eyes to a lot of things—"

He added: "I'm a fool. I let the expedition go to Tibet without me. Well, to the devil with them. You knew I would."

She said, "You should have gone, Peter."

"Would you have missed me?" he asked her.

"Very much."

It was true. She would have missed him dreadfully. But missing wasn't loving. She wondered, looking at him, at the lean, familiar face, the shock of gray hair, whether it was as much the man she would have missed as what he stood for. Consideration. Attention. Flattery. The warm happy feeling, admitted or not, that one was loved; whether or not one loved in return. But Acton was talking.

"It's bad for some people to read. They take to it too early—or too late—and they get themselves all muddled and confused with other men's thoughts, none of them perhaps very new. But you're just at the right age. And you've a crystal-clear little mind. Perhaps, I don't know, you're beginning to evolve a philosophy of life. Books might help; who knows? Besides, own up, you are lonely . . often?"

She answered that no, she was not. She had her work. She had Jenny's casual, pleasant, amiable companionship. She went out a good deal; had made friends; notably Dana and May Crossman.

During Acton's June visit she took him with her to the Crossmans'. Jenny had suggested it: "Bring him along on a party." Lola had asked, worriedly, "What will they think?" and Jenny had regarded her with some scorn. "They won't think anything. Why should they? unless you put it up to them? An old friend from New York. What of that? He'd like them. They'd like him."

So Lola took him. But she was anxious. Not because of what they would think. But because of herself; because she had hesitated; because Jenny had had to explain things for her, to her.

Acton was instantly at home in the Crossmans' studio. Able to talk to May about her books; to Dana about his landscapes. There was quite a big party that Sunday night. The room was blue with smoke and vocal with laughter, with music, with people singing, talking, arguing, chattering.

Taking Lola home, he said, "Can't I come in a moment?" Then, abruptly: "I'm sailing, next week. I didn't tell you."

She opened the door of the furnished flat and let him in. To have hesitated would have been stupid of her. Strain at a mouse and swallow a camel. Jenny would be coming in soon. She and Frank Lansing, to whom she would not admit that she was "seriously" engaged, had stayed at the Crossmans'. But Acton had intimated that it was growing late.

Lola switched on the lights. The small living-room sprang into being. It was furnished in a most ordinary, commonplace manner. But it was comfortable. Jenny had pictures all round the walls and mantels, mostly of personable young men. Jenny's mending-basket was strewing its contents on an upholstered couch. Millie's pictures were evident too. None of Ken. Ken's picture was in the bedroom, on the night table. A flat, lineless, unsmiling, self-conscious Ken. The only photograph of him that Lola possessed. But she had snapshots; taken at home; and that time, in Maine; and the dear, silly Atlantic City postcard. She carried those in her envelope purse. No one knew, except, perhaps, Jenny.

"Not bad," Acton commented, walking around, "not bad at all. But not exactly your setting. No . . . Lola . . ."

She was taking off her hat in the little hall and fluffing up her hair, running her hands through the heavy brightness. She turned, slim, overslim, in the little blue dinner dress.

"What? Are you hungry? I'll look in the ice-box. Want a cigarette? There are some in that brass box, on the smoking stand. It's late," Lola reminded him. "You mustn't stay long."

She came into the room. He was standing quite still, looking at her. He said:

"Yes, I'm hungry. Not that it matters. Wait"—as she turned—"wait!" He caught her by the hand. "Not for food, Lola . . ."

"Please, Peter."

She thought: I did make a mistake . . . a dreadful one . . . letting him come in . . . I knew I shouldn't . . . but it seemed silly of me, not to. As if I expected something—I couldn't bear to have him think that I expected—just this—or that I was afraid. I'm not afraid, she told herself wildly. . . . Nothing can happen.

Men didn't force their violent love-making on women. Men like Peter Acton didn't, anyway. Peter Acton wouldn't be content with anything gained by compulsion, a question merely of inferior physical strength. No, she was not afraid.

He took her in his arms, a little roughly.

"I'm sailing next week. I can't stand this much longer. How long has it been? A year, two years? Eternity. Forever. Lola, you'll sail with me?"

She said—"No!" trying to free herself. "No!" she said again.

"Be still. Just a moment. If I go, I won't come back. Not till I'm cured, if it takes my lifetime. But it won't. I'll be cured, all right. Don't think I don't know; I'm no youngster telling you I'll bear the wound to my grave. We're always cured; that's the hell of it." He was speaking, half to himself, eyes burning with a clear blue flame, holding her not hurtingly but close enough and hard enough. He put his hand under her chin and turned her face up. Her eyes met his own, as blue as his own, darker, the pupils dilated.

"You're not afraid of me?" he asked, as if in wonder.

"No." She added, "I *like* you, Peter."

"Perhaps. If people knew"—he was again addressing himself—"what a fool they'd think me! Perhaps I am. You wouldn't follow the usual routine. Wouldn't go away, quietly divorce that boy you married, marry me. Was it too conventional for you, too routed? Would you rather take it as an adventure? Sail with me, next week, let him divorce you? Why not? He would. Or, I think he'd let you divorce him. In Paris. Then, you'd have a lover before you had a second husband . . ."

"Peter!"

He said, remorsefully:

"I'm still a fool. And a bigger one when I tell you that if you like you'll have a second husband before you have a lover. Do you understand me? I'll swear it if you wish. Anything. Just to have you, Lola."

Suddenly he dragged her face to his, hard, his hand hurting her chin and soft throat. Kissed her, angrily, tenderly, with passionate longing and with compelling love. She tried to free herself. Could not. Her senses, starved so long, responded beyond the acquiescence of her mind or will. She found herself clinging to him, answering his kisses, found herself in that mindless moment forgetting him, forgetting everything, her eyes closed, and her hands along his throat shaking.

He said, deeply disturbed:

"Lola . . . Lola, darling? You do love me?"

She opened her eyes and at the look in them he freed her. She stumbled to the couch, and with her hands flung out and caught to her face leaned her head against the harsh, dusty upholstery and abandoned herself to tears.

"Lola?"

He was terribly anxious. He had never seen a woman cry quite like that, wildly, heartbrokenly, as vulnerable as a child. He sat down beside her and tried to take her in his arms again. She shook her bright head. "Leave me alone," she begged him, sobbing.

He sat there, silent. She did love him. Her response had convinced him of that. This was reaction, knowledge breaking in upon her, shattering her defenses. He lighted a cigarette with hands none too steady and leaned back waiting. He could afford to wait now. Whatever she wanted, she should have her way. If she wished him to go away and wait a little longer, he would, if he could have her promise. She'd keep her promise. She'd give it to him; and keep it.

He thought, practically, that if Jenny came in it would be rather a bother.

Jenny did not. She was out with Frank Lansing, in a car parked along a suburban road and they were deciding that a good automobile salesman made plenty to marry on, even if the automobile business was shot. "I could sell de-luxe sedans to the Arabs in the desert, if I had you," Frank was telling Jenny.

After what seemed a long time, Lola raised her head and turned a little to face him, a sopping wet handkerchief in her hand. He took it from her gently and substituted his own, a great square of fine monogrammed linen. He was shocked at her devastated face, swollen, almost unrecognizable. When she spoke her voice was unrecognizable too, husky, roughened.

"Please," she said, and her breath kept catching like a forlorn child's, "please forgive me, Peter. I've been so dreadfully wrong."

Even then his heart did not misgive him. He said merely: "You couldn't be, you know. Take your time, Lola. . . . Whatever you say goes, dear."

"I don't love you, Peter," she told him bluntly. "I love Ken. I don't want you, I want—*him.*"

He was gray under the shock, but controlled enough. A little angry perhaps, as a natural reaction, the reaction from pain which makes a man hit out blindly.

"Then why—the recent demonstration?" he asked smoothly.

She said: "I deserved that. Listen. . . . Peter. . . . It's always been Ken. As far as loving was concerned I mean. I liked you. It—flattered me. I mean, you were different; I'd never known anyone like you. The things you stood for—I don't mean just money, Peter. Try and understand. I came away against Ken's wishes. I wanted—I don't know what I wanted—not so much the job perhaps as my own way. I thought he was terribly unfair. I knew that if he were in my place he would expect me to do as he said. I couldn't see that it was any different. So I came away. I missed him—you don't know. But I saw you, now and then. You kept reminding me of yourself. And I've been lonely. And when you kissed me"—she looked at him and stumbled in her little speech.

He said quietly, "Go on, Lola," his anger gone.

She went on, the anxious swollen eyes fixed on his own, the poor mouth trembling—"When you kissed me, I knew. I didn't love you. But I loved you to kiss me. I—wanted it. Oh, don't you understand?" she cried pitifully. "*Any man*—at that moment. Any man who was attractive to me; whom I liked, whom perhaps I didn't even need to like."

"That's between the eyes," he said slowly. "I understand perfectly. Any man would, if he would admit it. And most women, although they'd never admit it, except you. So, it wasn't—Peter Acton . . . it was— Never mind giving a name to it," he said. "There's no use in my telling you what is possibly the truth . . . that if you'd come with me and let me give you all I have to give you—I don't mean just material things—I could go on kissing you and you'd go on—liking it, and some day you'd realize who it was you were kissing and be happy. No, no use. I never really thought you cared much for that lad of yours. I thought it was habit, pride, a certain convention of your—"

She said swiftly: "Class. Middle class. Go on, say it!"

"You have," he retorted. "Middle class, then if you'll have it. But what's wrong about that? Most of us are, you know. Money doesn't make the difference. Nor, often as not, a belted earl in the dim family background."

She said: "I've taken so much from you. I don't mean just things. I don't mean, even, your time. . . . Perhaps I mean your thoughts. Hopes, too. I haven't," she told him, "ever said yes, have I?"

"No, Lola."

"I've said no," she said simply, "and meant it. But I didn't let you go. I didn't I suppose want to."

"It's having your cake and eating it too," he reminded her . . . "all along, not alone with me, but with the job and with, too, this Ken of yours."

She said drearily:

"I don't think he's mine, any more. But—I've taken so much from you. So much, Peter. I needn't have, you know. If I were a good sport now"—desperately—"I'd be willing to pay for what I took. But I'm not a good sport. I couldn't, with Ken in my heart."

"I don't want that kind of payment, Ken or no Ken." He rose and stood over her, looking down. "I'm going," he told her gently. "Don't reproach yourself. You have nothing with which to reproach yourself. At least not many women would think so. You've made me, if not happy, then something near it." He leaned down and kissed her hot, wet eyelids. "Good-by, Lola," he said. "I can't advise you; I wouldn't if I could. I'm not unselfish enough. And God knows if I were I might not. Because I don't know what will make you happy. Anyway, you'll have to give up something. It depends on what matters most. You think it's money, don't you? I mean, the necessity for your earning it? It isn't. Not essentially. But you'll have to find out for yourself. I want you to be happy." He smiled. "If you're not, you can always let me know. But you won't. And I'll sail next week . . . and somewhat, as other people sail, to take the cure."

"Good-by, Peter. If—you'd forgive me?" she said dully.

"There's nothing to forgive. I can't quarrel with the destiny or the purely physical chemical components which made you a woman, can I?"

He stopped at the door and looked at her. She was sitting as he had left her, head against the back of the couch, hands lax in her lap.

"Good-by," said Peter.

She thought: I'll never see him again.

She never did.

A little later, cold for all the warmth of the June night, she rose and stumbled into the bedroom she shared with Jenny. An hour later Jenny came in flushed, her hair tumbled—her wild red hair. She switched on all the lights and danced about the room.

"Lola, are you asleep? It doesn't matter if you are. . . . Lola, wake up! Frank and I are engaged. Isn't it marvelous? Gosh, I'm crazy about him!" said Jenny.

Lola was not asleep. She opened her eyes, punched up

her pillow and sat up. Jenny thought: She's been crying. She looks terrible. All the cold water and witch-hazel had not effaced the traces. Jenny thought further: Is it Acton or Ken?

Lola said: "I'm so glad, Jenny. Are you—going to keep on working?"

"Well, no, I'm not crazy yet. We'll get along. I'll have enough to do keeping that lad in the strait and narrow and learning how to cook. Next fall I'll resign. You'll stand up with us, Lola, won't you?"

"Of course," said Lola.

A few days later she telephoned May Crossman.

"Could I come see you?" she wanted to know. "I mean, could I ever get to see you alone? I'd like to talk to you, Mrs. Crossman."

"Dana's going out to dinner tonight. I'd half planned to work but I'd rather talk to you. Come in then, Lola, at six-thirty. No, don't be silly. I don't want to work. I love having an excuse not to."

That was the basis of their pleasant friendship. "Lola," Mrs. Crossman said, after the dinner table had been cleared and they sat together in the cool, dusky gloom of the studio, "what's on your mind? And for goodness' sakes, can't you call me May? I'm not much more than ten or fifteen years older than you, and that brat Jenny . . . by the way, she and Frank Lansing have decided to call it a wedding day, haven't they? But you two youngsters make me feel like a grandmother."

"May, then," agreed Lola, laughing. "Yes, Jenny's engaged. I hope she'll be happy."

"She probably won't be," prophesied May comfortably, "but that doesn't matter."

She crossed her slim legs and regarded her slippers. She had dozens of pairs, being vain of her little feet. Tonight she wore bright green pajamas and a brocaded coat, and her small dark face was alert and interested.

Lola said: "I suppose not. Still—you and—and Dana are."

"Heavens, yes, if by happiness you mean the contentment, pleasantly interluded with domestic upsets, quarrels, reconciliations, and romantic outbursts, we have attained. Hello, infant!"

The little girl came in to say good night. A blond child, like her father. Tall for her age. Not shy, but reserved. She gave Lola her hand and kissed her mother. "Run along, lamb; I'll come in before I go to bed," May promised. A round-faced Irish nurse hovered in the doorway.

"Now," said May, lighting a cigarette and switching on one tall, indirect lamp by the divan, "what's the matter? You look as forlorn as the infant used to—and still does —when she broke a new toy or a finger-nail or something."

Lola replied evasively,

"Nothing really. I get lonely sometimes. You've been awfully good to us, May, to Jenny and me. You must think we are such bores. I mean, knowing the people you do—artists—writers—" she floundered helplessly.

"Saints, what an idea!" May said lightly. "Do you think I want to live in an atmosphere of ink, carbons, and rose-madder all my life? I like people. Lots of them. All kinds. I like audiences, too. Most of Dana's crowd and mine, the particular crowd you mean, couldn't constitute an audience. They're too busy talking about themselves. About editors, art and otherwise, about publishers; about one-man shows; exhibitions; royalties. God knows what. A little goes a long way. We like our audience too. And we happen to like younger people. It keeps us young—for our own sakes and the infant's. We

decided a long time ago that we wouldn't get so sunk in a
sea of typewriters and oils that she'd be left out, when
she grew up, in case she shows no tendency either way.
She doesn't. I think she's going to be an engineer. Even
at seven her faculty for mathematics is amazing and her
mind and hand are mechanical."

"Have you," asked Lola, leaning back in the big chair
and feeling astonishingly at home, "have you—a—a—"
she hesitated, recalling Acton's exact words—"a philosophy of life?"

May Crossman had been asked many curious things
during the last few overflowing years. She thought a
moment and answered:

"I don't think so. At least nothing static. I suppose
I started out with what I thought was a philosophy. But
it proved pretty fluid. I wonder if you don't mean something to live by? I don't know. My mother—she'll be
here to visit me from Vermont in a day or so and you'll
meet her—my mother used to say—'Live and let live; bear
and forbear.' I don't know that I've followed that homely
rule altogether. I'm a little too curious. That's what
makes me a novelist. But she lives by it; and it works,
in her case. I think that I was born with a strong sense
of justice and an insatiable curiosity. And that going
along, with work, and then Dana, and then the infant, I
learned something we'll call a sense of values. Let it go
at that, anyway."

Lola asked shyly:

"I suppose people tell you things? Private things?
And ask your advice?"

"Lord. Yes! They tell me—a lot. And ask advice
on everything from where to sell manuscripts to what
shall I do about my mother-in-law. They do this to almost all writers, you know. Partly, I think, because they

feel, rightly or wrongly, that writers have an interest in, and an understanding of, the way the human heart and wheels go around. Partly because of a sort of vicarious exhibitionism. They want to see themselves in print. But if they ever do, they either do not recognize themselves or else they sue the hapless author. That's that. I don't use my friends as material, Lola, if that's what you mean. Or, if I do—I'm always making reservations —they never appear in print very like the way they really are. It's like baking something from a new recipe. You use the ingredients but you mix 'em differently or the oven temperature isn't exact, and it comes out something else again, something slightly deviating, or greatly differing, from the original."

By eleven o'clock that evening, Lola had told May Crossman a good deal: about herself; her family; Ken; about even Peter Acton.

May said, smoking furiously, her shrewd dark eyes half closed:

"I can't advise you, any more than your friend could. By the way, he seems to me to be a pretty darned good scout. I liked him when I met him; I like him even better now. No, I can't advise. It's not fair, or wise. I— strange as it may seem—I dislike playing God to any of my friends; or, if not God, acting as a pair of crutches. I'd rather they stood on their own feet. It all boils down to one thing as I see it, Lola—what you're able to do with . . . and what you are able to do without. Happiness. You might have been happy with any one of a dozen men. Might have been happy with Acton, if circumstances had been a little different. It's the person you are unhappy without who counts most."

Lola said, sighing:

"I wanted it to be a partnership. Our marriage. Both

of us working. You know. It's not—unusual. Most girls of my upbringing and surroundings have to go to work. Most of us marry men who aren't earning much. So we keep on working. I can't see why it doesn't work out, can you?"

"Yes and no, to that," May told her, "human nature being what it is."

Lola said: "Perhaps it's—business? The professions —they're different. You—and Dana's. You're happy. You get along."

"We get along in spite of 'the professions' as you call them. Not because of them. There are just as many unhappy marriages among professional people, Lola. As concrete examples, do you remember Bill Peterson, the illustrator, and his wife? You met them here. They're separated now. Bill was jealous of Lily. And their working hours didn't dovetail. She worked, evenings, say; he, daytimes. Oh, of course, she had matinées and rehearsals too. And they didn't see much of each other. Also, as I said, he was jealous. Then, there's 'Happy' and Jerry Norton. Both writers. They've been divorced from each other once. Remarried now. But they'll be divorced again. They're—let's call it temperamental, although I loathe that misused word. Each demands quiet, consideration, the path smoothed. They can't do it for each other. Neither is willing to give up anything. And then there's professional jealousy creeping in. Happy is more successful than Jerry although she doesn't really do as good work. And so it goes."

"But professional women, writers, they can work at home. It makes things different."

"No, each is working at home. Or one at home and the other in an office. Look here, Lola, don't blame any failure of marriage on what people do for a living. Peter

Acton—he was married before, you told me. His wife didn't go to work, did she? Look at the divorce records. Idle women, restless. No, it isn't your earning or your not earning."

Lola said amazedly:

"It's—I suppose I sound foolish—it's a question of character, then, isn't it?"

"Character. Love. Triumph of circumstance and intimacy. Dana and I, we had to live pretty close together, at first. We were dog-poor. And it happens that both of us like privacy. Well, we didn't have it. It wore on us, some. But we stuck it out. Now we have plenty and take very little advantage of it." May laughed. "So that's that! You two—you and your Ken—are very like we were, very like any young married people in a way—most of your conversation together hinging on ways and means and money. If you can get out from under that, you'll be all right. Above it, I mean. That is, if you want to. If you're willing to stand the gaff. You've tried being on your own, before marriage and after. How do you like it? Do you like it better, for all its lacks, than the other sort of life? Or do you like the other life, with what compensations it has to offer, and what sacrifices it entails, the best?"

Lola said miserably:

"I promised if I found . . . I couldn't stand it, I'd go home. Ken said, if he couldn't, he'd come out. But he said, too, that he wouldn't come out, as things are now; not until he made good and could take me home again. So after all it was a sort of one-sided promise, wasn't it?"

Dana came in, big and roaring and in high spirits. He turned on the radio, kissed his wife, smiled at Lola, wanted to know why they were sitting in the dark.

Hadn't, he said, had enough to eat. May must make a rabbit.

Frank and Jenny drifted in, to be congratulated. Later Frank took his girl and Lola home. Lola lay awake most of the scant rest of the night.

To go home? To admit she had failed? To swallow her pride? But if you loved a person a lot you didn't think of pride. Yet Ken did. She thought: I'll have to go on working though. Things won't be any different. We'll just be where we were before. What'll be the good of it, after the first newness of going back to Ken has worn off?

She thought: If he makes a sign . . . or sends a word?

He did not. And Mannering said to her:

"If I'm ever called to the home office, Mrs. Hayes, I know whom I'll recommend to run this one. You are more than my right hand. You're my left and an eye or so thrown in."

She thought exultantly, I can get there. After all. And it wouldn't stop there.

She thought again: There was Peter, and the money, and the—the attention and coddling . . . funny places, new countries, yachts, houses, clothes. But that wasn't good enough. I wanted Ken more. Now, there's the job, another step up on the ladder and plenty of room at the top. Do I want that more? I can't have both, I suppose. Not with Ken. But then, she told herself, I haven't Ken— now.

He wasn't writing often. Too busy, he said, when he did write. "Ken," wrote her mother, "is working too hard we all think. Your father is hurt that he didn't come to him for the money he needed. But the boys are doing very well." Howard, she added, had had summer grippe. Millie was working very hard; they didn't see

her often.   She concluded, "We all wish you'd come
home."

Home.

Lola drew a pad toward her, there in the office and a
pencil.   "Ken," she wrote, "I'm willing to come home and
see if Mr. Jameson can use me in the home office, if you
want me to.   I'll resign here.   There must be something I
can do.   If not in this job, in another.   I'll have plenty
of references and all that.   But do you want me?   Or
have you got over wanting me, Ken?" she asked him.

The evening of the day her letter reached him she was
with the Crossmans, going with them to a performance of
the open-air opera, after a long drive through Tower
Park in the oppressive heat with Frank and Jenny.   On
reaching home she found that Jenny had not returned
ahead of her, and as she put her key in the latch the telephone was ringing violently, with the long sustained ringing that is somehow so frightening in a dark, empty room.

She pressed the light switch and ran to the telephone
table and lifted the receiver from the hook.   "Yes—" she
said.   "Yes—"

The brisk voice of the operator, calm, practical and
with rolling consonants reached her.

"Mrs. Hayes . . .   Mrs. Kenneth Hayes . . ."

"Speaking," said Lola.

"New York calling," said the operator.   "Ready with
that New York call—long distance—ready—here's your
party—hold the line."

A buzzing.   A silence.   Voices on the wire.   New York,
St. Louis.   Another silence and then Ken's voice, clear,
small, distinct.

"Hello—hello—get off the wire, damn you.   This is a
busy line.   Hello, operator, what the hell's the matter
with this call?"

Lola called, "Ken . . . Ken . . ." He did not hear her. He was arguing with his own operator. He said, presently:

"Lola?" He added, unnecessarily, "It's Ken."

Her hands shook. Her mouth. She steadied herself. A small clear voice over the miles of wire. A person. A personality. That voice, detached, speaking seemingly bodiless into a transmitter.

"Hello, Ken."

The wire was cleared. He said:

"You all right, Lola? I've been calling since nine."

"I'm fine. I'm fine. You"—she tried to laugh at him —"such extravagance!"

"Debil with that, Lola. I've your letter. Look here, I was going to wait, till you needn't work. Ever, any more. I wanted to wait. You know how I feel. I know how you feel. Let's compromise. Come home," said Ken, across the miles, "on any terms!"

She was crying, "I'll come, Ken. . . . I love you," said Lola.

A moment later Jenny coming into the living-room stopped dead. Lola, walking the floor, laughing at her astonishment, crying . . .

"Well, for Pete's sake . . . Frank, you go on home; Lola's upset or something."

"No. No. Let him come in. I'm resigning tomorrow. I'm going home," said Lola. "I'm so happy. . . ."

She was. But she was still crying.

Chapter XV

Mannering said, "Well, I might have known it!" with his integral gloomy surrender to circumstance, which, oddly enough, did not prove an obstacle to business efficiency.

Lola, hesitant, herself a chaos of warring emotions, tried to explain.

"I'm so awfully sorry . . . Mr. Jameson will think I've let you down—but I can't help it, Mr. Mannering. I'm needed at home. I suppose I shouldn't have attempted this anyway."

"You would get married," he reminded her. "And I hear that Miss Jones is contemplating the same fatal step. Not that I have anything against marriage, as an institution. However, this can't be helped. You won't leave us at once, will you? I'd like you to break in a successor. She will have to be a couple of other girls, I'm afraid!"

Lola promised. She stayed on for a month or more, in order to help him as much as she could. Now that it was definitely the end, she had to force herself to interest, had to dissemble her impatience. Now that she was leaving her work, and the work ahead of her was vague and complicated by the old routine, she realized how much she had cared for the job *per se*. She thought: If I hadn't married Ken, I'd be here forever perhaps . . . trying to get ahead. Succeeding, I think. Keen about it.

Jenny said: "Well, good luck, old top. I saw it coming. A girl can't be in two places at once. But, darn you anyway, I'll miss you—like the dickens."

"Frank won't give you time," Lola consoled her.

"Well, there's another thing. He'll use this as an excuse to hurry up the wedding bells. He's said already that there's no reason why we can't live on here in this flat, as long as you're moving out and I couldn't swing it alone. He'll take it over," said Jenny, complacent in her knowledge of her man's ability to do so, and without her help, "and we'll stay here a while till we find what we want and get furniture and stuff."

Ken wrote impatiently. He promised in one of the letters which reached her two or three times a week: "Look here, when you do come back I'll try to be sensible about this. If you think you have to keep on in the game, it will be O. K. by me. I know I said that before. But this time I mean it. I'll try damned hard not to gum things up again. I'm getting along all right. It won't be long before we'll start in making more than bare expenses; not long before I can swing an establishment—nothing very fancy, you know, plain roof and bed and board. But you wouldn't be happy, I guess. I guess you'll always want to be on your own. The fact that you are willing to give up the St. Louis job means a lot to me, Lola. I'm damned grateful. Yet I hate to think of your sacrificing something that means so much to you; I'd be a lot easier in my mind if I could believe it wasn't a sacrifice."

She answered:

"I don't suppose you'll believe me, but it isn't a sacrifice. Of course I like it; not the St. Louis part of it; not especially, even the job itself; but what it all stands for. But I find I don't like it well enough without you. I can't have both, as things are. I'd rather have you. So it isn't a sacrifice exactly, is it? I'm taking what I want most, after all."

When she told May Crossman, May nodded and said:

"I thought you'd come to that. Women have got to learn they can't have it both ways. The old story of having their cake and eating it too."

"That's what Peter said once," Lola told her.

"Peter is, and was, a wise person," May told her. "Lola, you aren't regretting Peter, are you?"

She said no, that she wasn't. She expatiated upon it frankly. "I miss him. He made me feel—oh—*important*. To him. To myself. But no, I'm not sorry. I didn't really care for him, May. I've thought—who wouldn't?— what it would be like to be the wife of a man like that— ease, comfort, absolute freedom from worry. You know. It's like a dream. You see everything pretty clearly, all that it would mean. Except the man. I could fit myself into that picture somehow—but I couldn't see him in it. So, I'm not sorry."

May said, idly:

"I've always thought that the most perfect fate which could befall any woman would be to be born a rich widow. Well, none of us are. That's something in line with the way you felt about Peter, contemplating his possibilities. Rich, free, the world before you, experience without consequences and a state of widowhood achieved without having to go through the preliminaries. So, you see, you saw yourself in the surroundings Peter could give you. But without Peter. That's that. And a pretty fair test of how far his attraction for you went. Not far, Lola. . . . We'll miss you here," she told her.

"Not very much," said Lola, smiling.

"No?" May laughed. "You're a funny girl. No, not very much," said the dark woman, regarding the ash of her cigarette, "but enough. When we come to New York —and we do sometimes, you know—we'll look you up."

"You probably won't," said Lola, "but I like your thinking you will all the same."

May remarked irrelevantly:

"I believe you're growing up. That philosophy-of-life business isn't so far off, after all. Here comes Dana, with his arms full of packages. I'll bet a sugar cookie he wandered into a super-delicatessen and went berserk buying, as he does sometimes. Now for weeks the place will be redolent of strange and exotic things—cheese, preserves, anchovies, caviar, and God knows what all. . . . Dana Crossman, have you been wasting our substance in riotous delicatessen?" she demanded severely.

Toward the end of Lola's stay in St. Louis, Jameson came out on one of his flying trips. He knew, of course, her plans, talked to her, there in the office, tilting back in his chair and regarding her from under his eyebrows.

"It was," he told her, "a little too good to be true. I didn't think you'd stick it, after all."

She said, "I'm sorry."

He nodded, "I believe you are. I think you are sensible, however."

"Mr. Jameson," she spoke timidly, "is there room for me in the home office? I know my old place with you is filled. But, is there room?"

He replied cautiously:

"I think we can make room. But not now. For your own sake, I mean," he added hastily. "Go home, take a vacation. You've been here almost a year and haven't had one. After that's over, come and see me. Take," he told her, "a month. You're entitled to it. More, if you like. Then, come to the home office." He was silent, as she thanked him; wondering, a little anxious, yet secure in her belief in his kindness toward her, his sense of fairness and justice, "Do you remember Harriet Conners?" he asked abruptly.

She remembered, with a little effort. A tall blond girl, once in Jameson's department, later transferred.

"She married, didn't she?" asked Lola.

"Yes, she kept on working. Her husband made very little. He had a mother and father who lived on an income which was practically invisible to the naked eye, but in a house they owned, their sole possession, tangible possession, that is. Harriet bore most of the burden; lived in the house; kept up the taxes; did most of the housework. She came to me, frantic. She looked—wretched. My assistant—you remember Martin?—had let her out, while I was away on a trip, for a bad record. For staying out, you know. Once or twice a week she'd be out. Dismissed, she was, with two weeks' pay. She was making twenty-three a week. She asked me if she couldn't be taken on again. Her people lived in the West, and she planned to go out there in the fall. She had to work, she said. Couldn't leave the old people to suffer. I asked her, 'How much does your husband make?' 'Seventeen a week,' she said. 'Then his brother is living with us too; he won't work. I don't know what's the matter with him. He's perfectly well; just lazy.' 'Go home,' I told her, 'and tell them you're fired. And see what happens. They'll do something. They'll have to. Then come back here in a couple of weeks.' "

Lola asked, "What happened?"

Jameson smiled. "She came back. The brother had found a job. The father-in-law, an able-bodied man, had found something also. She said, 'I'm through. My married brother wants me to live with him. I'll separate from Paul. May I have my job back?' "

"Did you give it to her?" Lola wanted to know.

"I did. She isn't living with her married brother, after all. She has an apartment with another girl in the office. I am pretty sure that her young husband visits her there. But I've no proof. What can I say or do? That's the way she has worked it out. Washed her hands of financial responsibility, not only toward her husband but toward his people. 'They're lazy,' she told me, that first time. 'They want things. They have them . . . on their little income. Porterhouse steaks, a good radio; a piano; why should I turn all my money in for that?' "

"Then she isn't separated from her husband?"

"Oh, ostensibly! He has to stay home, you see, and contribute his mite. That's all he can manage to do, buy himself a suit of clothes, lunches, cigarettes, and turn in a small sum. His brother does the same. They're all right without her. She has her money and her freedom . . . and, *sub rosa*, her husband. What could we do about it? It's all perfectly legal," said Jameson, smiling.

He added, seriously:

"But it isn't marriage. It isn't home-building. People, talking about women's independence and financial freedom nowadays, laugh a bit at the old-fashioned woman. They call her female—quite without flattery. Tied to her house and her children, couldn't call her soul her own, they say. I wonder. Such women raised a pretty darned fine brood of sons and daughters; such women stood back of their men, all the way. All this business of middle-aged men saying, in person and in print, that they wouldn't have succeeded without their mothers and their wives may be sob-stories, success blah and such, in the eyes of the sophisticates. But like most banalities, at which we snicker, it happens to be true. We're not as smart as we think we are. Men—men get along best when they're not free, either. Tied, too, in their own way, to their house and lot. To their families. Men get along best when they have dependents. No man is one hundred per cent hero, you know. But when he has to live up to the head-of-the-house business, he tries like the devil. When he doesn't, he slacks. That's human nature, Lola."

She stirred in her chair. He was twirling a pencil between his fingers. Talking to her; as a friend; almost as a father. He didn't call her Lola as a rule. She said hesitantly:

"I see—but—nowadays, isn't the ideal toward partnership in marriage?"

"What's that but partnership?" asked Jameson hotly. "Look at the men in this plant of ours, middle-aged men like myself, who have worked up from messenger boys, married young, raised a family on very little, carried a burden. Where would they have been, most of them, the average among them, without a woman back of them? Looking after their health, nagging them into caution, setting as good a table as their means allowed, watching the family economies? Where? Nowhere, I tell you! Women haven't changed much, Lola. A great many of those women were just as alert, just as fitted for a business life as you are. But they didn't want it. They put their talents to work instead in what people now think is a mighty narrow sphere. Well, I don't think it is. I think it's pretty darned near the most important sphere there is, and the biggest. Not much recognition in it, perhaps, no kudos, no spectacular publicity; but it has built up nations before this, by God, and will again."

He stopped, a little ashamed of his own vehemence. He said, "Sorry," under his breath. Not a profane man, Jameson. Nor was he profane then. Lola didn't hear the apology. She was thinking.

He said gently, touching her hand as it lay on the desk, tapping the back of it with his pencil.

"Take your vacation, Lola. Find out what you want. What you can do best. Then come and tell me. If it's a job you want, I'll see that you get it."

She said, "Thank you, Mr. Jameson," and as he rose, rose too, and stood looking up at him with troubled eyes.

"It's all so mixed up," said Lola.

"No, not really. It's all pretty simple, when you come down to it." He was silent, recalling his own years of struggle and comparative hardships and doing without. But had they really done without, he and his wife and children? Of course, they had not. They had always had essentials. Love, laughter, work, understanding; a roof over their heads and food on the table. And simple amusements. No movies then; no night clubs; no radios and player pianos and cars bought on tick. There had been gallery seats for a show now and then or a concert; and the parks; and visiting at the homes of young people like themselves; and, as their children grew up a little and things were easier, parties at home for those children. It was, he thought suddenly, harder for people, young people, nowadays. You might talk about the machine age having lightened a woman's work, her housework. Well and good. Was it any better done now? It was not. In less time, that was all. But what did the average servantless woman do with her saved time? Went to a movie, as a rule, or sat over a card table. No, thought Jameson, the reactionary, the die-hard, the conservative, damned if it's any better! And along with lightened housework came the machine-age luxuries, so threateningly within the reach of the majority of people; the luxuries that could be paid for as you went along, anything from a house and a fur coat to a car and a refrigerator. They had, he told himself, a good deal more to fight against nowadays after all. They had shorter hours and more leisure. Pick up the newspaper and see what they did with that leisure. Night-club raids and week-end automobile accidents were common head-lines. Leisure? Leisure to land in a hospital or jail!

Family life, thought Jameson. Where is it? Apartments like rabbit warrens. The necessity for speed, for excitement, the inability to relax, to let down. You didn't know your children's friends. Your children spent most of their time in school. Then on the streets; in the motion-picture theaters; in crazy cars, careering about the country. In his own experience in the personnel, he'd heard a lot. "Where do you think she is?" he would ask a frantic mother whose daughter had been missing for three days. "We don't know, we think she's married." "To whom?" "We don't know that, either." "You don't know the man?" "No, sir, you see she met him at her girl friend's. There's four of them that go around together. They go to work on the same subway; and have breakfast together somewhere down-town. We don't know anything about him except that his name is Harry. He never came to the house. We haven't much room for entertaining, you see. My mother sleeps in our living-room and there are three children besides Marie . . ."

And so it went. Where would it end? he wondered. Of course, this was in New York; any big city. Not wholly representative. There were the smaller cities, the towns. Different. But the trend was away from the land, from the farm, the village, and the small town. Statistics proved that.

He admitted, standing there alone in Mannering's private office and chewing savagely on the end of a cigar, his eyes unseeingly on the door Lola had gone through and closed behind her, that any smart-aleck modernist, any avid feminist, any, perhaps, dispassionate and impartial bystander could shoot his argument full of holes. What did he care? He stood where he stood. It wasn't the alleged looseness of the younger generation that bothered him. He didn't think they were any looser than other generations. More open about it, that's all. A bad egg's a bad egg, no matter what date is stamped on it. There are bolters in every generation. This wasn't the first era openly to discount chastity. No, he wasn't bothered by the morals of the youngsters. He was bothered by their lack of responsibility toward—what was it—an ideal? . . . the race? . . .

Family man. Family woman. Terms, nowadays, not exactly of approbation. Still . . .

"Vanishing Americans!" said Jameson aloud, and stumped belligerently to the door.

He'd given Lola a hint. Well, he'd see. If she came back, he'd keep his promise.

Thus, in early September Lola returned home. Ken met her at the station. He was almost painfully scrubbed and shiny. She thought, going into his arms, he hasn't had a new suit since I left! He kissed her, said simply, "Gee, I'm glad to see you." Pretty inadequate, after all these months. He held her at arms' length, regardless of the hurrying passers-by, the porters, the confusion and publicity of the station, "Gee, I'm glad!"

He looked at her. He said, "You're pretty thin." He laughed and took her arm, clasped his strong fingers tightly about it. He said: "You should smell the kitchen. Mother Davis has been baking for two days."

There was shared gladness; but an embarrassment; a shyness; a reticence; a sense of having to keep to trivial things; an awareness of the immediate necessity of light speech, of laughter, for no good reason. They were husband and wife, they were lovers; but they had been absent, one from the other, for a long period of time as love counts time. Barriers existed, things were unspoken that must finally be said. Not now. Now they laughed and talked about layer cakes and the weather and, "How's Millie . . . ? I'm so sorry I'm going to miss her, I had counted on seeing her before she went back to the Coast, but I couldn't get away before, Ken. I just couldn't!"

"Yes, I know. Mother is nearly frantic, she's been counting the days. Me, too," he told her.

"So have I. Howard? He's all right—all over that illness? And father?"

"They're fine. Lola—gosh, you sure look good to me," said Ken.

All the romantic, tender, poetic things he couldn't say. "Gosh, you look good to me." His language. But she understood it.

He took her trunk checks from her, left her a moment in the waiting-room, returned beaming. "O. K., let's go!"

The car—"ours, Jake's and mine . . . we're expecting to get a good turnover in it; look, good as new, only ran twelve thousand miles, and Jake did a swell paint job on it—" was waiting, parked. "Hope to heaven, I don't get a ticket." He didn't. They drove off, following the stream of traffic.

Home. Her city. She drew a deep breath. Down-town they saw the great building of the insurance company, the aspiring tower. Lola looked toward it. Familiar as her own hand to her, it was. Now she saw it with a sense of strangeness, her appreciation sharpened, detached. A beautiful structure, clean and soaring, a symbol.

Ken was talking about the gas station and garage. "Not much of a garage yet. You wait and see. Watch our smoke. It won't be easy, for a while, but we'll make it."

"No," he told her, in answer to a question, "no, I haven't seen anything of Garry or Amy lately. Too busy. Too dog-tired to go out much." He added, his words hurried: "That Smith kid—you remember her, Lola, the blonde?—gee, she stepped out and got married the other day. An orchestra leader. He makes good money. It was his third crack at it. She's got courage, I'll say! It was in the papers, and a picture of her," he said.

Lola said casually, "She fell pretty hard for you, Ken!"

"Can't kid me that way," he told her, "you know—a kid like that. Any man who'll take her out and pay for the drinks. I didn't rate much though, I was married, see, and likely to stay so." He halted, remembering; went on uneasily: "Afterwards, do you know what she wanted of me? To meet Millie! To get Millie to give her an introduction or something, show her the ropes, get her into the movies! I didn't fall for that, not much. It was pretty easy to see what she was after."

He laughed, shortly, shamefaced. That it had hurt— stung a little—was something he couldn't himself understand. Not that he had cared for Shirley, for the flickering of her mascaroed eyelashes, the pouting of her pomaded mouth. Empty-headed little idiot, as light of brain as of feet. He hadn't, he told himself now, and truly, given a snap of his fingers for her. She had bored him at times intolerably; her monotonous slang, the Brooklyn accent marked even to his accustomed ears; the senseless repetition, "Boy, you boin me up!" and all the rest. But the male reaction had persisted under the faint disgust, the "laugh that off" attitude; under the boredom and the utter lack of desire. Put into words it was the usual poor-little-girl reaction. "Silly kid *but* . . ." He didn't want her. But to know, or to surmise, that she wanted him, without grounded hope, was not unpleasant, especially to a spirit bruised sore by circumstance and by doubt and by its own love, which far from running smoothly appeared engaged in an obstacle race. Therefore, when he slowly awakened to the fact that Shirley's persistent attentions had turned from himself in person to himself as brother-in-law of a rising motion-picture star he knew an intellectually illogical anger. Lola would never know, would never understand why. He didn't exactly himself. So now he shrugged and laughed, and said to the girl beside him, "She was a washout!"

No man likes being a sucker, he consoled himself, when he felt even now that stir of anger against Shirley. Not, of course, he amended hastily still to himself, that he hadn't known it all along!

Lola was ready to dismiss Shirley from her mind. One thing remained to be said of her. Lola said, therefore remorsefully:

"I did think you—liked her, Ken. That day, when you were ill—remember? I'd about made up my mind to tell you I wouldn't go back to St. Louis. Not, I mean, for good, that is. Just to settle things up. But when she walked in. As if she belonged. Oh," she cried hastily, as he turned to look at her, "I don't mean that I thought anything wrong—or really serious. I didn't. Truly I didn't! But it hurt me. I thought, you were getting along all right without me. Having a good time. That you didn't need me."

"Didn't need you?" He made a curious sound in his throat, half mirthless laughter, half groan. "You were never more off in all your life, Lola."

She said, aware that already they were touching on the unsaid things, "Yet you didn't come out . . ."

"No. I couldn't. Not yet. After a while, when Jake and I made good—I meant to, then . . . meant to make you come back."

She asked, half laughing:

"At the point of a gun? You needn't be so fierce about it."

"I'm not fierce. Just happy."

She touched his hand, on the steering wheel. She said:

"So am I. And mother and father. Have you moved back to the house yet?"

"The day before yesterday. They were mighty good to me, seemed glad to have me there. Howard," chuckled Ken, "is a card. Buys about six papers a day and studies the market. His boss is going to invest for him, after he gets two dollars saved. He's a scream, Lola. He wants to get rich. Not quick, you know, but slow and sound and sure. He's always talking about safe investments and a return on your money. He gets Dad Davis nearly crazy sometimes, but dad listens to him all the same. Pretty soon he'll be talking about, 'My son in Wall Street.' You wait!"

"I never knew Howard could be serious about anything," Lola remarked, "except his neckties and his meals."

"I think," said Ken, "it's the McCarthy kid. He moons around there half the time. Harold Teen to the life. It's great to see him. But you can't kid him about it. He gets all hot and bothered. Wait till you see him."

Lola said, "Mother seems perfectly happy to have us live there a while."

"Yes. When you first wrote, I wondered—if it would work out. Lola, it won't be like having our own place. We know that. But—it's the best thing, isn't it?" he asked, for reassurance.

"I don't know what else we *can* do," she told him, sighing inaudibly.

They had arranged to live with the Davises. Until they could afford an apartment. "We could now," he'd written her, "with what I'm making and with your job too. But this way seems better. You won't have the housework to do, you won't get so dead-beat, Lola. And they want us there. Lots of ways I don't like the idea, but in other ways it seems the best thing we can plan. I want to save. Really save. This garage business may not seem much to you, but it's got big possibilities. If Jake and I can put it over, putting back as much money as possible into the business, we'll be able to expand. Perhaps we'll be able to own more than one place. That's what we'd like eventually. A string of stations. Under the same name. There's money in it, Lola. But not all at once. You have to be careful, and slow. So many of the little places go under, you know."

They were almost at the house when he asked abruptly: "Mr. Jameson promise you your old job?"

"Yes, or one like it. But I'm to have a vacation. A month at least," Lola answered.

"That's great. You need it. You don't look good," he told her, worried.

Now they were stopping. Mrs. Davis ran down the steps, Howard was ahead of her. Davis himself, in shirtsleeves, the pipe going full blast, followed. There were embraces and exclamations. "Gee," said Howard, much himself as far as Lola could see except for a more dapper, slightly white-collar mode of apparel, "it's swell to have you home again, sis."

Ken stood by, as proud as if he had produced her from a hat. Jake appeared around the side of the house, his homely, alert face creased into a wide grin of welcome, his big ears scrubbed till they stood out like little wings, scarlet with cleanliness. "Hello, Lola," said Jake. "What do you think of my partner?"

"He's pretty nice," she said.

Jake had come to take the car back. But no, he must stay and have something to eat, insisted Mrs. Davis, bustling around. "Millie was just sick that she had to miss you, Lola."

"Jake," commented Howard, as they went into the house, "fell for Millie like a ton of bricks. She told him he was a 'perfect type.' For the movies."

"Lon Chaney, the guy with a thousand faces," mocked Ken, "or maybe she meant Bull Montana?"

"Perfect American type," corrected Howard, "that's what she said, one hundred per cent American. She sure had him going. He thought she was the works, didn't you, Jake?"

Jake said, flushing painfully:

"She sure is a pretty girl. But I know better than to get serious over a movie queen. If I hadn't had a job"— Jake grinned—"I'd ask to drive her car for her. 'Home, James!'" He struck an attitude.

"Heavens!" asked Lola, "*has* she a car?"

"She has," said Ken, "and too darned bad, because we tried to sell her a reconditioned Lincoln—we took it for a bad debt—but it wasn't any use. She's got a new Ford, back in Hollywood."

Such was Lola's homecoming. It was all—so natural, she told herself in wonderment. As if all the quarreling and troubles had never been. It couldn't, she thought further, last. There must be more than half explanations, more than slurring things over, evasions, full stops when a barrier was reached, careful pacing around that barrier in order to avoid a stumble.

At the table she looked around in bewilderment. Ken, gray eyes crinkled in laughter, white teeth, brown hair brushed to smoothness; Jake, freckled and snub-nosed and amiable, lean brown hands gesticulating; Howard, talking of the market as if it were a girl he knew rather well and was fond of, in a lordly manner; Davis, rather silent, smoking; her mother, fluttering from pantry to table. . . . "Take a little more of the steamed pudding, Lola. You don't eat enough to keep a bird alive. It's your favorite. Just a little slice. There's plenty of hard sauce."

Just the same.

Ken said that night, shy as her bridegroom had been, as ardent, as inarticulately grateful: "I wish it could have been different, Lola. . . . I wish we could have gone away by ourselves for a little while."

"I know—"

Yet perhaps this was as well. In the accustomed surroundings the troubled sense of strangeness which had haunted her homecoming had left her. It was as natural as breathing to be in Ken's arms again. She had longed to be there, all the months of absence; yet had feared it, when the time came. A year had intervened: a year of estrangement and unhappiness and wonder and doubt. Yet now it was as if the year had never been. It wasn't, she thought, like beginning again. It was as if there had been no interlude of loneliness. It was, perhaps, because she belonged with Ken; to Ken.

He said blunderingly:

"There are things I ought to tell you. They don't count, really. But I think you should know. You see, Lola, I love you. I've never loved anyone else."

She laid her hand on his lips. She said, frightened, her heart brushed with the dark wing of fear:

"If you love me—and I know you do—that's all that matters. Don't tell me anything."

He said, dogged: "But I want everything on the square between us."

She told him, turning to press her cheek to his smooth, bare shoulder:

"Everything is. I've come back. That's all, isn't it?"

He said, relieved: "Gee, Lola, you're a peach. And a dead-game little sport."

She thought: I wonder. She said nothing. What had he been about to tell her? That he had been unfaithful to her? once? twice? Not Shirley, she knew that. Some-one else? Who, didn't matter. Couldn't. She'd been away a year. Connie—Connie had said: "There are other women, you know." But Lola didn't want to know, wanted nothing more concrete, nothing that was pitiless fact. For she'd remember always, if she knew. No matter how much or how often she forgave him for a past crime against their love. A drink too much, a loneliness too un-endurable, a disturbance of the senses . . . No, she'd rather not know. She might remind him, when she was tired or cross or unhappy. She thought of Acton. She told herself, I was lonely, too. I didn't betray Ken, though. She told herself further, in amazement, *but I might have*.

She would not, she decided, speak of Acton. Coming home on the train she had pondered seriously the neces-sity of telling Kenneth all that had passed between her and Acton. Now she said, silently, No . . . better not.

That was life. Each with his or her own secret. May Crossman had said to her once, "Sometimes it's kinder to be silent."

Silence then. She might wonder about Ken; she would, of course, wonder. She would never know. It might have been that the confession he had wished to make to her involved nothing serious, from her angle; yet certainly, even if it had been, still nothing serious from his. She thought with a flash of strong intuition that Ken, being Ken, would perhaps find her episode with Acton more truly serious than any casual infidelity of the body he himself might have committed.

She said drowsily, "I love you. . . . I'm so glad to be home."

He lay wakeful after she had dropped off suddenly to sleep. He held her in his arms, warm, breathing, as much his own as any human being could be; all his own, he thought with the tragic and unattainable hope that lovers have, the hope of absolute possession, of identification with the beloved. He told himself: I'll be good to her— I'll carry her on my hands. . . . I'll try not to get sore and grouchy over things. . . . We'll be happier than we ever were. He was deeply grateful that she had spared him the necessity of telling her—certain truths. Yet, had he told her, she wouldn't have understood. Women couldn't. And a year is a long time.

He told himself, exultant and drowsy: she came back to me of her own free will; that means a lot; I'll make it up to her, I swear it.

He slept, waking now and then to wonder, to remember, to the security and peace she afforded him.

Lola went with him next day to the gas station. He and Jake were as proud of the garage as children with a new toy; or as grown men with a yacht or a fast car or an airplane. This place was theirs. It meant something to them. Work, planning, ambition. They pointed out the tiling, washed clean, the shining color of the pumps; the cement reaches of the garage; the cars parked inside. Jake said:

"Ken is a natural. He can take a car to pieces and put

her together again and she turns over, sweet as an ice-cream cone."

They had a helper, a lank lad in overalls. Lola went into the little office, a cubbyhole of a place, and looked at the books.

Ken said hesitantly: "I'm not so hot on the typewriter. You could help, if you'd care to?"

"I'd love to," she instantly said.

She went home alone, walking. The early autumn air was clean and crisp. She smiled, thinking of Ken in over-alls waving to her as she left, with a dirty piece of cotton waste. She walked along Fourth Avenue, went down a block into Third, thinking of Ken. Her physical eyes saw pictures that remained stamped on her brain . . . a boy about eight years old sitting in the open second-story window of a wooden house, feet against the frame, a har-monica held lovingly in his cupped hands to his mouth . . . a little girl with yellow hair and the dirtiest face Lola had ever seen, curled up in a filthy white dress on the rough board outdoor counter of a small stationery store, her grubby hands clasped about the drab gray neck of an enormous cat . . . a policeman in the trim blue of the new uniforms, pausing there on the steps of the shop to speak to her . . . two women walking home, their mar-keting in paper bags, limping, one of them, on stilted heels . . . two more women stopping on a street corner to compare the bargain-sale dresses they carried, utterly devoid of wrapping paper . . . a red-headed kid on a bicycle, skinning out from under the nose of an outraged milk-wagon horse . . . two men quarreling in the door of what was obviously a speakeasy. . . .

Lola walked toward Shore Road. At the end of the inclined street the water lay blue and lazy. A ship was coming in, the French flag flying. She thought—

Home—

Chapter XVI

"It's funny, not working," Lola told her mother after she had been at home about a week, "like marking time, or something."

"You've had vacations before," Mrs. Davis reminded her practically.

"I know, but this is different somehow."

Yet the days went quickly enough. She helped with the house, helped plan and prepare the meals. "When you're back at work," her mother said, "I'm not going to let you do so much. It isn't right. That's half the trouble with you girls, keeping houses and working. You bite off more than you can chew."

Up the street, across the way, old Mrs. Carney fell sick. Mrs. Davis watched the doctor come and go; tiptoed, actually, across the intervening pavement to inquire, to talk to the daughter who stood in the doorway, one ear listening for the slightest sound from the sick room, the other attentive to Mrs. Davis's assurances that people, even quite old people, with pleurisy got well. . . . "Why, I knew a woman once . . ."

The Davis kitchen was a welter, an extravagant, neat welter of extra eggs and milk, boiling miraculously into cup custards; a steaming chaos of soup kettles. "Nothing like good strong home-made beef broth to keep the strength," said Mrs. Davis. Lola watched, amused; helped where she could; sat on the kitchen table and swung her slim legs and made observations,

"You work yourself to death for everyone."

"They'd do the same for me. Folks say people aren't neighborly in the city. That isn't true. On a street like this everyone knows everyone else. It may be different in your apartment houses," Mrs. Davis admitted scornfully, "but we've lived in this neighborhood for so long. Of course people don't depend on neighbors the way they used to. I remember when I was a girl . . ." She was silent, thinking back to the small upstate town. "All our pleasures came from neighbors. And I remember the things your grandmother—rest her soul—used to tell me. She grew up in a little town. Her mother was highly thought of, better than a doctor for a childbirth, they said. My mother, too, I remember the many nights she'd go out, sit up all night, and come home the next day, cheerful and tired, after making the new mother comfortable and bathing the baby and all. She'd pitch right into a batch of baking. There were six of us children, you know, although you never knew any of them except your Uncle Tom and your Aunt Ella. Six. And a big house and barns and a yard. Mother was sick at having to move to the city, when father died and the place went and she had to come down here where her sister could give her a home and we went out to work." She thought back, standing there, her apron twisted about her fingers. "Neighbors, in those days . . . even in my time it had changed some but not much. Mother used to tell me about the shingling and barn-building parties, and the haying time, and all. Hay rides. And in winter the big sleighs with hot bricks to your feet and singing along the hard white road, under a moon, with the river alongside, smooth as glass, frozen solid. That was in my day, too. Skating parties, we had; and barn dances. And if there was a birth or a death the neighbors came in. Food on your table and in your pantry. Clothes they'd bring, for the one who had died or the one just born. Home-made soups and jellies and wine. Nowadays folks in the country have radios and cars . . . and all that. They don't have to depend on their next-door neighbors so much. But still and all, more than most city people do. This street, now, it's friendly. That's why I don't want to move."

"Move?" asked Lola, amazed.

"Your father, now. He wonders sometime, about when you and Ken are settled and Howard married and all. If I wouldn't rather have a little place. This property has gone up in value, the restrictions being off help. But I say no. I've lived most of my life here. I'd like to die here," she said, without fear or sorrow, "and leave it to you children. The place you were born in. It ought to mean something to you. That's why even if Millie wanted us to—and I don't think she does, I think it's just duty to her—I wouldn't like to settle in California. No neighbors," said Mrs. Davis firmly.

"Neighbors? But there's lots of them," said Lola, laughing, "wherever you go. People wouldn't stay away from you long. You have a way with you—and father says he's crazy about California. Climate and all."

"Climate?" asked Mrs. Davis, disparagingly. "That isn't all there is to life. I don't like it much anyway. Too much sunlight. Times, I longed for a good sock-dolager. Rain, like a waterspout leaking. Earthquakes too—not that I ran into any. And the houses built so—stagey. Pretty it is, flowers and everything. But flowers grow out there too easy. You don't have to fret and stew over them like you do here . . . watch every bud and coax 'em along. They're too big," she criticized with finality. "Out there everything is. Everything's so much the same. . . . No weather changes—though when it does rain they say it rains for months. That's too much change. I like it here, good and hot in summer and freezing cold in winter, and spring and fall thrown in so's you get used to things. No, they wouldn't be very neighborly out there. I'd feel like a fool trying to make myself fit in with Millie's friends."

"I'd like to know why they're any better than you are!" asked Lola, hotly loyal.

"They're not," answered Mrs. Davis in mild surprise, beating things in a deep yellow bowl. "Whoever said they were? But different. Young things, most of them. No better-looking than you or Millie or Howard, and some of them with not as much education, and not many of them coming from better homes. But money-makers. You don't know how—how unlikely a whole lot of youngsters like that are, all making more money in a week than your poor father makes perhaps in half a year. And some of the mothers! You'd think I'd take to the mothers, now, wouldn't you? Well, I didn't. One or two were nice old ladies, sort of bewildered, just the way I felt. But you couldn't feel much at home out there. Things seem so—what's the word they use to advertise hotel rates?—'transient,' " she brought out triumphantly. "As if they were put up overnight like a movie set. Marriages, too. Just get to know some nice young couple, and the first thing they've changed partners, and you have to get used to a new husband and a new wife. Not for me," said Mrs. Davis. "I'm too old-fashioned."

Lola went down to the gas station occasionally. She brought home the books with her and studied them. Some days she spent hours in the cubbyhole office, regardless of the noise of cars driving into the garage and backing out, unheeding the mild—and sometimes not so mild—profanity, looking out of the little door now and then to catch a glimpse of Ken, in the stained and faded blue overalls, wiping his hands with cotton waste, or his forehead with a brush of the arm, arguing animatedly with this man or that; or dashing out to the pumps. . . . "How many . . . five? O.K."

She thought perhaps he really shouldn't be doing this. She thought of him as she had first known him. White collar. Utility-company salesman. Well, why shouldn't he be doing this, she told herself; what sort of snob are you turning out to be? He's happy, isn't he?

And she would turn back to her typewriter and the letters Ken had not time to answer, with Jake's notations scrawled on them.

She went several times to New York to see Agnes and felt the first time very conscious of her clothes. The last year's suit, well-worn in St. Louis with the bit of sable Millie had given her for *chic* and warmth. Agnes was terribly smart. Lola eyed her soft, fine tweeds, her impeccable shoes and gloves, her casual, expensive hat and handbag, with normal envy. If I could afford it! But she couldn't. Even if she could—she couldn't. Agnes was, however, unchanged. A bit more brisk perhaps, perhaps a little hardened. But not a hardening that would repel the onlooker. She was keen and alert and brimming over with her job. "Men," she replied, in answer to Lola's natural question, "lots of them. They don't matter. Except to take me out . . . dinner, and theater, a night-club now and then . . . dancing. I always liked to dance, you know. But that's as far as it goes." She added carelessly that Jim had remarried.

"He has? Oh, Agnes, who?"

"I don't know. A girl, out West. I heard in a round-about sort of way. Someone said she was young and pretty and something of a clinging vine. But his sort.

Débutante stuff, in a small-town way; a state college graduate, I believe. I hope he'll be happy," she said sincerely.

"You don't miss—I mean, you're not hurt . . . you don't think of Jim?"

"No. Oh, of course, sometimes. But it's . . . comic, rather. As if I'd been another person then. I'm detached about it. You see, for a long time I had to be or go crazy not knowing where I really stood, what I really believed and felt. Then after a while it got to be a habit. You get over everything," philosophized Agnes, "except failure. I don't get over the bare fact that I failed—in marriage. That's detached, too, apart from Jim. Just a sort of blot on the mental escutcheon. I won't fail at anything else," she said, confident.

Lola thought of Peter Acton. He'd "got over" things too, probably. She felt the normal stab of regret, of wounded vanity. And Agnes asked, as if she had been clairvoyant:

"Peter Acton? Do you see him now, or rather did you? I know he's abroad. I see his name in the papers now and then. There's a man I might have cared for in a big way," she added, laughing.

"I did see him," Lola answered. "Yes, he's gone away. I read his name in the papers too."

"When are you going back to work?" Agnes asked.

"Soon. I don't know."

Agnes speared some lettuce with especial care. She asked casually:

"You *are* going back, then, aren't you?"

"Well, yes," said Lola, astonished, "I suppose so. I have to."

"Necessity then, not choice?"

"Perhaps. I don't know. I seem to have got out of the

way of thinking about it. Yet I've only been lazy a little while. Funny, isn't it?"

"I don't know. Don't you miss it?"

"Dreadfully. And yet—" She stopped and repeated, "I am getting lazy, I guess."

"Seen Connie?"

"Yes. I'll see her again soon. She sent you her love, Agnes."

With Connie, a few days later, she felt as little at home as she had with Agnes.

Connie, far advanced in her second pregnancy, was placid and serene. The boy had grown into a good-looking, sturdy youngster, demanding a good deal of his mother's time. Louis came in and slipped a package into his wife's hands. She opened it, smiling. A glaring pink sweater-suit for the new baby. Connie regarded it, laughing. "It's very Italian," she told Louis without malice. "Well, why not?" he wanted to know.

He was amiable to Lola, discounted all he had done for Ken with a shrug and a gesture of his dark, plump hands. "Why not?" he asked again. "Ken's a good boy." His accent was, she thought, as marked as ever. "He and that Jake, they'll make money for me some day. I'm not afraid." His own business, he went on to say, was good despite the building slump. He reminded Lola again that he had "friends" in the city.

She herself stood, Lola told herself, somewhere between Agnes and Connie: not sure of herself, marking time. Agnes made her feel useless, shabby, uncertain; and Connie made her impatient. She went to see Rhoda; Rhoda had had to give up a good job because of an unwanted baby. She found her up to her thin neck in housework, looking dragged and frail and harried, all her good looks gone. "It's a great life," said Rhoda, "if you don't weaken. I weaken—a lot." She looked at the baby in his spotless crib, and Lola said:

"You keep him like a new dime."

"Well, I have to, even if it means more work. I couldn't let him go. You've seen some of the poor mites around here, haven't you?" She wrinkled her nose in disgust. "I'm getting this down to a system. Of course, it takes all my time. But Fred's working hard. He's doing well, too; I'll be able to have help with the work by next year, and we're saving to get a little house out on the Island somewhere. Lynbrook maybe. Not too far out."

She asked for office news. Lola had little to give her. Rhoda wistfully said: "It must have been swell in St. Louis. Weren't you sick at giving it up? Why did you, Lola?"

"Ken's in business for himself, with a partner, that is," Lola said, "and he couldn't come out. So I came back."

Rhoda nodded. "It will get you," she said slowly, "one way or another."

Lola asked: "The baby? You were pretty sore about it. Now how do you feel?"

"I haven't time to feel anything but tired. Then it's another day." She smiled, and her mouth relaxed. "I'd sell him for two cents this minute," she said, and laughed. "It's sort of worth it, after all," she contradicted herself seriously, "and Fred will get ahead. I won't have to slave long. Since the kid arrived he's been so ambitious that it's almost funny. He's got a college picked out and everything," she concluded.

And when Lola was leaving Rhoda said:

"Give my best to the girls when you go back. I don't see many of them, just Sally Bartel, since she married and came to live on this street. And one or two others. I haven't gotten over missing things."

"You'd go back if you could?"

"Like a shot, if I could afford someone to take care of the baby. I mean someone I could trust. Probably there isn't any such person; probably I'd be a total loss, sitting in an office and wondering if the kid was falling downstairs or getting his fingers burned or his stomach upset."

She laughed again and shook her head.

"I guess it's one too many for me; I guess I'll never go back, not even if Fred gets me a French governess and a flock of nursemaids, which isn't very likely. Lynbrook and a part-time maid's the best I can look forward to, and it looks like a millionaire's dream from where I sit now, believe me."

Lola asked curiously:

"If you could go back . . . to the time before the baby, I mean, would you?"

Rhoda evaded uneasily. "That's putting it up to me." She cast a defiant glance at her sleeping son. She smiled, suddenly. "Darned if I would!" she admitted.

Lola's month was up. Her mother said at breakfast: "Going over to the office soon?"

Ken looked up from his coffee. He asked nothing. He merely looked. And Mrs. Davis remarked: "Ken, eat your cereal! I declare the way you go off to work, hit or miss, it's a shame. You're as bad as father."

Lola answered, watching the toaster intently:

"Oh, a day or so won't matter, I suppose. I've some letters to get out for Ken and I want to finish that housedress you cut out for me."

Ken rose. "Off to the day's battle," he said gayly. "Got an operation to perform today on one of the world's oldest Renaults. Come down and see it, Lola; it will give you a good laugh. But the darned thing runs! You'd be surprised."

He bent and kissed her and in passing dropped his big hand lightly on his mother-in-law's shoulder. Outside the house stood the battered "service car." "Come along, dad. Hey, Howard!" he called to Mr. Davis and Howard, who were out in the back yard putting Howard's latest acquisition, a homeless pup picked up off the streets, through his clumsy, touching paces. "Time to step on it!"

He would drop them at the subway. Presently the door slammed and the three had gone and the loud and angry noise of the motor turning over was heard. Lola rose, smiling, and started to clear the dishes.

A day or so later she sat with Jameson in his office.

"Well," he said delightedly, "you look great. Put on weight, haven't you?"

"A little."

"That's fine. You could afford to."

Gladys and Dorothy, heads together in the outer office, speculated. "She's coming back!" "Bet she isn't." "Sure she is." "She looks like a million, doesn't she?" "Well, I don't know," said Gladys, regarding her own costume complacently and smoothing the skirt which showed below the short smock, "her dress has an even hem-line!"

"Ready to come back?" asked Jameson.

"Ready to have me?"

"Not," he replied regretfully, "at the old salary. There isn't a place, Lola. You know how it is here. But I can find something. How'd you like to work in Medical for a while? You're quick, you'd catch on."

She said, "I think I'd like it. But——"

"But what——"

She said desperately:

"Mr. Jameson, I don't know. I want to come back; and I don't want to. Yet, I feel I should. To help Ken."

"If that is the way you feel," he said—"and, by the way, it wasn't always 'to help Ken,' was it? It was something a little different, wasn't it? If that's the way you feel, perhaps you won't have to. If you're willing to do without things."

She said, low, "I'm afraid."

"Of what?" he wanted to know.

"Of making a mistake. Either way seems a mistake to me now."

"Either way you'll probably be sorry," he told her. "Don't decide now. Give it more time. And if we can't fit you in here, I'll see that you have letters. Most companies are faced with cutting down staffs and wages. You know all about that; and the unemployment problem. But make up your mind, yourself."

That day she did a strange thing on leaving the office. She went down into the B.M.T. and, changing at Fourteenth Street, took an express through to Coney Island. The sea was blazing blue under an October sky. The island was empty, save for the people who lived there, whose business it was to be there. Pleasure park and Ferris wheel stood closed and idle. The great steel dips and sweeps of the scenic railways were empty and still. There were some people on the board walk, walking or in chairs; a few boys fishing from the piers; an invalid or two sitting in the sun.

Lola walked along the board walk and looked out to the smooth, quiet swell of the sea. She told herself: I have to think this out. The best way. The way for all of us.

Ken had been happy since her return; happy to find her there at night, to leave her there in the morning;

happy to have her come into the cubbyhole office and sit down at the battered typewriter; happy to talk to her, nights, of this new scheme and that old problem. There had been very little friction between them. She thought, sensibly: But I haven't been home long. If things went on this way, there'd be trouble, same as always. Bound to be. You don't make things different easily as that. But different trouble, maybe.

She had remembered that he had promised that if she went back to work he wouldn't "kick" or "grouch." But there would be the same things over again to wear on them both: the frantic rush in the mornings, the frantic return at night; the business of money; the inevitable being tired; the quarrels that came from irritated nerves.

Not that Ken wasn't tired nowadays; and irritated, too, sometimes; gloomy, when things went wrong; appalled, looking over bills; frightened, wondering if he and the more stable Jake could swing things. But it was different. She wasn't tired or worried or irritated. Against her placidity, her assurance, her laughter, his irritation turned off, like blunt arrows striking a smooth wall. He'd laugh and say:

"Well, tomorrow's another day. Gee, I'm tired!"

She thought: It would be easier, if I were earning—and harder.

It was long past dusk before she turned back and went home to find her mother peering out of brightly lighted windows and Ken pacing the living-room floor.

"For Pete's sake, where were ya?" he demanded. "I thought you were run over or something. I was ready to phone the hospitals."

"Ken, don't be silly. Think of all the nights I've come home late, after you," she reminded him.

"Sure, but you haven't been doing it lately"—he

grinned, sheepishly—"so I got out of the habit of not worrying, see?"

Her mother said, bewildered, "You couldn't be with Mr. Jameson all that time."

"No." She smiled at them both.

Ken asked suddenly, "Out with the boy friend?"

She saw him trying to speak lightly of the possibility, saw her mother's amazement, heard her comment: "Ken, how you talk—as if Lola would . . ."

"Well, no," said Lola hastily.

Mrs. Davis sniffed at a pie burning. She left the room like a small, plump whirlwind, and Ken asked quietly:

"By the way, what became of Acton?"

"I'm sure I don't know. He's in Europe somewhere. I read it in the papers," she replied carelessly. "I was down at Coney, taking my daily dozen on the board walk if you must know," she said, after a pause.

She thought: They always "must" know. You have to account for your time whether you like it or not. In one way or another.

Ken asked, elaborately casual, "Get the job?"

"No."

"No?" His face was incredulous. He said quickly: "Gee, I'm sorry, Lola, I know you're fit to be tied sitting around doing nothing. Darned tough. What's the matter with them over there anyhow?"

"I'm not worried," she denied. "I can get work."

"Somewhere else?"

"I don't know." Suddenly she was tired of delay. She asked seriously: "Would you care? Could we make out? Mr. Jameson will give me a place, at a lower salary. Or letters, references—whichever I like. I—I think perhaps I should go back. We'd get along faster. But if I didn't go back? If I stayed? I mean, it would mean staying on longer with the family perhaps than we planned. And doing without some things."

His face was almost stupid with astonishment, with his willingness to understand, yet as if he lacked the ability to do so.

"You mean . . . you'd live on what I bring in?" he asked. "You wouldn't mind?"

"I'd mind," she said honestly, "in lots of ways. Not having new clothes now and then. Not getting away, vacations, and having to ask for money. I'd mind that most of all."

He said a little proudly:

"We've a business checking account, Jake and I. And I'll have one of my own soon. With you. A joint account. You won't have to ask me for money. Lola, can you stand the gaff?"

She rose and faced him. She said:

"I think I'll have to. I can't bear going back to—I think you know. It isn't *worth* the money it brought in. At least not to me. We can do without things, Ken. Without an apartment, for a while, without theater tickets and radios and vacations, and—and speakeasies. I won't mind much after I get used to it. But you've got to let me help. I can't just sit home and rust out, help mother with the housework, sew a little, and pay calls. You've got to take me in with you, if Jake doesn't mind. A silent partner, like Louis. Only I can't invest anything in it," she said, "except time. I'll take care of the books and do the typing. I can do a lot of it, at home. I—I've been thinking. I might have some ideas; I'm not so dumb, even if I don't know the engine of a car from—from the bumper. I'd go crazy if I didn't think I was helping in some way. Helping save too, for the business. Our business. Will you let me help, Ken?"

"Will I?"

He was across the room; he had her in his arms. Mrs. Davis, returning to the living-room, backed hastily out again. She went out in the yard and spoke to Mr. Davis and Howard, who had come home to rush out-of-doors and regard the priceless puppy once more. "Lola," said Mrs. Davis, "isn't going back to work!"

"Are you sure you won't be sorry?" Ken was asking.

"I know I'll be sorry, lots of times. But it won't matter. We'll try it this way, anyway. Your way. My way, too, perhaps. I don't know."

He said, his voice roughened:

"Gee, you'll never know. I'll work so *damned* hard. . . ."

Inches to his stature, somehow. Funny new sort of ring to his voice. She thought: It can't mean so much to him. Or does it, to all men, only they won't admit it? He was saying: "I've been a pretty rotten sort of husband. I'll make it up to you, Lola."

That night she lay awake, looking beyond the dim blur of the windows into the uncertain future. She would be sorry. Often. She'd miss—oh, not only the office and the other girls and the feeling of being something, the tiniest cog in the amazing machine, but the sense of belonging to herself. Yet she knew that she belonged to Ken as well. That was funny; you couldn't belong to yourself and to someone else, at the same time, could you? She'd miss excitement, rumor, gossip, competition. She'd hate the girls to come to see her, looking at her with curious, rather pitying eyes . . . Poor Lola, tied to a house and husband . . . and children . . . Children? That, too, perhaps. She'd hate growing complacent, as Connie had grown complacent, looking in her turn at the girls who worked, unmarried, or at the—what was it Ken had

called them?—at the part-time wives, with eyes, also curious and pitying. . . . "Poor devils, working themselves
sick for—nothing very much." She'd loathe, in a way,
not being able to say: "I'm on my own."

Ambition? Well, she could use her ambition for Ken.
It would be as much hers, wouldn't it? He was the sort
of person who was easily discouraged, who needed pushing
and prodding, and "Sure, you can do it!" Not that he
was weak. He was no weaker than any man in his position would be. Sensitive perhaps; a bit of an inarticulate
dreamer. Nervous. Brimming with a nervous energy,
the sort that lets down easily. She knew that much about
him now.

Pride? Well, she'd hated Ken's pride. And now she
had her own. His had remained, although he had managed to compromise with it. Hers would have to go.
They couldn't both have what they wanted.

She was not unhappy, planning her letter to Jameson:
"I've made up my mind not to come back. I want to
thank you for everything . . ." She wasn't happy,
either. Yet her heart was oddly light within her, and
there was a certain eagerness in her determination.

He'll make good. I'll make good.

That's what it amounted to. She'd soon find her routine, soon forget, except at moments, the things she
missed, the things she thought she'd had.

She flung out a hand and touched him, sleeping. She
thought: We love each other. If we can keep that, what
else matters? He's always thought we could keep it this
way. I didn't. But I know now that we couldn't keep it
the other way. So we'll try this.

She could not see very far ahead on the road. She
guessed at things dimly, not putting them into words.
The things which waited; struggle and discouragement;

short tempers and long endurance; laughter, happiness; failure and success; birth and death, and sorrows shared and hopes frustrated and dreams coming true. All ahead of her. Ahead of them both. She said to herself: Agnes will think I'm a fool and Connie will think I've come to my senses at last. Both of them right, both of them wrong.

She remembered some of the things Jameson had said to her in Mannering's office at St. Louis. She thought of Jenny fleetingly, Jenny writing her carelessly spelled, perfectly entranced letters. Jenny was happy, two months married. She'd have a lot to learn.

Doing without. The things she—and Ken—would have to do without were not important. They had only seemed so. Curious, that the reasonably small amount of money she was able to contribute to the running of a home should make all the difference, stretch out to cover those unimportant things. But they were things people expected nowadays, somehow took for granted.

Well, she could do without them. She could do without anything but Ken.

There were drawbacks living at home; there would be more, as time went on. But they would plan ahead. When it was safe for them, and sane, they'd make their own home. They'd have a foundation on which to build.

Not yet quite reconciled, yet unrebellious, she lay there and listened to Ken's quiet breathing. She made herself— and him—a promise, in the speech of her generation. She had made it before, three years earlier when they were married. She had not kept it—nor had he. Was it through any fault of their own? This time they would keep it, no matter what happened.

"We'll make good," she said.

THE END